What Matters Most

Cynthia Victor

AN ONYX BOOK

ONYX
Published by the Penguin Group
Penguin Books USA Inc., 375 Hudson Street,
New York, New York 10014, U.S.A.
Penguin Books Ltd, 27 Wrights Lane,
London W8 5TZ, England
Penguin Books Australia Ltd, Ringwood,
Victoria, Australia
Penguin Books Canada Ltd, 10 Alcorn Avenue,
Toronto, Ontario, Canada M4V 3B2
Penguin Books (N.Z.) Ltd, 182–190 Wairau Road,
Auckland 10, New Zealand

Penguin Books Ltd, Registered Offices:
Harmondsworth, Middlesex, England

Published by Onyx, an imprint of Dutton Signet, a division of Penguin Books
USA Inc. Previously published in a Dutton edition.

First Onyx Printing, June, 1997
10 9 8 7 6 5 4 3

  REGISTERED TRADEMARK—MARCA REGISTRADA

Printed in the United States of America

PUBLISHER'S NOTE
This is a work of fiction. Names, characters, places, and incidents either are the
product of the author's imagination or are used fictitiously, and any resemblance to
actual persons, living or dead, events, or locales is entirely coincidental.

BOOKS ARE AVAILABLE AT QUANTITY DISCOUNTS WHEN USED TO PROMOTE PRODUCTS
OR SERVICES. FOR INFORMATION PLEASE WRITE TO PREMIUM MARKETING DIVISION,
PENGUIN BOOKS USA INC., 375 HUDSON STREET, NEW YORK, NEW YORK 10014.

for
Carolyn Clarke
and Sarah Dick

With a lifetime of love

Acknowledgments

Grateful thanks go to the following people for their generous help, advice, and support: Aaron Astor, Harriet Astor, James Astor, Peter Astor, Carole Baron, Richard Baron, David Blum, Betsy Carter, Amanda Clarke, Mackenzie Clarke, Jill Danzig, Susan Ginsburg, Larry Goldstone, William Guzzardi, Sam Guzzardi, Joel Higgins, Stacy Higgins, Jean Katz, Dale Mandelman, Rebecca Mandelman, Susan Moldow, Janet Morris, Diana Revson, Jennifer Skurnick, Mary Smitham, Mark Steckel, Drew Tarlow, Elinor Tarlow, and John Vitka.

As always, warmest appreciation to Meg Ruley.

Finally, to Audrey LaFehr go special thanks and the utmost respect for her talented and insightful work, and to Leah Bassoff, her assistant, a warm thank you for her very valuable efforts.

Chapter 1

"Oh, Lainey," Riley Cole cried ecstatically, "these are dynamite."

The dark-haired little girl grabbed the blue sheets decorated with pictures of Supergirl out of the box so quickly, both the pillowcase and a small white envelope fell to the floor.

"And what do we have here?" Lainey Wolfe smiled as she bent down to retrieve the items, replacing the pillowcase in the box, then handing the envelope to Riley to open.

Eagerly, she tore at it, her eyes shining as she discovered what was inside. "That's me," she shrieked, delighted at the hand-inked cartoon of a little girl dressed in Supergirl's cape and boots. "But, Lainey, the letter in front's all wrong." She pointed to the enormous *R* right in the middle of the girl's chest. "It's supposed to be an *S*. You know, for Supergirl."

Lainey moved forward, her arms coming around the small girl's shoulders and pulling her into a warm hug. "No, silly, it's supposed to be an *R* for Riley Cole, the superest child in the state of Connecticut."

She turned to the girl's blond-haired older brother, who sat across from them browsing through a soccer magazine, and pretending to be paying no attention. "The superest child next to Timothy Cole, that is," she added, loosening her hold on Riley and reaching over to pick up another wrapped gift box.

Tim Cole put down his magazine and took the box from her, affecting all the nonchalance a nine-year-old could muster as he slowly undid the Christmas wrapping. When he'd lifted the lid off the box, however, he couldn't hide his excitement. "Oh, how'd you get this? Oh, wow, man, you're the greatest, I swear it."

Triumphantly, he removed the contents of the box and carried them over to his mother, who was observing from behind the couch, resting on her forearms as she leaned over, enjoying the camaraderie between her friend and her children.

"Look at this, Mom—it's a basketball signed by Patrick Ewing! And two tickets to the Knicks game next Saturday!"

"Is the other ticket for me?" Riley asked. She unfurled her new sheets next to the enormous, elegantly decorated Christmas tree that dominated the room. Spreading herself out on them, she closed her eyes as if she were about to go to sleep for the night.

"No, Riley," Lainey replied, tickling the bottom of her feet until she sat up and wrapped the sheets around herself like a protective cloak. "That particular ticket has my name on it."

Riley frowned. Farrell Cole came over to her pouting daughter and scooped her up in her arms, sheets and all. "Daddy and I have other plans for you that day, buster," she said, carrying her like a bundle to the foot of the stairway in the center hall. "If you get upstairs right now and change into a decent skirt and a clean blouse, you will reap the rewards when your brother goes out on the town with Aunt Lainey."

Riley squiggled out of her arms. "Lainey's not our aunt, silly." She clambered up three steps, then sat down and made herself comfortable.

"Well, then." Farrell lifted a finger to her forehead, pretending to be thinking deeply. "When your brother goes out on the town with Uncle Lainey."

"She's not an *uncle* either, Mommy." Her offended tone clearly indicated that she wasn't to be made fun of again.

Tim walked over to the staircase. "How would you know, stupid," he said airily, before bouncing his new basketball off his little sister's knees.

Riley grabbed the ball and leapt down to the bottom step, hurling the object back at her brother, who easily sidestepped the assault. Abruptly, he ran back into the living room. He returned within seconds, holding up the card that had been inside his gift.

For all of the children's lives, Lainey had been enclosing a cartoon in every Christmas and birthday present she gave Tim and Riley. Tim's first one had been when he was born. It was a sketch of a stork carrying a baby over the Connecticut state line, while a crowd of people who had climbed out of their cars stood watching and applauding. He kept it in his top desk drawer, along with all the others she'd done.

He beamed with pleasure as he examined the newest contribution to his collection. Lainey had drawn a boy with straight blond hair wearing a basketball uniform, leaping ten feet up in the air and stuffing a ball through the hoop, as three aged players watched from the sidelines, all seated in wheelchairs, shawls wrapped around their shoulders. *Guess we got to the nursing home right on time*, read the words coming out of one of their mouths in a ballooned caption.

"Who are they?" Riley asked, grabbing the card out of her brother's hands.

Tim pulled it back, giving his sister a derisive look. "Obviously, it's Larry Bird and Michael Jordan and Isiah Thomas," he said, pointing to each character in turn.

"Obviously, it's Karry Kird and Kichael Kordan and Kisiah Khomas," the little girl mimicked, jumping up and down on the steps.

"Stop it, both of you." Laden with bags of pretzels, nuts, and potato chips, plus an assortment of soda bottles, John Cole had come through the front door without anyone hearing him. "All this noise is going to scare off our guests, who will be here in"—he looked meaningfully at his wife—"approximately twenty-five minutes."

"You heard your father." Farrell grabbed each of the children by a hand and pulled them up the stairs behind her.

John put down the heavy bags and extracted several of the soda bottles, carrying them over to the large table in the living room that would serve as a bar. "Thank goodness one person here is ready for this shindig," he said approvingly, looking over at Lainey, who wore a snug-fitting, royal blue sweater dress that came down to the midcalf. He frowned at the clunky black boots that completed her ensemble. "Why do all you women from Manhattan dress like you're in the army?"

"It's on the instruction sheet hanging on the wall at Balducci's," she answered breezily. "Besides, it's a whole lot more comfortable than the five-inch heels you men would have us wear."

"Yeah," he agreed, "but where's the mystery?"

"The real mystery is how we can still be standing two hours later, given what we're doing to our feet." Lainey laughed. "Time to go and pretty myself up." She started up the stairs, blowing him a quick kiss. "I'll try to make my face as festive as possible even if my feet look as if they're going on maneuvers."

She didn't look back, but she knew just what expression John Cole's face would have. Some mixture of dismay and disapproval would quickly settle into fondness, just as it had been doing for the fifteen years since he'd married her best friend.

Lainey ran her hand along the smooth mahogany railing. The lustrous wood had obviously been polished that day, as had the rosewood table holding a large porcelain bowl filled with fresh flowers that decorated the landing halfway up. She stopped there, hearing the sound of Tim and Riley playing in the TV room, their noises hushed by the deep pile carpeting. The slight fragrance of Farrell's perfume mingled with the aroma of *bœuf Bourguignonne* and pears poaching in red wine that rose from the kitchen, all of it enhanced by the smell of the fires John had lit in the living room and the dining room.

This is what life is supposed to be about, Lainey thought, overwhelmed by a sudden sense of loneliness. She had rarely been jealous of Farrell, yet tonight the richness of her friend's life seemed undeniable. Here Farrell lived, in one of the most beautiful Colonial houses in one of Connecticut's most beautiful towns, surrounded by a husband and children who adored her, a housekeeper to do most of the boring chores, a figure to die for, and friends by the score.

Farrell's bedroom door opened, and Lainey watched her emerge into the hallway, a vision in white cashmere, her dark silky hair down around her shoulders, her face accented by freshly applied lipstick and mascara, tiny pearl earrings her only jewelry aside from the diamond wedding band she never removed. She stood there for a moment, lost in her thoughts. Lainey was startled to see her put her hand to her chest and take several deep breaths, as if she was having difficulty.

"Farrell, are you all right?" Lainey called up to her in concern.

Surprised by Lainey's presence, Farrell hastily dropped her hand.

"I'm fine," she said quickly. "What are you up to?"

"Well, I was coming up for last-minute facial repairs, but I decided to stop right here and feel sorry for myself."

Farrell looked at her in bewilderment. "You? Why would you feel sorry for yourself? You have the most exciting life in the world."

Lainey rolled her eyes. "What would be the exciting part? My tiny one-bedroom apartment, perhaps? My job as an assembly-line worker for the Carpathia Empire? My—"

"Hold on," Farrell interrupted. "You have a wonderful job. You're a full-fledged designer, for God's sake."

Lainey shrugged her shoulders. "Meaning I copy cartoon characters onto mugs and rubber stamps, and get my wrists slapped if I so much as have them facing left instead of right."

"Meaning you get to go to a fancy office every day and interact with glamorous, creative people, and get paid for doing it."

"And I get to look at the man I love as he leaves to go home to his wife every night." Lainey sighed, coming to join Farrell at the top of the steps. "Sorry. That was tasteless. But it just hurts so much, especially on a holiday like this."

Farrell took Lainey's hand, pulling her toward the master bedroom. "Let's get to that facial repair stuff before all the guests arrive," she said, forcing lightness into her voice. She led Lainey to the antique inlaid vanity table at one end of the large room, standing behind to observe as Lainey sat down and picked up a small brush, pulling it through her dark blond wavy hair.

God, life is crazy, Farrell thought as she watched her friend. Imagine Lainey holding my life up as a model when I'm about to turn my entire world upside down. Fear and exhilaration mingled in her belly, the same mixture she used to know so well and had courted through most of her life. But all that was so long ago, before her marriage to John, the birth of her children. Now those feelings were being reawakened, as tempting and tantalizing as a forbidden drug.

She thought for a moment of sharing her secret with Lainey. What a relief it would be. Quickly, she stopped herself. Lainey would never understand. My God, she thought, I don't understand it myself. No. No matter how dangerous this was, it was something she had to do, something she wouldn't be talked out of.

Farrell pushed her thoughts aside, gathering Lainey's hair in her hand and lifting it up as if to evaluate how it would look in a French twist.

Lainey met Farrell's eyes in the mirror. "Who'd have thought you'd be the one with the life straight out of *Good Housekeeping*?" She shook her hair back into its wavy disarray. Her lips turned up in a smile. "I used to imagine you ending up as a belly dancer or a bush pilot. Or, if not that, possibly in Leavenworth."

"You sound like my mother." Farrell's tone clearly indicated it was no compliment.

Lainey pursed her lips and raised her naturally low voice to a high soprano. *"Farrell may not come to the phone today. She neglected to wear her biteplate in school."*

Farrell began to laugh. "God, she was on my case all the time."

"Well," Lainey said judiciously, "you can't exactly blame her. Imagine if she had known all the stuff you did."

Farrell waved a hand dismissively. "Oh, come on. I was a model child."

Lainey laughed. "Practically a saint." She thought for a moment. "Like when you climbed out of the window at three in the morning to meet Larry Johanson in eighth grade? Or how about when you drove into New York City on a junior license and picked up that doorman from the little bistro on Second Avenue." Lainey chose a red lipstick and evaluated the color against her face before she began applying it to her mouth.

"Gee," Farrell said, nostalgia in her voice. "Kenny Purcell. I'd forgotten all about him."

Lainey looked at her disapprovingly. "Don't sound so sentimental. That shocked even me. It's a wonder you weren't raped or killed or something."

Farrell reached for the hairbrush and ran it through her long brown hair. "I loved to shock you. I loved to shock myself." And I still do, she thought.

Lainey got up and walked over to the window, peering out to observe a man and a woman leaving the house that bordered Farrell's from the back. She recognized Sugar and Helmut Taplinger, having met Farrell's neighbors once or twice.

"But that wasn't the biggest surprise you ever handed me," she went on.

"No," Farrell said, coming up behind her. "That would have been junior year of college, right?"

Lainey nodded in agreement, easily recalling the

phone call that had awakened her early one Saturday morning.

"You're marrying Mussolini!" Lainey had screamed into the phone when Farrell had announced her news.

"He's sweet and I love him," Farrell had replied, *"and you're the maid of honor, so stop hollering and start shopping for a long pink dress. And never use that horrible nickname again, would you please."*

"It wasn't my *nickname,"* Lainey had reminded her. *"As I remember, it took you all of three minutes to call him that on your very first date."*

"Well, if there were trains, he'd make them run on time, trust me. But let's forget all that. As of April twelfth, I'll be Farrell Beckley Cole, adoring wife of John Cole. And you'll be the proud godmother of our six girls and six boys, whenever they choose to arrive."

"Aren't godmothers responsible for a child's religious education?" Lainey had asked archly. *"You want me taking your kids to services at Temple Israel?"*

Farrell had laughed. *"I don't care, as long as you promise to throw in Santa Claus and my Aunt Charlotte's annual Easter egg hunt."*

Now, Farrell looked at her friend, her expression serious. "You thought I was nuts getting married back then, didn't you?"

"Completely," Lainey agreed, laughing. She noticed the intent look on Farrell's face. "Well," she amended hastily, "you turned out to be the big genius . . . look at all this." She glanced around at the large room, its warmth and charm maximized by the antique iron bed, the matching love seats covered in the deepest rose-colored silk, a handmade throw flung casually over one arm, the wealth of pictures in heavy silver frames covering fifteen years in the life of a family. To Lainey, it seemed perfect.

Farrell's eyes were unexpectedly sad. "Not such a genius, really. Maybe just in a hurry."

"What do you mean?" Lainey asked.

"Oh, nothing," Farrell replied a little too brightly. "It's just sometimes I wonder why I settled into adulthood quite so quickly. As you know, even perfect suburban moms get occasional urges for the fast life."

"According to my mother, you're already living the *ideal* life. 'Why can't you settle down like your friend Farrell?' I think you're the one she wishes she'd raised."

"She pretty much *did* raise me, as I remember it." Farrell started walking to the bedroom door.

They both heard the doorbell and the sound of John welcoming the first guests, followed by a huge belly laugh that carried loudly up to the bedroom.

Farrell tensed. "That would be the Taplingers, our neighbors," she said quietly. "You remember them? I've gotten kind of friendly with Sugar lately."

The bell was ringing again as they started downstairs. They saw John open the door.

"Hi, beautiful," John's brother, Charlie Cole, called out to Farrell as he walked into the house.

Farrell waved to him, then exchanged knowing smiles with her husband when she saw the woman standing next to Charlie. The brunette must have been at least six feet tall and was as slender as a willow.

"John and I had a bet, and it looks like I've won," Farrell whispered to Lainey just before they reached the bottom step. "I knew Charlie's last girlfriend wouldn't be around more than three weeks. John chose to believe Charlie when he claimed he'd finally fallen in love, but here he is with someone we've never seen before."

Lainey smiled. She'd first met Charlie at Farrell and John's wedding. John's younger brother was destined to be the handsomest man in just about any room. But he'd gotten into the kind of trouble he was forever trying to live down. At twenty-five, he'd been arrested for selling marijuana to some so-called friends, who turned out to be undercover police officers; he'd spent a year in prison.

"What's Charlie up to these days?" Lainey asked Farrell, as he and his date were led over to the bar area by John.

Farrell grimaced. "It's better I don't know."

She saw Lainey's look of concern and quickly softened her tone. "Not that he's been in any real trouble in the past few years, but with Charlie you can't be too sure of anything." She raised an eyebrow. "Actually, there is one thing you *can* be sure of, and that's his taste in women. It runs exclusively to models, and his staying power is shorter than the average lifespan of a housefly."

A large, red-haired woman in a purple-and-green caftan walked over to them, kissing Farrell on the cheek. "I'm Sugar Taplinger," she said, holding her hand out to Lainey.

"You two have met, haven't you?" Farrell said.

Sugar nodded. "You're Farrell's friend from the city, aren't you?" she asked Lainey.

Farrell answered for her, catching Lainey's hand for a second. "Daniel Webster School, New Rochelle, New York. Lainey has been my best friend since first grade."

"We bonded during a game of kickball, if you want to really nail it down," Lainey said.

Farrell turned to Sugar. "Fascinating, isn't it? Come on, guys, we've got a party to run."

Sugar linked arms with Farrell, then turned and captured Lainey on her other side. She walked toward the living room but stopped short of entering it. Focusing all their attention on Charlie Cole's date, Sugar spoke in a whisper. "Here are the two things I need to know. Number one, exactly how old is she? I mean, do you suppose she can legally vote in the state of Connecticut?"

Lainey smiled as Sugar went right on.

"And, number two, assuming we find out her age, is that number higher or lower than her IQ?" She left both women laughing and walked over to the bar where her husband, a spindly man with thin white hair standing straight up on his head, handed her a large goblet of red wine.

Farrell spotted a distinguished-looking older man in a dark gray suit standing stiffly across the room. She took a long sip of wine and plastered a smile on her face. "The gentleman who accounts for several digits of my husband's annual income is not having enough fun. Pardon me while I make his day."

Lainey moved off to one side, looking around, her earlier melancholy returning. Every man in the room seemed to remind her of Julian Kroll, the man she loved, the one man with whom she'd never get to spend any holiday. What would he be doing right now? she wondered, taking a seat on one of the matching white silk brocade couches. She envisioned him, dressed as he undoubtedly was in perfectly clean blue jeans or well-pressed chinos, his silky dark blond hair in a ponytail, his two little girls seated on his knee, hearing tales of Santa and Rudolph as his wife opened scores of presents at his feet. Then she imagined an explosion blowing the scene away.

Generous thoughts at Christmas, she reflected, forcing her attention back to the present company. Farrell suddenly reappeared, sinking down to the carpet in front of Lainey in one graceful move.

"I've been making nice to my husband's business associates," she said with a sigh. "Have I stopped smiling yet?" she added facetiously. She lay her head back affectionately against her friend's knee. Farrell rubbed her temples for a few seconds as if ridding herself of a headache before reaching into the pocket of her dress and removing a tiny parchment card. On it was a caricature of a woman, obviously herself, sitting on a sunlit cloud borne aloft by a handsome blond-haired man and two children, the boy the image of the man, the girl a dark likeness of her mother.

"It's the most beautiful card you've ever made me," she said, holding it up so its creator could appreciate it one more time. "Right now, you don't look quite so sentimental. Exactly what are you conjuring up as you sit here watching my life flash before your eyes. Will my friends and neighbors show up on my next Christmas card?"

Lainey grinned. "Yes, you and your friends will be the angels circling the ceilings of heaven, while I'll be the one in uniform sweeping up the grounds, waving up to you and asking if you need anything to drink."

Farrell shook her head. "I think you're just watching so you can embarrass all of us next year with devastating caricatures of our most humiliating selves." Farrell allowed herself a tiny yawn, carefully hiding it from her other guests. "And by the way, exactly which parts of my existence suggest a visit to heaven? Driving Tim to basketball practice or picking up Riley from her computer class?" She raised an eyebrow as she saw her husband walking toward them, two fresh glasses of Perrier in his hands. "Or maybe the really heady part is being chained to sobriety by my much better half."

"I don't chain you to anything, darling," John Cole said, easing himself into a chair. "I simply keep you informed of where the straight and narrow is so you can follow it if you choose to."

Farrell gave him an odd look, then pushed up off the rug and slid into his lap, her hands affectionately mussing his hair. "Who could be straighter and narrower than Mrs. John Cole, mother of two, grande dame of Meadowview, Connecticut?" She pinched an invisible bulge on her upper thigh, then raised her hand as if in horror at what it had found. "Well, perhaps there are those who are narrower."

Lainey's skeptical look said it all. "Fair is Farrell, lovely as a reed. Hear my passion, and please, please heed my need."

"Jesus, Lainey." Farrell laughed loudly. "How on earth did you remember that?"

"Please say you didn't write it yourself," John said, obviously appalled.

"The poetry," Lainey explained, "is courtesy of Fred Cioffi. Written, as I remember, in study hall. It was probably the only ten-minute period in Fred's sophomore year at New Rochelle High School during which he was paying full attention to the paper in front of him."

"I believe I rewarded him amply for those ten minutes." Farrell laughed at the memory, but stopped when she noticed the expression on her husband's face.

"Much as I hate to interfere with the 'Oh, to be a teenage girl again' hour, I have guests to attend to." He stood, gently pushing Farrell off his lap and depositing her on the chair. "We're running out of ice, if you two would like a more current project to keep you busy. We're down to the last bag." They watched him walk away.

"Poor John." Farrell looked dolefully at Lainey.

"He has nothing to worry about. After all, if you'd wanted to remain the old you, you wouldn't have married him. Right?"

No, wrong, Farrell thought, her stomach clenching in fear. Abruptly, she realized that Lainey was waiting for an answer. She tried to sound as casual as possible as she responded.

"The old me wouldn't have been hostessing this party. She would've been seduced and abandoned in some hovel in a foreign country looking forward to letters from you, describing parties like this."

Lainey shook her head. "Without the new you, I wouldn't be attending parties like this. Besides, you weren't exactly a scarlet woman. You just liked to have a good time."

"What are you two whispering about?" Sugar Taplinger plunked her large body down on the couch next to Lainey.

Farrell looked away, her expression curiously guarded.

"Farrell and I are reliving her wild youth," Lainey replied.

"And what were *you* doing all that time, Lainey?" Sugar asked.

"Oh, mostly envying Farrell, if I remember correctly."

"Mostly thinking I was an idiot," Farrell interjected.

"Well, that, too." She smiled briefly. "Truly, though, I was fascinated by your courage. That has never been my strong suit."

Farrell laughed. "Oh, you're courageous enough. That is, when you decide what it is you want to do. It just

takes you about a hundred years to make that decision."
She raised one eyebrow meaningfully.

"What decision are we talking about here?" Sugar
turned her attention to Lainey.

Lainey just smiled. "Nothing that monumental, I promise. Although we'd better see about getting some more ice
before John decides to fire us both."

Farrell stood up, stretching her hand to Lainey's and
pulling her up as well. "Yeah, nothing monumental. Just
what to do with her life, whether or not to have children,
whether or not to get married."

Lainey shot her a warning look. That Julian Kroll
would never leave his wife was not a subject she felt
comfortable discussing in front of Sugar. "So, Farrell,
will a supermarket or a liquor store be open on a Saturday night, or will we have to forage for ice someplace
else?"

"I've got a ton of ice in the freezer," Sugar offered.
"Let yourself in and take as much as you want. Now if
you'll excuse me, I'm going to force Charlie Cole to
dance with me. Your brother-in-law is the most attractive
man I've seen since the tight end I dated at Penn State."

She got to her feet and looked toward John's
brother, who was lounging against a door frame, visibly
bored as his niece and nephew tried to engage him in
conversation.

"Poor Riley," Farrell said as she watched Sugar extract
Charlie from the children and engage him in a spirited
fox-trot. "She's undoubtedly trying to fill her uncle in on
her adventures with the Internet. It's amazing, you know.
Somewhere in Denmark a fifteen-year-old computer whiz
has a profound relationship with my seven-year-old
daughter. They exchange E-mail and faxes about a hundred times a day. Eric or Ulrich—I can never tell which

name is coming out of Riley's mouth—evidently has no idea of Riley's age, and on the advice of her savvy older brother, Riley isn't letting that information out." They rounded the corner into the enormous kitchen. "My greatest fear is that one of these days, some Danish teenager is going to arrive for an unannounced vacation in the United States and break my little girl's heart when he finds out his best international friend has been out of diapers for only a little over four years."

"Who's in diapers?" Riley's voice surprised them.

"Riley," Farrell said, wheeling around to see her near the refrigerator, "isn't it time you were getting ready for bed?"

"We're helping Mrs. Miles with the trays."

Farrell looked over to where her older child was removing canapés from a large silver tray and stuffing them into his mouth almost as quickly as the white-haired maid was setting them down.

"Tim, both of you," she included Riley in her gaze, "let Mrs. Miles do her work, and get to sleep."

"With all these people in the house ... come on, Mom."

Tim picked up a stuffed mushroom and lobbed it over to Lainey, who caught it easily in one hand. "Thanks, sport."

"Please don't encourage them, Lainey," Farrell said, walking over to Tim and wiping his hand on a paper napkin. "When you go to Lainey's for the weekend you can have food fights all night long for all I care."

"Come on now, guys," Lainey said. "Time to get upstairs. We're out of here, anyway. We have to go over to Sugar's house to get some more ice."

"We'll go over there for you," Tim piped up, coming to stand near his mother.

Farrell leaned down and kissed him on the cheek before heading to the door. "Thanks, but no, honey."

"Are you gonna show Lainey Mr. Taplinger's plates?" Riley turned to her mother, excitement gleaming in her dark brown eyes. "I bet she can figure out the secret."

"And what secret would that be?" Lainey asked, walking over to the mudroom off the kitchen, where a number of coats and sweaters hung on hooks. She removed the jacket she knew to be Tim's, glancing at him to make sure borrowing it was okay as she placed it around her shoulders.

Farrell joined her, taking an oversized black turtleneck sweater and pulling it over her head. "You'll see soon enough," she replied as she unlocked the door. "I want you two in bed by the time we get back," she said, attempting menace. "And that's going to be in approximately two minutes, so you'd better get moving."

She held the door for Lainey. "Here, let me lead you through the forest," she said jokingly as she made her way in the darkness through the foliage toward the large house sixty or seventy yards back behind theirs.

"You think you're kidding," Lainey retorted, holding onto Farrell's sweater. To Lainey, Farrell's sizable house, with its expanse of white clapboard and tiny matching carriage house beyond the garage seemed like a baronial estate. The grounds did indeed seem like a forest. "Why is it I'm never frightened in Manhattan, but am completely terrified in America's wealthiest suburb."

"Oh, Lainey, you're not really frightened of anything. Or at least not of the things you *think* you're afraid of."

Lainey shivered in the cold night air. "Please, please, save the ambivalence lecture until we're in a well-lit room, okay?"

They reached the Taplingers' house, and Farrell opened

a side door leading to the garage, ushering Lainey in as she flicked on a light switch to reveal two Jeeps and a dark gray Chevy. "Now here's the 'secret' Riley's so tickled by." She walked Lainey behind the three vehicles and pointed. "What do you see?" she asked, adopting a professorial tone.

"Well," Lainey paused. "I guess cars wouldn't be the correct answer, huh?"

"Read the license plates. McClellan, Bragg, and Pickett. It's Sugar's husband's idea of a great time. He's the editor of some history buff magazine called *Armchair General*. But what gets me is that he didn't just arrange to have Civil War generals on his license plates. They're three *losing* Civil War generals. Three winners would have been too much competition for Helmut Taplinger. He likes to be the winningest guy on the road."

Lainey thought of the conversation she'd overheard as Sugar's husband had held forth earlier in the evening. The pale, skinny, white-haired man had been lecturing two men from John's law firm. "It's different *from* not different *than*," he'd been carefully explaining when John had brought Lainey over for an introduction. "And it's not *less* books; it's *fewer* books. Less is anything you can weigh. Fewer is anything you can count."

"I could see he liked to be the most correct," Lainey said now.

Farrell led the way over to a small door. "The best and the brightest, our Helmut." She laughed as she turned the knob and entered the bright yellow kitchen. She walked over to a large, white Sub-Zero refrigerator, pulling open the freezer door and checking out the shelves.

The Taplingers' kitchen was meticulously organized. Much smaller than Farrell's, it nonetheless projected perfect order, from the hanging copper pots artfully arranged over a marble-topped worktable in the center of the room, to the brilliantly clean butcher block table, already set for tomorrow's breakfast with bright blue cloth napkins gracing flowered china cereal bowls and coffee mugs, and sparkling silver aligned with almost military fastidiousness. Two walls held matching framed posters of one large red flower, their bold color the only hint of Sugar Taplinger's full-blooded personality.

Lainey thought of her own kitchen, a space of under twenty square feet, crowded with indiscriminate china and unmatched silverware, her refrigerator door decorated with photographs of friends, notes to herself, and pictures drawn by Tim and Riley when they'd been in nursery school. Not to mention, she realized, the dishes she'd probably left in the sink from her quick lunch that afternoon. I live like a child, she reflected, comparing her own surroundings to the houses occupied by Farrell and Sugar. Hell, she lived like a child compared to just about everyone else in the world, she admitted to herself, conjuring up other single women she knew. Even her most immature New York acquaintances undoubtedly managed to leave the house without providing evidence of their tuna on whole wheat for their return.

"Farrell. You in there?"

The voice calling from the garage sounded tentative and young.

"Yes," Farrell answered back, recognizing it immediately, "we're in here."

A pale, thin woman in her late twenties made her way into the kitchen, hugging herself for warmth. "Sugar sent me over to remind you about the refrigerator in the basement. She says there's lots more ice down there."

"I don't think we'll need it," Farrell answered, extracting two plastic bags filled with ice cubes from the bottom shelf of the freezer. "Here, Lainey, take these two. There are more over here." She started to dig around behind the containers of Häagen-Dazs, then turned back to the others. "Lainey, you've met Carol Anne, haven't you?"

"Actually, no." She held out her hand. "Lainey Wolfe."

"I'm Carol Anne Gisondi. How do you do?" She stood awkwardly, as if unsure of what to say. "Isn't Sugar's house beautiful?" she asked finally, looking around the kitchen and shaking her head as if in wonder. "I dream about having a place like this, with all these wonderful things in it."

"Well, I'm sure you will someday," Lainey said kindly.

The notion seemed to make Carol Anne more hopeful. "When J.J. and I got here last year, we thought we'd died and gone to heaven. I mean, it's so much prettier than Indiana—" She stopped and looked at Lainey. "That's where we're from, Evansville, Indiana. Anyway, J.J. and I are saving up for a house."

Farrell shut the freezer door. "The Gisondis are living in those nice condos a couple of miles north of here. You know, we pass them on the way from the train station."

"That's a route I know very well." Lainey smiled at Carol Anne. "I make the train trek up here at least once every six weeks or so."

Carol Anne looked at her with interest. "Do you live in New York City?"

Lainey nodded.

Carol Anne seemed amazed. "I would be so scared to do that."

"It's not as bad as you think, I promise." Lainey felt

unexpectedly annoyed. Why did every out-of-towner have to imagine her city as one of the layers of hell?

"Well, I think you're very brave." The young woman's big blue eyes opened wide, as if she were addressing some sort of celebrity. "If you need a ride to the station tonight, we could drop you off later. We pass right by it on our way home."

"You know, if you're going in an hour or so, I might take you up on that." Lainey looked at her watch. "There's a twelve thirty-eight I could make. That is, unless you're staying later. I'm happy to take a cab."

"No, no, that'll be just great." Carol Anne looked apologetically at Farrell. "The kids are with a new sitter tonight, so J.J. and I should be getting back."

"It's fine," Farrell said. "You know Meadowview. Even on New Year's Eve, everyone is home in their beds by twelve-thirty."

Showing no inclination to get back to the party, Carol Anne peppered Lainey with questions about her "fabulous" life. Farrell remained silent, although Lainey noticed her friend watching Carol Anne intently. What is Farrell finding so fascinating about her? Lainey wondered, bewildered by such interest in someone whose fawning gave Lainey the creeps.

Once back inside Farrell's house with a fresh supply of ice, Lainey wandered through to the living room. She noticed a crush of people, whispering and looking over one another's shoulders, abuzz with excitement.

"Alanna Hayden just walked in," a pleasant-looking man in his thirties whispered to Lainey.

That's *got* to be Penn Beckley's date, Lainey thought derisively. How very perfect. With a theatrically late entrance, the great Pennington Beckley had finally condescended to arrive at his sister's little party. And, of course, the sophisticated international news producer would have to have as his date the gorgeous superbrain who covered Congress on the evening news.

Well, it was nice to know some things remain the same, Lainey thought ironically, making her way to the buffet table. Penn Beckley, four years older than Farrell and Lainey, had been the apple of every eye—his parents, his schoolmates, the football and basketball coaches, every one of his teachers.

It had always seemed so unfair to Lainey, who visited the Beckley house almost daily all through her childhood. Everything Farrell did needed "fixing" or "improving" or "toning down," one of Mrs. Beckley's favorite expressions regarding her rebellious younger child. But Penn, *ah*, Penn, was perfection, his life oh-so charmed. As young as she'd been, Lainey could see his parents' pride every time he entered the room. *Behold the future senator, president, emperor*, they seemed to think as he lifted a glass of milk or tied his shoelaces.

Lainey reached for a plate and placed an assortment of vegetables on it. Her hip rested against the table as she chewed a carrot stick thoughtfully. It wasn't just the unfairness that bothered her all those years ago; it was the fact that Farrell never seemed bothered at all. She adored her brother, didn't seem to resent one minute of the attention showered upon him. To be fair, Lainey realized, Penn was never anything but kind to his little sister. And the truth of it was, every now and then, Lainey would watch him from the sidelines, guiltily admiring his longish, dark hair, the deeply set, almost black eyes that had girls from his classes calling him every night of the week.

But whatever schoolgirl crush she might have harbored was more than erased by his constant sniping at her. Sure he was kind to his sister, but he was horrible to Lainey. She could still remember her embarrassment at the scene he caused when she wore her first cashmere sweater in seventh grade. *Elvira Flatigan!* he'd yelled from the kitchen as Lainey walked upstairs toward Farrell's bedroom. She'd run into the room and slammed the door behind her, waiting to die of shame.

Sometimes he'd eavesdrop on their most intimate conversations, never hesitating to tease Lainey about her shyness.

"Why didn't you just go up to that jerk and ask him to dance," he once exploded as he overheard her pour out her heart to Farrell about Stevey Roth paying no attention to her at a Friday night mixer in the junior high school gym.

"What a surprise, seeing you here without a date."

The sound of Pennington Beckley's sarcastic words almost made her drop her plate. Screw you, she thought, keeping her face impassive as she turned to look at him.

"And what a surprise watching the crowds ogle your date. You undoubtedly picked her to impress the *pauvre citoyens* in their hopelessly provincial suburb." Lainey smiled sweetly as she tossed a raspberry into her mouth.

He eyed her disagreeably. "Your French is magnificent, I'm sure, but I happen to have been stationed in London for the past three years. Perhaps you could abuse me in a Cockney accent. It might have a *soupçon* more punch."

The response was quick, but the words came out slightly slurred and his gait was unsteady as he walked the length of the table, eyeing the spread of food with seeming distaste.

"I see you've already drunk your Christmas dinner," Lainey tossed out.

"And eating Christmas dinner alone must be so very comforting for you," he replied acidly. "I'm glad to see that, faced with a roomful of people, you still choose to stand here by yourself."

Lainey felt her face redden. "Perhaps if my parents had kissed my hem and invited an audience every time I brushed my teeth, I, too, would have the world eating out of my hand."

Penn looked at her more seriously. "Perhaps if you ever took any action whatsoever, you wouldn't be—what is it now?—thirty-six years old, waiting for the world to throw its riches into your lap."

Before Lainey could respond, Tim and Riley both came bounding toward their uncle. As if by magic, his sarcastic expression disappeared as he scooped both children up in his arms.

"God, it's great to see you two," he exclaimed, hugging them tightly before placing them back on the floor. "I might just have a couple of items out in the car that you'll be interested in," he added, grinning.

"Oh, Lainey, come with us and see what he brought." Riley's excitement had her just about jumping into the air.

Lainey smiled at both children, then raised her gaze to their uncle. She pictured the prince dispensing his magical favors; his adoring nephew and niece worshiping at his altar. "Sorry, guys, but it's about time I hit the road." Besides, she added to herself, it's never a good idea to throw up right before boarding a train.

Farrell lingered in front of the house as the last of her guests got into their cars. She watched Lainey climb into the back of the Gisondis' battered station wagon as Carol Anne's husband started the ignition. Carol Anne had stopped to say good night to the Hornbys, a couple whose son was in Little League with theirs.

Could it be true? Farrell wondered, watching Carol Anne and remembering what Sugar had revealed about her earlier that week. Could *she* really be doing that?

The last cars began to pull away, people still calling to one another through their open car windows. A sense of familiarity overwhelmed Farrell. It was all so normal, the ongoing flow of their well-ordered lives.

Slowly, the undercurrent of fear that had been there all night threatened to turn into sheer terror. She shivered. John came up behind her and she burrowed into his arms.

"We'd better get you inside," he said, kissing her briefly on the cheek.

But Farrell just stood as she was, turning her head to look up into her husband's face, his blond hair slightly windblown, his cheeks reddened by the cold. He's so solid, she thought, drinking him in, appreciating for the umpteenth time the straight line of his jaw, the ease with himself he'd had even as a college student.

For the past few months, they'd hardly touched each other, eating dinner together only to have him return to the office or retreat into his study until late into the night. The few times they'd made love, she'd felt a million miles away. It was as if he were turning into a stranger. Yet, here he was, the same boy she'd married, the one who loved her, who followed her around campus swearing eternal devotion.

Suddenly she knew she was about to make the biggest mistake of her life.

Chapter 2

Lainey gave a final wave to Farrell from the back seat of the Gisondis' station wagon as J.J. pulled away from the curb. Carol Anne's husband was as thin as his wife, his dark hair receding in front, combed carefully, strand by strand, over a balding space on top. Lainey saw his eyes in the rearview mirror, fixed intently on the road in front of him, as if afraid he would veer off if he looked away for even a second.

He's probably drunk, Lainey thought, feeling around for the seat belt and fastening it. Carol Anne turned at the sound and smiled at Lainey.

"Sorry for the mess," she said apologetically.

Lainey noted the mass of toys and magazines littering the floor of the car. "I don't mind a bit."

"Kids," Carol Anne said with a smile. "Eddie and Donna always leave such a mess."

"How old are they?" Lainey asked, not really caring what the answer was.

Carol Anne's face brightened. "Oh, they're nine and seven, just like Farrell's two." She looked inquiringly at Lainey. "Do you have children?"

"No. I'm godmother to Tim and Riley. That's about as close as I've come."

"Oh," Carol Anne exclaimed, "they're such nice

children. Of course with those parents . . . I think Farrell
and John Cole must be the smartest two people I've ever
met. And that house! Someday, J.J. and I will have a
house like that."

"Sure, when hell freezes over," her husband muttered
almost to himself.

Lainey smiled politely as Carol Anne chattered on.
Isn't it amazing, she thought as they rode. Here's this
woman wanting a big house, and there's Farrell envying
my freedom, and here I am, about to return to my one-
bedroom brownstone, dreading the silence, only wishing
for a minute of my best friend's life. God, is anyone
really happy with what they have, or is everyone like
some hamster on a treadmill, running in hopes of finding
something better and realizing they're right back where
they started?

She thanked the Gisondis as they dropped her off at
the station. The train was just pulling in. Was anyone
really happy at all? she wondered as she settled herself
into the dim, sparsely populated railroad car. She was
suddenly depressed at how little pleasure everyone she
met seemed to take in their lives. She catalogued the
people she knew. Was there anyone who even approached satisfaction? She stared out through the filthy
glass window of the train, suddenly imagining Julian
Kroll's face in front of her. That's who the one happy
person was. Julian. Happy with his wife, happy with his
two little girls, happy with his paltry hours with me.
Julian Kroll. Happy as a clam.

Her gloom continued all the way home, staying with
her in the cab as she rode toward her apartment on West
Eighty-ninth Street. When she got out ten minutes later,
she climbed the seven steps to the entrance and looked
around carefully before putting her key in the door,

making sure no one had come along behind her or lurked inside between the two sets of doors leading to the tiny lobby.

The stairway to her apartment on the second floor had been decorated by some zealous tenant, a long string of holly wrapped around the metal banister, making it unexpectedly cheerful. I bet it was Rhonda Hackett, she thought, opening her door. She could easily imagine the Barnard student who lived below her in 1B energetically beautifying the aging building for the holiday season. The idea reassured her, as did the fragrance of the potpourri she'd placed around her apartment a few days before.

She flicked on the overhead light, pleased and surprised to note how comfortable and attractive her home seemed to her. What was I thinking, she chided herself, as she took off her coat. Her living room, with its sixteen-foot ceiling and large windows, looked cozy and colorful, with Mexican print pillows decorating her mother's old navy blue couch and her own drawings and photographs framed along every wall.

She walked to her small kitchen. Even that looked good to her. She'd left only a dinner plate and a butter knife in the sink. Not so terrible, really, she comforted herself, thinking of the perfect neatness of the Connecticut houses she'd just come from. And the striped china mugs hanging from open shelves stacked with white porcelain dishes she'd bought cheaply at the Pottery Barn seemed welcoming and friendly. Even the haphazard pile of art books she'd been sifting through the night before slung along the wooden counter under the cupboards was a pleasant sight.

She opened the refrigerator and took out a bottle of diet soda, happy suddenly to be alone in her own home.

My palace, she said to herself ironically, unconsciously touching the refrigerator door, then the wooden counter as if they were lucky pieces.

Carrying the soda bottle with her, she walked through the living room, turning off the lights on her way, and on into her bedroom, feeling more content than she had all day. She stood peering out her large bay window, its view displaying the tiny backyards of the brownstones surrounding hers. There were signs of life all around, people still up well after two in the morning. The couple across the way was entertaining friends, their lights ablaze, the sounds of their CD player plainly audible. On the third floor of that building, she saw the familiar form of the young man lying across his bed and reading, as he did until after she was asleep every night.

Lainey shook her head in disbelief as she pulled her curtains shut and drew her dress up over her head. She remembered how envious and lonely she'd felt early in the evening. Now all that seemed ridiculous. This is my place; these are my people. She laughed at her grandiosity as she admitted to herself that she'd never even *met* any of the people whose lives she'd just looked into from afar.

But it's true in spirit, she thought, moving into the bathroom and grabbing her toothbrush. This is mine, nobody else's but mine, and it feels exactly right. She looked at her reflection in the mirror over the sink. For the first time that evening, her face seemed at ease to her, her dark blond hair cascading around her shoulders, her eyes a clear blue. She brushed her teeth quickly, then removed her makeup. Finishing her nightly routine, she turned off the bathroom light and returned to the bedroom, walking over to the bed with relief. She pulled back the Oriental bedspread she'd bought years before at Azuma, and climbed in. Everywhere she looked she saw pieces of her life: two stuffed bears she'd had since child-hood, photos of herself, Farrell, and an assortment of college friends covering the top of her crowded bookcase, mementos from trips she'd taken to Italy and France. She curled up in her blankets, happy to be alone in her own space. I must have been crazy, she thought, yawning, before she fell fast asleep.

At first, the sound of the downstairs bell seemed like a part of Lainey's dream. She was back at Brown, standing in front of her dorm, the shrill ring reminding her that she was late for class. Which class was it, biology or English? she thought frantically, uncertain of which way she should be going. Gradually, as the ring seemed to get louder and louder, the harsh sound pulled her awake.

Bleary and yawning, she sat up and listened for a few seconds before getting out of bed. Eight-thirty, she noted groggily, focusing on the clock and trying to remember exactly what time she'd fallen asleep the night before. Stepping into rubber thongs and pulling on an old flannel robe, she made her way to the living room and pressed the button that connected her voice to the building's entrance.

"If you're a salesman, please go away," she snapped, hoping she could go back to bed.

"It's me." Julian's baritone was unmistakeable.

She felt an immediate stab of excitement at the sound of his voice, followed by embarrassment at the power he had to make her turn to jelly that way. "Come on up," she said as she buzzed him in and unlocked her front door.

Which is worse, she wondered, evaluating the thirty seconds or so it would take him to get up the stairs, me or my apartment? Of course, it didn't matter how much notice she might have had. Julian Kroll was one of those people whose clothing and office—for God's sake, even his car—were perfectly stylish and perfectly neat, while she herself strove for the merest hint of order. She heard him enter just as she reached the bathroom, where she quickly washed her face and pulled her hair into a ponytail.

"So what brings Santa into Manhattan on a weekend?" she asked, coming back into the living room and noting the three large bags of gifts he carried. "I certainly wasn't expecting this."

"Aren't you glad to see me?" Julian asked, looking actually hurt as he dropped the bags down onto the floor. He held his arms open and smiled at her.

Lainey came to him, burying her face in his sheepskin jacket. Julian hugged her hard, then snaked his arms down her body, lifting the bottom of the robe and running his hands up the backs of her legs.

"Cold hands, colder heart," Lainey murmured, the complaint mitigated by her tunneling into him even more tightly.

"One of these days, you're going to realize how wrong you are about me, Lainey." Julian tilted her face up, kissing her first on each eyelid, then on her mouth, before letting her go and taking his jacket off.

She watched him hang his coat in the small front-hall closet, smiling as she realized she'd left her own coat lying haphazardly across the couch the night before.

"Here, my cynical beauty," he said, coming back to take several gifts out of one of the shopping bags. "How do I love thee. Let me count the ways." Expertly, he aimed the boxes at her, laughing as she caught one and dropped two others. Lainey bent down to pick them up, sinking to the floor as she began to open them.

"Oh, Julian," she whispered, extracting a long string of

pearls from the first box. "They're too beautiful." Lainey slid the pearls around her neck and ran her fingers over the smooth pebbles.

"Go on to the rest," Julian said, carrying the two remaining bags over to where she sat. Rather than joining her on the floor, he pushed her coat aside and made a place for himself on the couch facing her. Lainey opened the other boxes, delightedly exclaiming at each gift. Most were luxuries—an exotically colored Hermès scarf, a pair of luscious leather gloves, a silver fountain pen—but the last made her laugh aloud. She unwrapped the heavy package to find a Dustbuster.

"The one thing every American woman prays to get from the man she loves," she said with a grin, picking herself up from the floor and seating herself on his lap.

"You're always complaining about what a mess your place is, so I figured you'd like it." Julian eased her robe off her shoulders and began kissing her bare neck.

Lainey arched her head back, enjoying the warmth of his lips. "I complain about it mostly to make you think I might change."

"And perhaps one day you will," he murmured hoarsely, as if he were whispering words of love.

Don't hold your breath, Lainey thought even as she felt herself melting under Julian's attention. Her inability to get her life together seemed as complete now at thirty-six as it had been at thirteen. Unlike her, Julian always had everything together. The latest books? He'd read them. Newest restaurants? Eaten there. And even early on this Sunday morning, his clothes were impeccable.

He lay back on the couch, pulling her along so she ended up on top of him.

Lainey allowed herself to be led. "Why are you here, by the way?"

"To see you, of course."

Lainey couldn't make herself let it go. "Where does your wife think you are?"

Julian closed his eyes for a minute, then let out a long sigh and opened them. "I'm picking up Christmas presents for my in-laws." He slid his arms around her and pulled her close. "You don't have to worry about me, honey," he said slowly, clearly uncomfortable at having to answer.

"And how are you going to produce these presents if you're here with me?" she prodded, not quite giving in to his warmth.

He opened the belt of her robe and moved his lips down to her breasts. "The gifts have been in the trunk of my car since last Tuesday. Assuming it doesn't get stolen in the next two hours, my husbandly duties for today will have been fully executed."

An unpleasantly familiar feeling swept over Lainey, a combination of annoyance and humiliation. But she couldn't make herself stop him as he slipped off her robe, depositing it in a heap on the floor.

"I love being here with you," he whispered, encircling her legs with his own and teasing her nipple with his tongue.

Lainey ran her hands up along his arms and around his back, not wanting to think anymore, wanting only to feel him close to her. She closed her eyes, letting his heat take over.

Chapter 3

"So then, I get to the bottom of my red wine, and this metal thing bounces against my teeth. At first I almost choked, but I see the expression on Jimmy's face, and I put the glass down, and at the bottom is this diamond ring." Gail Salerno's round chipmunk cheeks reddened as her eyes went back and forth between Lainey and Carla Mirsky, as if waiting for a reaction. Finally, getting nothing from either one of them, she leaned forward in her chair and dropped her tuna sandwich on the tray in front of her. "I mean, I thought I'd die of shock. I wanted to kill him."

Carla wiped at her mouth with a paper napkin, as much to hide her smile as to remove the trace of strawberry yogurt. "How shocked can you be when poor Jimmy's been telling you he loves you for the past month?"

"Kenny loves me, too, but he hasn't leapt to any conclusions. I'm nowhere near ready for marriage," Gail answered in an outraged tone.

"You're right—Jimmy should be killed for doing such a vicious, despicable thing like proposing marriage," Carla retorted. "Frankly, most single women in New York show a bit of discretion about their affections. I mean, if I had been involved with fourteen different men when I first met Larry, he not only wouldn't have married me, he never would have spoken to me again." Carla finished her yogurt, replacing the top on the empty container, folding her napkin exactly in quarters and pulling out a tiny mirror to reapply her lipstick. Checking to see that her short brown hair was perfectly in place, she put the mirror back in her bag and once again faced Gail. "You can't date a batallion and expect to find happiness. One man is quite enough for me."

Gail's mocking grin was a challenge. "I know King Larry and the two little princes bring you personal ecstasy, but some of us need a little excitement, a bit of spontaneity before we line up to die."

"Jesus, Gail," Carla began to laugh. "Who equates a husband and children with the Bataan death march? I love married life. I also love my job and, until today, I was quite fond of my friends."

"Well, you may be perfect, but the rest of us aren't so lucky." Gail eyed Carla's well-tailored gray suit and matching gray suede pumps with ill-concealed disdain.

"Gail, do you think just once you could jump all over Lainey instead of me? Come on, it's almost my birthday, you can make it my gift." Carla leaned back in her chair.

Gail was just as happy to redirect her fire. "Now that you mention it, what *do* you do for a social life, Lainey? You're always so mysterious. A person could almost believe you're up to no good."

"There is no gooder girl than me, I promise you." Lainey joined in the conversation reluctantly. In the two years the women had been eating together in Carpathia's cafeteria, she'd managed to keep her affairs private, not an easy task considering how close a friendship had developed among the three of them. "I go home at night, wash my stockings, say my prayers, read a few pages of *Middlemarch*, and go to sleep."

Carla and Gail looked equally dubious.

"What do you two think I do?" Lainey demanded. "After all, where would all these men be, the ones I could be no good with?"

Carla decided to treat the question seriously. "How about the guys you deal with in California?"

Rick Dean and Jerry Struch were Lainey's contacts in the Los Angeles operations of Carpathia Merchandising. Each a full-fledged vice president, their mutual appreciation of Lainey's work plus their casual California style had made them the best part of Lainey's job. Rick and Jerry were also talented artists who were savvy about corporate politics in a way Lainey could never duplicate. For several months both of them had been trying to refine her behavior in ways that would catapult her beyond her mere designer's job, though so far what they'd accomplished had mostly been making her even less secure than she was to begin with.

"They're terrific, but they're busy dating each other." Lainey herself had regretted this.

"Listen, ladies." She pushed her chair back, longing to end the inquiry into her social life. "I know hundreds of nice men, all of whom are either gay or married, and thousands of fabulous women. Maybe my problems will be solved by divine intervention—after all, every night I go to bed praying to wake up a lesbian." With that she stood and picked her tray up from the table, waiting expectantly for Carla and Gail to join her.

Gail sighed and rose as well. But Carla continued gazing up at Lainey, her neutral look turning into a smirk when Julian Kroll passed their table.

"Carla, Gail. Ms. Wolfe." The tray containing fruit salad and herbal iced tea Julian carried seemed well suited to his navy blue double-breasted Armani jacket and the ponytail that rested against his elegant collar. The gold wedding band on his left hand looked newly shined against the tan remaining from his family New Year's in Antigua. "I hope Christmas was good to all of you."

"Santa was more than kind," Gail answered for the three of them.

Lainey acknowledged his greeting, but stared past him, hoping the rush of excitement she felt at the sight of him wasn't visible on her face. She tried to ignore the long study Carla was conducting, her eyes darting between Lainey and Julian. Lainey had kept her affair with Julian a secret for the entire year they'd been dating, but Carla was not fooled. She'd approached the subject a couple of times with pointed questions, but Lainey had avoided the truth. She felt bad about being dishonest with a friend, but opening this can of worms with someone from the office could only make things more awkward.

Lainey always felt self-conscious when she and Julian were in front of colleagues. She tried to lessen her own tension by talking about work. "Uh, Julian, have you heard anything about the layouts for Matilda and Mommy?" She had sent rough sketches to Rick and Jerry by overnight mail. Often they okayed her projects directly, but some of the time approvals went through Julian, whose job as creative director of Carpathia consisted largely of keeping the corporate image harmonious among its many divisions.

"No," Julian answered, his eyes fastened on hers. "I expect to hear later this afternoon. There were a couple of little things . . ." He seemed slightly uncomfortable.

"What kind of little things?" Lainey could imagine what the "little things" might just be. Carpathia was proud of its reputation as a staunchly conservative company. An extra-wide smile, a hair out of place on any of its characters and Corporate would react as if one of their characters had been assaulted and killed.

"Well," Julian said dismissively, as if it were unimportant, "there was some mention of a Dorset tone to several of the sketches."

Dorset was Carpathia's arch rival, a corporation almost as large, well known for colorful and exotic cartoon creatures and groundbreaking marketing techniques. To most of the Carpathia executives, having "a Dorset tone" was akin to appearing naked on Main Street. Lainey thought about the sketches she'd sent to Los Angeles. She'd used a lot of purple in one of them, and a drizzled brush stroke in another, finding both of these sketches more electric than her usual sedate work. I should have known better, she thought, her heart sinking. Carpathia provided steady work, but individual creativity was not only discouraged, it was often grounds for dismissal.

Julian patted her shoulder, his hand lingering just a little too long for Lainey's peace of mind.

"You'll call me when you know what's what," she said, moving away from him.

"Sure. I should hear something by three or so. You'll be in your office?"

Lainey nodded and walked toward the back of the cafeteria, where the trays were collected and washed. Carla and Gail fell into line behind her.

"God, that Julian Kroll is attractive," Gail cooed.

"And very, very married."

Lainey knew Carla's stern warning was directed more to her than to Gail, but she didn't bother to acknowedge it.

"See you later," she said to both of them, turning around quickly and striding toward the elevator.

* * *

"Hey, you!" Al Smile's impatient, booming voice preceded him down the corridor, so that five different people looked up expectantly as he barreled toward the suite of offices that comprised Carpathia's Division of Art and Development. Lainey gazed up from her drawing board as did Fran Myerson, whose space was across the large room the two shared.

Fran quickly pulled a hairbrush from her top drawer, running it through her mane of curly blond hair, letting her head fall forward, then briskly back, so it settled like a shower of gold upon her shoulders. She seemed to find Al's inability to call anyone on his staff anything other than "Hey, you" a challenge, daring her to find a way to become memorable. To Lainey, it was simply another piece of sloppy behavior from a man who couldn't keep mustard off his tie or spinach from his front teeth. As art director of Carpathia, Al's most important function was making sure that fifteen artists re-created exact copies of billion-dollar creations like "Matilda and Mommy," the mother and tot pair who'd starred in four full-length movies and graced untold millions of cups, backpacks, and lunch boxes. In his capacity as overseer, Al was a relentless perfectionist. In any other dealing, however, he couldn't even be called upon to button his shirt correctly.

"Hey, you . . . uh, Wolfe," Al called out, stopping at Lainey's desk.

Lainey put down the marker she was using to design yet another "Patsy Pony" T-shirt, and turned her attention to Al, who was chewing gum and practically dancing in place, two things he always did when forced to stand relatively still for more than a second or two.

"How's it coming?" he asked, reaching down and turning her drawing around without asking if she minded.

"Do me a favor, Al, and come back in an hour." Purposefully, she returned the drawing to its original position and covered it with her arm. "I promise the Patsy T-shirt will be so adorable, children will murder each other to get one. Just give me one more hour of peace."

"What'd ya hear from California?"

"Nothing yet. I'm expecting a call from Julian Kroll."

"Who's working on SnapDragon?" Al asked, his eyes wandering the room as if in search of enlightenment from the furniture.

Fran offered up the information immediately, taking the opportunity to lean forward provocatively as she gave Al the name he was seeking. Ever restless, Al didn't even notice the hint of cleavage revealed in the maneuver, turning on his heel and rushing out the door.

"God, he's so cute." Fran's sincerity was as startling to Lainey as her apparent taste.

"Al Smile?" she asked in disbelief.

Fran looked at her with surprise. "Don't you find him attractive? I thought everyone in the department did." She shrugged as she noticed Lainey's lack of response. "It's all that energy. Edgy men always get to me."

Lainey thought about that for a moment. "I guess I have less appreciation for the hyperkinetic than you have. Good luck to you though. God knows, Al could use someone who appreciates a high endorphin count." She smiled at Fran. "Or, at the very least, someone to take his stuff to the dry cleaners more than once a year."

The phone rang as she turned back to her work.

"Lainey Wolfe."

Julian's voice on the other end was an intimate caress. "Did I tell you how beautiful you look today?" he purred.

"Yes, sir, what can I do for you?" Lainey was aware of Fran's interest from across the room.

"How about we get out of here right at five and you call me 'Sir' in the privacy of your home. 'Please, sir,' 'Thank you, sir,' 'Can I have some more, sir?' Doesn't that sound about right?"

Julian's throaty voice suddenly annoyed Lainey. Why couldn't he ever arrange something in advance; why did it always have to be spur of the moment, precisely when it suited him, except for their regular Thursday nights together? Because he's the one who's married, schmuck, Lainey said to herself, answering her own question.

"I don't think that's possible," she said dispassionately for Fran's benefit. "Was there any answer on the sketches?"

Julian retreated into a corporate tone. "Well, yes, actually. L.A. wants a more standard visual." His voice became apologetic. "Sorry, Lainey. You know how those committee meetings go. Their taste was fixed in 1938, and they see no benefit to moving forward."

"Thanks, Julian." Lainey hung up the phone before he could say anything more. Why does every interaction with him upset me so much? she asked herself, turning away from Fran's curious gaze.

Why, indeed, she practically said out loud. Just because I have a job with no future and a love life with no future—why should that bother me?

Chapter 4

Farrell paid the cab driver and stepped out onto the street. Resolutely, she retied the sash more tightly on her black cashmere coat, still trying to ignore the terror that had been with her for the past twenty-four hours, ever since Sugar had called her to say today was the day.

Actually, Farrell had thought about little else since the morning in Sugar's kitchen when she had finally let herself be persuaded to do the unthinkable. It was as if Sugar had seen into Farrell's soul—and found the darkness there.

Over and over since then, Farrell had resolved to call Sugar and tell her that she couldn't go through with it. But something always stopped her. It had been so many years since she'd had this feeling, the delicious terror, the illicit thrill of doing something forbidden. She'd practically forgotten what it was like.

God knows, she loved her husband and their life together, and she would do anything for Tim and Riley; they were the most wonderful children in the world. But Sugar had been so frighteningly right. When Farrell had married John and moved to Connecticut with him, she'd pretty much left behind the girl she used to be. And, Christ, how she missed that girl.

She kept telling herself this was a mistake, that it

would have devastating consequences if she got caught. But something inside her resisted. She was going to do this. She had to.

It was bitingly cold outside, but clear and crisp. Farrell adjusted the knitted black hat under which she had tucked her thick brown hair. She squinted in the bright sunlight at the words *Hotel St.-Tropez* written in white script letters on a blue canopy. When she reached into her purse for her sunglasses, her hands trembled slightly with nervousness.

Good thing it's sunny, she thought as she pulled open one of the heavy glass doors to the lobby, but I'd be wearing these glasses even if it were the dead of night. I don't care if Glenvale is four towns away from mine. I have no intention of having anybody recognize me. Taking a cab here had been Sugar's suggestion, and it was a damned good one, Farrell reflected. The last thing she needed was someone she knew spotting her Saab.

She headed through the lobby toward the elevators, her long strides and determined air disguising her growing panic. It didn't look as if anyone was going to stop her. God, what would I say if someone asked me where I'm going? she wondered fearfully. Stop it, Farrell, you're acting like an idiot, she told herself. As if you couldn't handle a hotel clerk. You're going to see a registered guest, as anybody else might.

The elevator door opened and she stepped in, checking her reflection in the mirrored rear wall. She'd spent close to an hour that morning deciding what to wear, carefully surveying her racks of clothing in the enormous walk-in closet she loved so much, a renovation she'd treated herself to as a birthday present three years before. Finally, she'd chosen a beige wool sweater dress, elegant and simply cut, but close-fitting to show off her curves.

Pressing ten, the hotel's top floor, she removed her hat and dug a brush out of her bag, hurriedly yanking it through her hair, as she ran her tongue along her teeth to erase any traces of lipstick that might be there. She finished and shoved the brush and hat into her bag as the elevator doors opened again.

I'm really going ahead with it, she thought as she stepped into the hall. Her heart was pounding crazily in her chest. When was the last time she'd felt this electrified? All at once, it came back to her. It was the night when, on a sudden impulse, she'd taken off from her college dorm and hitchhiked through the night to Cape Cod. She'd waited there expectantly on the barely lit road, thumb out, knowing she'd miss her biology exam the next day, knowing her friends would be frantically looking for her, but happier than she'd been in months. She loved the anonymous freedom as she wove elaborate lies about her life for the men who stopped for her in their pickup trucks and sleek sports cars and tried to seduce her along the way. She remembered so vividly the way she had felt when she reached the Cape, shoes in hand as she meandered along the beach at dawn. There was something of that in how she felt right now.

My God, she thought, a smile lighting up her face. I actually feel *young* again.

The suite was at the very end of the hall. Room 1012. It had a name painted on the door below the room number. *La Plage*. Let's hope that this is indeed a day at the beach, Farrell thought, wanting to laugh aloud at her own giddiness. Her confidence suddenly restored, she opened her coat and smoothed down the front of her dress, then gave two sharp raps on the door.

Almost immediately, Sugar opened it, smiling in greeting. Dressed in her usual uniform of a silk caftan, this one in a paisley print, her rich red hair was swept up in a loose bun on top of her head, and she wore more makeup than Farrell was used to seeing on her. I guess this is her business look, Farrell thought wryly.

"Well, hon, here you are." Sugar gestured toward the living room behind her.

Farrell slipped off her coat as she entered and looked around. The suite's outer room was decorated with thick carpeting and voluminous drapery at the two windows, which shut out the light and noise of the outside world to create a cocoonlike effect. Farrell quickly took in the large sofa and love seat, some cherry-wood end tables, an enormous antique mirror, several paintings, and sterling bric-a-brac scattered strategically throughout. Next to the sofa, a silver ice bucket rested on a stand, the neck of a champagne bottle sticking out; two champagne flutes were in place on the coffee table, along with a small dish of black caviar and an assortment of crackers.

"This is beautiful," Farrell said sincerely, the surprise evident in her voice. Expensive suites might have nice furnishings, but the St.-Tropez didn't routinely have anything nearly as tasteful and extravagant as this, she was certain. The decor had been carefully planned, and it was obvious to Farrell that everything was of the best quality. Virtually all of it had been brought in from the outside by someone who wanted to give the room a richer look and an intimate feeling. But brought in by whom? Sugar? Farrell couldn't imagine that the same woman whose own house was decorated in country prints and frills had put together this sophisticated retreat.

When she'd imagined this suite, Farrell had anticipated that it would be pleasant and comfortable—Sugar would hardly send her to some dump—but she'd still expected a more standard-issue hotel room. More impersonal. Something less . . . calculated. It occurred to her that she would have preferred that. Sugar had mentioned that she kept the suite on a permanent basis, but Farrell hadn't thought about it much. Now, unbidden, visions appeared in her mind of the many people who might parade in and out of this elegant room, and what they might be doing in here.

Suddenly, this didn't seem like quite the spontaneous lark it had before. It was, in fact, a business. Sugar's business. And from the time and money invested in this room, she clearly took it very seriously.

Farrell's lightheartedness vanished as quickly as it had come.

Sugar seemed to sense her shift in mood. She came up next to Farrell and put an arm around her. "You look absolutely gorgeous, and this guy is going to be thrilled. You will be, too, honey, because I promise you, he's the best-looking man I've seen in only about a hundred years." Moving to stand behind her, she gave Farrell's shoulders a few firm massage strokes as she talked. "I promise you, this will be *fun*."

Farrell spoke uneasily. "Maybe I—"

"Oh, I nearly forgot," Sugar interrupted. "You're going to need this to lock up after you leave, and you can keep it for next time." She went over to a side table and extracted a large silver key from her purse. "Now that you know your way around, there's no need for me to meet you here again."

Biting her lip, Farrell took the key.

"The bathroom's inside, of course, and you'll find the bedroom completely wonderful, lots of pillows and lace, soft lights, that sort of thing." Sugar continued speaking as she retrieved a blue cape from the closet. "There are condoms in the drawer next to the bed."

Farrell nodded.

"And, remember, I'll get the money to you. Don't say a word about it to him. I know this guy, and he'll keep it simple, so you won't have to negotiate anything."

Farrell was too taken aback to reply.

Sugar glanced at her watch. "He'll be here in a few minutes, so I'm gonna run." She stopped to look more closely at Farrell. Slowly, a wide smile spread across her face and she let out a loud laugh, the same old Sugar that Farrell had always known. "You look as nervous as a cat. Now stop that, honey. Have some champagne and relax. You're in for a treat."

She opened the door and waved, the bracelets on her massive arm jangling. "Talk to you later."

Alone, Farrell just stood where she was for a moment. What am I doing here? she wondered. She should just leave, disappear. This man didn't know who she was; it made no difference. Sugar would understand.

Sugar. Farrell frowned. The woman who just left bore little resemblance to the Sugar who sat in her backyard on hot summer afternoons, mixing mint juleps and gossiping. Sure, her friend was a tornado of efficiency and organization. She was always cooking, cleaning, running from this charity function to that benefit luncheon. Her life seemed to Farrell like a whirlwind of community events and board meetings, and she still managed to find time to make the elaborate Easter decorations she thought Tim and Riley "might get a kick out of," or the magnificent centerpiece of dried flowers she'd "just thrown together" for Farrell's hall table. Farrell had always been slightly amused—and, if she was going to be honest, somewhat condescending—about what she called Sugar's Total Woman activities. Here she had envisioned Sugar as a lively, outspoken woman who nonetheless still measured her worth by the cleanliness of her guest bathroom and the gooeyness of her brownies.

But it turned out she had a secret life that proved she was nothing like the image Farrell had of her. Of course, who would have dreamed Sugar would oversee a bunch of women out looking for some excitement and extra cash? "For both fun and profit, absolutely, the two go hand in hand," was how she put it when she first confided in Farrell about the operation a month before. Today, though, there was an edge to her that Farrell had never seen before. She forced herself to push aside her mounting uneasiness.

Well, she's gone and I'm here, Farrell thought. Some gorgeous man is about to knock on that door. If I walk out now, I'll never know what might have been.

She turned back to look at the living room. Champagne, Sugar had said. Crossing over to the ice bucket, she lifted the bottle out of the ice chips surrounding it. She glanced at the label. *Cristal.* My, Sugar doesn't mess around, she thought, reaching for the white cloth draped through the bucket's handle to cover the cork as she eased it out of the bottle. She practically gulped down the first glass, then took a deep breath and poured herself a second. Sipping it, she sat down on the couch.

The champagne was delicious. She'd skipped breakfast and had only a salad for lunch, so the alcohol was affecting her already. Closing her eyes, she felt herself relax. Sometimes at night when she was having trouble sleeping, she would concentrate on a mental picture of a beach to help drive all her other thoughts away. She conjured up the picture now, imagining azure water lapping at the shore, the hot sun on her bare shoulders. She felt good, genuinely calm now. She interrupted her reverie just long enough to pour a third glass of champagne, then returned to the couch, noticing she was getting a bit hazy and not minding at all.

I am about to do something outrageous, she thought dreamily. And I'm going to have a great time doing it.

There was a loud knock at the door. Farrell jumped up with a start, her stomach flip-flopping, her adrenaline instantly pumping again. But she wasn't completely steady on her feet. She paused a moment to regain her equilibrium before she set down her glass and moved toward the door, her hands automatically reaching to smooth her hair back.

"Yes?" she managed to get out, the anticipation tying her stomach into a knot.

The voice that answered was deep. "It's Don."

Here goes.

She opened the door to reveal a man in a navy blue overcoat, carrying a briefcase. He was over six feet, with graying hair, and a narrow face, the long, bony nose and chin giving him a harshness, despite his friendly smile as he took in the woman before him. Gorgeous was how Sugar had described him. No, Farrell thought in dismay. Okay-looking, but that's all. Actually, kind of scrawny.

"Well, hello," he said pleasantly. "Mind if I come in?"

Farrell immediately took a step back to make room for him. He entered, and she watched as he dropped his briefcase against the wall, then hung up his coat in the closet. He was reed-thin beneath his well-cut gray suit. She noted his expensive shoes, the good silk tie, gold cufflinks she recognized from Tiffany. He's been here before, she realized, seeing how familiarly he moved about the room.

"I see you've gotten started already," he said, pointing toward the open champagne bottle on the coffee table. "Mind if I join you?"

She nodded. He looked at her more directly. "You *do* speak English, don't you?"

"Oh, yes, of course." She managed to find her voice. "Please, sit down and help yourself." What am I saying, she wondered. I sound as if I'm hostessing a dinner party instead of getting ready to have sex with a total stranger.

"Good." He was settling himself down on the couch and patting the cushion next to him. "Join me, won't you? My name's Don, and I think you're absolutely beautiful. You are . . . ?"

"F . . . Fay." And you're probably David or Douglas or something, she thought. But that's not my concern.

"Okay, Fay, let's play." He smiled at his rhyme.

Farrell stood there, tongue-tied. She was startled by a sudden surge of irritation at herself. Christ, she thought, I came here to have some fun, and I've done nothing but cower and worry. I know this guy's paying, but there's no reason I can't have a good time. I'm not going to stand here while he makes stupid jokes. I came to be wild, and I'm goddamned going to do it.

She strode across to the couch, lifting her glass and holding it out for more as she dropped down beside him, one leg underneath her. "I'm glad you could make it."

He turned toward her, his eyes traveling over her face, her body, liking what he saw. Slowly, he put out his hand and ran it up and down her arm, feeling the soft material of her sleeve. "I don't have too much time today, but I'm glad I could make it, too. May I kiss you?"

Farrell downed the rest of her champagne, then turned back to face him. Were all the men who came here so polite? Her head was getting foggier. Come on, Farrell baby, she told herself, loosen up. You've earned this with years of good behavior.

"I wish you *would* kiss me." She almost giggled, feeling like she was in some kind of bad movie.

He leaned forward and slowly brought his lips to hers. Farrell saw her husband's face in front of her, felt her husband's lips on her mouth. No, no, no. She shut her eyes, forcing herself to feel the strangeness of this man's tongue in her mouth, moving around, faster and faster.

His hands went to her breasts, stroking and kneading them. Farrell kept her eyes closed as he pulled away from her. She could hear his breathing grow faster, was aware of his hand slipping across her stomach, down her leg and under the hem of her dress. She tensed as he stroked her thigh, moving up until he reached her stocking top.

"Ohhh, you're wearing a garter belt," he breathed, his thin fingers trailing underneath the material. "You're so beautiful." Relax, relax, she told herself. She leaned her head back against the couch, putting her hands on his shoulders. She felt the bottom of her dress being shoved up to her waist.

"Oh, please . . ." he was moaning, his hands roaming across the new black silk garter belt and underpants she'd bought a few days earlier.

Suddenly, he was standing, and in one motion leaned forward to lift her from the couch in his arms, carrying her like a baby, surprisingly strong. Instinctively, her arms went around his shoulders to keep from falling as he hurried with her into the other room. The bedroom was dim, the drapes drawn closed, none of the lights on. He deposited her gently onto the enormous bed, then slid the dress up over her head, tossing it aside.

Farrell lay on the bed, realizing she was really and truly drunk now, unable to think. The man above her stepped back to gaze hungrily at her body as he quickly kicked off his shoes and yanked off the rest of his clothes. Farrell watched him coming closer, felt his weight upon her, inhaled his unfamiliar odor. She imagined her husband's broad shoulders, his familiar soapy-clean smell. *John.*

Dear God, she thought frantically, I must have been insane. This is crazy, wrong, the worst thing I've ever done. She wanted to run, to yell at this stranger to get away from her. But she couldn't seem to move. She'd come here of her own free will; she'd invited this madness into herself. What was she going to do?

He was grunting now, his hands moving everywhere on her. She felt her legs being pushed apart, his fingers insistent now, yanking her underpants aside.

"Yeah, yeah, do me," he was saying as he moved away from her for a moment. She realized he was reaching into the night table drawer, heard the condom package being ripped open. Then he was over her again. She felt his hardness pressing against her, pushing, pushing, until he found his way and shoved into her. She moaned in pain and misery.

God help me, oh, God, I'm sorry. She felt hot tears sliding down her cheeks. John, honey, I'm so sorry.

The man above her thrust again and again, mumbling words she couldn't make out. Farrell turned her head away, her eyes shut tight, her hands clenched into fists by her side. She felt his spasm, heard his final groan. He flopped down, his weight fully upon her, catching his breath.

It was as if she were suddenly able to move once again. Immediately, she pushed him off her.

"Leave now," she whispered hoarsely. "Right now."

He looked at her in amazement. "What?"

"Please leave."

His eyes narrowed, the pleasant demeanor of before

Chapter 5

"So, Lainey baby, when you come in tomorrow, make sure you're wearing something that reeks of adult." Rick Dean's usual laid-back California tone held an edge of excitement that came through clearly over the telephone.

Lainey glanced down at what she'd chosen to wear to work that morning. Her black leggings, over which her turquoise wool granny dress hung perfectly to midthigh, fit snugly into the black suede lace-up platform shoes she'd snagged in the flea market on Sixth Avenue the week before.

"And your hair, baby," Rick continued as fashion expert, "could you brush it or something? Make it nice, you know. Just don't do the ponytail thing."

Guiltily, Lainey pulled out the rubber band holding her makeshift ponytail before realizing that no one was there to see it.

"What is this about?" she asked finally, interrupting him in the middle of the same "bright lipstick brightens your whole face" tirade she'd had to live through years before with her mother.

"Never you mind what it's about, sweetheart. Just know it's about something you're gonna really like." Rick sounded uncharacteristically smug.

When Rick and Jerry had called earlier that day to

announce that something big was going on, something that had a lot to do with Lainey, she'd felt elated, just as they clearly meant her to. But two phone calls from Jerry and another one from Rick later, overwhelmed by instructions ranging from beauty notes to conversational tips, Lainey was becoming terrified.

"Rick," she said, trepidation creeping into her voice, "please just tell me what's going on. You and Jerry have succeeded in scaring me half to death, and neither one of you will give me any idea of what I've got to be scared of."

"Oh, Lainey, chill. There's nothing to be scared of. Believe me, you're going to love this. I would tell you what it is but I promised the guys here I wouldn't spill it."

The guys here. Lainey stayed silent for a moment. Rick and Jerry were the only people she ever communicated with in the Los Angeles office. She didn't know a soul at California headquarters besides them. So who were "the guys here" and what could they possibly want with her?

"Listen," Rick said gently, "I know I'm being oblique, but I promise this is not just good news, it's great news. They're gonna talk to you tomorrow and then you're gonna call Jerry and me, and . . ."

Lainey's other line rang.

"Rick, can you hold on for a second?" Lainey pressed the hold button and switched to the other line.

"Lainey Wolfe."

"Hey you, uh, Wolfe." Al Smile sounded even edgier than usual as he grunted into the phone. "Get yourself up to thirty-five. Patrick Fouchard wants to see you."

"What?" Lainey couldn't keep the shock out of her response. Patrick Fouchard, senior vice president of

Carpathia, Inc., wasn't only Al Smile's boss, he was Al Smile's boss's boss. What could a corporate hotshot like Fouchard possibly want with her?

"Just get yourself up to thirty-five, Wolfe."

"Can't you give me some idea of what I'm going up there for?"

"No," Al said peevishly. "Whatever it is, Fouchard didn't bother sharing it with me." With that, he hung up.

Lainey switched back to the other phone line. "Rick, Patrick Fouchard wants to see me upstairs."

"Oh, man," he said, plainly rattled. "They must have decided to do it today, instead of tomorrow. Okay, get on up there."

She started to hang up, hearing his "And make sure you call us the minute you get back downstairs!" just before the receiver hit the cradle.

Here goes nothing, she thought, shaking her hair into place as best she could and walking out to the elevator bank at the end of the hall.

The thirty-fifth floor of the Carpathia building looked unlike any other. Lainey felt her shoes sinking into a carpet inches thick. An array of Impressionist paintings graced the walls, and Patrick Fouchard's secretary sat directly under fifteen square feet of Monet's *Water Lilies*. Lainey was so stunned by the original masterpiece, she stood without speaking to the young woman at the desk.

"Ms. Wolfe, I assume." The dark-haired woman gently interrupted her staring.

"Oh, yes," Lainey answered, shifting her attention quickly.

The woman picked up a phone, announcing Lainey's presence, and nodded in the direction of a large white door to the left. Lainey walked through, entering an office half the size of a basketball court, fresh flowers in huge vases placed artistically on two tables, a large porcelain sculpture of a ballet dancer taking up the far corner behind the narrow marble table that apparently served as a desk.

"A pleasure, Lainey."

Patrick Fouchard walked toward her, a giant in blue pin-stripe, his enormous bulk making her feel absurdly Lilliputian.

"How do you do." She managed to hold her hand out.

Fouchard waved her over to a seating area just off the entryway, indicating a small beige silk couch for her and seating himself on the exact match opposite.

"Great work on Matilda and Mommy." Fouchard leaned forward, punching her lightly on the arm, and nodding his head up and down several times.

Lainey was so startled by his touch, she said nothing in return. Fouchard had the air of a heavyweight contender preparing for a big fight, his head continuing to bob, his arms occasionally jabbing at some invisible opponent.

"So what's next for you?" He leaned forward once again, this time feinting a playful right to her midsection.

Lainey tried to mask her confusion. "I'm sorry, Mr. Fouchard. Was there something I was supposed to know before coming up to see you?"

"Nah." He feinted again, once to the left, then quickly to the right. "Listen, Lainey, the guys in California have been telling us how terrific you are. Your stuff on Matilda and Patsy, all first-rate." He got up and began to walk around, his gait a small trot, his hands moving as he spoke. "We need someone like you, someone original to start up a new deal." He stopped in front of her. "Do you know anything about Marissa?"

Lainey shook her head. "No," she answered, bewildered.

"Well, neither does anyone else." Fouchard started to guffaw, his whole body shaking, as he appreciated his own wit. "All anyone knows about Marissa is that she's gonna appeal to girls between ten and fourteen. And she's gonna carry a half-hour television program in prime time, and about twenty million dollars in merchandising paraphernalia in her first year."

"What exactly *is* Marissa?" Lainey asked.

"Well, I guess that'll be up to you." Fouchard began his trot once again, jabbing constantly now.

"Up to me?" Lainey couldn't believe what she was hearing.

Fouchard looked at her as if she were a backward child, then shrugged and took the seat opposite her once again. "You're gonna start up the whole thing. Maybe you'll want her to have a sexy brother, you know, like Blossom does."

Taking in her blank face, he forced himself to slow down. "According to the California guys, you're just the person to create Marissa and see her through her journey. You know, just like Pevis did with Kathleen."

Kathleen the Wise Cat was Carpathia's queen of Saturday morning television. Early in her career, Lainey had done a quick pasteup of a Kathleen cup and saucer, which had sold over two million sets. Ernie Pevis, the guy who'd created Kathleen and overseen both the television and merchandising efforts, had been rewarded not just with enough bonus money to last several lifetimes, but his own six-story building in Culver City with a design team of over a dozen of Carpathia's best people.

"You're giving me a character to create?" Lainey couldn't keep the amazement out of her voice.

"They say you're the one." Fouchard gave her a brief grin. "Of course, it'll have to be done in L.A. I assume that won't be a problem?"

Lainey shook her head. Was she actually committing to this, right here, right now? The thought terrified her.

"You want me to move to Los Angeles?"

"To start with, we'll put you up at a hotel. When you have time, you can see about a house. A car comes with, of course." Fouchard smiled at her again. "It starts at one-twenty-five."

Lainey was openmouthed to realize that he was refer-ring to the salary. He didn't seem to notice.

"When is this supposed to happen?" Lainey finally asked.

"Is four weeks from now okay with you? We're going to start the research right now on the East Coast."

"Mr. Fouchard, I don't understand. Not that I'm not interested. I'm just, well . . ." Lainey couldn't think how to end the sentence. *I'm just flabbergasted that you know my name, let alone like my work, let alone want to make me rich and happy,* was what she felt like saying. *I'm a peon and you're Mr. Big and you must have the wrong Lainey Wolfe. I'm only a little girl and this is a dream and I'm going to wake up and feel really embarrassed.*

I'm just petrified.

"You're just what, Lainey?" Patrick Fouchard walked toward the door, obviously intending to open it and bring the meeting to a close.

"I'm . . . I've just never been more excited in my life." Lainey rose and walked over to where he stood, putting her hand out to be engulfed by his enormous paw.

Chapter 6

Farrell glanced at her watch. She didn't want this to take one minute longer than necessary. All she had to do was tell Sugar what she'd come to say. She grimaced as she walked into the lobby. As nice as the St.-Tropez was, nothing on earth could ever induce her to set foot in this hotel again.

She sighed, wishing she could have done this over the telephone. But it wasn't something she wanted anyone overhearing, and Mrs. Miles, her housekeeper, was in today, bustling around, too close for comfort. Still, when Farrell had called Sugar to tell her it was urgent that they talk in person, her heart had sunk when Sugar replied that they would have to meet at the suite. Just riding up in the elevator now was making the bile rise in Farrell's throat.

She got off on the tenth floor and hastened down the hall, completely unnerved at the prospect of talking to Sugar. Of course, Sugar had called after Farrell's nightmare here, but Farrell had simply confirmed that, yes, everything had gone as planned, both of them understanding that they would talk further about it another time. Now, Farrell realized she was actually fearful of what Sugar's reaction might be when she heard that Farrell wanted no part of this ever again.

Why am I suddenly so afraid of this woman? Farrell

asked herself. It was as if some instinct was telling her to
be careful. She frowned, not liking the feeling.

I'll never be able to look at Sugar the same way again,
she thought. In fact, after this escapade, we may never be
able to look at each other again, period. She cursed
inwardly, wishing Sugar had never told her about this,
wishing she'd had the brains to stay away. No, I wanted
danger, *risks*, she mocked herself silently. I thought I was
nineteen again and entitled to be the bad girl. All I did
was play Russian roulette with my entire life.

Her lips drawn tight with self-loathing, she stopped at
the door to 1012 and knocked. She waited, tapping her
foot, wanting desperately to be anywhere else in the
world.

Muffled voices were coming from behind the door.
What now, she wondered. She *had* to get out of here. She
raised her hand to knock again when the door was
yanked open. Farrell found herself face to face with a
woman she'd never seen before.

The woman, in her late thirties, was clearly furious and
in a hurry to leave. Short and slightly stocky, she wore
jeans, sneakers, and a white T-shirt. Beneath her blunt
brown pageboy haircut, her face was without makeup.
She had a dark red birthmark about the size of a baseball
on one cheek. What were they called? Farrell thought.
Oh, yes, port wine stains.

Was she one of the women who worked for Sugar?
Judging from her outfit, Farrell doubted it. But then
again, she reflected, what do I know about what goes on
here? Her own experience had been with straightforward
sex, just as Sugar had told her it would be. But Farrell
was certain that many of the other men requested something far more . . . *exotic* would be a polite way to put it.

Would I have been faced with that eventually? she wondered with an inward shudder.

"We'll see about that, won't we." The woman had turned her head to spit out her disdainful words as she was stepping into the hall. Her eyes registered Farrell's presence with utter disinterest. Brushing past, she lost no time in heading toward the elevator.

Tentatively, Farrell stuck her head into the room. The sense of dim quiet that she remembered from before enveloped her once more. It took a moment before she spotted Sugar sitting on the love seat, furiously drumming her fingers on the sofa's arm, her face flushed, eyes ablaze, unaware that anyone else was in the room.

"It's never going to be enough for that fuckin' bitch," she muttered in rage. "I don't need this crap. I really don't."

Farrell shrank back. This was yet another side of Sugar she'd never seen before. The ugliness of her anger was frightening. But of course, Farrell thought, I should have expected it. The woman runs a call girl ring, for Christ's sake. That simple housewife I imagined her to be had never existed. She forced herself to take a step forward inside the room.

"Hello, Sugar."

Looking up, the other woman instantly composed herself. She rose, smiling. Farrell was amazed at the speed with which all traces of her anger disappeared.

"Hi, hon. Come on in and sit down. No one's due here so we can be comfortable and talk awhile."

Farrell only took another step forward. "No, I really can't stay." She hesitated, but was unable to keep herself from asking. "Who was that I just saw leaving?"

Sugar frowned briefly. "Nobody, nobody at all." She changed the subject with a grin. "But you haven't told

me what happened with Don. I'm dying to hear." Eager-
ness in her voice, she appeared to have completely forgotten whatever it was that had so infuriated her only
seconds before.

Farrell fiddled nervously with one of her coat buttons,
but forced herself to look directly at Sugar. "Yes,
well . . . It didn't go quite the way . . ."

Sugar came over to her and put a hand on her arm. "I
know, I know. Don and I spoke. But that's just first-time
jitters. And I blame myself—he wasn't the right one for
you. Forgive me, please. I swear I'll do better next time."

Relieved that Sugar wasn't giving her a hard time
about what had undoubtedly been an angry customer,
Farrell was able to speak up more firmly. "There isn't
going to be a next time."

"Believe me, I understand." Sugar nodded. "I do. But
you can't let this throw you."

"It's over. This whole thing was a mistake." The deci-
siveness in her voice belied her jittery nerves.

"Oh, no, you can't just walk away. I mean, of course
you *can*. But that would be a real mistake. Please give it
another try," Sugar wheedled.

Farrell was both surprised and emboldened by Sugar's
response. Whatever dark side she might possess, she
had apparently chosen not to reveal it to Farrell. Still,
she didn't seem willing to take no for an answer. Farrell's tone grew slightly harsher. "There won't be any
other tries. As far as I'm concerned, I don't know anything about what goes on here. And none of this ever
happened."

Sugar walked over to one of the plush, upholstered
chairs, but instead of sitting down, she rested her hip on
its arm, one leg swinging quickly up and down. Farrell

assumed she was nervous, but when Sugar spoke this time, her tone of voice revealed barely suppressed rage.

"So, Miss High and Mighty has decided that none of it ever happened. I'm interested in your perception of that decision as unilateral."

Sugar's sudden mood change had occurred in seconds, a fact that Farrell found almost more harrowing than her words. Yet it seemed a mistake to lash back at her. The last thing she needed was to make Sugar even madder.

Farrell put one hand on the doorknob, as she forced a conciliatory edge into her voice. "I apologize for starting all this up and then backing out. But, in this case, we both made a very wrong call. Let's just forget about it, okay?"

Sugar shrugged. "Why do I think you're never going to forget about it." She smiled grimly, then continued. "And I damned well know *I'm* never going to forget."

Farrell's hand whitened as she gripped the doorknob. "What is it you're saying? What are you intending to do?"

"I'm not exactly sure." Sugar smiled broadly, a perfect replica of the person she had pretended to be for all the time Farrell had known her. "Why don't we wait and see."

Thoroughly frightened, Farrell turned the knob and stepped out of the room quickly. She hurried down the corridor, pressed the elevator button over and over until it arrived, and then rushed through the lobby to her car. Sitting at the wheel without starting the engine, she felt as if her body were on fire, licks of panic rushing through her at top speed. But after a few minutes, she managed to calm herself down. Sugar couldn't possibly do anything to her. After all, anything that would hurt Farrell would also hurt Sugar. If she let John know what had happened, Farrell would expose the whole business. For Farrell, it would mean the end of her marriage. For Sugar it would mean years in jail.

A silence for a silence. As long as she kept Sugar's secret, Sugar wouldn't reveal what Farrell had done that afternoon. That had to be the bottom line. It was the only thing that made sense. Yet she felt a chill go up her spine.

She had composed herself by the time she drove her car into the Meadowview Elementary School parking lot. Pulling into a spot, she jumped out and raced into the large brown building that housed the school's skating rink. Tim hated it when she was late to pick him up from hockey practice. Sure enough, there he was, standing by the railing, skates and backpack slung over one shoulder, scowling at her.

Still wearing his uniform, he nonetheless appeared clean and neat, his hair freshly combed, his socks pulled up straight. Ever since he was a toddler, Tim had had that odd way of looking exactly the same at the end of the day as he did at the beginning. He simply didn't get dirty and rumpled the way other kids did, even though he played just as hard. Farrell marveled at it, certain he'd inherited the trait from her mother, who could have posed for a magazine cover at any time of the day or night with ten seconds' notice.

"Hey, Gretzsky, how'd it go?" she asked playfully, ruffling his blond hair.

He batted her hand away. "Knock it off, Mom. And stop calling me that." He glanced around to make sure no one had heard his mother's corny joke. "I've told you a hundred times it's dumb."

She hung her head, exaggerating her remorse. "No, I'm sure you've told me a *million* times, maybe a *trillion*. I'm hopeless. I don't know why you put up with me. But it's true. You happen to be great."

"Mommmm . . ." Tim rolled his eyes, but the grin on his face told her that he was secretly pleased by her words of praise. "Gimme a break."

She smiled as they exited the building together and walked around to the school's front entrance. Tim was a natural athlete, and she and John were vastly proud of his accomplishments in hockey, basketball, and baseball, evidenced by two shelves filled with trophies in his room.

They went into the elementary school and down the hall to the last classroom, stopping just outside the door. Riley wouldn't be done with her computer club meeting for another ten minutes, so the two of them waited there, Farrell trying to glean whatever information she could about Tim's day at school, Tim giving his typical evasive responses to her questions.

Finally, Riley burst out of the room, her shirttail hanging out of her corduroy skirt, which had ink smeared over one pocket. If neatness was inherited, the gene for it was clearly absent from her daughter.

"Mom, hey," she yelled, catching sight of Farrell, waving a piece of paper. "You're not gonna believe what I'm gonna do here next week."

Farrell stooped down to tie the open lace of her daughter's right shoe. She never understood a word of what Riley told her about computers, which were currently her greatest passion in life. She was continually nonplussed by her seven-year-old's ability to converse so easily on a topic Farrell found virtually incomprehensible. "I want to hear all about it, darling." She gave Riley a kiss on the cheek as she smoothed back her unruly dark hair, full and thick just like her own. "Tell me in the car."

Riley talked during the entire drive home, regaling

Tim and Farrell with the abstruse details of her latest computer project. Farrell nodded at what she guessed to be the appropriate spots, while Tim gazed out the window, ignoring his younger sister altogether.

As they stepped inside the house, the telephone began ringing. For a split second, Farrell was petrified that it would be Sugar.

"Hello." Farrell dropped her bag and keys on the kitchen counter as she answered.

"Farrell. Hello, darling."

"Oh, hello, Mother."

"I'm glad I caught you in."

Farrell's relief quickly turned hollow, as she dropped onto one of the chairs at the pine breakfast table and listened. Talking to her mother ranked as one of her least favorite activities in the world. It was only by dint of her most strenuous efforts that she maintained the surface civility that permitted them to remain cordial to each other. And it had taken her nearly thirty years to reach the point where she could manage even that. As she recalled, back when she was away at college, she and her mother had spoken no more than four or five times a year, and those conversations were restricted either to Farrell's finances or her travel plans for summers or vacations. When she went home for the school breaks, the two of them usually tangled over something or other within the first twenty-four hours, and the remaining days would be spent in frosty silence until Farrell could escape back to Wellesley. Christ, Farrell thought, between not talking to me and not talking to Dad, theirs had to be the quietest house in New Rochelle.

"How are you doing, Mother?"

Doris Beckley got right to the point. "It's your aunt Marjorie's birthday next week, and we're taking everyone out to dinner on Saturday night. That means the children, too."

"This Saturday?" Farrell asked, trying to keep her voice even. Absolutely typical, she thought. Of course, her mother wouldn't see anything wrong with calling on Thursday and expecting them to make themselves available for a Saturday night two days away.

"We thought we'd go to Fabriccio's. Eight-thirty."

Farrell immediately thought about how tired and cranky Riley would be, sitting down to dinner that late in a formal restaurant. But she knew better than to waste her time saying anything about it to her mother. When Doris Beckley made her dinner plans, she wasn't interested in whether or not they were convenient for anybody else.

"By the way," her mother went on, "the other day, Aunt Marjorie happened to mention that she could use a new clock radio, so you might want to pick one up as a present from you two."

"Thanks for the suggestion," Farrell replied. *Directive* was more like it.

"Oh, and Farrell, dear, be sure the children have something to read or play with in the restaurant so they don't get fidgety."

Farrell bristled, saying nothing. Her mother had no appreciation for how well-behaved her children actually were. If they expressed so much as a hint of boredom at the prospect of sitting around a table while a bunch of grown-ups drank coffee—as happened every time there was one of these family get-togethers—her mother acted as if they were a pair of spoiled brats, permitted to run wild in the streets by their incompetent parents.

"Come to the house for drinks first. Let's say seven-thirty."

Farrell had had enough of these orders. "That part

might be a little difficult. Why don't we meet the rest of you at Fabriccio's?"

Farrell could hear the disapproval in the long pause that followed. However, Doris apparently decided to let the matter pass.

"That will be fine. See you then. My best to John."

Feeling reprieved, Farrell hung up. She sat at the table, waiting for the knot in her stomach to unclench, amazed that her mother still had the ability to rile her so easily. I might as well be five years old, she thought ruefully, the way I let her get to me.

She recalled her most recent conversation with Lainey on the subject of their parents. Farrell's mother said practically nothing, while Lainey's mother said far too much—yet both mothers managed to have the exact same infuriating effect on their daughters. It was a familiar topic, one they'd analyzed countless times over the years, although they'd long ago acknowledged they were never going to come up with any answers.

Farrell went over to the refrigerator and pulled open the freezer door as she made a mental note to call Lainey later that night after the children were in bed. Right now, though, she wanted to get started on dinner.

Idly surveying the assortment of frozen chicken, fish, and steak before her, Farrell's mind went back to the conversation with Sugar. It would be okay, she reassured herself. It had to be.

Suddenly, her shoulders sagged. What on earth was I thinking, getting into something like that? she asked herself, her horror at her behavior mounting. I practically dared the gods to obliterate my marriage and my life. If I'd sat up nights planning it, I couldn't have devised a more perfect strategy for my own destruction.

But it was going to be all right. She'd made a terrible,

a ghastly mistake, and now it was over. Somehow, she was going to be lucky enough to get away without the catastrophic consequences that might very well have been the result of her temporary lunacy. She was sure of it.

I'm sorry, John, she thought. I can never be sorry enough.

Chapter 7

Lainey could hardly believe what she was hearing.

"Watch out for Harmon. He looks like your grand-father, but he'd chop you up and eat you if you gave him half a chance." Rick Dean drew his finger across his throat for emphasis.

Jerry Struch looked at Lainey across the expanse of white carpet. "You think he's exaggerating," he said almost accusatorily. "I once saw him kill a whole division because some vice president asked him if he'd put his cigarette out until the meeting was over."

"And during the five or ten minutes it took to announce that forty people were out of work, he smiled and smiled . . . like he'd just distributed Christmas bonuses or something!" Rick looked fierce, his green eyes ablaze as if fueled by some independent power source.

Jerry walked over to the window of their sparsely but elegantly furnished living room and pulled open the shutters. "But Harmon, at least, has brains. McGregor is the real stumbling block. Forty-five years on the board of directors, maybe forty thousand shares of preferred stock, and not an iota of new thought."

"Of *any* thought," Rick added. "Every now and then, he comes up with a memory of long ago, like 'Remember the time Beanie got out of his cage?' " He shook his head in disgust. "A damn cartoon bunny from before World War Two—*that* he has time to think about."

Lainey was exhausted. A quarter moon was visible through the window Jerry had uncovered. She could hear the comforting sound of waves lapping at the shore. Last she'd noticed, it had been one in the morning, her plane having landed at LAX around nine. Rick and Jerry had picked her up and begun their tutoring session the moment they'd brought the car around. The first important meeting on Marissa was scheduled for that afternoon, and there wasn't a moment to waste. So here she was, still on New York time, her bags barely unpacked back in her hotel room, drinking her fourth cup of coffee in Rick and Jerry's Malibu house.

"Is *anyone* decent or smart or on top of things in this company?" Lainey asked, rubbing her eyes exhaustedly.

Rick was thoughtful. "Well," he said finally, "Cassava is smart, but not what you'd call decent. Wiley's more or less decent but dumb as a post." He peered at Jerry as if to ask if anyone fit the third category.

Jerry responded with a laugh. "Farley's on top of things . . . things like your head, your expense account, your underlings—"

"How long it took you to go to the bathroom," Rick continued for him, "how many times you call your mother, whether your socks match your tie. All the important stuff."

Jerry finally noticed how tired Lainey was and grew more serious. "There are some guys in the room with brains. The problem is, even the brainiest guys are afraid to move forward too quickly."

"Or at all," Rick interrupted. "Listen, Lainey, Carpathia didn't become a multibillion-dollar business on

the backs of idiots, but even Salisbury himself"—Rick
and Jerry gave each other mock salutes at the mention of
Carpathia's internationally famous chairman—"thinks
the world's still run by men like Dwight Eisenhower and
Charlton Heston, with hourly coffee delivery by females
in shirtwaists calling them 'sir.' "

"Well, you two aren't exactly standard issue," Lainey
countered.

"Don't ask, don't tell," Jerry responded. "Just so long
as we keep producing tremendous profits, the big guys
will keep asking us when we're going to meet some nice
girl and get married. You'd be amazed how stupid even
the smartest people can will themselves to be."

Lainey sneaked a peek at her watch. It was already
two-fifteen. Any chance of sleep before the meeting was
melting quickly, and the guys were making her even
more nervous than she'd already made herself. "So what
am I supposed to do with all this? Dress like Doris Day
and keep my mouth shut?"

Rick shrugged. "Beats the shit out of me."

Exhausted, nervous, and annoyed at their flippancy,
Lainey began to feel anger rising in her stomach, until
both Rick and Jerry started to laugh.

"I'm sorry, honey," Rick said, walking over to her and
putting his arm around her. "What you're supposed to do
is be as smart and creative as you are, and you'll do just
great." He walked her over to where her jacket lay tossed
across a chair.

Lainey pulled it around her shoulders as a familiar stab
of fear lodged inside her. Be as smart and creative as you
are, she repeated to herself cynically. In her case, it was
more like try to fool more of the people more of the time.

Spinning around to face him, Lainey saw Rick notice

the apprehension in her eyes. "Hey, what's going on?" he asked in bewilderment.

Lainey knew that a true professional would fake her way through the answer to that question. Nothing, she would say with perfect self-confidence. Everything's fine. But she could never pull that off. Besides, these two had staked their reputations on her, and they had a right to know just how likely it was that she would fail them utterly.

"Listen, guys," she said, sitting down on one of the pear-green brocade dining-room chairs and holding tightly onto its arms for support, "I know you're counting on me, and I'll try like crazy to do my best, but you have to be aware of just how far out of my league all of this is."

Both Rick and Jerry looked at her in perplexity. "All of what?" Jerry finally asked.

Lainey looked at him earnestly. "You two, Owen Salisbury—you're people who know exactly what you're doing, who have actual talent. Even those people you're busy making fun of, they're experienced professionals with real knowledge."

Jerry walked over to stand in front of her, eyeing her as he might an exotic animal. "And just what is it you think you are? A rank amateur? A six-year-old child, perhaps?"

Lainey felt her cheeks redden in shame. "Well, actually yes."

Rick and Jerry looked at each other in astonishment. Then they looked at Lainey once again.

"Lainey," Rick said, as he pulled up a chair opposite hers and sat down, "you're the most accomplished thing to come out of the New York office in years."

Lainey looked at him in obvious surprise.

"Why in hell do you think you were picked for this?" Jerry added, resting his hand on the back of Rick's chair.

"Why, for God's sake, do you think Al Smile has such a hard time dealing with you?" Rick chimed in once again. "Every manager we deal with recognizes your ability. We've been searching for an opportunity for you since the Carolina promotion two years ago."

Disbelief radiated from Lainey's face. "But half the time, I can't even decide what shoes to wear."

"Who cares what shoes you wear?" Rick asked, exasperated. "I've never seen you at a loss about anything that really matters."

"Jeez, Lainey," Jerry said, obviously still mystified by what he was hearing, "you can't be that blind to what people think of you. I mean, you may feel like Jell-O, but to the rest of the world, you're the goddamn Rock of Gibraltar."

Lainey sat back, trying to take in what the two of them were telling her. Were they serious, or were they lulling her into some false security that might allow her to get through the next twenty-four hours.

"Enough of this," Rick said. "By the time Marissa is finished, you'll realize just how good you are—you'll be the hottest ticket in L.A."

He held up his hand to forestall any response she could make, and went on talking. "Right now, we're taking you back to the Bel Air, and singing you lullabies until you fall blissfully asleep."

Lainey smiled at him gratefully. "Just make sure I wake up in time."

"Oh, don't worry about that. We're gonna do everything you need for the next twelve hours. Now may I suggest you catch an hour or two of sleep before the most important meeting of your career?"

Lainey's shoulders sagged with relief at the prospect. "Oh, thank you, warden."

"Not at all," Rick replied airily. "I'm a *most* benevolent despot."

"I remember my daughter's excitement when Annette Funicello came onscreen. Cassie used to dance around the room, singing along with the television, her very own set of ears on her head!" Tom Wiley's eyes closed in nostalgia as several of the other men around the enormous oval table nodded.

Bill Farley leaned forward in his chair. "I think it's important to remember values. You know, like politeness and respect for your fellow man. It seems to be that's what prime time is missing. I mean, take 'Lassie,' for example. She wasn't just a dog. She was a savior. Thirty minutes after the program started, kids could feel good about themselves, good about the world."

Lainey sat back, listening. She and Rick and Jerry were the only members of the creative team allowed in this meeting. Everyone else at the table was a senior vice president of one of Carpathia's nine divisions. Owen Salisbury presided at the end of the oval, silent and expressionless. She wondered what he was thinking, sitting there, omnipotent, playing his cards so close to the vest. Was there even the tiniest possibility that he found all of this as inane, as old-fashioned as she did?

As if reading her mind, Salisbury turned to Lainey. "So what do you make of all this, Miss Wolfe? After all, this is your baby."

I think you're all about a thousand years behind the times. That's what she would like to have said.

"Well," she began hesitantly, "it's interesting to remember how touching television was. I loved watching

Lassie pull the kid out of the well. And," she smiled nicely at Tom Wiley, "I owned my own set of ears. In fact, my mom still keeps them in a drawer in my old room, just in case I decide to move back home."

Several of the men around the table chuckled appreciatively.

"But, frankly, I have a different concept of Marissa." Here goes nothing, she thought, sitting up straighter in her chair, and looking at Rick for just a second, as if for courage. "I did an informal sampling before I came out here, and the ten- to fourteen-year-olds I spoke to don't have much in common with me, or with most of you as a child."

Tom Wiley's smile disappeared.

"If you ask a ten-year-old what she likes to do—and ten is the youngest of our target audience—her answer is likely to be going to the mall, and reading fashion magazines, like *Seventeen* and *YM*. They watch Janet Jackson and Salt-N-Pepa and Boyz II Men and Pearl Jam on MTV, and they love jewelry stores that sell cheap earrings and hair accessories. Half the kids I spoke to were considering getting their navels and noses pierced."

There was a collective gasp of distaste in the room, but Lainey went right on.

"Kids this age, particularly girls, are into 'Melrose Place' and 'General Hospital,' even if they're still picking up Betty and Veronica comic books once in a while. The age range for *Aladdin* and *Pocahontas* is at least three to five years younger than the kids we're trying to reach."

John Cassava glared at her. "The stuff you're talking about is disgusting."

There were grumbles of assent from all around the table.

Robert Broadhurst, senior vice president of marketing, took the floor. "You may be right about some of the things you say, Lainey, but Carpathia *stands* for something."

This time, even more voices rang out in agreement. Owen Salisbury, however, remained silent.

As the chorus of opinions began to rise in volume, Rick scrawled a note on the yellow pad in front of him, one that only Jerry would see. *If Lainey's ship does down, I'm going down with her,* Jerry read to himself.

"You know," Rick started, loudly enough to make himself heard, "the things that Lainey is saying are supported by our research. In fact, if I'd suspected that informal chats with the children of friends could accomplish that level of accuracy, I could have saved Carpathia several hundred thousand dollars in research fees." He leaned back in his chair and spoke slowly, eager to lessen the tension in the room. "If we want to change our specs, to try to appeal to a younger age group, we can go in a kinder, gentler direction. But if we're after the ten-to-fourteens, we'd better be ready to stand up to MTV and Brad Pitt. Ready or not, that's the competition."

"This is all very interesting." Owen Salisbury's voice created immediate silence. "So, Miss Wolfe," he said, turning to face her. "Exactly what is your version of Marissa?"

Lainey breathed deeply and reached into the large black leather bag at the foot of her chair. She extracted a large pad of drawing paper, turned back the cover, and displayed the sketch on the first page.

"I see Marissa as one of the girls at the mall. But she's older than our core group. Probably about seventeen or so. And she's not a customer; she's a worker. A salesgirl in one of those jewelry stores they all love to hang out in."

Tom Wiley reached across the table and grabbed the pad. "Is that a tattoo on her shoulder?" he asked, obviously outraged.

"Marissa is not exactly a role model. In fact, she's what we might not want our kids to be. Doesn't have much and doesn't care, and isn't particularly polite to the grown-ups." Lainey took the pad back and turned to the next page. Here, Marissa was blowing a large bubble with her gum, and waiting on a young customer whose shocked expression indicated that the unconcerned Marissa had just delivered some verbal zinger. "Marissa's got an edge, but she's also got a wicked sense of humor."

Robert Broadhurst gripped the arms of his chair. "America's children are not about to tune into some tramp with a tattoo."

Owen Salisbury cut him off. "Like Roseanne, for instance? You know, men," he said, looking around the table, "the last I heard, Carpathia was a profit-making corporation, not a historical monument. It seems to me America loves its characters to be *characters*."

Lainey stared at him, shocked by his show of support. She felt a buzz of exhilaration coursing through her body.

"Go on, Lainey," Salisbury continued. "Tell us more about this Marissa of yours."

I love you, Owen Salisbury, she thought, as she picked up the pad once again and began walking everyone through its pages.

Chapter 8

As soon as Farrell awoke, she knew she was alone in the bed. Rolling over, she peered groggily at the glowing red numbers on her clock radio. Three-twelve. When she'd gone to bed at eleven that night, she'd left John downstairs, going over some papers in his study. Surely he hadn't been working all this time.

She got up and went to check on Tim and Riley, going into Riley's room to cover her again with the quilt she had thrown off in her sleep, and smoothing her hair back off her face. Then she padded downstairs, seeing the light on in the kitchen.

Much as she appreciated the rest of the house, it was really the kitchen she'd fallen in love with when she and John had first come house-hunting in Meadowview. The previous owners had been gourmet cooks, and had torn out the existing kitchen to install beautifully crafted cabinets and state-of-the-art appliances. Farrell had envisioned an enormous antique wooden table beside the large bay windows and French doors leading out to the backyard; it had taken her nearly eight months, but she'd finally found what she wanted in a store in Litchfield.

That was where John was sitting now, still dressed in the sweater and pants he'd been wearing earlier, eating vanilla fudge ice cream directly out of the carton. He was eating slowly, an unhappy expression on his face.

"Hey," she called out softly. "You've been down here all night?"

He looked over at her distractedly. "Yeah."

She sat down in the chair across from his. "Something wrong?"

John took a moment before answering. "I was handling this woman's divorce, back about a year and a half ago. It was pretty straightforward, but, of course, it dragged on the way divorces do. Anyway, she just got killed in an accident."

Farrell's expression turned pained. "Oh, Christ. How?"

"Car accident. She was a cop, actually, but they tell me she had something of a drinking problem. The blood test indicates she was drunk when it happened. Swerved off the road into a cement wall. Thirty-nine years old."

"Did she have any children?"

"No. I got the idea she led a pretty simple life. You know, cop's salary, owned a car and a condo, and not much else. She never said anything to me outside of the subject of her divorce. She was actually kind of curt. Not rude, really, but not especially nice either. It turns out she made me executor of her estate. Never mentioned that she was going to do it."

John pursed his lips. "You know, I never really understood why she came to me to handle her divorce. She didn't need someone like me for such a simple, uncontested sort of thing. She could have found someone much cheaper. But after going over her papers tonight, it turns out she had a good reason for getting me involved in her life."

Farrell tilted her head questioningly. "Yes?"

"This cop was taking payoffs from a whole string of people. I don't know what their connection was to her or why they were paying. I'm assuming protection money, or maybe she had something on them. Who knows. But she kept a list of all of them. Names, dates, amounts. A lot of local people. And it added up to a hell of a lot of money."

"That's pretty incredible," Farrell said, sitting up straighter.

"That's not the incredible part. She had someone handling the money. Laundering it, investing it." He jabbed his spoon into the ice cream, leaving it there.

She waited.

John sighed heavily. "My brother."

"What?" Farrell's eyes opened wide. "Charlie?"

"The very same baby brother we all thought was doing so well," he said bitterly. "The big success story. Made a youthful mistake, had a bad patch, but pulled himself together and turned his life around." He leaned forward, putting his head in his hands. "Except he didn't. He just had us fooled. Went from one kind of hustling to another."

"Oh, God, John, are you sure?"

"Positive. Of course, that explains why I was the perfect lawyer for her. She must have figured if I'd found out what she was up to in the course of handling her affairs, I wouldn't blow the whistle on her because that would mean getting Charlie into trouble. And if she'd gotten caught some other way, who would have had better motivation than me to defend the hell out of her. Once her story came out, my own brother would be on the line."

"But now . . . ?"

He turned his palms up to indicate his confusion. "I'm at a loss to figure out why she chose me as her executor."

"Did she have any other family?"

"Nope."

They sat there in silence for a moment. John retrieved his spoon, tapping it on the table.

"You know," Farrell said reflectively, "she was a young woman, and you have to assume she wasn't planning to die right now. She had to name *some*body as executor. Maybe she just thought you were a good lawyer, and figured you'd be the best person to handle it."

"I hope you're right. I hope there are no other surprises connected with this woman." John picked up the ice-cream carton and walked over to the refrigerator to replace it in the freezer. "Come on, I'm beat. Let's go to bed."

He started to leave the kitchen as Farrell rose and reached across to pick up the spoon he'd been using. She was putting it in the sink when he turned back to her and spoke again.

"Oh, I almost forgot," he said. "You're not going to believe this."

Farrell looked at him. "What?"

"One of the people on this cop's list—one of the people giving her payoffs—was none other than our beloved neighbor, your buddy Sugar Taplinger. Now what the hell reason do you suppose Sugar could have for doing something like that?"

"This is a bad time, John. Maybe tomorrow."

John's voice grew quiet, a sure sign he was growing angry. "*Now*, Charlie. I'm coming over now."

He hung up the telephone without waiting for a response. It was hard to guess whether Charlie would actually hang around until John showed up. As soon as he'd uttered the words, John regretted having told his brother it was urgent they talk. Just the suggestion of something serious, something that might involve words like *responsibility* or *obligation,* was a red flag, signaling Charlie to disappear until someone else took care of whatever it was.

It took John nearly half an hour to reach the condominium complex in Stamford where Charlie rented a two-bedroom apartment. With relief, John heard the television being turned off and his brother's footsteps coming to the door in response to his knocking.

"Good, I'm glad you're here." John entered, but stood in the foyer, not removing his coat.

Barefoot, his blond hair tousled, and dressed only in jeans and a red sweater, Charlie Cole's appearance somehow had the casual, unstudied perfection of a model in a sportswear catalog. When they were adolescents competing for dates, John had desperately envied his younger brother's good looks. But once they'd both reached their thirties, Charlie's life of revolving jobs and endless parties seemed pathetically empty to John, his younger brother's constant parade of vapid girlfriends nothing more than a big bore.

Now, though, his perspective on Charlie's life was different. Charlie hadn't simply been changing jobs all this time, trying to find something that suited him. He'd been searching out new and better angles.

"Why are you barging in here, ordering me to stay put?" Charlie demanded in annoyance. "We're not eight and ten anymore, you know."

"You might as well be eight for all the brains you exhibit," John snapped back. "I'm here to save your ass, so don't give me a hard time."

"What's that supposed to mean?" Charlie folded his arms across his chest.

John shook his head in disgust. "You know, I'd do—hell, I *have* done—anything to help you, to bail you out of trouble." His voice rose with his anger and frustration. "But how the hell am I supposed to help you when you go *looking* for trouble?"

"Listen," Charlie retorted, "I don't ask for your help. Whatever you're getting pissed off about, you can just stay out of it, okay? Don't give it another thought."

He turned away and walked into the living room, sitting down on the armchair in the corner, indifferent to whether his brother followed him. John came to the room's entryway and stopped.

"Marina Paulsen." He waited.

Charlie looked over at him sharply. "What about her?"

"You know she died in a car accident?"

"Yes, of course," Charlie said irritably. "She was my client. Not that it's any of your concern."

"I handled her divorce a while back. She made me executor of her estate."

Charlie was genuinely surprised. "*You?* How come?"

"I'm not exactly sure. But here's what I do know. She's been taking payoffs, and you've been laundering the money for her."

Charlie snorted. "Where'd you get a stupid idea like that?"

In a few quick strides, John was standing right in front of him. "From her papers," he snapped. "Where, *in writing,* it's as clear as day that you are committing crimes, which, with your record, will get you put away for a good, long time."

"She kept notes on her business transactions?" Charlie asked, a flash of fear in his eyes.

"That's right, genius," John said contemptuously. "She was smart enough to have this little setup, so it stands to reason she was smart enough to write it all down in case she should need a little protection later on. Why do you think she hired *me* for her divorce in the first place? Because if push came to shove, I'd protect her ass to save yours."

A sly look appeared on Charlie's face. "This stuff is in papers *you* have?"

John nodded.

"I mean, I'm not saying I did anything wrong. But, even so, you don't have to show them to anybody. You can just hide them, or better yet, destroy them." Charlie spoke with relief, as if the matter were already settled.

John's eyes blazed. "And that's it? You're off the hook, no problem."

His brother spoke beseechingly. "John, come on. Marina wasn't hurting anybody. These people she took money from, most of them were royal scumbags. She needed someone to help her with the cash, and I needed some decent accounts to show the firm I could bring in business. It was no big deal."

John stared at him. "I don't even believe what I'm hearing. You're doing something you know to be illegal and you don't give a damn. You're still looking for the easy way out."

Growing more agitated, he began to shout. "You're a common criminal, Charlie. Do you understand that?"

The younger man jumped to his feet. "Knock it off, John. I haven't done anything so terrible." His eyes narrowed in anger. "And you've got a hell of a lot of nerve, walking in here like you're God, telling me what I am. You've always had it so easy. Everything just came to you. You may not be aware of this, but it isn't that way for everyone else in the world."

John was momentarily stunned by the verbal attack. "I didn't know you felt that way . . . You never—"

"Well, now you know." Charlie paused. "Not all of us can afford your moral superiority. I myself have no desire for it. In fact, I'd go far out of my way to be nothing like you."

Wounded, John bristled once more. "Listen, I'm just telling you that you'd better get rid of whatever the hell you've got connecting you to Marina Paulsen. And if you have half a brain, you'll clean up your act."

Charlie regarded him coldly. "Thanks for the brotherly advice."

John exploded in exasperation. *"What's wrong with you?* I'm trying my best to help you."

"You're a saint," was the sarcastic reply.

Without another word, John spun around and left.

Driving home, he struggled to contain his fury. All this time, Charlie had stayed out of trouble, yet here he was inviting disaster. But maybe he'd been involved in shady deals for years, without John knowing. It's not as if that would have been difficult to do. If Paulsen hadn't died, John would never have discovered their connection unless they were caught by the police. The *noncorrupt* police, he amended grimly.

By the time he pulled into his driveway, he felt more sad than angry. Charlie hadn't been able to find a way to be successful in life without giving in to greed and laziness. John thought back to his brother's angry words about how easy it had been for him. He had worked hard for what he had, but obviously Charlie hadn't taken notice of that part; all he knew was that his older brother had everything a man could want. And I do, don't I? he reflected gratefully.

Maybe Charlie didn't enjoy his so-called playboy life the way he appeared to. I always accepted what he said at face value, John thought. Why is it I never looked beyond what he chose to present, never questioned what he was saying. Or what he might be doing.

Chastened, he stopped the car at the end of his driveway, and got out to retrieve the day's mail. Getting back into the driver's seat, he quickly flipped through it. The town's semiweekly newspaper was on the bottom. There on the top of page one was a photograph of Marina Paulsen in her uniform. LOCAL POLICEWOMAN DIES IN CAR ACCIDENT.

God, he wished this whole business would just go away.

Farrell stared at the ceiling in the darkened bedroom, afraid to move, her heart pounding. She was certain John was asleep, but she waited a few minutes more nonetheless, listening to his deep and even breathing. Finally, satisfied, she slipped out of the bed and left the room, quietly closing the door behind her.

Downstairs, she went directly into his study, dimly lit by the moonlight peeking in through the curtains. She made her way to his desk, fearful of tripping over something, then turned on the brass lamp there, wincing as the small room was suddenly flooded with light.

There it was. The carton had arrived by special messenger. It contained the rest of Marina Paulsen's effects, John had explained. A few odds and ends, plus whatever was in the car with her at the time of the accident. Farrell had nodded as if she were disinterested at the time, but she had known instantly that she would have to go through it as soon as John's back was turned.

Carefully, she opened the box, noting just how the flaps overlapped so that she would be able to reassemble everything later to hide her tampering. Her stomach was tight with tension, a feeling she'd been living with from the first moment she'd seen the photograph of Marina Paulsen in the *Meadowview Ledger*. She had recognized her face right away, the port wine stain on the cheek only serving as final proof. The dead policewoman was the same person Farrell had seen leaving the hotel room at the St.-Tropez, the one who'd called out over her shoulder with such contempt, and left Sugar inside, cursing her.

It was bad enough when John told her that Sugar was on the list of people paying off the cop. Of course, John would have had no idea what possible reason their neighbor could have had for bribing a police officer—or succumbing to blackmail, whichever it might have been. But Farrell certainly had an idea.

She'd frozen when the words came out of her husband's mouth, relieved that he'd gone upstairs ahead of her, and was unable to see her agitation. Sugar was making payoffs to a corrupt cop to cover up her prostitution ring, and now Farrell's own husband had all the information he needed to lead him right to it. From there it would be just a small step to his discovering Farrell's participation. She had lain awake the rest of that night, her fear only growing stronger.

But when her husband had dropped the newspaper on the kitchen table the next evening, and she spotted the woman's picture, her heart had nearly stopped. When she'd imagined Sugar making payoffs, she envisioned an envelope left someplace, a tidy, impersonal transaction.

Now she recalled the fury in Sugar's eyes, the way she spat out her words once the policewoman was gone.

"It's never going to be enough for that fuckin' bitch. I don't need this crap. I really don't."

Two weeks later, Marina Paulsen was dead. But it had to be a coincidence, Farrell told herself. She had a wildly overactive imagination, she was crazy even thinking there could be a link. It wasn't possible that the Sugar she knew could have done such a thing. Besides, the cop was drunk, and had driven right off the road. No one was with her; she had crashed her own car. As she reached into the box, Farrell prayed that that was truly what had happened.

She lifted out a large plastic bag and began removing its contents. An empty pocketbook, a wallet and checkbook, an envelope with several credit cards, driver's license, and police identification. She noted a receipt from the dry cleaners; Paulsen's skirt and pants had been ready to be picked up a week ago. Shuddering, she put the envelope down and unzipped a small black makeup case; lipstick, blush, mascara. She went on. A copy of the *New York Times*, dated the day of the accident, still unread. An unopened bag of potato chips, a half-empty box of tissues, a hairbrush, several pens, and a Toyota Corolla owner's manual, along with half a dozen maps of Meadowview and the bordering towns.

Flattened by having been packed in with the rest was a large white shopping bag from Horner Fashions, a discount clothing store on Route One that Farrell had often passed in her car but never gone into. She looked inside the bag to find a pink silk blouse, now crushed into a wrinkled mess. She was about to put the shopping bag off to the side when something caught her eye. There was a word, written by hand in blue ink, down near the bottom of the bag. It was scrawled, as if someone had made the notation in a hurry.

She stared at it, moving the bag closer, then farther away, trying to make out the letters. The first one was definitely a *P*. Would that be *P*, then *I*? The last two letters were *T-T*, and there was a *K* in the middle. Okay, she thought, *P*, *I*, something *K*, something *T-T*. P-I-C-K-E-T-T. Definitely, that was it. PICKETT. Why was that word so familiar?

With a gasp, Farrell dropped the bag on the desk. PICKETT was the license plate on one of Sugar Taplinger's cars. Helmut Taplinger had that series of three vanity plates, the three Civil War generals. She could picture the car, a Jeep, parked next to the other Jeep and the Chevy in Sugar's garage, the license's white letters against a dark blue background.

Marina Paulsen had written the word on the shopping bag the night she died.

Farrell sank down into John's desk chair, her heart pounding. She took a few deep breaths, certain even before she had completed her train of thought that she knew what had happened.

Marina Paulsen had stopped into Horner Fashions and bought a blouse. She could have put her purchase into the trunk of her car. But it was only the one item, and, as Farrell herself was more likely to do with smaller bags, she probably dropped it onto the passenger seat next to her. The bag stayed there for however many hours were left in Paulsen's day—Paulsen's *life*, Farrell corrected herself. The policewoman eventually stopped somewhere for a few drinks, maybe dinner, it made no difference. But she had been drinking, the blood tests had proven that. And when she was driving at some point after those drinks, she wanted to write down the work PICKETT, and to do it quickly, so quickly that she didn't have time to find a piece of paper. She'd reached over and scrawled it onto the shopping bag.

Paulsen had seen a car, and hurriedly made a note of its license plate. Maybe she wanted to trace it later. Or, maybe, Farrell thought with dread, she knew the driver of the car was coming after her.

Then why hadn't she simply written the driver's name instead? Farrell answered the question for herself almost as soon as she had posed it. Paulsen might not have known who was driving the car; she only knew that she was in danger. Maybe she realized it was her last chance to leave a clue. Of course, the word wouldn't make much sense to most people.

But to the right person, it was the most telling message Marina Paulsen could have left.

Sitting on the park bench, Farrell held her gloved hands tightly together in her lap, not so much from the frigid February day as from nervousness. She blinked away tears caused by the wind, and when she could see clearly once more, started at the sight of Sugar approaching from the far end of the park, her black cape billowing out behind her. Farrell would never have imagined she could have felt such fear at the simple sight of her neighbor, the woman whose home she'd had dinner in, whom she had once counted as a friend. But that woman was gone forever, Farrell reminded herself. If she ever existed at all.

Sugar moved with surprising swiftness for a woman of her bulk. She came upon Farrell with an expression that mixed amusement and exasperation.

"Honey, you'd better have one hell of a good reason for wanting to get together out here," she said, sitting down alongside Farrell. "I'm freezin' my little tootsies off. There's coffee and muffins back in my kitchen, but, no, you have to see me in the middle of nowhere."

Farrell had trouble finding her voice. "It's not something I wanted to talk about at home."

Sugar nodded. "I figured it was about that." She brightened. "You've changed your mind and want to give it another try?"

Farrell shifted uncomfortably. "No, no, it's not about that. Well, not directly." She searched for the words. "Sugar, the second time I came to the hotel, I saw a woman leaving. It was obvious the two of you had had an argument."

Sugar appeared to be trying to remember. "I don't know who you mean, hon."

Farrell's voice grew quiet. "I didn't know at the time, but I know who it was now. Marina Paulsen. The policewoman."

Sugar twisted in her seat to look directly at Farrell. Her eyes had suddenly turned so flinty, it took all of Farrell's restraint not to move away.

"Why would you be bringing this up, may I ask? I can't imagine what interest you would have in her."

Farrell clenched her fists. It was hard to know what was worse, accusing an innocent woman of murder or ignoring the possibility that Sugar might have killed someone. But she had to see Sugar's reaction, *had* to find out if any of her suspicions were justified.

"As I'm sure you know, she died in a car accident."

Sugar nodded. "Yes, I know, just like everybody else in this town does."

"But what everybody else doesn't know is that you were giving her money. I know, and John knows, because he's the executor of her will, and she's got your name down on a list."

Sugar considered this. "Does John know what it was for?"

Farrell shook her head. "It's not as if it would be hard for him to find out."

Sugar regarded her for a moment, then looked away as if unconcerned. "Farrell, we're all grown-ups here. I'm sure you can understand that there are certain people who have to be paid off in order for me to run my business. Don't blame me if the woman was greedy." Her face took on an expression of annoyance. "Just because you got a trifle shaken up by your little adventure, let's not get all righteous."

Farrell flinched at her words. "That's not what this is about."

"Oh, isn't it?" Sugar asked sarcastically. "You weren't up to it, Farrell, and that was a big disappointment to me. But you wanted to walk away, and you did. Now drop it."

Farrell took a breath. She found she was suddenly tired of being afraid, tired of backing down from the bullying of this woman. She'd had enough of the barbs, enough of the whole sordid mess.

"There's more to it," she said, her words clipped. "Marina Paulsen wrote down the word PICKETT on a shopping bag in her car the night she died."

Sugar said nothing, but her eyes never left Farrell's face.

"Most people wouldn't put it together, but you and I know who drives a car with that license plate," Farrell went on, her confidence returning as she sensed herself on surer ground. "Maybe you can tell me why a woman would write the letters of your Jeep's plate in the final moments before she died? Were you there, Sugar? Did you have something to do with what happened?"

Sugar didn't move for a moment. Then she burst out laughing. "Where do you get these ideas? What a hoot. Baby, you've been watching too many TV movies."

Farrell ignored her condescending tone. "The prostitutes are real. The bribes are real. It's a pretty logical question."

"Oh, brother, you're somethin' else." Sugar waved a hand at her dismissively.

"But can you explain why she might have written PICKETT?"

"Honey," Sugar said with amusement, "I'm not even gonna try."

Farrell stood up. If someone had accused *her* of murder, she would have been horrified, angry, shocked beyond belief. Sugar was none of those things. Rather, she appeared to find the whole thing humorous. It just didn't ring true to Farrell.

"You know," she said slowly, "when they talk about murder, they talk about motive, means, and opportunity. As far as I can tell, based on what this woman left behind, you had all three."

Sugar rose and brought her face close to Farrell's. "Now you listen to me. I didn't do a damn thing to that cop, not that she didn't deserve it. But I didn't. What's important to you is that, even if I had, what are *you* going to do about it? You bring all this out into the open, you have to tell them what you were doing at the hotel."

She took a step back and looked at Farrell appraisingly as a smile played across her lips. "Think of your marriage. Think of what this would do to your husband's law practice, the whole world knowing that his wife tried her hand at being a high-priced hooker. He can kiss his career good-bye, and you can kiss *him* good-bye. Is that what you want?"

Farrell looked into her eyes, seeing the enjoyment Sugar was getting from this. She shivered.

"Well?" Sugar's tone was more insistent. "Is that what you want?"

Farrell turned and ran out of the park, her head bowed as she fought against the biting wind.

Chapter 9

Impatiently, Sugar Taplinger tossed a can of tomato soup into her cart before looking to see what the next item was on her list. She had more important things to concern herself with today than shopping. But this was her weekly grocery-buying day, and Helmut would notice right away if the refrigerator wasn't restocked, the plastic bags used to carry the groceries home neatly folded in the cupboard beneath the sink for use in the garbage can.

Besides, they were almost out of Shredded Wheat, and she was genuinely hard-pressed to imagine what Helmut would do if he couldn't have the breakfast he had eaten every morning since they'd been married. Exactly one cup of Shredded Wheat with half a cup of skim milk, every day, no matter what. In the winter, it was accompanied by a half grapefruit; in summer, that was replaced by quarter of a cantaloupe. He was no less consistent at lunchtime, she knew. At eleven-fifty, his secretary at *Armchair General* brought him a turkey sandwich, lettuce, no mayo. He would bite into it at noon, and a few minutes later, throw the other half into the trash basket. That was Helmut. Regular and utterly predictable.

Which was fine by Sugar, especially right now. She didn't need any further surprises on any other fronts.

Damn them, she thought. Damn them all. That bitch

Marina Paulsen had forced Sugar's hand, pushed and pushed until she'd had no alternative. But how the hell had everything gotten so tangled up—not just one of them, but *both* Farrell and John Cole on her tail.

She wheeled her cart around to the next aisle, and savagely began dumping packages of cookies into it. Mallomars, Oreos, half a dozen of the white Pepperidge Farm bags—she didn't even bother to see what flavor cookies they contained. For Helmut, she told herself, knowing full well that her husband would starve before he would touch a cookie of any kind, and she would wind up eating them all. The truth was, she would probably hide them from him. He might have guessed, but she wasn't going to draw attention to the fact that she had put back on most of the hundred and fifty pounds she had lost in the first three years after they got married. But, still, she comforted herself, he'd loved her back when she weighed three hundred and twenty, so he probably didn't mind.

That had always been the amazing thing about Helmut Taplinger. He hadn't minded her being overweight, hadn't seemed to care at all about the enormous folds of fat that made up her double chins, the repulsive flesh that hung from her stomach and arms, that sagged around her thighs and knees. He was the only one who didn't look at her with disgust, as if he thought she should be blotted off the face of the earth. But everyone else did. And always had.

"Hey, pigface, you've got food all over yourself."

"You're soooo *gross*."

"Beatrice, there *isn't* any more. I kill myself to put dinner on this table, and you eat like there's no tomorrow. One hamburger was enough for Mary and Larry, and it'll have to be enough for you."

Childhood mealtimes were burned into her memory, the endless taunts of her brother and sister, her mother's annoyance and revulsion. And Sugar just sitting there, still craving more after a second helping, unable to stop eating despite her own humiliation.

No one in her family ever considered how Sugar might have felt about her weight. Rather, everyone understood that Sugar's obesity was the crowning injustice in her *mother's* life. And it certainly wasn't the only one. As Jeanette Lawton had made clear every day, providing for three children all by herself was sheer torment. How could she be expected to do it, she would ask, a woman of forty-five who had conceived a third child totally by accident, and then lost her fifty-year-old husband to a heart attack only six months after the baby was born. Holding down two jobs in the small Pennsylvania town where they lived was no easy task, and as far as she was concerned, it was a thankless one.

The way she looked at it, her mother would say, fate had killed her husband, and then forgotten all about her. Sugar could still recite the litany of complaints from memory, repeated almost nightly as her mother sat in a tattered armchair, rubbing her tired, stockinged feet, the television blaring nearby. Whatever was happening on the screen would somehow connect to how ridiculous it was to have a baby when she'd already raised her first two to the ages of twelve and thirteen, or to how unfair it was for her husband to have died and left her without life insurance or a dime in the bank. If anyone on the tiny black-and-white television went on a date or out with a friend, she would plaintively wonder how she was expected to have any kind of life stuck in this dump of a house in this dump of a town.

For Jeanette, having a fat child was simply the final

indignity. When Sugar had grown overweight as a child, people used to pinch her cheeks and say how adorably plump she was. But as she got older, she was no longer cute. She could tell people viewed her as nothing more than a disgusting fat kid, a ball of pasty-looking dough. And her mother's opinion was no different. Sugar often caught her wincing at the very sight of her daughter coming into the room. Jeanette herself gave Sugar her nickname, sitting at the tiny kitchen table one Sunday morning with her coffee and a cigarette, observing through narrowed eyes as her six-year-old daughter consumed three jelly doughnuts.

"Some mothers might call their daughter Peaches or Pumpkin," she had said dryly, taking a long drag on her cigarette, "but, Beatrice, there's only one thing we could call you."

Jeanette apparently never saw any reason to keep her thoughts about Sugar's eating to herself. If something set her off on the subject, she raised her eyes heavenward to ask God why the third mouth she had brought into this world was always open, and how was she ever going to fill it. "If she could, she'd just swallow my paychecks whole," Jeanette would say. "Look at her, my fat little accident."

Sugar's brother and sister would inevitably guffaw at these words, glad to have Sugar instead of themselves as their mother's target. Sugar would turn beet red, wanting to take one of the long knives in the kitchen and slit herself open to stop the feeling of shame. On balance, it had been easier to deal with Mary and Larry, with their nasty barbs and occasional hitting. They were like phantom tormentors, appearing at odd times according to their more grown-up schedules, avoiding her one minute, attacking her the next.

But Sugar had found weapons of her own, ones that brought an exotic pleasure she never would have expected. It began the afternoon of Mary's junior prom, when she and two of her friends were trying on their long dresses, toying with their long layered hair for hours on end, all the while taunting Sugar whenever she happened to pass by in the hallway.

"At least Lardo will never have to struggle over her prom outfit," Mary said to her pals in a loud stage whisper as Sugar entered her own room across the way. "That is, unless they start doing beauty checks on the tubby selling punch in a dark corner of the gym."

All three girls had laughed hysterically, with Mary's precious yellow canary, Snowbird, cackling along.

But, Sugar noted with pleasure, as she stood at her bedroom window to watch, Mary wasn't laughing when she found the bird on the doorstep, its neck twisted and broken, when she arrived home at three that morning.

Mary could never prove that Sugar had done it. Nor could Larry absolutely point to his youngest sister when he found his good gray wool trousers on the floor of his closet, the crotch torn out in jagged cuts. Both of them had gone to their mother, but their complaining was oddly muted. In fact, from the second incident onward, they tended to tiptoe around Sugar, eyeing her strangely only when they were sure she wasn't looking back at them. As soon as they finished high school, they had moved out of the house. Sugar lost contact with them, and didn't know or care where they were now.

Her mother was a different story. She had an endless supply of cruel comments for her youngest child, and every one of them had permanently etched itself into Sugar's brain. Until the day she died, Sugar would never forget the expression on her mother's face the night she accidentally came into the bathroom as a then-thirteen-year-old Sugar was just stepping out of the shower. All Sugar had to do was close her eyes to summon up the look on her mother's face, frozen with revulsion. Sugar herself had stopped looking in mirrors long before, and only glanced down at her body when she had to. Still, she could imagine what her mother had seen. Had it been possible, Sugar would have hated herself even more at that moment. But her self-loathing was already complete.

Somewhere around ninth grade, Sugar stopped hearing the teasing, stopped noticing the stares of the other children at school. She gave up trying to make friends, and she never even entertained the idea of talking to a boy, much less going out on a date. Instead, she found herself consumed by needs she didn't understand. She felt compelled to wash her hands over and over, sometimes as often as one hundred times a day. When that somehow wasn't enough, she began cleaning, scrubbing every inch of the run-down house every single day.

But late at night, lying in her small dark room, she was still driven by some nameless urge. Her hand would snake up to her head, as if of its own volition, and she would pull out her hair, one strand at a time, until she fell asleep. Her thick, red hair, the one part of her that was actually beautiful, was soon limp and thinned, white patches of scalp showing through.

One year flowed into another with the only noticeable change being the continual upward creeping of Sugar's weight. When she graduated from high school, the need to tear at her hair seemed to diminish. The absence of her peers' vicious taunts freed her from that particular compulsion.

Jeanette's arthritis, always a problem, grew more severe as she reached her late sixties. Finally, unable to work at all, she became dependent on Sugar. The arrangement wasn't that different from the way it had always been, other than that it was Sugar who now went to work instead of Jeanette, making breads and rolls in a bakery. The two women had spent nearly every evening at home together for all of Sugar's life, and they continued to do so. If Jeanette Lawton noticed her daughter's withdrawal from the world, she never commented on it.

"Look at us," she'd say, holding up her gnarled, painful hands. "A cripple and a hippo. We're some pair, huh, Sugar?"

But by then, Sugar had stopped feeling sorry for her mother; she had stopped feeling anything at all for her. When Jeanette died of pneumonia at seventy-two, Sugar immediately sold the house for the little she could get, splitting the money with her brother and sister in what proved to be her final encounter with them. She used what was left to take a bus to New York City and rent a studio apartment in a building on Twenty-third Street.

Twenty-eight years old, three hundred and twenty pounds, Sugar roamed the streets of New York looking for work. For months, she went on interviews for every job that sounded halfway decent: receptionist, salesgirl, waitress. No matter how pleasant she was, how neat her appearance, no one ever offered her a position. Finally, it dawned on her: she wasn't going to get a job anywhere she was visible. She would never be permitted to work in a front office or a store. Fat people like her had jobs *in the back*. They baked, they stacked boxes, they washed up.

For days, she raged at herself, at her freakishness, at her desperate inability to be normal. Once again, she tore at her hair, all the while understanding that a bald patch would provide yet another excuse for her to be overlooked and cast aside. Then, on a rainy Friday afternoon, she spotted the man who had refused her the last time she'd tried to find a job. He was waiting for the subway at Union Square. Sugar remembered the man's name, Norman Fidler. He was the night manager at a small hotel in midtown, and he'd been looking for an assistant bookkeeper willing to work late into the evening. She moved up right behind him, taking in the folds of flab obvious even under his brown twill suit. Another couple of years and he'll look like my twin brother, she thought. But no one will stop *him* from working. She stood there, infuriated by what seemed an outrageous double standard.

She never really *meant* to nudge him just as the train was roaring into the station. It kind of just happened, she decided, backing away as his body was carried underneath the screaming metal wheels. So many people were milling about, it was impossible for any witnesses to point to her, although several people glanced her way more than once when the police arrived. And, strangely enough, she wasn't very worried about getting caught.

In fact, she realized a few days later, she'd stopped pulling at her hair. For a few weeks, she stopped stuffing her face, finding herself eating vegetables and fruits, not much thinking about the cakes and cookies that spilled out of her kitchen cabinets. She even eased up on her cleaning, realizing one Saturday afternoon that she hadn't vacuumed or dusted since the previous Wednesday.

And magically, with her money nearly gone, she found a job. She became the telephone receptionist for an escort service on the Upper East Side.

"Hi, Sugar."

Sugar looked up from the selection of mustards to see Tracey Eiger pushing a cart past her.

"Hi, hon, how are you?" Sugar answered with a broad smile, automatically resuming what she thought of as her Meadowview face. "Haven't seen you in a dog's age. The kids okay, and Bill?"

"Everybody's great, thanks."

Sugar gave a small wave in farewell, grabbing a jar of Dijon mustard before moving on. Tracey had been someone she'd actually considered recruiting, but, in the end, she'd decided against it. Choosing the right women to approach was the most delicate part of the entire operation; she couldn't afford to make a mistake. She listened to her gut, and if she had the slightest hesitation, she bypassed the candidate. Despite Tracey's efforts to cover it up, it was obvious to Sugar that she wasn't happy in her marriage. That immediately put her on the list of possibles. But there was something about her that Sugar didn't trust.

Learning to rely on her instincts about people was one of the many things Sugar had discovered back on that first job in New York. Manning the phones, she was in charge of coordinating the schedules, keeping the books, and matching the appropriate girls to the men. The man who owned the business was delighted to have someone he could trust to take over the day-to-day operation, and soon stopped coming in altogether, just checking in with her once or twice a week.

The vast majority of the so-called dates were routine sex-for-cash arrangements, although sometimes a man actually needed an escort for the evening. Some men were straightforward and specific about the type of girl they wanted, and what they expected her to do; others spoke in vague terms, pretending they had nothing more in mind than a little conversation over dinner. In the years she spent there, Sugar became an expert listener, learning that the most important messages often lay in what went unsaid.

The women who worked for the escort service would hang around the small office, waiting for their assignments. They compared notes on everything from the fastest ways to make a man climax to the best gynecologists and child care. Sugar was intrigued by their casual patter about threesomes and fellatio, anal sex and fetishes. The name of the game was to get the customer satisfied, then take off as fast as possible, and the women loved to one-up each other with outrageous tales of how they got away with doing the minimum for the maximum amount of money.

Sugar derived vast amusement from the fact that, having had virtually no close contact herself with men, she figured she knew far more about them than most women. All in all, men seemed to her simple-minded fools.

She had been with the agency nearly three years when she met Helmut Taplinger. He had called one Thursday late in the afternoon, most likely to set up an appointment with one of the girls, but his attempts at asking for what he wanted were so pitiful, he hung up abruptly without even getting to the point. When he tried again several days later, she recognized his voice, this time making jokes with him, easing the way for him to get the words out of his mouth.

Even then, he didn't go through with actually setting a time. Instead, he asked a hundred questions, all of them irrelevant. Sugar enjoyed the conversation. It was liberating to find someone even more pathetic than herself. And when he called back a few days later, she once again listened to his every word and made him feel like a somebody.

She'd mentioned him to some of the girls, and when his calls became a daily event, Randi, a tall blonde whose obvious intelligence was overwhelmed by a laziness so vast it would keep her on her back all of her working life, began to make fun of him, even while Sugar was on the phone with him.

"Tell him to come and see me," Randi had said loudly, obviously hoping he'd overhear. "I'll sing him a lulluby and tell him that's what sex is. Believe me, he'll never know the difference."

Sugar had shushed her cheerfully, covering up an emotion that surprised her: she actually felt sorry for this guy, even protective of him. And when he finally asked her out on a date, she found herself saying yes. Not that she expected anything to happen. She knew that her weight made her virtually invisible to men, so when the tall, skinny man with the thick shock of graying hair met her for the first time outside the building she worked in, and took her to dinner at an elegant if reasonable French restaurant, she never bothered being nervous. After all, she told herself when he graciously offered her a second cocktail, he'd never be romantically interested in her. He just wanted advice on how to approach real women, the ones he could pay to see if only he knew what to say.

But, unexpectedly, he continued to call her in the weeks that followed. One Thursday night, he asked her if she would be interested in going with him to a concert at Lincoln Center. It was all she could do to keep from blurting out "Why?" instead of "Yes."

Despite what she had come to expect from men in her years at the escort service, Helmut had none of their bluster, none of their sense of entitlement. It was as if he were the student and she a revered teacher. He would look to her for approval as he would help her on with her coat and hold the door open. To the girls, she would joke that dating Helmut was like having a baby born at the age of forty. After she raised him and taught him how to be a man, he could come back and shower the girls with the fruits of her fabulous instruction.

But, in fact, she didn't feel cavalier about him at all. She got a kick out of his adoration, found herself feeling sorry for him, almost eager to repair the damage his own terrible upbringing on a poor Wisconsin farm had caused. The only child of a mother who died when he was a year old, he'd gone from the isolation of the farm to the rigors of a small, all-male, Catholic college nearby, staying on for graduate work. Still living at home with his father, a man who was in bed by eight every night, Helmut barely even saw a woman until he got his first job in New York City when he was well into his twenties.

He worked as an editor for a history buff's magazine called *Yesterday*, and Sugar's conversations with him typically consisted of Helmut's holding forth on some historical incident. Although she was rarely interested in what he was saying, she marveled that he chose to say it to *her*. She couldn't get over the way he looked at her without seeming to notice that she was fat, that he never referred to it, never commented on what she ate or how much.

On their sixth date, he kissed her good night. On their eighth, they sat on his couch and kissed more deeply, Helmut stroking her hair and her back, asking her politely if he could go further. Sugar had never considered him handsome, and there were times she found herself bored, listening to him go on at length about some obscure treaty or dead politician, but she was surprisingly moved by his entreaties, by his appreciation when she would lead his hands over her breasts, guide his fingers inside her. It was titillating to be in charge, to be the one with the upper hand for the first time in her life.

Sometimes, in the privacy of her apartment, she would wonder when he would come to his senses and realize he was insane to be having sex with a pig like herself. But when they were together, it never felt like that. He was grateful for her favors, eager to know what would please her. For her part, she almost drowned in the sensation of his bare body against hers. She'd never dreamed such a thing could actually happen to her. Night after night, she encouraged him, slowly making him an expert in her body. He would travel her massive flesh thankfully, making her feel like an empress. If she never approached ecstasy, she at least came to understand the concept of satisfaction.

With her new sex life came a self-confidence that Sugar had never imagined she could possess. Feeling more sure of herself every day, she suddenly wondered why she was running the escort service for such a small salary. After all, she did all the work. Her demand for more money and her change in attitude quickly caused friction between herself and her boss, and it became obvious to everyone he would get rid of her as soon as he found a replacement.

Sugar found herself wanting a level of control she'd never had. She began to understand how much better she was at business details than most other people were. She longed for a business of her own, a real life of her own. When Helmut asked her to marry him, she said yes without hesitation. He was getting a new job at a magazine called *Armchair General*, which was located up in

Connecticut, and he wanted Sugar to move there with him as his wife. He understood that she intended to found a business up there as well, one that most men wouldn't have tolerated. But Helmut wasn't most men; he was her disciple, her most ardent fan.

They married in a civil ceremony at City Hall the next week, then moved up to Meadowview. Later that year she went on the first diet of her life, an excruciatingly slow process that dropped her weight by a miraculous one hundred and fifty pounds. Oddly enough, Helmut never commented on the radical change in her appearance; he just never seemed to notice what she looked like.

Sugar reached into the dairy section to pick up a quart of skim milk and a pint of half-and-half for her coffee. She remembered their first house, a tiny two-bedroom Cape on a narrow, tree-lined street. She had to smile, recalling how grand it had seemed to her at the time, all the space of a house and yard compared to her studio apartment back in New York. As Helmut had moved up at the magazine, they had moved up in the community. Their current house wasn't overly big by Sugar's newer standards, but it was in one of the best neighborhoods in Meadowview, a well-kept Colonial with, as their real estate broker put it, "good bones." And what had seemed so expensive when they hesitantly put down the ten percent cash necessary for their mortgage quickly became a financial bargain when the real estate market boomed the following year. These days, they often laughed to each other as they perused the real estate column in the *Ledger*—they could get five or ten times what they'd paid.

Stopping in the store's bakery section, she grabbed a chocolate chip cookie from the open display, munching on it as she began to fill a plastic bag with bagels. Even though she had never wanted children, it seemed that having babies was expected in this town, and she had planned on following the program. After a year of trying unsuccessfully to get pregnant, they learned that Helmut's sperm count was practically nil, so she was off the hook. And she had her business to sustain her. She'd started slowly, carefully analyzing each woman and each customer before enlisting them.

Helmut knew little of what she did with her time. She understood that the fewer facts he had, the happier he was. Not that he would ever have stopped her, but if she spoke about it, he would get frightened, and that was a waste of her time. So, night after night, he would be completely self-absorbed in his work and his nightly reading, and she would do whatever she had to in the privacy of her study. It was a perfect arrangement: he didn't want to know, and she didn't particularly want to tell him.

Their sexual relationship had peaked years before, with neither especially interested anymore, but they were happy together in their own unique way. His pedantic lecturing and perfectionism were a bit boring, and he was less than thrilled with her career, but they would always be grateful to each other. He had treated her like a person when that was what she needed more than anything else, had even provided her with a nice house and car, respectability—hell, a whole new world. And she had taken a frog and turned him into a prince.

If she no longer seemed to turn to him in bed, he didn't mind. He'd been redefined by her. Never again would he be a pitiable nerd, the oldest male virgin on the eastern seaboard; he was a man.

And, with the success of her business, Sugar had discovered her real passion: money. All that cash—

tax-free—turned her on as no man ever could. Without ever rubbing it in to her husband, Sugar helped pay for their expensive furnishings, the gourmet take-out dinners, and the silk caftans and costly shoes she wore. Without ever bothering to inform him, she stuffed enormous sums of cash into shopping bags in the back of her closet.

She had a gift for managing this particular kind of business, no question about it. She knew which women to approach. She knew how to spread the word to attract customers without exposing herself to the law, and how to make payoffs when she had to. She had a proper life as Mrs. Helmut Taplinger, and then she had the life she enjoyed, the one that made her feel alive, as Sugar, the madam. For years, everything had run as smooth as silk.

Until now.

Sugar found an open checkout line and hurriedly loaded her groceries onto the conveyor belt. At first it had been such a coup, getting acquainted with the high-and-mighty Farrell Cole. Sugar had relished it. Here she was, the fat nobody from nowhere who had brought herself to this point, gossiping in the backyard with this elegant, sophisticated number. Sugar was accepted, respected. Somebody. Of course, with her secret life, she had always laughed to herself, she was even *more* of a somebody than the social scions of Meadowview ever dreamed.

But she should have known that a high-class bitch is a high-class bitch. And that's what Farrell was. For a while, it had gone all right, the Coles and the Taplingers socializing every so often, Sugar really feeling that they were being accepted into the Coles' golden circle of friends. But then came that night when Sugar and Helmut were having dinner over at the Coles' house, a meal that, as usual, appeared to be straight out of *Gourmet*. As always, Farrell and John looked and acted the perfect couple. Sugar wanted to spit when she thought about it now.

They had been discussing some man in a nearby town who had killed his wife. Focusing on her crème brûlée, Sugar wasn't paying much attention as Helmut complained about the liberal treatment the man would undoubtedly get for such a vicious crime.

"He'll get away with it, that's a foregone conclusion. The court system is a disgrace. There's no question he did it, but you mark my words, the man won't spend a day in prison, much less get the execution he deserves. It will all be a huge waste of time and money."

Farrell wiped her mouth with her napkin. "Helmut, would you rather we just got out our rifles and went over there to gun him down?"

Sugar raised her head at the gaiety in Farrell's tone.

"Save the cost of a trial altogether."

The smile never left Sugar's face, but she put her spoon down and sat very still. She caught the amused look that passed between Farrell and John. Her stomach lurched. So that was what they really thought of Helmut. He was a buffoon to them. A big joke.

She didn't know if she could make it through the evening. After dessert, she hastened Helmut back home, fuming over their superior attitude, at the same time wanting to crawl into a hole and hide. She couldn't get Farrell's words out of her mind, the condescension in her attitude. Who the hell did Farrell think she was, judging Helmut that way, making *fun* of him, for Christ's sake. Sugar suddenly recalled other incidents revealing the Coles' arrogance toward Helmut, comments she had missed at the time but which in retrospect were blatantly obvious as put-downs. Her rage grew.

The idea had come to her a week later, striking in its simplicity. Sugar would convince Farrell to come to the hotel to meet a trick. It was the perfect payback.

"Paper or plastic?" The checkout girl asked in a bored tone.

"Plastic." Sugar pulled out her wallet, then waited impatiently for her groceries to be bagged. She unloaded the bags into the trunk of her car and quickly pulled out of the parking lot, heading for home.

Sugar had always known Farrell wasn't the right kind of woman to get involved in a call girl operation. She may have had a lost wild girl inside her, but at heart she loved her husband. Sugar would bet big money she'd never cheated on him or even seriously considered it. And she just wasn't the right kind of personality for the business. Going into a hotel room, having sex with a stranger for money—for some women it was a perfectly reasonable way to make a buck. Some of them did it for kicks, or their own sick reasons. But Farrell didn't fit into any of these categories. Sugar knew that if she could get Farrell to cross over the line, actually to go through with it, she would be psychologically devastated by the process. Miss Manners might get through it exactly one time, but it would tear the fabric of her perfection forever.

Let's see how high and mighty you are then, she'd thought. Let's see who's the big joke when you've blown your comfortable little world to bits.

When she finished unpacking her groceries, Sugar was finally free to make herself a cup of coffee and sit down to think. But she was too restless to sit there and drink it. She went over to the sink, grabbed a sponge and a can of Comet, and got down on her hands and knees to scrub behind the refrigerator.

Farrell had reacted to her experience at the St.-Tropez just as Sugar anticipated she would, and Sugar had enjoyed every minute of the entire episode. But the whole thing had backfired on her in a way she could never have foreseen. Farrell was actually accusing her of killing Marina Paulsen. If Farrell were to be believed, she and John might be able to prove it.

"Why, goddammit?" she spat out as she ran the sponge back and forth almost savagely across the linoleum. "Why did this happen to me?"

Clearly, the situation couldn't be permitted to continue. What she had to do now was contain the problem. In the end, one of them would survive this, nothing more, nothing less. Sugar was going to make damned sure that it was her.

Chapter 10

Tim Cole turned onto Lilac Lane and breathed a sigh of relief. Nobody in sight. Grasping the straps that held his backpack in place over his down jacket, he picked up his pace; he was definitely going to be late for school. He shook his head, annoyed with himself. He'd never taken this route before; he should have allowed extra time.

He envisioned himself coming into the classroom after the morning bell, Ms. Miller giving him the hairy eyeball and questioning him as he made up some lame excuse. Frowning at the image, he broke into a run, dodging the random rocks and branches in his path.

Not too much farther to go. According to the street map he'd studied in his room, if he made a right at the end of Lilac onto Milford Street, and then another left after that, he would wind up right behind the school.

He careened around the corner onto Milford. Then, with a sharp intake of breath, he stopped short.

There they were, not twenty feet away. Garth Hober, lanky and taller than most of the other sixth graders, slouched against a parked car, a shock of thick black hair protruding from beneath his dark green knitted cap. Jay Zubett, wearing earmuffs, was kneeling down a few feet away, relacing one of his hiking boots, his schoolbooks on the ground beside him. It was Jay who looked up and spotted Tim first, pulling his lace tight with a flourish and standing up, a sly smile on his face. He said something to Garth, who also looked over in Tim's direction. The two of them moved to stand together, facing Tim, blocking his way.

Tim stared at them, sick to his stomach. He couldn't believe it. Every Monday for four weeks, they'd waited for him on Lantern Street. How on earth did they know he would choose *this* Monday to come a different way?

For a moment, the urge to cry was almost overwhelming. There was no getting away from them. They were going to be everywhere, forever. Sure, he might be a big deal on his baseball team and at the Y's Saturday morning basketball games, but that didn't matter when it came to Monday. One fourth-grade pipsqueak was no match for these two sixth-graders, and never would be. It was hopeless.

"Hey, Cole," Garth Hober called out to him contemptuously, "you're late." His voice turned singsong. "Gonna get in trouble with your teeeeacher."

Tim forced himself to move forward. He might as well get this over with.

"Whadda you care?" he retorted with the little bravado he was able to muster.

Jay Zubett grinned, his words taunting. "But we *do* care, Timmy. A good boy like you shouldn't get yelled at."

Tim didn't answer. Trying not to look at them, he kept walking. When he got close enough, Jay reached out and shoved him hard on the shoulder.

"Hold it. We got some business to conduct."

Tim stopped and sighed, knowing what was coming.

"Well?" Garth held out one hand, palm up.

"I don't have it today." Tim stared directly at Garth,

trying to sound convincing. "My dad forgot to give it to me."

Garth looked over at Jay. "You believe that? You think Timmy's daddy would forget to give him his allowance?"

Jay shook his head. "Nah."

"Me neither." Garth's eyes were reproachful as he turned back to Tim. He reached out and, as Jay had just done before, gave Tim a hard shove on the shoulder. Jay joined him, striking out at Tim's other shoulder.

"Hey, stop it," Tim protested loudly.

The two boys continued silently, advancing as Tim was pushed back by the force of each shove, stumbling for balance.

"Cut it out!" he yelled. He lashed back, but his arms didn't reach them, and he found himself swinging at the air.

Garth took two quick steps forward and punched him on the ear. Tim yelped, his arm going up to cover his head.

"You know how to make us stop," Garth said, shoving Tim again, this time on the forehead. "Hand it over."

"All right, all right." Fighting back tears of pain and humiliation, Tim turned away, pulling off his backpack. He yanked open the zipper of the small front compartment and reached inside to pull out the crisp dollar bill his father had given him the night before. Garth snatched it from his hand.

Jay gave him a last push on the back. "Now get out of here."

Tim busied himself by zipping up his backpack again as he stepped out into the street and crossed over, his head down, not bothering to see if any cars were coming. I wish a car *would* run me over, he thought miserably. At least this would stop. His ear was starting to throb. He could hear the two boys behind him laughing and talking, their voices growing fainter as they made their way down the street.

He slipped his backpack on, thinking about how late he would be if he went to school now. What would he tell Ms. Miller? *I stopped to give my allowance to two morons from the sixth grade, just like I do every week.* Everyone would laugh at him, make jokes about what a total wimp he was.

He felt so angry, and so completely *stupid*. He had been trying for weeks to figure out how to make those two jerks leave him alone. But what he thought was such a brilliant idea—changing his route to school—had proved to be of zero use.

Of course, he didn't dare tell anyone what was going on. That would have made him look like the dweeb of the century. He remembered all too clearly how, at the end of the first week of school, Ben Sorel had complained to their teacher about Teddy Adams teasing him on the bus. Teddy had been reprimanded in front of the whole class, but everyone stopped speaking to *Ben* for weeks afterward. And telling his parents wouldn't be any better. He knew what they would do: go to the school and complain. Hober and Zubett would only get a lecture from the principal. But they'd beat him up a lot worse the next time they got hold of him.

His ear was really hurting. Rubbing it, he decided he just couldn't face school. All he wanted to do was hide in his room. So what if he missed a day? It was no big deal and it wasn't like he did it all the time. He turned around to go back the way he had come. Then he hesitated. If his mother was still home, she'd expect a good explanation about what he was doing back all of a sudden. Well, he'd tell her he'd gotten a stomachache on the way or something. He set off at a brisk pace.

When he got there, he let himself in the house through the door to the kitchen. His mother didn't come to greet him, so he figured she must have gone out. He could hear the washing machine starting up in the basement. Mrs. Miles must be doing the laundry, he thought. But then he heard his mother's voice in the living room, low and urgent. It was odd that she hadn't come in at the sound of the door slamming. He stood there for a moment, but he couldn't make out what she was saying. As he put his backpack on the kitchen table, he was startled to hear his father reply to her. Why was his father still home? He always drove off to work right after Tim left for school. Tim took a few steps closer to the doorway so he could hear what they were talking about.

"No, no one else saw me," his mother said.

"You did this without a thought to any of us. Let's not even get into what it says about our marriage. Did you ever stop to consider the children?" The fury in his father's voice made Tim shrink back against the wall.

"John, please . . ." His mother sounded close to tears.

Tim heard the angry sarcasm in his father's response. "At least it was a *suite*. A suite is so much more appropriate. I wouldn't want to think of you in some unpleasant place. Something *beneath* a woman of your stature."

What was a *sweet*? Tim couldn't imagine what on earth they were talking about. Did she eat something his father had wanted for himself, or maybe for him and Riley?

"Okay. I know I deserve that." His mother spoke quietly. "You're going to have to decide whether you can live with this." Her tone became grim. "And if you're going to hold it against me for the rest of our lives."

His father's shout was sudden and loud. "I'd be god-damned entitled to."

Tim cringed inwardly as his father continued to yell. He'd heard his parents argue before—not often, but sometimes. Yet there was something about their voices now that was different. Their arguments tended to be short and pretty quiet. Usually it was his mother who seemed the more upset, while his father would respond in his typically calm manner. In fact, Tim could barely remember hearing his father shout the way he was doing now. Whatever was going on, it was something very bad.

"What did you expect? That I'd hold your hand and say, sure, it's all right, honey, I know you had to *find* yourself again." Tim heard his father pacing as he yelled. "Poor little Farrell, trapped in this horrible life, in this terrible house with two terrible children, with a husband who loves her and would give her anything. It's gotta be *hell* for you."

What was he talking about? Tim was getting panicked. Did his mother hate them and want to leave? Please, he begged silently, make them stop. Whatever this fight was about, make it go away.

There was a pause before his mother replied. "I'm not going to pretend it's all right. It's not. But now I'm trying to do what's right."

"What's right?" His voice grew even more furious. "You sure as hell didn't worry about what was right when you traipsed off to have your little bit of fun. And how about a few other minor items, like my career. And Charlie—is this going to help my brother, bringing this out when his name is attached to it? It's not enough you're going to expose what *you* did, and ruin me as a

lawyer. You're just throwing my brother in for good luck here, huh?"

His mother's voice had a tremble in it. "I can't help that he's involved."

Tim chewed on his lip. What did Uncle Charlie have to do with this?

"We'll have to move. We can't stay here with everybody knowing." There was anguish in his words. "Farrell, how *could* you?"

They were silent. Tim was genuinely frightened now.

"Damn, it's really late." From the shift in his tone, Tim guessed that his father had suddenly looked at the clock on the mantelpiece. "I have to get to the office." Tim heard him stride quickly to the living-room entryway, heard his clipped words. "We'll finish this conversation when I get home."

Tim craned his neck to get a glimpse of his father's back as John Cole picked up his briefcase and suit jacket from where they had been resting at the base of the staircase. Realizing his father would come this way to get to the garage, Tim turned and ran out into the dining room, his heart pounding with the fear of being discovered. But his father hurried out of the house, and there was sudden quiet.

Tim waited, but he didn't hear anything from the living room. He wondered what his mother was doing in there.

Well, no matter what, he couldn't let her know he'd been here listening all this time. Moving as carefully and quietly as he could, he retrieved his backpack and tiptoed from the kitchen to the staircase. As long as she didn't come out of the living room, he would be okay. If she stuck her head out, there was no way he could hide.

Holding his breath, he started up the stairs. Silence

from the living room. He continued. The third step, the fourth step. There was a loud creaking beneath his foot. *Oh, no.*

Almost at once, she appeared. He looked over at her. She was pale, and there was an unfamiliar expression on her face, a look of intense unhappiness he didn't ever remember seeing.

"Tim? What are you doing home?" Her surprise and concern erased the expression, returning her to the mother he recognized. "Is everything all right, darling?"

He gave her a look of misery to reinforce his story. "It's my stomach, Mom. I don't know why, but it started hurting like crazy. I couldn't make it to school."

"Oh, *sweetheart.*" Her voice full of sympathy, she came to join him on the stairs. "That's really unlike you. Let's go see what we have in the medicine cabinet."

She put an arm around him and they proceeded upstairs together. Tim sneaked a glance at her face. Whatever she'd been thinking about before, she had put it aside to deal with him. She looked down and smiled, giving him a reassuring squeeze.

It didn't matter what his father had said. She wouldn't do anything to hurt him or Riley. And she *couldn't* think they were terrible. His father was wrong. Whatever he thought had happened, he must have misunderstood. But it would get straightened out, later, when his father got home from work. Tim just knew it would.

Farrell moved quickly around Riley's room, packing a blue canvas overnight bag. She wasn't too pleased with the prospect of her children having a sleepover on a school night. Still, when Carol Anne had called that afternoon to say that her children were driving her crazy, begging to have Tim and Riley stay over, Farrell realized the invitation was actually a godsend. She and John had to resolve things, and heaven knows, they couldn't talk with the kids around.

Much as she dreaded the conversation with her husband, at least she wouldn't have to go through another day like this one. It was actually a blessing that Tim had come home sick; tending to him enabled her to get her mind off John if only for a few minutes at a time. Of course, she wouldn't have sent Tim out if his stomachache had persisted, but by three o'clock, he reported he was completely better.

The worst part of the day had undoubtedly been when Sugar dropped by unexpectedly, bringing Farrell a coffee cake and chatting as if nothing had happened. Stunned by this performance, Farrell had said practically nothing, vastly relieved when Sugar left after a few minutes, gaily telling Farrell to stay put, she would let herself out.

Farrell heard their housekeeper's voice calling out to her as she opened the front door to leave. "Good night, Mrs. Cole."

"Good night, Mrs. Miles," she answered, emerging from Riley's room. "Thank you." Tim and Riley were downstairs in the family room. "Kids, it's time to go," she called, heading that way, zipping up the bag as she went.

She came upon her children sitting on the floor cross-legged in front of the television, credits rolling onscreen to indicate that whatever they had been watching was now over.

"Listen, folks," she said brightly to the backs of her children's heads. "J.J. Gisondi will be here to pick you up any minute."

Tim twisted around to look at her, his tone unhappy. "Do we really have to go?"

Riley also looked over, screwing her face up. "Yeah, Mom, I don't feel like it."

Farrell felt terrible. Her children didn't dislike the Gisondi children, but they weren't particularly close with them either. Here they were telling her they didn't want to go over there tonight, and she was about to force them.

But her marriage was at stake, and the talk she was about to have with her husband was more important than anything else right now.

She spoke cheerfully. "It'll be fun."

Tim scowled. "No, it won't."

Farrell smiled. "Come on, don't be such sticks-in-the-mud. Here your old mom gives you a chance to sleep out on a school night, to stay up late and cause chaos at somebody else's house. I'd think you'd leap at it."

She caught Tim's eye. He was staring at her, as if trying to figure something out. Abruptly, his tone changed.

"Okay, Mom. We'll go." He stood up, retucking his already-tucked-in shirt.

"I don't *waaannt* to," Riley whined.

Tim looked down at his sister. "Come on," he said sternly. "Get up." He bent down, tugging on her arm. Reluctantly, she allowed herself to be pulled to her feet.

Farrell watched him in surprise. Whatever had caused this sudden change of heart, he was apparently now eager to accommodate his mother. His cooperation made her feel even guiltier for pushing this on the two of them. "Carol Anne will drive you to school tomorrow," she said.

Tim nodded. Sulking, Riley bent sideways to scratch behind her knee.

Farrell sighed and held out the overnight bag. "I've packed your stuff."

They all turned at the sound of the garage door indicating that their father was home. The tension Farrell had felt all day returned in full force, but she certainly didn't want it to show.

"Good," she said brightly. "You'll get to say good night to Daddy."

Farrell hung back as the children ran to greet their father, saying their good-byes just as J.J. pulled up outside. She and John barely even looked at each other until they had seen them off and were back inside the kitchen.

"So." Farrell spoke only the single syllable.

John sat down heavily on one of the chairs. "This had to have been one of the longest days of my life."

"Mine, too." Farrell joined him. "I feel so terrible. I don't know how to apologize. It was the worst thing in the world I ever could have done. I don't know what made me do it."

He began tracing patterns with one finger on the table. "I've been over and over it. Of course, you're right. We have to go to the police with what you know. Whatever you might have done yourself, whatever it means to us as a family—we're not the kind of people who could live with knowledge like this and do nothing about it."

He looked directly into her eyes. "I don't know how I'm going to be able to deal with this. I'd like to believe we can work it out together. My job, the kids . . . I can't address all that right now. But we may be talking about a murder here. We have to go to the police."

There was a long pause. Finally, he continued. "I have one demand, and it's a critical one. I don't want my brother implicated in this. It's unnecessary, and it could mean prison. I can't do that to him."

"What do you want to do?" Farrell asked.

He inhaled deeply, then let his breath out slowly. "This

goes against everything I believe in, and everything I stand for as a lawyer, but I want to destroy whatever evidence there is linking Charlie to this business. We'll tell the police the whole story, with that one piece left out. That part of it just never happened."

Farrell looked at him in surprise. "Can you live with that, lying that way?"

He nodded unhappily. "I'm going to. It's one thing for us to reveal our own involvement here. It's another thing to expose Charlie. He's on the edge as it is."

Farrell nodded.

"We've been through a lot together, Farrell, but nothing like this. Still, I have to believe we can survive it."

Farrell rose and came closer to him. He stood to meet her.

"John," she said, her voice breaking, "I love you so very much. You have to know that."

They embraced, and remained that way in silence, wrapped in each other's arms. Farrell's eyes filled with tears. Finally, John pulled back.

"It's done then," he said.

"Thank you," Farrell whispered. "I'm so sorry, John. I know it'll be hard, but I'll do anything I can to make it up to you. Anything at all."

She began to cry in earnest. John stroked her hair. "Sssshh. We'll worry about that later."

They went into John's study, and looked over all the papers and materials they would be turning over to the police. Anything that might lead to Charlie was torn up. They discussed what they would say and how they would present the story. Nearly two hours later, satisfied that they had covered it all, they made some sandwiches before going upstairs to go to sleep.

It wasn't late, but Farrell was exhausted. She washed up, gazing at her reflection in the mirror above the sink, unable to believe she was actually going to the police in the morning. Slipping on her nightgown, she got into bed to wait for John, who had gone back downstairs to make his daily entry in his computer journal, something he did every night, no matter what was happening or how tired he was. He came upstairs about ten minutes later, already wearing the pajama bottoms in which he slept.

"What time should we go?" she asked him.

He shrugged slightly as he joined her in bed. "I don't know. Eight-thirty? Does it matter? I'll have to call the office and tell them I won't be coming in."

She reached to turn off the light on her night table, then moved over to be close to him.

"I admire you, John," she said quietly. "Every piece of this is at the most incredible personal cost to you. You're a very courageous man. I know why I was so right to marry you." She paused. "And why I was so horribly, unforgivably wrong to do something that could drive you away."

He stroked her arm. "We have a big day tomorrow. Let's get through that and then we'll face the rest of it."

They were quiet. He turned out the lamp on his side of the bed.

"Good night, Farrell," he said softly in the darkness. He kissed the top of her head. "I do love you very much, you know. I always will."

Farrell put her arm across his chest and tilted up her face so she could kiss him on the mouth in return.

"To say I'm sorry doesn't begin to fix this mess. But I love you, John. More than you can ever know."

He sighed and put his arm around her. "I have to believe that. I couldn't go on if I didn't."

Chapter 11

"Well . . . if Marissa were a car . . ." The eleven-year-old girl groped for an answer, bouncing around in her seat as if she heard music from some invisible radio inside her head. "Uhhmmm . . . I'd want her to be a big, white convertible with a red stripe on the side." Triumphant at having thought of something to say, she smiled at the other six girls in the room, before nodding her head in satisfaction at the heavyset woman who conducted all of Carpathia's focus groups.

Lainey munched on what must have been her seventy-fifth potato chip, wondering what in the world she was supposed to do with such wisdom. Should she design a character with a red stripe down its side, for God's sake. For almost two hours now, she'd been seated in darkness on the other side of a one-way mirror that enabled the marketing and creative team from Carpathia to see without being seen. Boredom had set in immediately; now she was beginning to feel drowsy.

After her apparent success with Owen Salisbury in Los Angeles, she was astounded to learn that the other corporate honchos still wanted her to go through with these focus groups—and he had agreed to it. It was as if they needed to feel they were still important in this process, as if marching forward with the original plans meant they

still counted. She supposed this was some type of corporate gamesmanship she didn't understand. Clearly, however, Owen Salisbury did. Much as he liked her ideas for
Marissa, he was willing to let his vice presidents spend
the company's money on what seemed to her like a
pointless exercise, just to let them save face in the end.
Maybe, she reflected, I could learn something from
him. Or maybe he was simply trying to keep her on her
toes, leaving her not quite secure that her idea would
automatically be approved once she fine-tuned it. With
that thought came new anxiety that refused to leave her.
These were the corporate big leagues, where outguessing
everyone else's true agenda was part of the routine
workday. The problem was, she wasn't so sure she
wanted to play on this rarified field.

This was the fourth group she'd attended since she'd
returned from California. The first three meant consecu-
tive nights of traveling out to Short Hills, New Jersey,
with a number of Carpathia colleagues right after work,
sitting through hours of what seemed to be ridiculous
questions. Today's installment was an all-day session
with five different groups of kids scheduled straight
through from nine in the morning until eight that night.
Lainey looked at her watch. It was only eleven and she'd
already had enough of "what kind of car-animal-person
would she be" to last her a lifetime.

Rick had assured her that the questions weren't as
senseless as she might think, and these groups were considered so important that he and Jerry had come east
specifically to attend them. Julian was also sitting in, and
he had warned her that she should pay close attention in
case her idea for Marissa was suddenly vetoed, and she
had to come at it from another angle. His words only
intensified her anxiety. After each group, the leader

would come back into the darkened room and explain what she was supposed to have gleaned from that particular group of children. And it did make a kind of sense, even she could see that, but it was certainly not related in any way to the creative work she'd been doing since coming home to New York.

She'd already come up with a final design for Marissa, one she loved. The only person she'd shown it to was Julian, who had been genuinely impressed, his eyes lighting up at her ingenuity as she described some of the situations she had in mind for Marissa's early adventures. He insisted she keep the sketches to herself until the focus-group process was played out. "Let 'em believe their money went for something," he'd said. "And don't forget, after they see your work, there'll be ten or twenty more groups combing through every inch of it before they give it a go."

"This should wake you up a little," he murmured in her ear now, placing a can of Coke and a huge bowl of peanut M&M's in front of her.

"Has anyone ever actually eaten himself into a coma during one of these?" Lainey asked the room at large, keeping her voice low as if the children on the other side of the mirror might hear her.

Rick Dean leaned forward from the row behind Lainey and Julian. "During the Matilda and Mommy focus groups in Los Angeles eight or ten years ago," he whispered, "the marketing guy from the publishing division had a heart attack right in the middle of the sweet and sour pork. His widow threatened to bring a lawsuit against the company, claiming they had murdered her husband." Rick laughed, covering his mouth to muffle the sound. "The best part is Carpathia gave her over two hundred thousand bucks."

"Did she actually bring suit?" Julian asked incredulously.

Rick shook his head. "Nah, they told her how sorry they were and promised never again to serve Chinese food in a focus group."

Lainey stood up and walked to the back of the darkened room. This whole experience was beginning to feel like a bizarre dream. The notion of traveling to a town in northern New Jersey and bringing a bunch of kids together at a round table, paying each of them fifty bucks and asking them questions like what kind of object a certain character might be seemed planets away from the creation of Marissa.

"Back in a minute," she whispered, opening the door to the long corridor that led to a small kitchen.

Lainey stood in front of the tiny refrigerator, not particularly intending to open it but glad for the opportunity to be alone in a well-lit place. She didn't hear Julian's footsteps as he approached her from behind.

"It helps if you splash water on your face," he said, taking a quick peek to make sure they were alone before kissing the back of her neck. "The New York guys think you're the greatest thing since Wonder Bread." He reached past her to open the refrigerator door and remove a bottle of Perrier.

"Sure, they do," Lainey replied, turning around to smile at him ironically. "That's because they haven't seen the sketches yet."

Julian placed his hands under the bottom of her sweater, knowing that his body shielded his actions from anyone who might be in the corridor behind them. "They're going to love them, don't worry." He glided his hands up under her bra, stroking her breasts lightly until his fingertips rested on her nipples. "By the way, I've got a surprise for you."

"Animal, vegetable, or mineral?" Lainey responded, keeping her eyes on the empty hallway.

He thought for a moment. "Well . . . animal, I guess. Human beings are animals, right? Tonight this animal gets to spend the night with you."

"How come?" Lainey removed his hands from under her sweater and took a step back, thinking she heard a door open somewhere near them.

"Because, as I explained to my wife, these groups may run all night so I'm forced to stay in Jersey." His voice lowered in response to her move, so no one could hear what he'd said. He then spoke in a conversational tone, so anyone walking by would definitely overhear. "I'll run you back to Manhattan later. I have to pick up some files before I make my way home."

Lainey knew she ought to be happy, but guilt threatened to overwhelm any pleasure she might take from his news. How much joy was there to be taken from sleeping with a married man?

Plenty, she admitted to herself, sighing at the thought of Julian lying beside her for an entire night. She brushed an imaginary hair off his shoulder just to have an excuse to touch him. "How many more groups do you think there are before we can blow this popstand, anyway?"

Julian took her hand in his, bending his head to run his lips over her fingers. "Only about eight hours' worth . . ."

His response was interrupted by footsteps in the hallway.

"Miss Wolfe?"

The young blond receptionist who'd greeted them each day came up behind Julian. He dropped Lainey's hand abruptly and moved back.

"They told me I'd find you here."

Julian left the room, taking his bottle of Perrier with him, smiling briefly and impersonally at the woman before making his way back to the group.

"There's someone on the phone for you. He says it's important."

Lainey looked quizzical. Who would call her in the middle of New Jersey? "Where can I take the call?"

"I'll switch it right in here," the young woman said, indicating a phone on the small table near the stove. "Just pick it up when it rings."

She left, and moments later Lainey heard the phone beeping quietly. She walked over to pick up the receiver.

"Lainey Wolfe."

"Lainey, it's Charlie."

The voice sounded familiar, but she couldn't place it.

"Charlie Cole, John's brother."

"How did you track me down here?" she asked.

"It wasn't easy," he responded, a strange catch in his throat. "Listen, you've got to come help. Something terrible has happened."

Lainey glanced around the room, not realizing that she would think about this exact moment, this exact setting for the rest of her life. "What's the matter?"

"Oh, God," Charlie was crying now. "It's John and Farrell. There's been an accident. They're gone, both of them."

Lainey felt an explosion of terror and dread. "What do you mean, they're gone?"

"They're dead," he said, the words a strangulated cry. "Some kind of gas leak or something. Please come on out here. Riley's screaming for you, and I just can't handle this all by myself."

She thought she would choke from the pain in her

chest. She lost track of the phone in her hand, dropping it to the floor. Maybe Charlie had made a mistake. Maybe it wasn't true.

Lainey felt her knees buckling and made her way to a small stool near the cabinets. She didn't dare sit down on it, just grasped the wooden seat with both hands, breathing deeply, afraid she might be sick. Farrell. Her best friend was dead.

And John, too. Jesus. Tim and Riley. She pictured them saying good-bye the last time Farrell had driven her to the Meadowview train station. Riley had been chomping on a huge lollipop, cheerfully leaving Lainey's cheeks wet and sticky as she kissed her good-bye. Tim had teased his little sister about it, lobbing snowballs at her as they walked back to Farrell's car. How were they going to survive this? What would happen to them?

Suddenly, she felt as if she'd been struck by lightning.

Oh, my God. She drew in her breath sharply. *Oh, my God.*

When Farrell and John chose her as godmother, they'd also made her legal guardian. It was in their will, in black and white, signed, witnessed, and notarized.

In case both parents died, it was Lainey who was to raise the children.

She would never forget the day they first brought it up. Tim was not quite three and Riley was an infant. They had been asleep upstairs, while the three adults were relaxing over coffee. Farrell and John had been to their lawyer's office the day before, and they shared with Lainey the queasy business of making decisions that would only come into effect after death. Arranging the financial details of their lives had been easy enough, but when it came to guardianship of their children, it got trickier.

Neither of them thought Farrell's parents were young enough to step in. John's parents were both dead, and Charlie Cole was clearly out of the question. Certainly, the kids loved Farrell's brother Penn, but he didn't even live in the United States. In fact, his work as a news producer meant he didn't live anywhere for very long.

"How about you, Lainey?" The question had sounded almost casual as John asked it, reaching for a cup of coffee, smiling at her for just a second before taking a sip. It was only as they talked about it, discussed her closeness to the children, their love for her, that Lainey began to realize how much thought John and Farrell had already put into the notion. But even as she said yes, as she agreed she would move up to Connecticut to provide some stability for Tim and Riley if something as horrible as the deaths of their parents came about, even as she nodded solemnly at her oldest friend in the world, it had seemed little more than a flattering request, an affirmation of how close their bonds were. Something that would never happen.

But it had happened. Lainey felt as if her heart were breaking. She sank onto the stool, dropping her head down into her lap. Grief and terror overwhelmed her in equal measure. She willed herself to stand up once again, to walk over and pick up the phone receiver. She dialed the Coles' number in Connecticut, waiting tensely until Charlie answered.

Farrell and John Cole were gone, and she was the one who was supposed to pick up the pieces. Oh, dear God.

"I'll be there as quickly as I can."

Chapter 12

"I know, honey, I know," Lainey murmured soothingly to Riley, one arm around the little girl, the other stroking her hair. "It's okay, sweetheart."

Riley only cried harder. "*Mommy*. I want *Mommy*."

Sadly, Lainey gently kissed the top of her head. The truth was, she had no idea what words of comfort to offer Riley, who had sobbed without letup throughout the funeral service, at the graveside, and, so far, during this drive home. What platitudes could possibly help a seven-year-old child who had just watched both her parents being buried?

The limousine was turning onto Fielding Drive, and the Cole house came into view. Finally, Lainey thought with relief. Maybe once she got Riley inside and back into her room, she could calm her down. The child had to be exhausted by now. The best thing would be if she permitted herself to be put to bed early, so at least her body could recover from this terrible day. At what point her mind would recover was another issue altogether.

Lainey looked across at Tim, seated next to his grandfather on one of the car's pull-down jumpseats. In contrast to Riley, Tim hadn't shed a tear the entire day. In fact, she had yet to catch him crying since she'd arrived at the house. He had remained stoically silent, speaking

only when spoken to, his eyes downcast, treating Lainey
as if she were some casual visitor he barely knew. And,
like Riley, he had hardly eaten a thing, no matter how
much cajoling went on. Now, she saw, he was gazing out
the window as if it were an ordinary day, and they were
all out for a drive in the country. As if his parents hadn't
died two days before of carbon monoxide poisoning in
their sleep. Lainey didn't know what it was going to take
to get through to him, but she suspected that, for the
moment, it was best to let him handle things in his
own way.

She was glad the funeral was over at last; the anticipation had only made it worse for all of them. And, her personal distaste for Farrell's brother aside, she felt terrible
that Penn Beckley hadn't been here. The absence of their
favorite uncle was yet another blow for the children,
especially Tim. But Penn had been unreachable, on
assignment somewhere in Eastern Europe, and Farrell's
parents couldn't hold up the burials with no hint of when
he might get their messages.

She felt Doris Beckley's hand on her arm and turned
toward the older woman. At the cemetery, Lainey had
observed her through her own tears, struck by how self-
possessed Doris was even at that moment, a lacy white
handkerchief clutched in one hand the only sign that she
might be upset. Seeing the Beckleys standing together
beside the two open graves, their eyes hidden behind
sunglasses, so impeccably dressed, so proper even in
their grief, part of Lainey wanted to scream at them. *Why
don't you cry out? Why don't you get down on your
hands and knees and curse the heavens for taking Farrell? What the hell kind of parents are you?* She had
turned away from the sight of them, her own heart
swollen with pain, giving herself over to the luxury of

finally being able to cry for her friend after willing herself to stay dry-eyed in front of the children up until then.

Now, she admonished herself for judging Farrell's parents that way. What do I know, she thought, about what it feels like to have my child die before me? They are who they are, and Farrell herself had never been able to change them, neither in life nor in death.

"Lainey, dear," Doris said to her quietly, leaning over Riley between them to be heard. "You've been so wonderful, staying with us all this time, helping out. And we're ever so grateful you'll stay with the children until we get back. It's just the most unfortunate timing. But, of course, it's too late to call off the conference. I don't know what they'll do if Hugh doesn't come to speak."

Lainey nodded, hoping her face didn't betray her utter lack of understanding of the logic behind this. Who the hell cared what happened to the stupid conference, when Tim and Riley were here, desperately needing love and attention. The children had no other grandparents, their uncle Penn was who-knows-where, and it wasn't like their uncle Charlie was of much use. Besides, where was it written that Doris had to accompany Hugh to Michigan tomorrow, instead of staying behind? But that was the way they did things, she reminded herself. They lived in their own world, on their own schedule, and very little interfered with it.

Suddenly, an alarm went off in the back of Lainey's mind. She'd been so busy being annoyed with Doris, she'd almost missed the significance of what the woman had just said. *We're ever so grateful you'll stay with the children until we get back.*

Oh, Jesus. The Beckleys didn't even know she was the children's permanent guardian.

The limousine came to a stop, and the driver hurried

around to open the door. Lainey saw cars parked up and down the street in the darkening evening. Another limousine pulled up behind them, and she watched Charlie Cole and several of John's other relatives getting out. As she approached the front door, Riley still clinging to her, she could see through the windows that the house was full of people.

Sympathetic eyes turned toward them as Lainey shepherded Riley upstairs. Along with a sea of unfamiliar faces, most of the people Lainey knew from Farrell's world had come back to the house: the Taplingers, the Gisondis, women she'd encountered during past visits, couples she recognized from the Coles' parties. They'd all been at the service earlier, but Lainey hadn't been interested in talking to anyone besides the children, and she still preferred to avoid them now, glad to be able to escape with Riley.

At the landing, she looked down to see Tim shaking his head vehemently to his grandmother before turning and bolting upstairs, right past Riley and her, and on up into his room. He slammed the door loudly. Lainey sighed. Doris had undoubtedly wanted him to stay downstairs with the guests, receiving their condolences, but he wasn't having any part of it. She didn't blame him.

"Come, sweetie, I know it's not bedtime yet, but let's get you into some pajamas." She and Riley went into her room. "Are you hungry?"

Riley rubbed her swollen eyes and sniffled. "I just want some water."

Lainey went to the bathroom and brought back a glass for her. They sat down on the bed together, Lainey holding Riley and rocking her slightly as the little girl drank. Then Lainey helped her change. Although it was nowhere near bedtime, Riley immediately crawled under the covers.

"I'm going to sleep now," she said in a voice so fragile Lainey thought her heart would break. "You'll be here tomorrow, right?"

"Of course I will. Every day, angel." Lainey leaned down to kiss her. Riley had clung to her from the first moment she'd arrived at the house, as if terrified Lainey would vanish if she turned her back for a second.

"You promise?"

"Absolutely. Try to go to sleep."

It was fully dark outside by now. Lainey switched off the light and started to leave the room.

"Don't go," Riley begged suddenly. "Stay with me."

Lainey turned back. "Okay, sweetheart. How about if I sit in the rocking chair?"

Riley nodded her head in agreement. Lainey went over to the wooden rocking chair Farrell had used to breast-feed both her children in their infancies. She rocked quietly, listening as Riley's breathing went from a ragged sniffling to the deep, even breath of sleep.

Lainey knew she should go downstairs to join all the people there, but she didn't want to move. She looked around the large bedroom, making out the shapes of toys crowding every inch of space, posters all over the walls, computer games in precarious piles on the window seat.

From the moment she had gotten the news of the Coles' deaths, she had refused to think about what was happening; she had just put one foot in front of the other, packing a bag, telling Al Smile she would be away from work for a while, just moving forward, knowing that she had an obligation to keep. Suddenly, the weight of these past forty-eight hours came crashing down on her. For the first time, she permitted herself to face the enormity of the situation.

I can't do this, she thought. I can't. I'm supposed to move in here and act as if I'm the children's new mother, just like that. I'm supposed to know how to take care of them, how to run their lives, what to teach them, how to love them like a parent.

Her eyes filled with tears. Oh, Farrell, she thought. How could we have made such a monumental decision so glibly, so casually. We just agreed that I would drop my entire life, move in here as if that were the simplest thing in the world, and take over where you and John left off. I certainly never spent a minute thinking about the reality of raising two children. Two children who had lost both parents, no less.

She rose and went to the window to look out. The suburban shrubbery took her back to her childhood in New Rochelle. Her eyes welled up with tears again as she saw herself and Farrell walking home in fifth grade, doubling back toward Lainey's house the moment they neared Farrell's because they didn't want to say good-bye yet, then returning to Farrell's only to turn around yet again.

Lainey had always associated the Coles' house with warmth and love, with the bustle of activity. But, of course, Farrell was at the heart of all that. Now there was only a cold silence. Now there was no heart. I can't fill a hole that big, Lainey thought, turning back to Riley and seeing the pain evident on her face even as she slept. What do I have to give these children? She felt inadequate and ashamed of how far short she fell from being up to this job. Farrell had entrusted her with the most important treasures she had in the world, and now Lainey couldn't imagine why she had made such a terrible mistake.

"I'm so sorry," she whispered in the darkness, as much to Farrell and John as to Riley.

She heard the front door slam downstairs. The sound jolted her from her thoughts, and she left, crossing the hall to the guest room where she was sleeping. The Beckleys were staying in the carriage house, and Lainey had immediately unpacked in the guest room where she always stayed when she visited. It occurred to her that she could sleep in Farrell's bedroom from now on, but the idea was too awful to contemplate, and she knew instinctively that would be bad for the children. For the time being, she would stay in what she always laughingly used to call "her" room. Standing before the mirror, she slowly brushed her hair, gathering her resources to face the guests. She reminded herself that she had to call Carla later: her friend had generously offered to pick up more of Lainey's things from her apartment and drive them out to Meadowview. She needed more clothing, but she was uncertain what else to transport just now. Should she be bringing her art supplies, her address book, her favorite coffee mug—all the things that would signify that this was going to be her home? She knew this arrangement was permanent, but none of it seemed real.

She stared at her reflection, and her voice came out in a whisper. "Thinking of backing out?"

She turned away, tossing the brush down on the bed. Emerging into the hallway, she stopped in front of Tim's closed door and knocked.

His response was low. "Go 'way."

She opened the door to see him standing near the foot of the bed, still in the navy blue blazer and gray wool pants he had worn to the funeral.

"Hi, honey," she said, coming over and attempting to encircle him in a hug.

He shook her off, but didn't demur when she stroked the straight blond hair back from his forehead. "Is everybody still here?" he asked.

"Afraid so," she said sympathetically. "You must be hungry. It's dinnertime."

He shrugged, uninterested.

"Come on downstairs. These ladies have made some great stuff, I know." She took his hand, intending to walk with him, but he held back. Kneeling, she put a hand on each shoulder. "Tim, you *have* to eat something."

"Then you bring it upstairs." He eyed her dully, obviously not caring whether she did or not.

What should I do? she wondered helplessly. She didn't want to pressure him, but it didn't seem right to let him hide out up here, walled off from the people who cared about him. Two days here, and she was already at a loss.

"I'm sorry, honey," she said finally, trying to sound firm. "I really want you to pick out something you'd be willing to eat. And your grandparents aren't going to want to leave without spending a few more minutes with you." Gently, she tugged at his arm and urged him toward the door.

"Are they going tonight?" Tim asked, his voice strained.

She nodded, wondering how upset he would be without them. "They have to, remember? Did you want them to stay longer?"

"Wow, no." Tim's response was a small explosion. "They just sit there, drinking and asking questions. I can't stand it."

Lainey was surprised at his reaction, although she was pleased to see some animation on his face, regardless of what had elicited it. "They're just concerned about you, Tim. You know that."

"Yeah," he said, his tone dull again, retreating into himself. "I know."

He shuffled behind her as she descended the stairs, his eyes aimed at the carpet. Lainey saw that the crowd of guests had thinned out considerably.

"Well, Tim, you must be famished." Farrell's mother appeared before them. She went over to the boy and started to walk him toward the kitchen. "There's roast beef and salad, and about half a dozen different cakes," she said brightly.

"Lainey's gonna give me something," Tim said irritably, pulling away from her.

Doris glanced at Lainey, then tried again.

"Lainey won't always be here to cater to you. Don't you think the two of us can rustle up something tasty?"

Tim looked from his grandmother to Lainey, his eyes filled with panic. "What do you mean she won't be here? Of course she will. She's always gonna be here. Right, Lainey?"

"Of course I will, sweetheart." Lainey came over, enveloping him in a tight embrace. She had to straighten things out with Doris Beckley without any further delay, that was clear. Loosening her hold on Tim, she spoke to him softly. "Can you start choosing what you'd like from the platters on the table? I'll be there in a minute."

A worried frown on his face, he nodded and left.

Lainey turned to Doris, wondering how to start. "Let's talk for a minute," she said, indicating that they should take a seat on the stairway.

The older woman sat down beside her. "What's on your mind, dear?" she asked, impatience creeping into her voice.

Lainey paused. This was a sensitive matter, and dealing with Doris Beckley wasn't easy under the best conditions. Staying under one roof with her and her husband for just these two days had practically driven Lainey crazy. They were obviously trying to be agreeable and keep the mood of the house cheerful for the children's sake, but there was a constant undercurrent of disapproval, of *judging*. No matter what she did, she sensed they thought she wasn't doing things properly, down to the smallest task of something as minor as setting the table. Doris Beckley would look and smile, but Lainey saw the hesitation, the subtle way she communicated her disapproval. Lainey's own mother was critical, but at least she came right out with it, only too glad to tell Lainey what was wrong with her and how to fix it. Doris Beckley's approach was maddening beyond all endurance. Farrell's father wasn't much better, obviously used to having things done in a certain way in his own home, and apparently not seeing why it should be any different elsewhere. He didn't say anything, but his annoyed frowns were enough. She always understood why Farrell had had such difficulty with her parents, but she had never experienced it so directly before.

Still, there was no point grousing about them. They were Tim and Riley's grandparents, and she had better stay on good terms with them, no matter what it took. God, she thought, it's as if I have to work out a relationship with a second set of parents now.

She chose her words as carefully as she could. "I'm sorry to seem insensitive if this is a surprise, but we need to discuss it. Farrell did tell you about me and the children, didn't she?"

"Tell me what?" The woman gave her a piercing look.

"That I'm their guardian."

The shock on Doris Beckley's face confirmed Lainey's fear: the woman knew nothing about it.

"Farrell and John asked me right after Riley was born. We agreed that if anything happened to them, I would move in here and take care of the children ... permanently."

"You?" The disbelief in her voice made it clear that Farrell's mother thought Lainey was just as poor a choice as Lainey herself did.

"You know how close we all were." Lainey watched the way Doris stiffened, the magnitude of the news sinking in. Lainey was struck with the impulse to take her hand, to show her that she realized this was a shock. After all, she had known her all her life, been in and out of her home since she was little. But she didn't dare; Doris Beckley wasn't the sort of woman you touched. And with every passing second she was looking less and less kindly disposed toward Lainey.

Farrell's mother sat quietly for a few moments, shifting her expression from displeasure back to neutral. Then she stood, smoothing her skirt and smiling thinly at Lainey.

"It's getting late. There will be time to talk more about this later."

She returned to the living room, seeking out her husband, who was sitting in a wing chair off to one side, talking to two men.

"Hugh, we have to leave now."

Hugh Beckley looked up at his wife sourly before glancing at his watch, then put his glass down on the end table and went to join her. Lainey stood at the foot of the stairs, silently watching them say their good-byes.

"Lainey, can I get ya something?"

She turned at the sound of the voice, the broad Boston accent readily recognizable as belonging to Megan Burke, Farrell's closest friend in Meadowview. Before this week, Lainey hadn't seen her for quite a while, and the Burkes had been away on vacation the night of the Coles' Christmas party. But Megan had been in and out of the house over the past two days, stopping by on her way to and from work to drop off food and offer her help. She was the one person Lainey wouldn't have minded talking to during this terrible day. Other than exchanging brief hello's at the funeral, they hadn't had a chance.

Of all Farrell's Connecticut friends, Megan had always been Lainey's favorite. Tall and skinny, she had a thick, unruly mane of black wavy hair that she continually brushed back from her face with her hands, usually revealing wildly dramatic earrings. Lainey loved how completely down to earth she was, glad to discuss virtually anything with anybody. She was always joking about how so many of the women here were perfect mothers, with their beautiful faces and figures, effortlessly managing children and charity work and social engagements.

Lainey had been drawn to Farrell's friend immediately. She remembered laughing the first time she met Megan on one of her visits, coming downstairs on a Sunday morning to find Farrell and Megan talking in the family room. "So, big deal, I left Michael's sandwich out of his lunch box yesterday, and sent them both to school with stained shirts," Megan had been saying in her nasal voice. "Take me out back and shoot me."

Despite her self-deprecating remarks, she had raised two delightful, friendly children in a well-ordered household while holding down a full-time job. The biggest surprise was when Farrell had informed Lainey that Megan commuted into Manhattan every day to her job as a particle physicist at Fallows University, a job that Lainey could never quite comprehend, no matter how many times she got Megan to explain it. The incongruity between her unpretentiousness and her intellect never ceased to intrigue Lainey.

Megan was extending a plate with roast beef and potato salad. Her eyes were red and swollen from crying, but her tone was cheerful. "You want this? You gotta be staahhving. And you know that food is always the answer to everything."

"Thanks, Megan," Lainey said gratefully, putting a hand on her arm. "But, no, nothing for me." The words reminded her that Tim was waiting in the kitchen. "Oh, I've got to get to Tim."

She was interrupted by the sound of the doorbell. More guests, she thought with an inward groan. She opened the door to find a short broad man wearing a beige uniform on the front steps.

"I've got somebody in the car, refuses to wake up," he said, obviously annoyed.

Lainey followed his sausage fingers as they indicated a taxicab in the street, its back door open to the cold night air.

"This was the address he gave," the driver went on, his tone accusing, as if Lainey were to blame. "How 'bout you get him outta my cab and pay the fare."

Clutching her arms around herself against the cold, Lainey hurried down the walk, approaching the taxi warily. She peered into the back seat, taking in the smell of alcohol that permeated the vehicle. A slender, dark-haired man in worn blue jeans and a black sweater lay across the seat, a navy jacket covering him loosely as he slept. Leaning in, she took a closer look at his face.

"Oh, for God's sake," she exploded in exasperation. She reached in to shake his shoulder. "Penn. *Penn.* Wake up."

There was no response. She regarded him with displeasure. The prince was back. A day too late and dead drunk. "Wake up, damn it." She shook him again, more roughly this time. Nothing.

"What's going on?"

Hugh Beckley had come up behind her. Lainey moved aside so he could see into the cab. He took in the situation at once, his face impassive.

"Doris," he yelled back to his wife, who was standing in the doorway observing them, "get Charlie out here."

They stood there in silence until Charlie Cole joined them.

"Go on back inside," Hugh instructed Lainey curtly as the two men maneuvered into position to pull Penn out of the cab.

She went back up the path, shrugging her shoulders helplessly at the other guests who had gathered in the doorway to watch.

"Perhaps it's time to leave the family alone," Doris announced to the assemblage, her dignified embarrassment enough to send all the guests hastily filing out into the night. It seemed that within moments, the house was empty again.

Tim walked in from the kitchen, undoubtedly having waited until all the intruding adults had left. Lainey moved quickly to guide him upstairs, not wanting him to see the limp form Hugh and Charlie were just about to drag in across the threshold. "Come, honey. It's time to go up to bed."

Wordlessly, he permitted her to take his hand. Behind her, she heard Doris Beckley speak.

"Poor Penn," she murmured sympathetically.

Lainey gritted her teeth.

When she returned downstairs twenty minutes later,

having gotten a listless Tim into bed for the night, the house was dark. They've all gone, she thought, relieved. Suddenly, a light was switched on in the living room. Frightened for a second, she realized who it must be.

"So, you're awake," she said to Penn Beckley, who was sitting up on the couch, looking around as if trying to figure out where he was. Still fully dressed, his eyes were bleary and his dark hair a tousled mess.

"Lainey Wolfe," he said in a low voice, as if telling her something she didn't already know.

"That's me," she answered. "And exactly who are you—Ray Milland in *The Lost Weekend*?"

His eyes narrowed. "I'm the man whose little sister was buried today."

His remark stopped her. "I'm sorry." She struggled to find something else to say. "Will you stick around tomorrow? I know it would mean a lot to the children to spend some time with you."

"Are you the new social director?" he retorted angrily. "What the hell are you still doing here, anyway?"

"I'm the children's guardian. I live here now," she shot back, his anger fueling her own.

His response was a derisive snort. She watched him lean over to remove his shoes, then settle himself back down on the couch, clearly not interested in talking with her any further. Easing a pillow under his neck and closing his eyes, he established a comfortable position and seemed to be drifting back to sleep.

She heard his muttered comment as she turned off the lamp.

"Guardian. That should last about a week."

Chapter 13

"I'll have it in by ten tomorrow."

Lainey knew from the silence on the other end of the phone that Al Smile was anything but pleased by what he was hearing. She saw Fran Myerson peering at her curiously from across the office.

"I promise," she added weakly, finally hanging up.

The Patsy Pony sketches were overdue by three days, and ordinarily she would have sat there and finished them even if she'd had to stay until three in the morning. But this had been Riley's first day back at school, and Lainey had to catch the two forty-two if she was going to make it home in time to be there for Riley when she walked in the door. Thank God Mrs. Miles can drive, she thought, grabbing her coat and stuffing the sketch pad into her carryall before rushing out of the office.

Emerging outside, she glanced at her watch, then anxiously looked up and down Sixth Avenue. Getting to Grand Central would take only a few minutes, as long as she was lucky enough to find a cab. After a couple of nervous moments, an empty cab screeched to a halt in front of her. Ten minutes later, she was sitting on the train bound for Meadowview, leaning her head gratefully against the back of the seat with her eyes closed.

It was the first uninterrupted period of tranquillity

she'd had in a week. Since the funeral, Lainey had had to deal with a million details, each of which was completely new to her. People came in and out of the house at all hours, everyone wanting to help, everyone needing attention.

Decisions had to be made about meals, about shoveling snow, about all the things that went into running a large house. And hardest of all, there were Tim and Riley, one refusing to leave his bedroom, closed off from everyone and everything, the other refusing to leave Lainey's side, in tears that threatened to go on forever.

Lainey had put off going back to work as long as she could, but this was the day she'd had to return, at least for a few hours. Not that it was long enough, she thought, gazing momentarily at her carryall, the Patsy sketches weighing on her conscience. I'll get them done tonight, she thought, allowing herself the luxury of doing nothing as she sat on the train. There would be plenty of time this evening, once the kids were asleep.

"Hi, there."

Lainey opened her eyes at the unmistakable sound of Megan Burke's voice.

"How's it going?" Megan asked, taking the empty seat beside Lainey.

"It's going okay, I guess," Lainey responded. In spite of Megan's warm overture, Lainey still felt compelled to try to put her best foot forward.

Megan looked at her thoughtfully. "Really? You look like warmed-over crap."

From anyone else, the remark would have been the height of hostility, yet somehow from Megan it seemed utterly sympathetic.

"Well, to tell you the truth, I've been a little

overwhelmed," she answered, relieved even to be slightly honest.

"A little overwhelmed? You mean, your best friend is dead, you're suddenly the mother of two, living in a strange town, handling a home and a full-time job? Yeah," Megan actually chuckled, "I guess you would be 'a little overwhelmed.' "

Lainey found herself laughing along with Megan. What heaven to talk to someone who seemed to understand. The words began pouring out of her. How torn she felt leaving for work on the children's first day back at school, or at least Riley's first day, since Tim refused to leave the house.

"Oh, Megan, it's so heartbreaking. Half the time, he won't come out of his room. And when I brought up taking them for some help—you know, just suggested talking to someone—he wouldn't hear of it." She shook her head at the memory. "In fact, he looked at me like I was his executioner."

"How about Riley?" Megan asked.

Lainey sighed. "I never knew what grief looked like before last week. She's been attached to my hip, afraid to let go for a minute." Lainey felt tears coming into her eyes. "This morning, when I drove her to school, she cried all the way there and begged me not to make her go. She finally gets out of the car and trudges toward the entrance, then she stops and looks back with empty eyes. You know, the way concentration camp victims looked right after the war." Lainey pulled a tissue out of her pocket and blew her nose. "It's so sad, I can barely stand it."

Megan caught Lainey's hand and held it, a gesture Lainey found supremely comforting.

"She'll pep up tomorrow at the recital," Megan said

reassuringly. "You know how much she loves her ballet."

Any feeling of comfort fled. "Recital? What recital?" Lainey knew she sounded as hysterical as she felt.

Megan regarded her, clearly aghast. "Tomorrow afternoon, three forty-five, Pembley Auditorium. It's the Winter Snowfest or whatever they're calling it this year. Big stuff, actually. Riley didn't mention it?"

"She certainly did not," Lainey responded. "Oh, God, what does it entail?"

"Not that much really. She's been studying the routines since September. All she needs is to show up, tutu and slippers in hand."

Lainey thought frantically of the things she had seen in Riley's closet that morning as she'd helped her get dressed for school. She could swear she'd seen a pair of ballet slippers lying around. But a tutu? She certainly hadn't seen one of those. Where would she find one at this late date?

Megan could see how agitated Lainey had become. "You know, Riley can miss one recital. I mean, for goodness sake, it's so soon after Farrell and John . . ."

What a relief it would be to agree, but Lainey knew she couldn't. "Oh, Megan, you're a very nice person, but you know as well as I do that these kids have to get back to some kind of normal routine. Missing a recital she's spent months preparing for doesn't seem like such a good idea."

"Listen," Megan said encouragingly, "if there's anything I can do to help, don't hesitate to ask."

"You mean for all the free time you have between raising two children and splitting the atom, or whatever it is you do all day?"

"Ah, you'll see," Megan said warmly. "This job and

kid thing, it's not so hard after you get used to it. Trust me."

"Sure thing," Lainey answered, rolling her eyes before burying her face in her hands.

"I think it's the next block." Riley strained against the seat belt, twisting around to look at both sides of the coming intersection.

"Left or right?" Lainey asked, understanding from Riley's blank stare that oral directions might never get them to their destination. "This way or this way?" Lainey pointed first one way then the other, deflated when she noted the confusion on the child's face.

"I'm pretty sure it's *that* way," she said, pointing her tiny hand toward the left, "but it might be the next block. I'm not exactly sure."

Lainey tried not to sigh out loud. At least Riley was talking, which was a lot better than the long silences she'd offered when Lainey had gotten home from the station. When she questioned Riley about the recital, the girl had barely responded.

"I don't feel like doing it," she finally whispered when Lainey had pressed her.

It had taken two hours of cajoling to get Riley to agree to go, so, now, at almost six o'clock, Lainey had to sew or buy or somehow obtain a white tulle tutu. Five frantic phone calls to Riley's classmates' parents had yielded the name of a mother who claimed to have several extra yards of fabric, which Lainey could have the pleasure of measuring, pinning, and sewing tonight until the early morning hours, just in time for Riley to get to her performance, and for Lainey to get to designing the sketches of Patsy Pony she'd promised.

Even if she managed to make the damn tutu and complete the sketches, she couldn't quite figure out how to transport her work to New York and be back in time to get Riley to Pembley Auditorium. I'll work it out somehow, she thought.

"Take it one day at a time," Patrick Fouchard had said when she told him her plans for California had to be, at the very least, put off for a while. But she still had her old job to do, and with two children, there didn't seem to be any uninterrupted hours in which to do it. I should quit and stay home with Tim and Riley, she thought for the hundredth time. But she knew she couldn't do that. A decision that big shouldn't come in the same month you lose your best friend, move to the suburbs, and become an instant mom, she had told herself. This wasn't the time for any more major changes. The problem was, combining two kids in Connecticut with a full-time job in New York seemed impossible. And, as understanding as everyone at Carpathia tried to be, there was work to be done. The Patsy project couldn't wait for kids or ballet recitals or a period of mourning. It had to be finished when the movie came out, and the movie was scheduled to open in two months. Without her work, the production people couldn't proceed, and without the finished product, hundreds of thousands of dollars would be lost in the opening week alone.

But how could she take the time away from Tim and Riley—two kids who could barely function. I have to find them some professional help, whether they want it or not, Lainey thought, wondering if Megan Burke might know of someone good in town.

She felt slightly more hopeful as she spotted the street name they'd been searching for. Meadowview was a town she had visited scores of times during the years Farrell and John had lived there, but visiting a town and living in a town were two very different things. In the many times she had accompanied Farrell to a soccer game or a trip to the dry cleaners, she had come to recognize certain streets, identify some of the different neighborhoods. But being alone in the driver's seat was quite another matter. Meadowview was a mystery to her. She could get from there to Manhattan practically with her eyes closed, but the way from Skylark Road to Breedlove Road was a perfectly landscaped maze.

"That's it over there." Riley's high-pitched voice shimmered with victory. "It's the yellow house with all the lights on."

Gratefully, Lainey pulled into the wide circular driveway behind which the house glowed like an oversized jack-o'-lantern.

"You know how many hours a hundred-watt bulb will burn before it goes out?" Riley began an informed stream of nervous chatter about electricity. It was clear to Lainey that, at seven, the child had a better grasp of the subject than she herself would have if she lived to be a thousand. The girl's extraordinary range of factual information started almost as a parlor trick when she was three or four. By now, she had collected a trove of details that in and of themselves probably could have gotten her through high school by the time she was seven and a half.

Lainey knew that the science lecture was a stalling tactic, but she chose not to say anything about it. "Okay, pal, let's get a move on," Lainey urged Riley, leaning over to unlock her seat belt and pushing the passenger side door open from the inside.

Riley sat immobile as Lainey opened her own door and eased herself out of the car. She walked around the front and looked back toward Riley expectantly, but the girl continued to sit there, silently staring ahead.

Without meaning to, Lainey looked at her watch impatiently. Six-thirty already. Time was whizzing by. "Riley, honey, let's go on inside."

The girl refused to answer, and Lainey found herself losing patience. *I'm doing this for you,* she felt like yelling, until she noticed the tears coursing down Riley's face. Quickly, she came back to pull open the car door and kneel down next to her.

"What's the matter, honey?" she said, cupping Riley's face in her hands.

"I can't go in there," Riley sobbed.

"Why not, sweetie?" Lainey fought to remember the name of the little girl whose mother was to be their salvation. It took only a few seconds to come up with it. "Wendy is in there. You two can play for a few minutes while her mother and I talk."

Riley lowered her head, seemingly engrossed in the sight of her fingernails, which were bitten to the quick.

"Riley, please tell me what's going on." Lainey leaned into the front seat, pulling the little girl out of the car and into her arms. The two of them knelt together, hugging for dear life, until Riley finally came up with the words.

"Wendy won't play with me. Nobody will play with me. All day today, no one would even talk to me." She wept into Lainey's shoulder.

Dear Lord, Lainey thought, remembering back to her own childhood. Eunice Gold's sister had died when Lainey was in third grade. Pneumonia during a flu epidemic. And it was true. The day Eunice came back to class, no one could figure out what to say to her, so they left her alone. How horrible it must have been for Eunice, Lainey realized.

How horrible for Riley, she thought, the girl's heaving sobs making her wish she could sob right alongside her.

"You know what, sweetie?" Lainey kept her voice bright. "Why don't you just stay in the car. I'll run in and talk to Wendy's mom, and then we'll go home and get your outfit together, and you don't have to worry about any of it." She loosened her hold on the child and lifted her back into the car. "I'll be out in a jiffy," she yelled over her shoulder as she walked up the pathway to the front door.

Well, that was the coward's way out, she chided herself, ringing the doorbell. I should have used that as an opportunity to get some of her feelings out about her parents' deaths, to reassure her, to help her through a crisis. Oh yeah, she said to the absent Farrell, I'm a great choice as guardian. A caring nurturer. That's me in a nutshell.

Lainey checked the baking potatoes, then shut the oven door and opened the broiler. I hope there'll be enough left for tomorrow's sandwiches, she thought, eyeing the flank steak she'd only remembered to start marinating ten minutes before she'd stuck it in to broil.

Now what else have I forgotten? she thought, hearing the sound of *Beauty and the Beast* in the family room. Watching that particular movie was the only activity Riley was willing to perform without her.

What dinner was missing was a vegetable, Lainey suddenly realized, wondering where on earth she was supposed to find anything green at seven-thirty at night. Certainly she hadn't thought to do any supermarket shopping during the week. For days, they'd been living on casseroles and home-baked sweets that had been left by thoughtful friends and neighbors of Farrell and John. Finally, they were down to one serving of pot roast and a few stale brownies.

She opened the refrigerator and searched through the

shelves, coming upon a half-empty bag of carrots. Ah, success, she exulted. In three tries, she had located the drawer containing the carrot peeler, and hurriedly peeled and sliced them, placing them in a large pot and setting the flame much higher than she would have had she thought about them earlier.

She opened the window over the stove and watched Tim, who'd been shooting baskets alone since she'd forced him out of his room when she and Riley got home.

"Tim, come on in. It's almost time for dinner."

Tim heard her calling, but refused to answer. Admitting he heard her would lead to his agreeing to go inside, and that would only lead to having to sit around a table and make small talk with Riley and Lainey for half an hour. That, he just couldn't do.

He dribbled his way over to the basket and began aiming layups off the backboard. Making basket after basket, he strove to lose himself in the activity, but his thoughts wouldn't leave him alone. No matter how hard he tried, he couldn't get the sounds of the last morning he ever spent with his parents out of his mind, the odd sound of his mother's voice, his father screaming at her. And the next morning, they were dead. Supposedly a gas malfunction in the basement's heating equipment.

It happened that way, he knew it did; at least, for the past few weeks people had been *saying* it did. But every time he tried to relax into the belief that that was what had occurred, he would hear his father yelling.

Out of the corner of his eye, he saw Lainey watching him. He turned his back to the house, stepping away from the basketball net, and stared up at the sky. It *had* to have happened that way, he reassured himself, dribbling the ball on the grass, steering it first with his left hand, then with his right.

My father killed my mother.

Hearing the words inside his head made him drop the ball. He watched it roll down the lawn. It took a few seconds for him to follow it down the grassy slope, and scoop it up into both hands. He stood there, twirling the ball in his outstretched fingers, the horrible sentence rolling over in his brain. My father killed my mother. My father killed my mother and himself. It couldn't be. It had to be. The ball continued to circle in his hands, as he heard Lainey's voice calling him yet again.

"Honey, dinner's gonna be ready in five minutes or so. Come on in and wash up, okay?"

Tim didn't even acknowledge the sound of her voice, let alone put down the basketball.

Lainey shook her head, trying not to panic as she considered everything still to be done. One thing at a time, she thought. Dinner, tutu, Patsy Pony, sleep. Everything would be all right if she stuck to her schedule.

The moment she and Riley had gotten home, Lainey had laid the yards of white tulle out on the dining-room table, and pinned the pattern pieces to the fabric as neatly as she could. Not since junior high school had she attempted to sew anything, and she didn't remember having any special competence then. Taking a break to make dinner had been her reward for actually cutting the material in five neat pieces with a pair of huge shears. Sewing them together was the hurdle that would wait until the meal was over.

"Is it time to eat?" Riley appeared in the kitchen, tightly hugging the white satin-bordered blanket she'd stopped needing when she was three.

"Why don't you wash your hands while I try to get Tim to join us." Lainey checked the meat one more time, then walked over toward the back door. She pulled a sweater from a hook and buttoned it down the front. "He doesn't seem that eager to eat," she said in explanation as she made her way outside.

She watched him miss a shot off the backboard. "Tim," she called softly, "come inside, won't you? You must be starved."

Once again, there was no response, as he picked up the ball and dribbled it back to where he would have to make a three-pointer.

She tried again. "You have school tomorrow. And really, honey, tomorrow you have to go." She looked at him beseechingly. "You must have some organizing to do, maybe a few phone calls to your friends to see if you need anything special."

Tim stared past her as if she didn't exist, and threw the ball toward the basket, missing it by several feet, then running for it and trying again.

"Tim." Lainey walked over to him and took the ball out of his hands. "You don't have to suffer alone. Honestly, you don't. I'm going to call Mrs. Burke tomorrow morning and get the name of someone we can all talk to." She tried to keep her voice light. "You know, I could use some help, too. Your mom and dad were my best friends."

Tim looked right through her. To Lainey, it seemed as if a sullen stranger had entered the body of the child she'd known since birth.

I give up, she thought, the taste of failure once again in her mouth.

"Let's eat," she called out to Riley, who was busily setting unmatched plates and assorted silverware on the kitchen table, a chore Lainey had forgotten about entirely.

The flank steak was gray and overdone, while the cooked carrots were still uncomfortably crunchy as the two of them ate in silence.

"What's your favorite dinner, Riley?" Lainey asked, eager to start up a conversation.

Riley merely shrugged in response.

"Do you know what you're going to wear tomorrow?" she tried one more time.

But again, Riley wasn't willing to join in.

Lainey thought about all the meals she'd had with the Coles over the years. Riley was the chatterbox, the one who'd talked months earlier than babies were supposed to, and had rarely stopped for a moment since. Now the child was practically mute.

The sound of the doorbell interrupted their silence. Lainey looked up at the kitchen clock. Who would be arriving at eight o'clock on a Monday night? she wondered, going through the long hallway toward the front door. She could hear Riley pushing her chair away from the table and heading back to the family room. Two men were standing outside. A knot of anxiety found a home in the pit of her stomach when she realized these were probably friends expecting to make a condolence call.

"Hello," the taller of the two men said, shaking Lainey's hand and making his way into the house without being invited. "I'm Tom Williamson and this is Alderman Rafferty."

"Peter," the other man amended, following behind them and drawing the door closed.

"We were good friends of John's and we wanted to see if you needed any help." Williamson put a patronizing arm around Lainey's shoulder, leading her toward the living room and making himself comfortable on one of the twin sofas.

Yes, I need help, she thought to herself ungraciously. I need you two to leave.

"Thank you," she said out loud, wondering where to go from there.

The two men gazed at her expectantly, as if she were somehow to entertain them, and she looked back without even a notion of what to say.

"Did you know John and Farrell for very long?" she finally offered, having no interest at all in their response.

But her question opened a floodgate of memory, both men eagerly exploring their years of acquaintanceship with Farrell and John Cole for at least ten minutes without pausing. It was with relief that Lainey heard footsteps from the kitchen, a genuine smile on her face when Penn Beckley came into the room. Penn had been staying in the carriage house since he'd arrived just after the funeral. He'd been coming and going on his own schedule, and she was never sure when he might appear.

"Do you know each other?" Lainey said, desperation obvious in her voice.

"I'm Penn Beckley, Farrell's brother," Penn said easily.

Williamson and Rafferty immediately switched their attention to him, repeating almost verbatim the anecdotes they'd been telling Lainey. After listening respectfully, Penn looked over at her.

"Tim seems to be playing basketball for the blind," he said questioningly. "It's pitch black outside."

"I tried to get him in for dinner, but I can't seem to find the magic words. He really has to go back to school tomorrow." And, she wanted to add, I don't begin to know what to say to him and these men won't leave and I have my own work to do, not to mention a tutu to make.

Penn smiled as if he could read her mind. "You know," he said to the two men, "my nephew's having a tough time, as you can imagine. Maybe if we made it four for basketball, it would be a little easier for him."

"Well, sure," Williamson answered for both of them, standing up at once and laying his topcoat across the arm of the sofa.

Lainey returned to the kitchen, where she could hear the sounds of *Beauty and the Beast* once more. Within ten minutes, she had cleared off the kitchen table and set the dishes in the dishwasher. Time to face the tutu, she thought, a sudden image passing through her mind. It was eighth grade, Mrs. Closkey's home ec class, and out of the mismatched darts and uneven hem of her yellow wraparound skirt, Lainey had received the first and last *D* she would ever get in Albert Leonard Junior High School. Here goes nothing, she said aloud, procrastinating yet another few seconds by looking out the kitchen window toward the garage.

Gee, she thought, I don't believe it. She watched in amazement as Tim, the same boy who'd said under ten words in a week, smiled tauntingly at Tom Williamson, then feinted to his left and passed the ball to his uncle. As Penn whirled the ball gracefully through the net, Tim leapt up to give him a high five, smiling and cheering as if he didn't have a problem in the world.

Whatever the magic, she prayed silently, please make it strong enough to get him through his first day back at school tomorrow.

Figuring out how to use the old sewing machine Farrell had bought in the earliest years of her marriage turned out to be easier than she had imagined. By ten o'clock, she had tried the tutu on Riley, and gotten her into bed, cheered by the vision of white tulle. Now she was ready to tackle Patsy Pony.

She returned downstairs to find Penn and Tim engaged in a lively conversation with Tom Williamson and Peter Rafferty. From the empty bottles on the coffee table, she could see that the men had gone through several rounds of beer, while Tim was sucking on a ginger ale.

"The Knicks look pretty good in the Eastern Conference," Tim was saying enthusiastically, "but I don't think they're going to be able to pull it off. I mean, Orlando's really strong . . ."

"Did you get something to eat?" she asked when Tim finished his thought, hoping she didn't jinx the boy back into silence.

"Oh, yeah," he replied airily, "Uncle Penn made me a sandwich."

"*Pfft*, you're a sandwich," Penn inserted, making his nephew wince at the oldest joke in the world.

"Well," Lainey said uncertainly, "I have some work to do. Do you mind if I excuse myself?"

Tim looked unconcerned, while Penn merely smiled at her.

"You know," she added gingerly, "you have to be up by seven-twenty."

"Don't worry," Penn responded for him. "Tim and I have an agreement. Two sodas and he's in bed." Penn reached over to the boy and ruffled his blond hair. "Right?"

Tim nodded enthusiastically.

Feel free to stay as long as you like, Penn Beckley, she thought to herself as she walked upstairs to get to her sketches. But when she came back downstairs well after midnight, her spell of goodwill ended abruptly. There in the living room sat Penn, the empty bottles of Budweiser replaced by a half-filled bottle of Glenfiddich and a large tumbler.

"I think it's time you get yourself back to the carriage house," Lainey said in annoyance.

Penn did not bother to acknowledge her request. In fact, he gave no sign he had even heard her come in. Moving only to take another sip of Scotch, his dark brown eyes seemed to bore into the Oriental carpet. All the charm he'd displayed earlier in the evening had melted away. Now he was expressionless, unfathomable. Disgusted, Lainey flicked off the overhead light switch, leaving him in the dark, sodden and still as a statue.

The morning sun streamed through the window, waking Lainey out of a fitful sleep. Exhausted and tense, she considered trying to go back to sleep, but changed her mind when she remembered how much more she had to do on Patsy. Hazily, she caught sight of the time on the clock radio.

My God, she thought, seven-thirty. Hurrying out of bed, she pulled a robe around her and went out to the hall.

"Tim! Riley! Get up, both of you." She realized she was more than a little hysterical when a tiny voice called up from the bottom of the stairs.

"We're down here, Lainey." Already dressed in a clean white blouse and red plaid pleated skirt, Riley looked up at her quizzically. "We're in the kitchen."

Lainey returned to the bedroom and sat down for a moment to collect herself. Then she pulled on a pair of black slacks and a gray sweater, ran a brush through her hair and pulled a lipstick across her mouth. If she drove the kids to school, she could get to the office by a little before ten. She probably had another couple of hours' work to do on Patsy, which could get her back to the house just in time to pick up Riley for her recital. Assuming everything went the way it was supposed to, that is, she reminded herself, as she looked for her watch and located it on one of the night tables.

She walked downstairs, checking the living room to make sure Penn was not still sitting there, drunk out of his mind. The room was neat, all the detritus of the night before gone. When she walked into the kitchen and picked up a paper napkin from where it lay on the floor, intending to toss it away, she saw that the plastic trash bin was filled with empty beer bottles, topped off by an empty bottle of Glenfiddich.

She felt a second's irritation, then forced herself to get past it. I have more pressing items on my agenda this morning, she thought, turning around to watch the kids eating their breakfast. Riley's tutu was hung on the back of one of the kitchen chairs.

"It looks nice," the little girl said shyly, her pleasure brightening Lainey's day.

But Tim was another story. Still in pajamas, he sat in front of the cereal bowl, twirling his spoon in the milky liquid. His ebullience of the previous night was a thing of the past. Now, Lainey noted, his face had that white pinched look his father's used to get when he was upset about something. She came over and sat down at the table across from him.

"School starts at eight, right?" she asked, as if she hadn't been informed already.

Tim just shrugged.

"I'll drive you over there this morning, guys," she said, including both children in her glance. "Riley's recital is

right after school. Do you want to come and watch?"
This time she looked only at Tim.

For a moment, he didn't respond, simply staring into
the bowl of Cheerios as if searching for buried treasure.
"I'm not going," he said finally, looking up at Lainey
defiantly, then laying down the spoon, standing up, and
leaving the room.

Riley regarded Lainey expectantly, making her feel
even worse. I don't have a clue what to do, she thought,
wishing she could admit it to the child, but knowing that
would only make things worse. It would be no comfort
for Riley to know just how far in over her head her
guardian felt at this moment.

Unable to think of a better idea, Lainey decided to go
for help. "See you in a minute," she called out as breezily
as she could, opening the back door and walking outside.
Okay, Penn, she said to herself as she approached the
carriage house. You were great with the boy last night.
Let's see you do your stuff one more time.

No sounds came from the cottage as she knocked on
the wooden door. "Penn," she called out, knocking again
a little more energetically.

After getting no response, she turned the doorknob,
again calling out his name as she let herself in.

The small white entrance area was ablaze in winter
sunlight. "Penn," she yelled, walking through a tiny
hallway to the cottage's main room.

Not only was Penn nowhere to be found, but the bed
was made, as if no one had slept in it. She looked around.
There was the suitcase he'd brought with him from
London. A small pile of shirts sat on top of the oak
dresser, a pair of black loafers and some clean socks
were neatly set down beneath a small table. A pair of

gray wool slacks was slung over the top of a wing chair in one corner.

Damn you, she thought. There would certainly be no help from this quarter.

She heard Riley hanging up the telephone as she opened the kitchen door.

"Someone named Julian called," the little girl reported. "He said you could call him back at the office."

Lainey felt a pang of loneliness, followed quickly by disappointment at missing his call. Of all the things she could use right now, a word from Julian would be just right. But there was no time. She looked at her watch. Almost five to eight. She had to deal with Tim fast and get both kids to school. And then, she had to complete her work on Patsy. She hurried up to Tim's room. He was sitting on his bed, his eyes expressionless.

"Tim, you're getting dressed and going to school right now, period."

Lainey went over to his dresser and pulled out a maroon shirt and a pair of corduroy pants. Having little idea of what she was doing, she pulled the boys pajama top over his head and replaced it with the shirt. Tim didn't fight her; he sat there passively, like a helpless prisoner of war, allowing her to have her way, compliant if not cooperative. Finishing the task of getting him dressed, she tramped downstairs, pulling him like dead weight behind her.

Sugar Taplinger stood at the bottom of the stairway, two brown paper bags in her hand, smiling at them as if it were a holiday.

"I thought the kids might like my special Monte Cristos for lunch today," she said, beaming. "Plus chocolate cupcakes and seedless red grapes." She held her hand out to Tim, who grudgingly accepted one of the bags and trekked off toward the kitchen.

"I hope you don't mind, Lainey," Sugar said, as they followed behind him. "They've always been his favorites, and I thought he might need a little something fun."

Lainey looked at her gratefully. "Thank you," she said, not bothering to add that she had forgotten about their lunches completely, and without Sugar, both kids would have starved on their first day back.

The rest of the week went no more smoothly. Tim had to be coaxed out the door each morning, and Riley spent every free moment glued either to Lainey or to *Beauty and the Beast*. Penn had returned early Wednesday evening, two days' growth of beard on his face, his eyes heavy-lidded and bloodshot. He'd passed Lainey outside as she carried in bags from the supermarket and gone straight to the carriage house, where he remained almost constantly for the next few days. As far as Lainey was concerned, that was just fine.

Two children and a full-time job are quite enough to contend with, she thought to herself as she straightened up the living room early Friday evening in preparation for a visit from the children's grandparents.

Hugh and Doris Beckley arrived just before seven, their arms filled with gifts for Tim and Riley. They seemed ill at ease, their greeting to Lainey distant, even their hugs for their grandchildren awkward and strained.

"Let us know if we're in your way," Doris said to Lainey pointedly, as she held out a large baby doll to Riley, who climbed gratefully in her grandmother's lap. The older woman raised her hands slowly, as if she didn't quite grasp the concept of a hug, but would gamely try for the sake of the child.

Meanwhile, Hugh Beckley sat on the carpet with his grandson as the boy opened several boxes containing new additions to his already massive electric train system. Lainey noted the disappointed expression on Tim's face. When she saw what was in the boxes, she understood why. With the exception of one green boxcar, Tim already owned all of the new ones his grandfather had brought.

As soon as the packages were opened, Doris turned to Lainey. "We thought we might take the kids out to dinner. Maybe even bring them to our house for the night."

"Of course," Lainey heard herself respond, noting irritably that Hugh and Doris should have checked this with her privately, before causing the kids possible disappointment.

"When is Penn going back to London?" Doris asked as she helped Riley into her jacket on their way out.

"Actually, I'm not really sure," Lainey said, realizing that she and Penn had exchanged barely a word since Monday night.

"Tomorrow." Penn's voice was a surprise to all of them. He had entered the house so quietly, nobody had heard him come in. "How are you, Mother," he said, leaning down and kissing his mother briefly somewhere near her forehead.

"Fine, dear," she replied. "We're taking the children for tonight. Would you like to come along with us for dinner?"

"Can't," he offered without elaboration. He turned to Tim, who was neatly repacking the train cars in their various boxes. "Maybe we'll play with those when I come back from London next time."

The boy looked at him sadly.

"You have to go?" Riley came across to her uncle and held up her arms so he would pick her up.

He smiled at her as he lifted her into the air and kissed her on the cheek. "I'll be back sooner than you think, you'll see," he said, putting her back down on the floor.

Lainey felt like a stranger suddenly, the children, their uncle, their grandparents seeming to form a Norman Rockwell painting.

"I'll see you tomorrow, kids," she said, expecting and getting no response from anyone but Riley, who smiled at her briefly before taking her grandmother's hand and walking her out of the room.

Lainey heard the front door slam a few minutes later. She sat at the kitchen table, contemplating the telephone, considering the coffeepot. Picking up the phone, pouring out the coffee, both seemed more than she could handle. In fact, she hardly knew what to do with herself. On the one hand, she'd been searching for free time all week long. But it was hard to concentrate on anything. She felt like a stranger in someone else's house. The large kitchen, the snow-covered lawn outside the window, the cheerful yellow paint on the walls, the line of sweaters on hooks near the door—all of it was someone else's life. No, she realized. Not just someone else's life. Farrell's life.

That's who she wanted to talk to right now. Farrell. That was the one person who'd understand. She felt tears welling up inside her as she pictured her friend, smiling at Lainey, making fun of her attempts at sewing, at cooking, at keeping house. If only you were here, she thought, overwhelmed by sadness.

She forced herself to lift the telephone receiver. She'd call Julian. She'd hardly spoken to him all week. It seemed as if every time he called, she either wasn't home or was in the middle of something that just couldn't wait. Julian. That's who she needed. But she hesitated as she started dialing his number at work. It was too late for him to be there, and of course she couldn't call him at home.

"Thanks for putting up with me." Penn Beckley's voice intruded on her reverie. "You okay?" he added as he walked over to her chair and looked down at her.

She found herself wanting to talk to him. He was definitely a drunk and pretty much of a louse, but he might understand what she was feeling. "I'm missing Farrell," she said simply.

"Me, too," he said, pulling a chair close to hers and sitting down. "I had this image when I woke up this morning of Farrell coming in with her concoction."

"What concoction would that be?" Lainey asked.

"Oh, some home remedy she knew about for those who overimbibe," he answered, leaning back in the chair so it balanced precariously on only two legs.

"Do you ever think about imbibing a little less?" she asked before she could stop herself.

Penn looked at her, angry for a moment. "Not right now," he answered brusquely. Pushing the chair back, he stood up and walked out of the room for a moment. When he returned, he held a bottle of Beaujolais under one arm, a pinot noir in the other hand.

"Here," he said, placing them down on the table. "I'm about to compensate you for the accommodations by making dinner. Do you prefer meat or fish?"

Lainey watched him make his way to the freezer and contemplate its contents.

"How about swordfish?" he asked after a minute or

two. "That would call for the white." Without waiting for any response from Lainey, he walked back to the table and opened the Pinot Noir.

"Dinner should be ready in fifteen or twenty minutes," he announced, winking at her briefly before he poured the wine in an empty coffee mug that happened to be nearby.

"Piss elegant," she observed, taking a small sip of the cold liquid.

He walked back toward the refrigerator, calling behind him as he started pulling an assortment of ingredients from its interior. "Not elegant, maybe, but at least dinner will taste pretty good."

He hadn't been bragging, Lainey discovered when she bit into the grilled fish half an hour later. "Delicious," she acknowledged, holding up her glass of wine as if to toast him.

"I was taught by a master," he said, raising his glass in return and emptying it. He reached across to the bottle of white wine and poured another glass for each of them. "Do you remember our summers up in New Hampshire?"

"Yes, of course." Lainey hadn't thought about that in years. Each August, while she herself was baby-sitting or off in some arts camp somewhere, Farrell and her brother would be packed off to Hugh Beckley's parents up in northern New Hampshire. "I remember Farrell going there all the way through grade school and maybe a couple of years into junior high, but not much after that."

Penn nodded sadly. "Grandpa died during my senior year, and Grandma didn't feel she could handle us alone. Not that anyone could ever handle Farrell. God, she was wild when she was a kid."

Lainey felt her throat close with emotion. She hadn't

heard anyone else talk about the real Farrell, her Farrell, in so long.

Penn continued to speak, looking past Lainey, his eyes darkening with emotion. "She once crawled out of bed in the middle of the night and left us a note saying she was climbing Mount Keersarge alone and would see us when she got back." He chuckled and took another sip of wine. "She must have been about six and a half. My grandparents were petrified until we found her asleep along the road, about half a mile from the house."

He watched Lainey drain her wine, and reached out once again to the bottle. "Finished," he said, lifting it up and pouring the last dregs into her glass. "Time for red." He raised the corkscrew and applied it to the Beaujolais.

Lainey felt herself relax. She was getting glassy-eyed, and it felt good. After Penn refilled her glass with the red wine, she took a long sip. "So what does New Hampshire have to do with your ability to grill a fish?"

"My grandfather was a great cook. Didn't Farrell ever mention that?" Penn smiled at her.

"You know," Lainey said, reaching as far back in her memory as it would go, "maybe she did. I seem to remember her talking about breakfasts—big pancake-and-egg breakfasts, with everyone eating enough for an army."

Penn looked at her thoughtfully. "We knew we'd starve once we got back to New Rochelle. My father had no intention of following in *his* father's footsteps, and my mother's idea of a feast was one slice of cinnamon toast."

"I know." Lainey almost hugged herself with the pleasure of her memories. She took another drink of the red wine. "Farrell and my mother had a special understanding. Every time my mother made some grotesque stuffed cabbage and brisket feast, Farrell would come over for dinner. She was like some adopted *shiksa* daughter." Lainey felt the tears running down her face. She looked away from him. "I miss her so much," she said almost to herself.

Suddenly Penn's arms were around her, holding her as if he could make it all better. And for a few minutes, it felt almost as if he could. He comforted her with his hands, smoothing her hair, rubbing her back, murmuring words of solace. Drunkenly, she thought, God, this is Penn Beckley. His comforting touch was transformed into an unbearably exciting caress.

She wasn't sure how they ended up in the living room, curled around each other on the sofa, his lips moving on her hungrily, his hands claiming her with assurance. She pulled back from him for a moment, wondering if he were any more clear-headed than she herself was. But she couldn't stay away. The warmth of him, the solidity of his body—she needed so much right now, and this was the only thing she could hold onto.

She didn't know how her clothing came off, but she shuddered with pleasure as he entered her, the rhythm of his body rocking her slowly and securely into climax. She held onto him as she came, wordlessly begging him to stay inside her, as if as long as he remained, nothing bad could happen. Afterward, they remained on the couch, clinging to each other tightly.

A whisper of the night's passion tantalized her as she opened her eyes the next morning. But she found she was upstairs in her own bed. She took her time going downstairs, wondering what in the world she would find to say to Penn. But the carriage house was empty, a hurried note thanking her for the previous week the only sign that he had ever been there. She went back out the door, embarrassment and a headache the only real remnants of their night together.

Great, she thought to herself, walking slowly to the house. I fall into bed with Farrell's brother in a drunken stupor. Smart, very smart. The phone was ringing as she entered. She wondered if she had time to grab a few aspirin from the cupboard before answering the insistent ring. No, she decided, reaching for the receiver and managing to say hello.

"Lainey?"

The voice was familiar, although she couldn't place it for a moment. "Yes," she answered tentatively.

"Patrick Fouchard."

Lainey tried to pull her professional self together, standing up straighter and clearing her throat before she spoke again.

He didn't wait for her to talk. "Listen, Lainey, I realize things are very difficult right now, but we want you to know that the job in California is still very much yours."

Lainey stood immobile. She hadn't even thought about the Marissa job in days. She'd been too busy with tutus and dinners and homework. "Well, Mr. Fouchard, I don't really know what to say. You know, right now I seem to have inherited a whole life, someone else's life, that is." Lainey cursed herself for her awkwardness. "What I'm trying to say is that it seems out of the question right now."

Fouchard was quiet for a few moments. "My name is Patrick. And Lainey, the job was made for you, we know it is. Preproduction won't be starting for several months." His voice grew more urgent. "Think about it. Don't rush to any decision. We're not planning to make any other arrangements for a while yet. Obviously, at some point, we'll have to . . ."

She wanted to die at the thought of what she might be giving up. "Yes," she answered.

He said good-bye to her and hung up. She rested on her arms for a moment, staring out of the kitchen window at the snow-covered trees. She could see California in her mind's eye, almost hear the exciting hum of a creative studio. She thought about the thrill she experienced when a few lines on a page became a whole character.

She lay her head down on the counter's ceramic tiles, the cool surface a balm to her throbbing head. Suddenly she missed more than Farrell. She missed getting up for work in her tiny brownstone apartment, sitting alone with her coffee, getting ready to face the day. She missed the *B* train she'd taken every morning on her way to the office, the secret thrill when she would run into Julian unexpectedly, the familiar comfort of her lunches with Carla and Gail. Who the hell am I? she thought as she raised her head and looked around the room someone else had decorated. She could barely remember.

Chapter 14

"When we finish with the vegetables, are we gonna get the meat? Or maybe should we do the milk stuff first?" Riley asked as she watched Lainey select a bag of fresh spinach.

"First, we'll pick up some chicken, and then we'll get the dairy," Lainey answered.

Riley stuck her right thumb in her mouth and rocked back on her heels, her left hand clutching the grocery cart for support. "And after we leave the Grand Union, are we going home or are we going to another store?"

Lainey had to work at maintaining her patience. Riley's need to know every single step they were going to be taking had become an obsession since her parents' deaths. "We're going to take the groceries home, and then you're going to stay with Mrs. Miles for an hour or so while I go to see someone, and then pick up Tim."

Lainey walked over to the bin containing a variety of lettuces, and within seconds Riley was right beside her, her fingers wound around the belt loops of Lainey's black wool slacks. "Why do I have to stay with Mrs. Miles? Why can't I come with you?"

Lainey sighed. "Honey, I have an appointment with Mr. Moses, the man who handled your mommy and daddy's legal affairs. If you came with me, you'd get bored." She looked down at Riley, whose eyes were beginning to fill with tears. "Honestly," she said, giving her a warm hug, "you'll be fine at home."

Lainey had had to leave work right after lunch in order to pick up Riley. The first-graders had been let out early for some teacher planning conference. It seemed like a good opportunity to kill several birds with one stone, namely finish the grocery shopping and finally get to Philip Moses' office, as she'd been promising she would for the past two weeks.

"Can I watch *Beauty and the Beast*?" Riley asked as Lainey walked back toward the shopping cart.

Lainey nodded her head resignedly. "Sure, Riley." After all, she thought, heading for the cashier, you've already seen it nine thousand times. How can nine thousand and one hurt you?

Lainey checked her watch as she closed the car door behind Riley. It was already three-thirty, and she was due at Philip Moses' office at four. If she got back to the house quickly and got Riley settled in with Mrs. Miles, that should make her only fifteen minutes late. She looked over at Riley as she got in behind the wheel. The girl was already clutching her white blanket, which Lainey had forced her to leave in the car while they were inside. With her thumb back in her mouth and the blanket clenched in her lap, Riley looked years younger than seven.

Lainey couldn't bear how sad she looked. "Are you okay?" she asked helplessly, both grateful and guilty when Riley didn't respond.

A few minutes later, Lainey was surprised to hear Riley's voice as she opened the door to the mudroom.

"Why is everyone so sad around me?" Riley asked, her voice barely a whisper in the cold air.

"Well, sweetie," Lainey put the bags she was carrying down on a counter and turned back to shut the door, "everyone feels very bad about Mommy and Daddy."

Riley walked over to the kitchen table and sat down on a chair, her blanket firmly in hand. She seemed unable to speak for a moment, then looked straight at Lainey. "Did they go away because of me?"

Lainey could see the pain in the little girl's eyes. She quickly walked over to her. "Of course not. They didn't go because of you," she said gently, picking her up and holding her in her arms. "It was an accident, just a horrible accident." Lainey rocked her as she'd done when the girl was an infant.

"So when are they coming back?" Riley asked, her voice muffled by Lainey's shoulder.

"Oh, Riley, baby, Mommy and—"

The harsh ring of the phone interrupted her sentence. The interruption seemed to make the girl lose her nerve. Suddenly tensing, Riley uncurled herself from Lainey's arms and hurriedly began walking toward the family room.

"Riley," Lainey called out to no avail. Finally, she picked up the ringing phone, catching sight of the clock on the wall as she did so.

"When am I going to get to see you?" Julian's voice had a demanding edge to it.

"How about July twelfth in the year two thousand?" Lainey couldn't keep the exasperation out of her voice. Yesterday, he had called her office twice while she was in meetings, and this was the fourth or fifth time he had tried her at home. At least this time he hadn't gotten the answering machine. "Julian, I'm sorry, but I can't talk right now."

"Lainey . . ."

She could hear that he was taking great pains to maintain his patience.

"Perhaps if I come out right now for a couple of hours," he said insinuatingly.

Lainey was growing annoyed. "How can I explain this to you? I have an appointment with Farrell and John's lawyer in fifteen minutes." She looked at her watch. "Shit, make that ten minutes, which means I'm already five minutes late. I just found out that Riley doesn't actually understand that her parents are dead, and I have to pick up Tim for his orthodontist appointment by four, and get Riley to her soccer practice."

"Well, I guess that leaves me out," Julian answered petulantly.

For the first time, Lainey had a notion of what Julian must be like at home. *Please don't treat me as if I'm your wife,* she felt like responding, then realized how crazy that would sound. Besides, she didn't have time for the fight it would undoubtedly cause.

"I've got to get to the lawyer's office," she answered in a placating tone. "Maybe if you call later on this afternoon"—she realized even as she said it that there was going to be no good time at all that day—"maybe tomorrow morning we can talk at the office." She felt a stab of loneliness, the distance between them starting to feel like a continent instead of just one state. "Maybe one day next week we can go up to my apartment, have a long lunch."

Julian's voice warmed up considerably. "Now that sounds like a very good plan. How about Monday?"

"That's perfect." Lainey hoped she wasn't promising more than she could deliver. What was it Tim had mentioned about Monday? A doctor's appointment? A class trip? Well, one way or another, she'd find a way. Even if it kills me, she thought grimly, hanging up the phone. But what does it mean when planning a romantic tryst becomes this difficult?

She checked the calendar for the address of Philip Moses. The lawyer had called practically every day since Lainey had moved in with the children. "We *should* go over the terms of the will," he'd said the first few times, which changed to a much sterner "you *must* come in" by his last call the day before. Lainey hadn't meant to dismiss him; she'd just found herself without enough hours in the day. But no more excuses. This was it.

She thought about her reluctance as she walked out to the garage and climbed in the Saab that had belonged to Farrell. She understood it a little. After all, she admitted to herself, going over the details of a will meant Farrell and John were really and truly dead. Not that she had any belief in the supernatural or anything. Just that this seemed so damned final. Meaning I'm suffering from the same delusion that Riley is, she realized bitterly.

Another thought came to her as she pulled out of the driveway and headed toward the Merritt Parkway. Reading the will meant seeing herself as guardian, right there in black and white.

She drove along the narrow, winding road, opening the side window and appreciating the freshness of the cold air as it blew in. Meadowview certainly is beautiful, she thought as she looked for the sign that led to the parkway's entrance. I might be in nomansland, but the scenery couldn't be better.

Even the parkway was beautiful, she noticed, as she made a left turn and entered the northbound lane, pale winter sun shining through thick branches that in a couple of months would be a hundred different shades of green. The state of Connecticut smelled better than New

York City on its best day, and the hushed sounds of birds, of wind blowing through naked branches that woke her up every morning, was constant comfort.

Not that it made up for everything she was missing. If I could have just one thing, what would it be? she mused as she drove toward the Bridgeport exit. An entire afternoon of making love with Julian? Going to a movie at the Sony 84th Street on the spur of the moment at three on a Saturday afternoon? Her mind practically reeled with the impossible pleasure of those things. Guiltily, she remembered how lost she used to feel most weekends in the summer, the blazing heat of an August Sunday filling her with an aching sense of isolation, always accompanied by the bitter jealousy of everyone else on the planet, all of whom seemed to have something to do, someone to love.

What I would give for a weekend by myself, she almost said out loud in the protected privacy of the speeding automobile. Nice, she chided herself as she pulled off the highway onto the road that would take her to the lawyer's office. A lovely thought as you're about to see your life with these two kids laid out in legalese.

Disgusted with herself, she pulled into the parking lot in front of the L-shaped, two-story professional building that housed Philip Moses' law office. Climbing the stairs to his second-floor suite, Lainey tried to think of everything she needed to ask him about. Random questions had been going through her mind since she'd set up the appointment, but right now, she could think of none of them.

"Good afternoon," Moses said, as she walked past his secretary into the main office. He rose from behind the large desk and motioned her to a small gray sofa across the room.

"How do you do." Lainey put out her hand and smiled before sitting down.

The elderly white-haired lawyer sank into a brown leather chair to her left, laying out several long, white legal pages on a low walnut table. "Since you're coexecutrix, I'm going to walk you through the entire document. I hope that's all right with you."

"About how long will that take?" Lainey wanted to kick herself; why hadn't she thought to ask how long she needed when she'd set up this appointment.

"Well," the lawyer said thoughtfully, "a couple of hours should do it."

Lainey's heart sank as she looked quickly at her watch. Two hours would leave Tim without a ride to the orthodontist and make Riley late for soccer. Without realizing it, she let out a small sigh.

"Is that a problem?" Moses was polite, but his impatience was just beneath the surface.

Lainey thought for a moment. There weren't too many people she felt comfortable asking for favors. "May I use your phone?" she finally answered.

"Of course," he responded, getting up and walking into another room to give her privacy.

Lainey dug around in her purse. She knew she had Charlie Cole's number somewhere. There it is, she thought, relieved, as she pulled the business card out.

"This is Charles Cole." His voice at work sounded an octave below his social tones.

"Charlie, it's Lainey. I have a big problem, and I thought maybe you could help."

"Sure, what's going on?"

Hurriedly, Lainey explained her situation, but her hopes for a solution were dashed quickly.

"Gee, Lainey, you know I'd do anything for those kids, but I'm just leaving for lunch."

Her silence moved him to further explanation.

"I mean it's business and all, you know."

Lainey realized that arguing with him would be useless. "Next time," she said, knowing there would be no next time.

She sat there trying to come up with an alternative plan. Finally, she dialed a number that had become familiar in the past weeks.

"Sugar. It's Lainey."

The request took only a minute, Sugar's immediate acceptance leaving her mind free to wander over something Philip Moses had said.

"What did you mean by 'coexecutrix' ? " she asked as he came back into the office.

"Oh," he said, slightly disconcerted, "I assumed Farrell and John had made that clear. You're one of two executors. The other is Pennington Beckley, Farrell's brother."

For Christ's sake. Penn. A perfect capper for a perfect day, Lainey thought, attempting to keep her chagrin to herself. She tried to pay close attention as Moses described the various life insurance policies, special bequests and trust fund issues covered in the complex legal document, slowly coming to realize that whatever financial problems she had had up to this point, Farrell and John Cole had left her future secure. In addition to the fee she would be paid as executrix, she also was to inherit over two hundred thousand dollars outright, in addition to an annual stipend to cover household expenses plus management over the several million dollars left to Tim and Riley, at least until they reached the age of twenty-five.

I had no idea Farrell and John had so much money, she thought as she was driving home. Yet she guessed it made sense; after all, the house covered several acres in a very expensive community, John's law practice had also been a thriving one, and she'd heard Farrell talk about Alicia and Herbert Cole, John's parents. John and his brother Charlie had shared their inheritance about ten years before, and it must have been sizable.

Her mind went back to the surprise Moses had sprung. Pennington Beckley as coexecutor. Dear God. First you fall into bed with a near-stranger, someone you haven't seen since you were a kid, she reproved herself, and then you get him as a life partner.

Twenty minutes later, her mood wasn't helped any by the sight of two cars in the driveway: one, the navy blue BMW she recognized as belonging to Doris and Hugh Beckley; the other, the cream-colored Oldsmobile Cutlass her parents had been using for years.

"Hello," she yelled, letting herself in the front door.

All four voices answered back. "We're in the kitchen."

She forced a smile as she walked to the back of the house. Which would be harder to take this afternoon, she wondered, the well-meaning intrusiveness of Saul and Helen Wolfe or the exquisite politeness of Hugh and Doris Beckley? Dead heat, she decided as she entered the kitchen and took in their faces.

Her own parents were resplendent in retirement chic, namely matching royal blue running outfits, her mother's accessorized with oversized silver earrings, which in New Rochelle were a sure sign that the bearer was a member of the liberal wing of the Democratic party. Doris and Hugh Beckley were dressed in standard-issue Connecticut afternoon: she in a gray wool dress, he in a dark blue wool jacket with gray wool slacks.

Lainey blew a general kiss at all of them, a move her mother had no intention of letting her get away with. Rising from her chair and coming over to Lainey, Helen Wolfe put her arms around her daughter and hugged her tightly.

"Sweetheart," she said comfortingly, "what a time you've been through."

Her mother couldn't see the glaring look Doris Beckley aimed at her, as if to say, what a time *she's* been through, but Lainey caught it easily. The Wolfes and the Beckleys were never at ease under one roof. She disengaged from the hug as quickly as she could. At least she didn't have to stay there with them; the bad news was they were all there, but the good news was she had to leave to pick up Tim from his orthodontist's and Riley from her soccer.

"You know, guys," she aimed her words at all of them, "I wish I had known you were coming, 'cause I have to leave in a few minutes to pick up the kids."

"Oh, don't be silly, dear," Doris Beckley had visibly relaxed at Lainey's words.

Lainey knew just what was coming.

"Hugh and I will get the kids."

Lainey comforted herself with the thought that at least only one set of parents would remain.

"Well, that would be great, thank you." Her smile at the Beckleys was almost beatific. "Shall I give you directions?"

She saw the angry glance that traveled between Doris and Hugh, understanding that somehow her question had wounded their pride.

"We'll find our way," Hugh answered for both of them. "Just give us the addresses."

Lainey watched them walk down the path to their car.

She was too far away to hear Doris Beckley's words to her husband as he held open the car door for her.

Lainey returned to the kitchen and sat down across from her parents, feeling like an accused felon in the glare of an angry bright light. The questions began immediately. How long will you be staying? What are you doing here every day? What are you doing about your job? Why do you look so tired? When are you going home?

Lainey didn't know which question to answer first. "Listen, folks, I guess there's something I haven't explained to you."

Her mother leaned forward in her chair, looking over briefly at her husband as if to say *See, I told you she wasn't telling us everything.*

"I'm the guardian for Tim and Riley. I'm moving out here to take care of them, lock, stock, and barrel." Lainey saw the stunned look on both her parents' faces. "Actually, I was just at the lawyer's office, going over the will."

"How could Farrell have done this to you!" This time it was Saul Wolfe who was doing the talking.

Lainey tried to hold her temper. "She didn't *do* it to me; it's a decision we came to together a long time ago."

"What kind of stupid decision?" Her mother couldn't help but get into the act. "You're a single woman. You have your own life to live, such as it is."

"Such as it is? What exactly do you mean by that?" Lainey's voice was rising.

Her father's words were placating. "What your mother means is that we love you, and we want the best for you." He leaned across the table and took her hand. "You know, we want you to have a husband and children of your own. How are you supposed to do that out here, saddled with someone else's kids?"

Lainey stood up, unable to cope with her parents a minute longer. "Listen. I'm godmother to Tim and Riley. I am also their legal guardian." She glowered at her mother and father. "They are, for all intents and purposes, *my* children, and you'd better get accustomed to that."

She turned away and walked toward the door. "I'm sorry to leave, but I have work to do upstairs. I'm still employed by Carpathia, you know, and my afternoons are not my own. If you want to stay for dinner, feel free. I'll see you in a few hours."

She could hear her parents arguing as she marched out of the room to the staircase, but her mind really wasn't on them and their reaction. What am I so self-righteous about? she thought as she climbed up to the second floor. If I felt any more overwhelmed by all of this, I'd yell "Mommy!" and fall into a dead heap right here on the landing.

Chapter 15

"Come on, one more." Jackson Frye, a reporter who had worked with Penn in London for three years, signaled to the bartender for another round.

Penn pushed off the barstool a little unsteadily, shaking his head. "Can't do it, pal. Gotta get back to the office. I've got some stuff to go over before I meet Sarita."

Jackson snorted derisively. "Ten minutes more won't make any difference."

"Have one for me," Penn said with a grin as he turned to go.

The other man nodded. "Will do. As long as it's *on* you."

Penn laughed. "Naturally."

He gave a wave as he made his way out of the crowded, smoky pub that served as the local hangout for staff members of the London news bureau. With its dark interior and worn wooden stools, Addy's was one of Penn's favorite spots in the world.

If I had a nickel for every drink I've bought at Addy's, he thought to himself as he pushed open the door to the street. Zipping up his leather bomber jacket, he smiled; even better would be if he had the money he'd spent on the drinks themselves. But what difference did the money make? He loved working in news, it was the one part of his life with which he was completely satisfied, and after the long hard hours he put in, one of the bonuses was the time spent hanging out with colleagues, trading stories until late into the night, getting loaded, and getting into trouble.

It was just after six o'clock, and the sky was dark. He shoved his hands in his pockets and picked up his pace in the chilly night air. The office was just around the corner.

Suddenly, he stopped. Oh, Christ, the notes. He wanted to go over the new budget, but his preliminary notes were still back at his apartment on the hall table; he'd forgotten to pick them up on his way in to work this morning.

"Damn."

He knew from past experience that he wouldn't get much done if he tried to work at home. There was nothing to do but drive back to pick them up and then return to the office.

Irritably, he hurried down the street to where his black Austin-Healy was parked. Standing beside it, he fished in every pocket for the keys. Where the hell were they? He began to regret having had that last Scotch; he didn't really feel like driving right now.

The keys were in his back pants pocket. It took him a few fumbling tries before he was able to insert the key into the lock, but, finally, he was inside and on his way. What an utter waste of time, he thought in annoyance as he pulled away from the curb. At the corner, he made a left turn.

A little boy of four or five and his mother suddenly appeared out of nowhere, holding hands and crossing in front of the car as it came around the corner. Penn slammed on the brakes and jerked the steering wheel as hard as he could to the right. Tires screeching, the car careened wildly to the side, skirting the little boy and missing him by only inches before it hopped the curb. Penn saw the black lamppost looming, as if it were coming at him. The car smashed into it with a sickening noise, the impact propelling him forward, his seat belt harshly jerking him back.

Then there was silence. Penn sat, immobilized, his hands still clutching the steering wheel. He could hear the blood pounding in his head. He turned to see the woman in the street bending down to grab up her child, her face white, her eyes wide with fear. His heart beating wildly, he looked down at himself, reflexively feeling his chest and legs, realizing he was fine. Slowly, he unclasped his seat belt and opened the car door.

"You okay?" he called out to the woman.

"Bleedin' maniac," she screamed at him, fury quickly starting to replace her terror. "What're you, drunk? You nearly killed us both." The little boy, visibly upset, started to cry.

Penn stepped out of his car. "But you're all right?"

She clutched her now-wailing son and hurried over to the sidewalk. "No thanks to you."

Penn watched her walk away, hearing the child's sobs, feeling, suddenly, stone cold sober. The woman was right, of course. He had nearly killed her and the boy. It was only sheer luck that he hadn't.

He turned and saw the front end of his car, dented into a V-shape around the lamppost. Putting one hand on the roof of the car, he noticed that his hand was trembling.

His arms crossed behind his head, Penn lay on the living-room couch, looking out the apartment window as he had been doing for most of the morning. He had been too mentally shaken up to go in to the office, but he kept telling himself he might manage to get some work done at home. So far he hadn't even glanced at the notes resting on the coffee table in front of him, the same notes he had been driving home to retrieve the night before. He was unable to do anything but think about what had happened.

Instead of the incident fading, his horror at what could so easily have occurred grew worse with every hour. He replayed the moment over and over in his mind, how quickly he had swung the car around that corner, not even looking to see if anyone or anything might be there. Had the boy and his mother been only a couple of feet more to the right, he would definitely have hit them. There would have been no way to avoid it, given the speed at which he was going and the alcohol in his system.

He grimaced. *That* was the part that was gnawing at him. He'd been drunk. He'd been driving in that condition for years, but it wasn't until this moment that he forced himself to put the label on it. Hell, the way he'd always seen it, a few drinks like he'd had yesterday didn't mean anything, and he had always possessed sharp reflexes. Whenever he thought he'd had a few too many, he wouldn't drive at all. God knows, that had happened often enough, and he was proud of himself for knowing his limit.

But last night he had barely swerved in time. Though he would never admit it to another living soul, his head had been foggy and his reaction time piss poor. In the light of day, he knew full well that he shouldn't have been behind the wheel at all. It was a damned miracle he hadn't killed those people.

And what were the odds that this was the first time he

hadn't realized how far gone he was? On how many other occasions had he not realized it?

At least he felt secure that drinking had never affected his work. Grabbing the half-empty mug from the end table nearby, he went into the kitchen to spill out the cold remains of his last cup of coffee and pour himself a fresh one. He was good at his job, he didn't doubt that, but he had always believed his concentration remained unaffected by two or three Scotches. Could he have accomplished even more in his career without all the social drinking that went on?

He let out a long, resigned sigh. It wasn't social drinking. Who the hell was he kidding? He'd always known the truth, he'd just never had any reason to do anything about it before. He'd drunk his way through the past fifteen years. Some kind of natural talent had enabled him to skate through professionally without getting caught. It was as simple as that. He frowned. Maybe it was just a miracle that he had gotten this far. Maybe yesterday's incident was the warning signal that his guardian angel was packing up and leaving, that his good luck was running out.

It wasn't as if there hadn't been signs along the way that he drank too much. He winced at the one that immediately came to mind: the days he spent in Connecticut after Farrell's funeral.

He'd tried not to let anyone see how profoundly upset he had been at having missed the burial service. But that wasn't much of an excuse for the fact that he'd spent most of his time at the house with a drink in his hand. Of course, he had been doing his best not to think about Farrell. It just couldn't be borne, remembering his little sister, feeling how much he had loved her and what had been lost. It was better to keep all that locked away. Back in London, he had continued to run from thoughts of Farrell and John.

But what he really couldn't bear was Tim and Riley's pain. It was simply more than he could stand. So, as always, he drank. He had told himself it was only to avoid the image of Farrell, but, as the days passed, it was just as much to block out the children's anguish, the silent Tim and the crumbling Riley. He'd hung around for a week, offering the few token words of comfort he could come up with. Big hero that made me, he thought sarcastically. The truth was that he had blown in and blown out, making it all as easy for himself as he possibly could. He had really done nothing at all.

To top it off, he had walked into the unspeakable nightmare of their deaths to discover Lainey Wolfe, of all people, in charge of things. Christ, what the hell was his sister thinking? There was nothing wrong with Lainey, but, Jesus, this was a woman who had never stuck with anything since she was a kid, who had a hundred talents and squandered them because she could never take any action. She hadn't changed a bit since high school. Still unmarried, unable to commit to one man, floating along in some job far below her potential. He'd seen her work, and someone with a little more hustle would have turned that kind of talent into something.

She might have agreed to take on Tim and Riley, but he didn't believe for a second she was going to stick with it. The excuses would come slowly, but they would come. Eventually, she would be out of there, back in her safe little world in Manhattan.

He suddenly realized where these thoughts were taking him. Somebody needed to be there to pick up the pieces for the children when she left.

Penn carried his coffee over to the window and looked

out. He had never considered himself father material, never given any thought to having kids of his own. It was the last situation he ever would have pictured himself in. He really hadn't even been around his niece and nephew all that much in the past. But that didn't mean he didn't love them. They were his sister's children. And they had never needed him before. Now they would.

A light rain was falling outside. He rested his forehead against the cold windowpane. He had to be there for them. It was the only right thing. And he couldn't be there drunk. The image of the woman and son from the night before came back into his mind. No more drinking. It was all over, as of right now.

"I'll need a few weeks to wrap things up here." Penn paced back and forth behind his desk as he spoke into the telephone, ignoring the noise around him in the busy office.

"Of course. But make it as fast as you can and try to give us a firm arrival date by, say, Tuesday. Okay?" The executive producer from New York spoke more quickly than any of Penn's London colleagues.

"Thanks, Mike. Talk to you then."

Penn hung up the phone and stood, motionless, for a moment, letting it sink in. He was sorry to leave London; it had been a great few years here. But it was damned exciting, going back to a great job in the States. NBC's "Images" was one of the top-rated newsmagazine shows. Being invited to come on board as a senior producer was actually more than he had hoped for when he'd started sending out feelers two weeks before.

"Luck and timing," he murmured. "The laws of the universe."

Glancing at his watch, he hurried over to the side

closet to grab his jacket, pulling it on as he ran for the stairway. He was already half an hour late to meet Sarita. She was practically fanatical about being on time herself, and she could never accept his habitual lack of punctuality. It was the one serious bone of contention between them. Of course, she had made it clear from the start that their relationship was primarily about good times and good sex. He knew she would never get seriously involved with a working producer with no real social standing. Still, the two or three nights a week they spent together were perfectly satisfying to both of them.

"Coming to Addy's later?" Jackson Frye looked up from his word processor to call out to Penn as he raced by. "We haven't seen you there for ages."

He shook his head as he was pushing open the door to the stairway. "Sorry, buddy."

He ran the four blocks to Zone Two, some hot new place Sarita had wanted to try. She was always taking him to London's hip and trendy spots; it was important for her as an art gallery owner to stay on top of what was happening and be seen at the right places.

Thank God this place was close to the office, he thought, looking at his watch as he entered and scanned the busy pub. The conversation would be difficult enough. He caught the eye of an attractive brunette sitting at the bar. She smiled at him.

"Penn, darling."

He heard Sarita call off to the left, and turned to see her sitting at one of the tiny tables arranged around the room's perimeter. She was dressed in a bright red silk suit with a short skirt revealing her extraordinarily long legs. Making his way through the crowd, he leaned down to kiss her, inhaling her perfume, briefly stroking her long, black hair. With her exotic dark beauty, she always reminded him of a cat.

She tapped her watch. "Thirty-five minutes today."

"I know. I'm sorry." He hung his jacket over the back of the chair. "I was on the phone with New York."

Sarita shrugged. "You're hopeless."

The waiter came over to their table. "May I get you something from the bar?"

"A Coke, please. Lots of ice." Penn glanced over at her wineglass questioningly. "Another for you?"

"No, thanks." The waiter left. Sarita waved to someone she recognized, then turned back to Penn. "Any word on when your car will be done?"

"It's a big job. You don't want to know."

She smiled. "On to more pleasant things. I met with a sensational new artist today."

"Really? Tell me."

Penn made an effort to listen as she described her discovery, but he couldn't concentrate. He quickly downed the soda placed before him and ordered a second. There was no point putting off what he had to say.

"Penn? Did you hear me?" Sarita had realized his attention wasn't on her.

He leaned forward and took her hand in his. "I have something to tell you."

She regarded him. "I don't like the tone in your voice. It's not something good."

"Not something good for us, I'm afraid," he said gently. "I'm going back to America. I've got a producing job there."

She frowned. "I see."

"I told you about my sister's death." He paused. "I think her kids could use having me around."

"Oh." She smiled politely.

Penn waited, but she said nothing further. Somehow, he had expected her to want to know more. The subject of his niece and nephew had never come up until Farrell's death, and though Sarita had been sympathetic about his sister, she had shown little interest in hearing about the children.

"When do you leave?"

"Soon. When I get things taken care of here."

She withdrew her hand from his. "I know this is selfish of me, but does this mean you won't be going to the benefit with me on the twelfth?"

He shook his head. "I have to get to the kids."

"How come?" she asked with a frown. "Obviously, someone's been with them all this time, and will be until you get there. Would a little more time hurt? They're not alone, right?"

"No, of course they're not alone."

Penn envisioned Lainey in his sister's house, sitting on the couch in the living room, moving about the kitchen. The children loved her, he knew that.

Suddenly, unbidden, an image came to him of Lainey lying naked on the couch the night they had made love. He recalled the feel of her soft skin beneath his hands, the way she had moved in response to him. That had been a surprise, falling into bed with her, but, of course, there was the wine, and the strain of the whole business for both of them. It was one of those inevitable one-night stands brought on by stress and proximity, like the kind that went on between male and female colleagues working on an intense news story until all hours of the night. He'd had his share of those flings. No, he'd never wanted Lainey Wolfe in all the years he'd known her, and he wasn't about to start now. In fact, she was part of the whole problem.

"What do you think?" Sarita's voice interrupted his reverie.

"Sarita, I'm sorry, but it's time for me to go back to the States."

"Well, I suppose you'd best be getting back to your flat to pack." She sounded mildly sarcastic. She rose and came around to his side of the table to give him a kiss on the cheek. "Good luck, darling."

He watched her go, a striking figure in her sleek red suit. He'd like to believe she was putting on a brave front, holding on to her dignity as he was breaking up with her. The truth was, she just didn't seem particularly upset.

"Bit of a blow to the old ego, that," he muttered under his breath.

He observed several men turning to watch as she passed by. It wouldn't take her long to find someone else.

Perhaps this move wasn't such a bad idea. It was the right time to make a few changes in his life.

Chapter 16

"So, if by seven-thirty, you have the kids ready, yourself ready, and breakfast on the table, there's no reason you can't get them to school and be here by nine-fifteen." Carla Mirsky clicked her compact shut for emphasis.

Lainey leaned back in her chair and pushed the Styrofoam tray away from her, half a tuna sandwich remaining on the paper plate. "Carla, if I could manage even one of those things, I would stand up and yell 'hooray.' I can't even get Tim out of bed without an hour of threats. And Riley thinks I'm going to disappear into thin air every time I drop her off in front of the school."

"You're taking them to see someone, right?"

Lainey nodded yes. "Megan Burke recommended a woman in New Haven. All three of us went to see her last Friday. This week, she's seeing the kids separately." Lainey ran her hands through her hair nervously. "I hope to God she's good. Those two need more help than I seem to be able to give them."

"Don't underestimate yourself. You're crazy about them, and they feel the same way about you."

"Oh, I love them, that's for sure."

"What is it you're not so sure about?" Carla's self-satisfied smile indicated there was a right answer to that question—one she already knew.

Lainey didn't feel like playing the game. "I don't know what you're talking about." She sat up straighter and reached for the half sandwich. "By the way, where's Gail today?"

"Gail is home with the flu, as you already know." Carla glared at Lainey. "Stop trying to change the subject."

Lainey put the sandwich down. "What on earth are you so angry about? I mean, honestly, I'm the one with the problem."

Carla leaned forward. "Lainey, your problem is you don't know what you want." She hesitated for a few seconds before her final shot. "As usual."

Lainey stood up angrily. Most of the time Carla's perceptive swipes made her laugh, but today they were making her uncomfortable. "I know *your* whole life is under control, but I've had a few complications not of my own making lately, so give me a break."

Carla stood up as well, and both of them picked up their trays, making their way to an oversized trash can and depositing everything inside. Carla nodded to someone in her department as they continued to walk toward the exit.

She stopped for a moment as they reached the doorway. "Listen," she said, resting her hand lightly on Lainey's shoulder, "no one would wish all this on you, least of all me, but there are basic decisions to be made in this life, and until you're willing to go on record with something—raising those two kids, doing the California job, doing your old job, living in Connecticut, living in New York—whatever it is you really want, you're hanging yourself by your very own thumbs." Carla once again began moving and Lainey followed, both stopping as they reached the elevator bank.

Carla looked at her gravely. "The minute you make real choices, everything will fall into place, I swear. Just make a decision, and go with it."

Carla's monologue was interrupted by the appearance of Julian Kroll, hurrying past them on his way to the cafeteria. He stopped when he saw Lainey.

"Oh, Ms. Wolfe," he spoke haltingly as he noticed Carla standing next to her, "we have that four-thirty off-site today." Getting no response, he nodded self-consciously and moved on.

Carla leaned her shoulder against the wall as Julian walked away and shook her head disapprovingly. "And until you get that one out of your system, you're not going to be able to handle anything."

Lainey fought to keep herself from blushing. "I don't know what you're talking about, and I very much resent the implication."

Carla stared at her, forcing Lainey to look back. "You're playing with fire, and I don't think you even know that the matches are in your hand."

Lainey suddenly realized that other people were beginning to regard the two of them with curiosity. Slowly, she pushed the 'up' button. "Carla, I'm raising the white flag. Please put your weapons down." She had lowered her voice to an intense whisper.

Carla, too, answered softly. "I'm sorry to be so tough on you, but I love you. You're my friend. I can't stand to see you mess up your life."

Lainey heard the bell indicating the elevator's arrival and entered as soon as the doors opened. She looked straight ahead as Carla joined her, not knowing what to say. What a relief it might be to talk honestly about Julian, she thought as the car began to rise, to share her fears, her frustrations. But she knew she shouldn't actually do it.

"I'm a big girl now, you don't have to be my mother," she replied at last as they reached Carla's floor.

Carla sighed loudly as she left Lainey behind, holding the elevator door open and turning back for just a moment. "Well," she said adamantly, "I'll *be* your mother. Here's your mother's advice. Be careful what you wish for, honey." She raised an eyebrow. "I suspect you already know the rest of the phrase."

"An off-site!" Lainey stretched languorously in Julian's arms. Her bedroom looked strange to her, just as her living room had when they entered the apartment an hour before. "What a slice of improvisational genius."

Julian slid his hand over the curve of her belly and laid it to rest on her mound. "So I'm lousy with words," he said softly, moving his fingers in a slow circle.

"You're creative director of a major American corporation." Lainey laughed, unconsciously fitting her body into his hand.

"I feel very creative," he answered, sliding his fingers inside her.

Lainey allowed herself a moment of giving into the sensation, then peeked guiltily at the clock. "Not again, darling. I have to get back to the kids." She pushed away from Julian, groaning as she sat up against the pillow.

Julian sat up as well, and pulled her back toward him, encircling her with both arms and trailing tiny kisses down her neck. "I can't stand this," he said, bending his head to hers and kissing her hard. "I need time with you. I need *you*, damn it."

Lainey couldn't deny the pleasure his words evoked in her. The ferocity of his longing was almost worth having spent over a month apart. "Julian, I need you, too, but I have to get back to Connecticut. You've got to understand."

Julian pushed himself away and looked at her. Wordlessly, he got out of bed and began pacing around the room. Lainey, too, stood up. He watched her as she picked up the articles that had been tossed in a careless heap on the floor and began to put them back on.

"What if we got married?"

Julian's question stopped her cold. In a tiny corner of her mind she heard Carla's voice. Be careful what you wish for . . . She fought to put it out of her mind.

With only one arm through her white silk blouse, Lainey found herself sitting back down on the bed. "Excuse me?" she whispered nonsensically, struggling to put the other arm into the second sleeve but succeeding only in tangling it up.

Julian sat beside her, patiently removing the garment and replacing it on her correctly. "I mean it, honey. I love you. I want to be with you." He buttoned the blouse carefully, as he might have done for a child.

Lainey could hardly speak, hardly think. For several agonizing moments, she felt as if she were inside a coffin, the lid closing slowly but inexorably, shutting off her air supply for eternity. "But it's not just me anymore," she answered finally. "I have the children to consider."

Julian took her face in his hands, kissing her softly on the mouth. "I know that. I understand. I want you and anyone else you bring with you."

There was an ocean of muffled sound rushing through Lainey's head, making real thought impossible. I'm making this up, she thought dazedly. I'm dreaming. In one minute I'm going to wake up and feel really stupid.

Julian saw the confusion on her face. "This isn't something you have to decide right now. I know that I've sprung it on you."

"Why now?" she breathed in desperation.

Julian took her hands in his. "The last few weeks, with you in Connecticut. You're so busy here at work, I almost never get to lay eyes on you. So busy at home with the kids, I never get to talk to you. I've missed you so much. I realized how much I love you."

My God, Lainey thought, this is really happening.

Julian stood up once again. "I'll call you later, sweetheart. Please think about it."

He dressed quickly, kissing her once more before walking out of the bedroom.

Lainey heard the click of the front door as it closed. She looked again at the clock. Six-fifteen. I've got to make the six-forty-seven, she thought, trying to rouse herself out of what felt like a waking coma.

"Julian just asked me to marry him," she said out loud, trying, once more unsuccessfully, to move.

It was nine-thirty before she'd served dinner and finished the dishes. For some reason, everything was taking twice as long as it usually did. Even Riley had noticed how distracted she was, asking three times if everything was all right. Lainey had done her best to reassure her; after all, the last thing Riley needed was one more person to worry about.

But it wasn't okay, she admitted to herself after the kids had gone upstairs to watch television. She felt pure terror every time she replayed Julian's proposal in her mind. She wished she could claim that her fear was based on concern for Julian's children, even for his wife. But she knew that wouldn't be honest.

In fact, faced with a marriage proposal, she realized she barely knew Julian. She conjured up the handsome face in her mind, his brown eyes so earnest as he spoke to her that afternoon. It was a portrait of a stranger.

And marriage, that connectedness she thought she'd longed for—it felt like an iron gavel banging down on her future.

She heard the phone ringing, but couldn't bear to reach for it. One of the children finally picked it up.

"Lainey, it's for you," she heard Riley call down from the TV room.

"Who is it, sweetheart?"

"I don't know," she answered. "I think it's that Julian guy who calls all the time."

Lainey trembled as she reached for the receiver, not hearing the door open behind her as Penn Beckley entered, unobserved, from the mudroom carrying two large suitcases.

Penn watched Lainey, aware that she didn't realize he was in the room. Quietly, he set down his suitcases. He saw her holding the telephone receiver, hesitating before she spoke. As she said hello, he noted the way her fingers were clutching at a linen napkin, as though hanging on for dear life.

"Julian," she murmured, her voice anguished.

Penn saw her expression of torment as she responded to something the caller said.

"I can't do it," she said, even more softly now. "It's not just your family. It's not any one thing. . . ."

He noted the slouch in her shoulders as she tried to explain herself.

"I just can't marry you."

With interest, he realized there was relief in her posture when she hung up the phone.

Sensing something, Lainey turned around suddenly, almost crying out in surprise as she saw him standing there. "What are you doing here?"

Penn smiled wryly at her. "And warmest regards to you, too."

"How long have you been standing there?" she gasped.

"Just a minute or so," he said, walking over to the kitchen table and pulling out a chair. "You don't mind?" he asked perfunctorily before lowering himself into it.

"Uncle Penn." Tim's excited shriek preceded both children's entry into the room. Within seconds, they were hugging him fiercely, attached like iron filings to a magnet.

"How long are you staying?" Riley asked eagerly, pulling away from her uncle and looking at him as if making sure he was really there.

"Well, actually, that's up to Lainey." Penn's level gaze met hers across the large room.

That's really fighting fair, Lainey thought, momentarily enraged. As if she could deprive these kids of their heroic Uncle Penn.

"You can stay as long as you like," she said angrily, flashing on their last encounter. "If I remember correctly, you left your bed very neatly made." She strode out of the kitchen, fighting the urge to look back.

Would today never end? she wondered, cursing the butterflies that were crowding her stomach.

Chapter 17

"Are you coming, Tim?" Penn took Riley's hand as he leaned down to talk through the car's open window.

"No." Sitting in the front seat, Tim crossed his arms and stared straight ahead through the windshield. "This is a stupid idea. Stupid and weird."

The truth was, Penn had his own doubts about this whole plan, but he couldn't share that with the children. "C'mon, kiddo," he said encouragingly. "Later on, you'll be glad."

Tim set his mouth. "Like hell I will."

Penn raised his eyebrows in mock horror. "The language. Okay, my good man, wait here, and we'll be right back."

Riley clutched his hand tightly as they crossed the parking lot to enter the florist shop. It took less than five minutes to purchase a dozen roses and get back to the car. Then they drove a half mile to the bakery, where Tim again sullenly refused to leave the car while Penn and Riley went inside to pick up the cake Lainey had ordered two days earlier.

There was silence on the way home. Penn was pulling the car into the driveway before Tim spoke again.

"But it's nuts," he protested as if they had been in the middle of a conversation. "It was *her* favorite kind of cake, not ours. She doesn't even know it's here. It's not as if she's going to come down like some ghost or something and have a piece."

Riley spoke up from the back seat. "We can still have a Mother's Day even if she's not here. She's still our mother." She addressed the back of Penn's head. "Right, Uncle Penn?" she asked anxiously.

Penn guessed she was repeating some version of the way Lainey had explained what they were going to do. "Of course, Riley, of course," he agreed vigorously. "She'll always be your mother."

He parked the car and the three of them went into the house. Lainey had set out cake plates and forks. Four glasses and a container of milk sat on the counter nearby, next to a vase for the roses.

Lainey came into the room to meet them. "Thanks for picking these up," she said, taking the flowers from Penn and inhaling their fragrance. "They're beautiful."

She busied herself arranging them in the vase, which she set in the middle of the table. Riley sat down in one of the chairs, watching, while Tim stood off to one side, an unhappy expression on his face. Penn took the cake out of the box, his eyes on Lainey. She was obviously nervous, attempting to cover it up with cheerfulness. He hoped she knew what the hell she was doing.

"So, folks, let's eat some cake. No big deal." Lainey began serving.

The tension in the kitchen was becoming unbearable. Penn suddenly realized he was just standing around, like Tim, waiting for Lainey to make this work. Until now, it hadn't occurred to him how difficult this must be for her. The least he could do, he thought, was give her a hand.

"Right," he agreed cheerfully. "A snack of mocha crème cake is always a good plan in my book. And a cold glass of milk to go with it is perfection." He grabbed the milk and the glasses and brought them over to the table.

Sullenly, Tim took a seat. "I don't know why I have to," he muttered.

"Along with the roses and her cake, Daddy would have gotten Mommy a present," Riley said as she took her plate of cake from Lainey. "We always made her cards, too."

"Oh, brother," Tim exploded in exasperation. He turned to glare at his sister. "You think we should make her cards? What are you, crazy? Why don't we just pretend she's still here and start talking to her." His voice was growing louder and nastier. "Maybe we can set a place for her and Dad at dinner, leave them plates with food on it and stuff. I mean, really, why stop there?"

Tears had formed in Riley's eyes. "I only—"

"That's enough, Tim," Lainey cut in sharply. "If Riley wants to make a card, I think that's fine. In fact, I think it's great."

Savagely, Tim cut a chunk of cake off his slice with the side of his fork. "You're all nuts. Celebrating Mother's Day for a dead mother is just plain nuts."

Penn observed Lainey quietly taking a deep breath. He wasn't sure if she was trying to calm herself or figure out what to do next. He jumped in.

"You know, Lainey said we're going to be talking about memories, and I've got one I bet none of you know about," he said. "It's about the first Mother's Day, the year Tim was born."

Lainey looked over at him gratefully. "You were here?"

He shook his head. "I was working in D.C. back then. But I remember that John had planned this big night out for Farrell. He'd arranged everything and it was all supposed to be a surprise. Some concert and then a fancy dinner in New York, the whole deal. He had to go to the office in the afternoon to meet with some client, somebody important enough to summon him on a Sunday. But after that he was going to take her out royally."

He saw that Riley was drinking in every word, while Tim picked at his cake indifferently. He addressed his next words to Tim. "Anyway, at the last minute, your mother—who had no idea what was planned—told your dad that her big wish for Mother's Day was to do something, all three of you together. Him, her and their new baby. No distractions from your dad's office, no phone calls. Getting your dad away from the office was a big deal back then. He was still building a reputation as a lawyer, and that meant putting in a lot of hours."

He took a long drink of milk. "So your dad did what she asked. He never told her that he'd already bought tickets, or anything about the client, who raised holy hell and tried to have him fired, just for canceling the meeting. But the three of you went to the beach or something, and then spent a quiet night at home."

Penn looked at Lainey. "I remember this because Farrell said to me later it was one of her all-time favorite days in her life. She said that for some reason, everything about it was perfect."

Lainey smiled. "I never heard that one."

Penn took a forkful of cake. "It's sort of a story about both of them, isn't it?"

Abruptly, Tim broke in. "Dad did lots of nice things for Mom. That wasn't the only time." He spoke almost ferociously. "He loved Mom. He *did*."

Startled by the intensity of his outburst, Penn and Lainey stared at him. "Of course he did, Tim," Lainey said hastily. "We weren't suggesting that was unusual. It was just especially nice."

"I remember when Mommy let me stay home from school one day, and the two of us went on a picnic, just us alone. It was last year." Riley's tone was dreamy, and they could see that she was picturing the scene in her mind. Then she frowned. "It was when Chelsea Moore didn't invite me to her birthday party because we'd had a fight. I was the only one left out."

Lainey nodded. "I heard about that party. The two of you made up the day after it, right?"

"Yeah." Riley drank some of her milk.

Penn leaned back in his chair. He hadn't realized how involved Lainey had always been with Tim and Riley, how much attention she had paid to the details of their lives. *They do have some kind of special relationship,* he admitted grudgingly.

He regarded her more closely. Tendrils of dark blond hair were escaping from her ponytail. He had a sudden urge to reach over and smooth them back.

Christ, he thought. For the first time since he'd come back from London to stay, he had to acknowledge that he *was* attracted to her and had been all along, that sleeping with her that one night hadn't been such a drunken accident after all.

Riley's voice intruded on his thoughts.

"Mommy and I drove somewhere—I don't know where, it was far away—and we had the best day. We ate our picnic, and then we found this fair. There was a merry-go-round and a magician, and even pony rides. I had cotton candy and popcorn, both." She looked at Lainey, her voice slightly awed. "And you know what? Mommy never told Daddy or Tim or anybody that I skipped school. She wrote my teacher a note saying I'd been sick."

Tim snorted. "Big deal."

Lainey laughed. "Your mother did the same thing for me. Actually, lots of times, now that I think about it. I remember this one day in particular, when I skipped work because I was so down—about a few things, it doesn't matter what anymore. But your mom drove in to the city, and took me to lunch at some great Italian restaurant, and for a facial at Georgette Klinger's. Then we had a drink at the Carlyle Hotel, which I love. Neither one of us got a single useful thing accomplished the whole day."

She looked away, remembering. Penn saw her eyes filling up. There was a tremble in her voice when she spoke again. "She was so great. There was nobody who could cheer me up like Farrell. She was the most fun to be with of anybody."

Penn was afraid she might dissolve into tears. "Hey," he said, "she could be a royal pain, too, right? When we were kids, she drove me crazy. Stole my stuff, was always borrowing my records and my sweaters—and, of course, they never came back. She hung around me and my friends, making a nuisance of herself."

Lainey smiled as she wiped a tear from her cheek. "It was more like they were hanging around her."

"Yeah, yeah." He made a face. "Not that I paid any attention to that. If they wanted to moon after her, that was their problem."

"What are you two talking about?" Riley asked.

"Your mom was popular," Lainey replied lightly. "Everyone wanted to be around her, girls and boys. That never changed. People always loved her."

"She was the most beautiful of all the mothers at

school." Riley's voice was quiet. "At the Christmas play . . . she was the most beautiful mother there."

Riley sat still for a few seconds, then suddenly burst into tears. *"I hate her!"* She jumped up, knocking her chair over. *"I hate her! And I hate Daddy, too."* Her voice had risen to a scream. *"How could they die and leave us alone?"*

She turned and ran from the room. Tim got up without a word and walked out of the house, slamming the kitchen door behind him.

Penn and Lainey looked at each other. It was Lainey who finally spoke first. "I don't know what to do to make them stop hurting," she said sadly.

Penn stood up. "I'll go to her."

When he got to Riley's bedroom door, he could hear her crying inside. He knocked, but there was no reply. Pushing the door open, he took only a step inside the room, leaning back on the doorjamb. Riley was on the bed, her face buried in her pillow. Her shoulders shook with the force of her sobs.

"I don't blame you a bit," he said softly.

She didn't acknowledge him, continuing to cry.

"I don't blame you for hating your mother," he repeated. "Sometimes I hate her, too." He knew that Riley might think he was saying it just to appease her, but, in fact, he was telling the truth.

Slowly, Riley lifted her tear-stained face to him. "W-what?"

"I mean it. I *really* hate her sometimes. I hate her because I love her and I miss her, and I can't stand that she died and left us without her." He walked over to sit down on the edge of the bed. "I want to yell and scream at her, to say how *dare* she go and die on us."

"Y-you do?" She was trying to catch her breath between sobs.

"You bet I do." He regarded her seriously. "I love her, but sometimes I hate her at the same time."

"Oh, Uncle Penn," she said in a small, sad voice. She crawled into his lap and curled up as tightly as she could, her breath still coming in short spasms.

He put his arms around her. "Your mom and dad wanted to be with you for your entire life." He pulled back and looked into her eyes. "They loved you and Tim more than anything in the world. They would never have left you if they could have helped it. You know that, Riley, don't you?"

Slowly, she nodded.

"But you can still feel whatever you want to. Sad, angry, whatever. And it'll be perfectly okay."

She sighed quietly. Then she buried her head in his shoulder. He held her tightly. They sat that way, in silence, for a long time.

Chapter 18

Lainey watched Riley push Cheerios around glumly with her spoon, building a stockpile of them on one side of the bowl, then aiming the few she'd left on the other, one at a time, toward the cereal mass.

"Honey," Lainey said gently, "not to interrupt World War Cheerio, but we have to leave in a couple of minutes. Is your project ready to go into the car?"

Riley brightened for a moment, then pushed her chair back and ran toward the stairway. Her class assignment from the previous day had been to make a sculpture out of recycled materials, a more interesting form of homework than any Lainey remembered from her own second-grade experience years before. Using plastic soda bottles, old buttons, the cardboard tube from a roll of toilet paper, milk cartons, used cans, and popsicle sticks, Riley had fashioned a large and colorful robot.

Within two minutes, she was back downstairs, the robot sculpture proudly in her arms.

"I think the eyes are my favorite part," Lainey said, smiling appreciatively at the colorful buttons that were attached with Scotch tape. She walked over to Riley and gave her a brief hug. As she pulled away, she looked at the robot once again. "Actually, the whole thing's my favorite."

"Yeah, it's great if you like piles of trash." Tim's entry into the kitchen was punctuated by the sound of his heavy book bag crashing to the floor.

Riley looked at her brother with disdain. "It's not trash. It's recycled material. It happens to be not just art, but environmentally healthy art."

"It happens to be not just garbage, but environmentally healthy garbage," Tim taunted mercilessly.

Lainey was relieved to hear them behaving normally even if they were fighting, but she had to keep the battle from escalating into a war that would make them late for school, and her late for work.

"Who wants what for lunch?" she asked, getting up from her chair and walking over to the refrigerator.

"Peanut butter and jelly." Riley's response was the same every day.

"You, too?" Lainey looked back at Tim as she opened the door and reached for the strawberry jam.

"Yecchh," he responded, the expression on his face echoing the spoken sentiment.

"What then?" Lainey leaned on the refrigerator door impatiently as he tried to make up his mind.

"I don't know," he mumbled, pouring an enormous amount of Sugar Pops into his bowl and drowning them in milk.

Lainey looked at the clock nervously. "We've got exactly seven minutes before the bell rings, so please eat that quickly."

Tim placed an enormous, soggy clot of cereal into his mouth, making Lainey sorry she had tried to hurry him.

"The last thing we have time for is an emergency Heimlich maneuver, kiddo," she said, shaking her head. She waited for him to swallow the dense glob and repeated her earlier question. "So, lunch. What's it to be?"

"Turkey," he said finally, milk dribbling down his chin as he took another huge mouthful of cereal.

Lainey pulled out a loaf of whole wheat bread and the half pound of turkey breast she had bought a couple of days before. "Mustard? Mayo? Ketchup?" She looked questioningly at Tim.

"Sure," he answered unhelpfully.

Lainey glanced once again at the clock and decided not to pursue it. Hastily, she mixed some ketchup with a dab of mayonnaise and spread it on one side of the bread. She hadn't blended it thoroughly and the mixture looked like pink slime with odd white traces here and there. I am my mother, she thought none too kindly, viscerally recalling her disgust when this particular substance would turn up in her own school lunches. "Mix it," she used to whine on Monday mornings, horrified when Helen Wolfe would claim Russian dressing status for two distinct trails of red and white swiped at lazily once or twice before being slathered on the brisket or roast beef remains of Sunday evening's dinner.

The memory reminded her of another family tradition.

"Guys," she said, looking up from her sandwich preparation, frowning at how long it had taken her to think of this question. "Do you two get an allowance?"

Tim shifted uncomfortably in his seat. I guess he's been too embarrassed to ask about it, Lainey thought, wishing she had time for a long conversation about what they had a right to expect from her. Quickly, she cut through the turkey sandwich and placed it inside a zippered Baggie. Wiping her hands on a dish towel, she walked over to the door where her shoulder bag hung from the knob. "How much?" she asked.

Riley looked up. "I don't remember," she said, holding her hands up in confusion.

Tim glanced at his sister contemptuously. "She gets fifty cents, I get a dollar," he mumbled, obviously still uncomfortable with the notion of asking Lainey for money.

Lainey pulled her wallet out of the large black leather bag. She removed two quarters from the change purse, then riffled through the bills, finding some twenties and tens, plus a couple of fives. She walked over to Riley and handed her the coins. Then she turned to Tim.

"This will have to do," she said, holding out the five-dollar bill.

He eyed it, but refused to reach for it.

"Take it, honey," Lainey said reassuringly. "You can bring me change later on today."

Tim avoided her eyes, looking down at the floor instead. "One dollar, Lainey, that's all I need, honest."

Lainey felt the clock ticking. She plunked the bill down on the table in front of him. "Sorry, it's all I have. Now hurry, both of you, we have absolutely no time left."

Riley rose from the table and picked up her robot sculpture, carrying it to the mudroom and pulling her jacket down from its hook. Lainey looked at Tim expectantly, but he seemed unwilling to budge.

"Tim." Her voice was firm now. "Let's go." She put her hands on the back of his chair, attempting to pull it out from the table, but stopped as she heard a small sob. Her hands fell to his shoulders. She sat down on the chair beside him and forced him to look at her. Tears were streaking his face.

Lainey put her arms around him. "What is it?" she

asked soothingly, stroking his silky hair and resting her cheek against his.

Tim raised his head and glanced toward the mudroom.

"Riley," Lainey yelled out, understanding immediately, "take the robot to the car and strap yourself in. We'll be out in a minute."

At the sound of the back door opening and closing, Tim looked at Lainey gratefully.

"So what is it?" Lainey said, wiping his tears away with a paper napkin.

For a few seconds, the boy hesitated. Then the story poured out of him: the robberies, his fury and helplessness as he'd round a corner and see Garth and Jay standing there, just waiting to jeer at him and take what was his.

"It's bad enough they get a dollar," he said, his tears now at an end. "Five bucks will only make it worse."

Lainey hugged him hard, wishing she had some magic solution that could end this problem, but the only thing she could think of, she knew he'd never let her do. She decided to try it on him anyway. "How about if I talk to the school principal, tell him what happened?"

Tim jerked up in his seat. "Are you crazy? They would kill me!" There was true fear in his eyes. "Besides," he added as he searched her face to make sure she understood, "nobody else would ever talk to me again."

Reluctantly, Lainey caressed his cheek and stood up. "Tim, I'm going to solve this."

The boy remained seated. "Like how exactly?" he replied cynically.

"I don't know," she said grimly. "But I mean it. I'm going to make this stop. I promise."

Tim rose reluctantly and allowed himself to be led away from the table. Lainey walked out to the mudroom, shutting the kitchen light off behind her and pulling her coat and Tim's jacket down from their hooks. The words 'like how exactly?' echoed in her head as she made her way to the car.

Lainey looked up from the conference table as the doors opened and a large cart filled with platters of sandwiches and cans of soda was wheeled into the room. The meeting on Marissa had begun hours before, and several people in the room seemed delighted by the interruption.

"We'd better break for fifteen minutes," Patrick Fouchard said, yawning slightly and getting to his feet.

Lainey saw that Julian, who was seated just to Fouchard's left, was trying to catch her eye, but she pretended not to notice. The truth was, she found she could hardly look at him since his proposal of marriage.

Rick Dean, seated on Lainey's other side, smiled at her. "What do you think?" he asked, straightening the stack of computer pages in front of him.

Lainey simply shrugged, eliciting a quizzical nod from Rick.

She joined the crowd of Carpathia executives who'd already made their way to the sideboard, where the sandwich platters had been unwrapped, first making sure that Julian was still on the other side of the room. Rick fell in behind her. When they reached the front of the line, they were the only two standing there.

"So what's the problem?" he asked, keeping his voice low.

Lainey looked around at the roomful of men and women busily munching down ham and cheese. Nobody was paying any attention to the two of them. Even Julian was deep in conversation with one of the marketing directors from Los Angeles.

"I feel stupid being here, that's all."

Rick laughed. "Sweetie, you're many things, but none of them is stupid."

Lainey grabbed a sandwich and a soda, and indicated two chairs in a far corner of the room. Rick nodded, taking two sandwiches and a club soda, and walking beside her.

"So?" he said expectantly as they made themselves comfortable and deposited their food on a small wooden table between them.

"So I don't belong here," Lainey said, frowning as she bit into a sandwich.

"Of course you do." Rick sounded outraged. "You invented Marissa, for Christ's sake."

Lainey chewed her sandwich thoughtfully. "And now I'm giving her up for adoption."

He took a drink of his club soda. "Maybe so, but for right now, you're still on the project, at least here in New York, and there's no reason to feel out of place. That's just crazy."

"It's not 'for right now,' " she replied bitterly. "Tim and Riley are not going to disappear, suddenly freeing me up for a California sabbatical."

"Would you like them to?" Rick asked gently.

Lainey shook her head vigorously. "Of course not," she replied. "It's just that when I'm sitting through a meeting like this one, I can't help getting excited. That's really ridiculous because when the thing takes off I won't be anywhere near it."

He nodded sympathetically. "You never know what the future will hold," he said encouragingly, "but for the moment you seem to be carrying off the worker-slash-suburban mother dilemma very well."

"With my left hand," she said hollowly, thinking of

Tim's revelation of the morning. "Were you ever bullied as a child?" she asked suddenly.

"Excuse me?" he answered, confused.

"Tim was being mugged for his allowance every week by some older kids."

Rick scratched his chin. "I was, actually," he said, sounding slightly embarrassed. "Jim Chapman was his name. God, he was huge." He smiled. "I must have been seven or eight."

"What'd you do about it?" she asked, putting her sandwich down and giving him her complete attention.

He grinned delightedly. "As I remember, my brother Billy caught up with him one Saturday on his way to baseball practice and beat the crap out of him. He ended up in the emergency room." Rick laughed so loudly that several people around the room began to stare. "My parents grounded my brother for a month." He stopped laughing and looked at Lainey. "I wouldn't consider that solution if I were you. Adults don't get grounded, they get a prison sentence and headlines in the *National Enquirer*."

Lainey noticed Rick's glance at something above her head just as she felt a familiar hand on her shoulder.

"Do you mind if I borrow Ms. Wolfe?" Julian's amused tone was directed at Rick and Jerry. He never even glanced at Lainey, as if fearing that actual eye contact would allow her to say no.

Lainey knew she had no choice. Outright refusal would only spark curiosity.

"Thanks, guys," she said to Rick and Jerry as she allowed Julian to guide her toward the door.

Both she and Julian maintained neutral expressions as they walked across the room, but the moment they were out the door, Julian grabbed her hand and pulled her into an office nearby, barely checking to make sure it was empty.

"Jesus, I've missed you," he murmured, putting his arms around her and nuzzling her ear.

Lainey stiffened, making Julian draw back.

He stared at her for a few seconds. "What's going on?" he asked, his hands trailing down her back. All too aware of her lack of response, he allowed his hands to drop to his sides.

Lainey couldn't think how to answer. Here was the man she'd been in love with, the man she could have sworn she wanted to marry, and he seemed as strange, as foreign as someone she'd never met. She vaguely remembered her passion for Julian, whole nights devoted to thinking about him, longing for him, but right now she couldn't have brought herself to shake his hand.

"Lainey, I never meant to push you into marrying me. Honestly, honey, things can go on just as they were, I swear it."

Lainey fought to say something, anything to escape from the emptiness that was keeping her frozen. "Julian, we can't just go on. It's wrong, it's immoral, it's not fair to you or your wife or your kids."

Julian looked at her, puzzled. "Why is that such a problem suddenly? How long has it been, almost two years, and it's never bothered you before."

A wave of anger rode through her at the glibness of his response. It felt good to be mad. Not that she was kidding herself—it was a relief to feel anything at all. "What kind of answer is that?" she asked accusingly.

"Hey, Lainey," Julian said, stroking his ponytail nervously, "I mean, I'm ready to marry you. I'd move in with you this minute, if you'd let me."

His self-righteousness only made her angrier. "You

mean, now that I'm not so available. How about all that time I was completely at your disposal? What was wrong with me then?"

Julian's face began to redden. Suddenly, she wasn't the only one who was angry.

"Listen," he said, his voice rising out of its usual smooth cadence, "I've been nothing but honest with you from day one. I don't know what's going on with you, but don't blame it on me."

Lainey walked to the door and put her hand on the doorknob. She turned back to him, her eyes as cold as winter. "You want to marry me because you can't. If I had said yes, you'd have been in the middle of some other magical affair within three weeks."

Julian's brown eyes gleamed dangerously. "Maybe you're the one thinking about another affair. Why bother with me when your friend's brother is right on the premises."

Lainey's eyes widened in fury. "Here's what I'm thinking about, since you're so interested. I'm thinking about just how frozen a day would have to be in hell before I ever talk to you again."

She pulled the door open and strode down the corridor toward the ladies' room. Relieved to find herself alone, she stood at the sink, rinsing a paper towel in cold water and holding it against her face. For several minutes, as she tried to calm the flush that rode from her neck through her forehead, her fury at Julian built. He was a bastard, a cad, a jerk. She had fallen for the oldest con game in the world.

Then her eyes met her reflection in the mirror. What a phony she was, she acknowledged silently. The moment Julian had proposed, he'd stepped from delicious fantasy into terrifying reality. A reality that suffocated her, that made her feel as if she were an animal trapped in a cage. Not only couldn't she conceive of being married to Julian; she could hardly bear to look at him.

She turned on the cold water and rinsed the towel once again, this time holding it to her neck. Julian's last accusation ran through her mind. Was she attracted to Penn? Nonsense.

Of course, it was certainly helpful to have him there, playing with Tim and Riley, filling in for her occasionally when she needed to go somewhere. She pictured him, comforting Riley on Mother's Day, holding the girl tenderly as Lainey had passed by in the hallway.

Okay, she thought, unconsciously lowering the paper towel to her chest, it was true that sometimes, when she'd run into him unexpectedly in the kitchen or the garage, she could hardly be blind to his dark good looks, the slender but muscular body that couldn't be hidden in a T-shirt and a pair of blue jeans. She closed her eyes for a moment, conjuring up how smooth his skin had felt that one night they'd spent together, how expert his hands had been as they'd awakened her deepest cravings. He'd been like a jungle cat, sleek and beautiful, but with that margin of danger that had kept her at the outermost edge of desire.

Her eyes opened in disgust. What kind of person are you, she thought as she crumpled the paper towel and flung it into a waste basket.

However much anger Julian felt, it couldn't be a hundredth as much as she deserved. She had accused him of only wanting what he couldn't have. But she knew who was really guilty of that particular crime. She'd adored Julian when he was home with his family. And here she was, fantasizing about Penn Beckley, a man who didn't give a damn about her, someone with whom she'd had one night so meaningless it never even occurred to him to try again.

She felt her cheeks reddening yet again, but this time she couldn't pretend it was caused by anger. No, this was utter mortification.

Al Smile nodded to Lainey sourly as she passed him on the way back to her office. Sitting down at her desk, she could hear him striding down the corridor, his "Hey, you" evidently aimed at Bob Stillman, the designer in the office at the end of the hall who had been with Carpathia for twenty years at least. She shook her head in annoyance. Maybe Al would have learned his name by the time Bob's retirement dinner rolled around.

She looked at her telephone messages and thought about how much she could accomplish in the hour or so before she had to leave for Grand Central. But she found herself unable to concentrate on anything. She was damned if she was going to allow herself to dwell on Julian Kroll, or, worse yet, Penn Beckley.

There was one problem she really had to figure out, namely, what was she going to do about Tim. She understood the boy's reluctance to have her go to the school authorities. And she couldn't very well hire a hit man to gun down two children, however appealing the notion sounded for the moment.

Absentmindedly, she pulled a piece of bond paper from the top drawer of her desk and began doodling on it with a medium-tipped art marker. Without much thought, she found herself sketching the figure of a devil flying through the air, a pitchfork in one hand. In the other hand, he held two struggling boys in ski masks, one of them clutching a dollar. Using a pen with a finer point, she etched the words "illegal tender" onto the face of the bill.

She looked at the cartoon with some satisfaction, then pulled another piece of paper out of the drawer. On this one, she showed the devil, the dollar now in his own hand, flying alone above a cavernous burning hell. Several inches below were the two boys, now dropping precipitously toward the hellish conflagration. Chuckling, she wrote a line at the bottom. *Hey you! Admission only a buck,* it read maliciously.

It was no solution to Tim's problem, she thought, carefully folding the sheets of paper and putting them inside her briefcase, but at least it might make him smile when he opened his lunch box the next day.

"It's someone from the *Ledger,*" Mrs. Miles called out as soon as she heard Lainey come inside the house.

Mrs. Miles was cradling the phone against her heavily padded bosom as Lainey entered the kitchen carrying two bags of groceries. Awkwardly, the two women exchanged their burdens, Lainey carrying the portable phone over to the table while Mrs. Miles began unpacking the bags.

"Hi," Lainey said, wondering why the local Meadowview paper would be calling her.

"Is this Lainey Wolfe?" the man on the other end of the phone asked ingratiatingly.

"Yes," she answered politely, imagining that their subscription had run out. She watched Mrs. Miles leave to put the laundry detergent and bleach down in the basement.

"This one that came in today is the best of all," he said.

Lainey had no notion of what he was talking about. She sighed impatiently. It was Saturday morning, and she'd promised the kids she'd take them into the city this afternoon. Not that they were dying to go. It was her own idea that Tim and Riley get some sense of the world she'd been living in all these years. She was planning to show them her office, a place they'd never been. She had also researched karate studios, and arranged to take both children to a noon class. Megan had suggested it to boost Tim's self-confidence, but to Lainey it sounded like a great idea for both kids.

Whether it turned out to be helpful or not, she had a lot left to do before she'd be ready to leave, and this mysterious phone call was the last thing she had time for. "I'm afraid I don't know what you're referring to."

There was a short silence on the other end of the phone, then the man continued. "This is Bill Carpenter at the *Meadowview Ledger,* the one you sent the cartoons to. They're really very good. I especially loved the one with the sumo wrestler in the ballet class."

Lainey knew just which cartoon he meant. That first cartoon of the devil she'd left in Tim's lunch box a few weeks before had been such a hit, she'd started making them for both him and his sister every few days. The one Bill Carpenter was singling out had been drawn for Riley last week. Still, she had no idea how to respond. Eventually, the man spoke once more.

"We were hoping to sign you up weekly," he said, then started to laugh. "Free blind mice, indeed," he chortled, referring, Lainey knew, to the sketch she'd done of rodents in sunglasses, leaping out of a large cage marked "Meadowview Elementary School."

"Can I get back to you?" Lainey asked, unwilling to say anything before figuring out what was going on.

Carpenter gave his office number eagerly, urging her to respond quickly before hanging up.

Lainey walked out to the staircase and yelled for the children, waiting until they'd both joined her in the kitchen.

"Anyone have any idea of why a man named Bill Carpenter from the *Ledger* would be calling me?" she asked, watching both of them closely.

Riley shook her head no, but Tim gave her an odd smile. "Well, yes."

"Well, yes, what?" Lainey asked, crossing her arms in front of her chest.

Tim walked to the table and slung his legs over one of the chairs. "I just thought your cartoons were really good, so I gave some of them to this kid in my class whose father works at the paper. I didn't think you'd mind."

"I don't mind, exactly," Lainey started to say, then stopped.

Do I mind? she wondered, walking over to the table and pulling out a chair for herself.

She was jostled by Riley's lowering herself onto her lap and laying her head down on Lainey's shoulder. "How would you two feel about actually seeing them in print?" she asked, running a comforting hand down the girl's back.

Tim just looked at her. "That's why I gave them to Sam in the first place."

Lainey lifted Riley's head. "It's okay with you, too?"

Riley's 'yes' was immediate.

"Well," Lainey said, smiling now, "in that case, I guess you're going to get to see it each and every week for a while."

Mrs. Miles reappeared and picked up a six-pack of soda, laying the cans in the refrigerator individually.

"How about you, Mrs. Miles," Lainey called out,

"would you like to be immortalized in the *Meadowview Ledger*?"

Mrs. Miles turned around to face them as she answered. "Just so long as it's not in the police blotter," she said, evoking a laugh from her audience. "Oh, by the way," she added. "Mr. Cole called while you were out shopping. He wanted you to know he'd be out of town for a while."

Lainey bundled Riley off her lap. "Did he want me to call back?"

"No," Mrs. Miles responded. "He said he was walking out the door when he called."

Lainey stood up and urged Tim out of his chair as well. "We have to be on the road in five minutes if we want to make Mr. Nagato's class," she said, her words propelling the children out of the room.

What could make Charlie Cole move so early on a Saturday? she wondered. Given how late his Friday nights usually ran, she would have been surprised to hear he'd called before two in the afternoon. And why tell Lainey he was leaving? After all, he'd dropped by maybe twice since the funeral. Perhaps he feels closer to his niece and nephew than he's let on, she reasoned, surprised but also oddly touched.

"Did he say how long he'd be gone?" Lainey asked Mrs. Miles.

"No," she said, shutting the refrigerator door and walking over to the sink. She picked up a yellow sponge, rinsed it under the cold water tap, and gave the table a fast wipe before saying anything more. "Charlie Cole doesn't give away that much of himself unless the receiver is thirty years younger than I am." Mrs. Miles's smirk underlined her disapproval.

Lainey nodded. "The Cole brothers weren't exactly

identical, were they?" she said, picturing the solidity and strength John Cole had carried with him everywhere he went.

Mrs. Miles's expression softened. "He was one fine man, that John Cole. And, oh, how he loved his family. Never an unkind word or a raised voice . . ." She stopped in midsentence and scowled. "Almost never," she ended weakly.

"What do you mean?" Lainey asked, certain the woman had something specific in mind, something that seemed to disturb her.

Mrs. Miles gave her an evaluating stare. "I'm not one to open my mouth, you know," she began portentously, "but there was a bit of a row just before the tragedy."

"Whatever do you mean?" Lainey asked, surprised.

"Well." Mrs. Miles seemed hesitant, but Lainey's urgent gaze forced her to continue. "The day before they died, they were having some kind of fight, Mr. and Mrs. Cole. I was in the basement doing laundry and I heard their voices all the way down there."

"What kind of fight?" Lainey asked, somehow frightened to hear the answer.

Mrs. Miles lay the sponge down. "Oh, I couldn't make out the words, but Mr. Cole was screaming something awful." She turned to Lainey. "You know, I'd never heard them fight before, not once in all the years I've worked here. Mr. Cole slammed out of the house just as I was bringing the basket of clean whites upstairs to put away."

"Did Farrell say anything to you?" Lainey asked.

"No, of course not," she answered, as if shocked at the very concept. "And I heard Tim upstairs after that. He'd come home sick at some point. Mrs. Cole spent most of the day looking after him." She was quiet for a few moments, then looked earnestly into Lainey's eyes. "But it was sad, I tell you. I heard her later that day, in the privacy of her room. She was crying, real soft so no one would hear her. But hear her I did."

"Do I have to wear something special?"

The sight of Riley bounding into the room startled both women. Mrs. Miles returned abruptly to wiping the table, while Lainey reassured Riley that Mr. Nagato would find her blue jeans acceptable for that day.

As if on automatic, Lainey called out for Tim and urged them into their coats and out to the car. But all the time she was driving south toward Manhattan, inside her head she was replaying the information Mrs. Miles had given her. Of course, it was perfectly normal for married people to fight. But maybe there had been more going on between the Coles than she had realized. She recalled Farrell's preoccupied air at the Christmas party, the odd dissatisfaction Lainey had heard in her voice. By the time she paid the toll at the Triborough Bridge, she was upset and strangely disconcerted.

Chapter 19

"I'll be going in a minute."

Mrs. Miles stood in the doorway of the master bed-room, watching Lainey move around among the large cardboard boxes that covered most of the floor. Almost everything that used to occupy John Cole's large maple dresser now lay in piles at the foot of the bed or had been neatly packed in the boxes.

"I've left a pot of stew for you and the children. Mr. Beckley should have them home in an hour or so, I would think." Mrs. Miles viewed the stacks of clothing and shook her head sympathetically. "Is there anything else you need?"

Lainey looked up and sighed. "Thanks, but no." She reached toward the back of the topmost drawer and pulled out an enormous stash of white T-shirts plus a handful of handkerchiefs. After depositing them into the carton at her feet, she stretched her arms up over her head, attempting to release the tension in her neck. She'd put off this task far too long, but getting it all done in one afternoon was proving to be harder than she'd thought it would be.

Carla Mirsky had called an hour earlier, offering Lainey a ticket to a new revival of her favorite Tennessee Williams play later on that night in the East Village. She wondered if she could finish what she was doing in time to go into the city. Maybe she could make some arrangement about the kids with Penn. Although he spent most of his time working at his new job at NBC, he had taken a surprisingly active role with the children, occasionally staying with them at night and frequently taking them places on Saturday or Sunday. But Penn had already done his part for the day, she thought guiltily. Thank heavens he'd agreed to take them to a double feature in Stamford and keep them away from the house for the afternoon. The last thing Tim and Riley needed was to witness the dismantling of their parents' lives.

"You'll be moving into this room soon?" Mrs. Miles asked.

Lainey found she had no answer.

"It's about time, if you ask me," Mrs. Miles added emphatically, before walking out of the room.

I wasn't asking you, Lainey felt like shouting after her, realizing she was reacting like a spoiled ten-year-old, even if she would never have said it aloud. Momentarily discomfited, she rechecked all four drawers to make sure they'd been completely emptied.

With even greater trepidation, she walked over to the chest that had been Farrell's. She reached her hand out to the narrow drawer on top, then pulled it back. It's not a live grenade, she thought, wondering at her own panic. What is it I'm so damn frightened of? She stood staring at the dresser as if it held the answer.

Disgusted with herself, she retreated to the foot of the bed and sat down. Suddenly, an image from two days before came into her mind. She was back in Dr. Shaffer's office in New Haven, alone with her, as the family therapist had requested. They'd spent the first thirty minutes or so going over questions Lainey had about the children, the therapist making a note every now and then on the small spiral pad she kept in her lap. They had even discussed the advisability of transferring Farrell and John's possessions into storage.

"You were wise not to do anything precipitous," Dr. Shaffer had said. "It was important to keep things as stable as possible. But it's time now to begin moving ahead as a family."

Lainey had no idea what had prompted Dr. Shaffer's next comment. All she knew was the deep discomfort she felt as the words came out.

"Why are you with these children?" the therapist had asked, a new intensity in her voice.

Lainey had felt as if she were back in elementary school, searching for the correct answer. "I was Farrell Cole's best friend. She and John wanted me here." How lame, she'd thought, knowing these words were nowhere near adequate.

Only after a considered pause did Dr. Shaffer speak again. "You know, taking on a family is a very big task, a life-altering decision, really. When you elect to do something so challenging, it's important to have a clear idea of *why* you're doing it."

Lainey began to respond, but Dr. Shaffer raised a hand to silence her.

"I'm not questioning your loyalty to your friend Farrell Cole or your love for these children. I can see how much you care for them, believe me." She leaned forward in her chair. "I'm only suggesting you think about why *you* want to be here, not why the Coles elected you, or even why Tim and Riley might have reason to be happy about it." She had nodded in finality and placed the notebook on the table at her side. Obviously, the session had come to an end.

Those last five minutes had haunted Lainey ever since that night. What am I doing here? she'd asked herself over and over. Was she giving these children something they needed, or, after the greatest tragedy they could ever experience, was she going to prove the biggest cheat of all?

The reality of where this question could lead horrified her. Unwilling to think about it any longer, she stood up suddenly and returned to Farrell's dresser. Hastily, she tore open the bottom drawer, and began pulling cotton sweaters out in piles. She pushed forward, erasing every thought from her head. Only when the chest was completely bare did she slide over a large cardboard box and begin restacking the clothing for storage. As she began to refold a red cashmere sweater that had come undone, a shiny metal object dropped down to the floor.

Lainey bent down to retrieve it, then turned it over in her hand. It was an oversized silver key, much heavier than a normal housekey. How odd, she thought, noticing the marking *ST-T* in a fanciful script decorating one side in raised black lettering. On the other side was the number 1012. Thinking little about it, she eased it into the pocket of her jeans, and continued packing the carton.

It was after five by the time Lainey took the cartons upstairs to the attic. She had left the bedroom looking just as she had found it, at least from the outside. In fact, the kids probably wouldn't even notice that anything had changed while they were gone, she thought, as she pushed the boxes across the bare wooden floor into a neat pile in one corner. At least Farrell and John's clothes were packed away where, someday, when Tim and Riley were ready, they could go through all of it and take what they wanted.

One step at a time, Lainey said to herself, feeling

pleased that something had been accomplished. She was on her way back downstairs when she heard Penn's car in the driveway.

"How was it?" she called out as she met both children in the kitchen.

"We had hot dogs and soda and big chocolate bars," Riley said excitedly.

Tim's response was less enthusiastic. "The first movie sucked and the second one really sucked," he answered, nodding at Lainey briefly before walking out of the room.

"Siskel and Ebert," Penn said, laughing as he entered and made his way over to the refrigerator where he pulled out a Coke.

Lainey smiled. "Since they're such appreciative little things, how would you feel about staying with them again tonight? I have something in the city I'd really like to go to."

"Sorry." Penn didn't sound sorry at all. He poured the soda into a glass and gulped it down. "I'm supposed to be somewhere in half an hour." He shrugged his shoulders and returned the bottle to the refrigerator.

Lainey watched him leave. She should have known better than to ask.

"Can I have something to eat?" Riley made herself comfortable at the kitchen table.

Lainey looked at her and smiled. "I can't believe you're still hungry after all the junk your uncle fed you."

"I'm a growing girl," Riley answered contentedly.

At least one of these children is capable of a moment's happiness, Lainey thought gratefully, basking in the normalcy of the exchange. "How about some carrot sticks to tide you over until dinner?"

"Okay," Riley said, reaching for a spoon that had been

left on the table and pushing it across so it came almost to the edge without falling off the other side.

Lainey felt an unexpected lump welling up in her throat. The almost-but-not-quite game was one that the kids had often played when their parents were still alive. John had always claimed to be disapproving, but actually all of them, including Lainey, had indulged during long Sunday morning breakfasts, with every piece of silverware a possible source of ammunition. She turned away from Riley, concentrating on the vegetable bin in an effort to control her emotions.

"How would you feel about staying at the Gisondis' tonight?" Lainey asked as she pulled a bag of carrots out of the drawer and carried it to the sink. She picked up the peeler, which was drying in the dish rack. "I have something I'd like to do, and I thought staying with your friends might be more fun than a sitter."

Riley made a face. "Yecchh."

Lainey looked up. "But you always stay with those kids."

"I *never* stay with those kids." Riley thought about what she'd said. "Only that one time," she added softly.

Tim came into the kitchen, his collection of baseball cards in his hand. "Only one time what?" he asked.

"I thought you guys slept over at the Gisondis' all the time," Lainey said questioningly.

"Are you kidding?" Tim said indignantly. "I don't even like those kids."

Odd, Lainey thought, deciding not to pursue the matter any further. But who was she going to get to baby-sit tonight? She suddenly felt tired. Maybe this isn't the night to go into New York anyway, she decided. She walked over to the telephone intending to call Carla. There were bound to be lots of people eager to use that ticket. She looked out the window just as the sun was beginning to disappear below the horizon. The house was warm and cozy, and the idea of an early dinner with the children was sounding more and more attractive.

Lainey glanced at her watch and grimaced. "Damn."

It had taken her over an hour to go all of about fifteen miles from Meadowview. Either she had taken a wrong turn or something hadn't been right in the store owner's confusing directions. It was late on a Thursday afternoon, and she had returned from work early to pick up a baseball bat Tim needed before the start of softball. The only store that carried it was in Glenvale, a town Lainey had never been in before and hoped she'd never have to try and find again.

Lainey was relieved to see MCLEAN'S in big red letters over the front of a large corner store, happier still to see a sign announcing public parking around the corner. Making the left turn, she drove down a long street, then followed another sign into a parking lot.

She pulled into an empty space just in front of a tall modern building, its entrance marked HOTEL ST.-TROPEZ. Realizing it would cut through to the street where McLean's was located, Lainey approached the entrance, magnetic doors swinging open as she neared.

"Hi!"

Lainey's voice came as a surprise to Carol Anne Gisondi, who was making her way out of the lobby.

Startled, Carol Anne took a moment to register who it was greeting her. Instead of the smile Lainey would have expected, Carol Anne's face took on a nervous, unhappy expression. "Oh, hi," she finally responded.

"Imagine running into you here, when we almost never

bump into each other in Meadowview," Lainey said, attempting to make polite conversation.

"Nice to see you, too." Carol Anne's edginess belied her pleasant words. She quickly peeked at her watch as if she were afraid she was late for an appointment.

"What are you doing here?" Lainey asked.

The young woman looked blank for a moment. "Oh, there was some stuff I had to do for J.J."

Lainey began to describe the trouble she'd experienced trying to locate the town when she noticed the hotel's logo above the reception desk. She recognized it immediately. That key she'd found in Farrell's drawer, it must have been from this hotel, she thought, smiling with the satisfaction of one small mystery solved.

"Boy, oh, boy," she said to Carol Anne, interrupting her own story, "you and Farrell must have really liked this hotel. She even had a key to this place. Did you used to come here together?"

Carol Anne's face reddened abruptly. "I have an appointment," she added almost rudely, moving past Lainey quickly and exiting the building without further explanation.

Now what was that about? Lainey wondered, making her way across the lobby to the front entrance, then going outside and over to McLean's. She asked for and got the Louisville Slugger that Tim had requested, before returning to the parking lot, this time going the long way around the block.

She mentally replayed the conversation with Carol Anne Gisondi as she started the engine, suddenly feeling uneasy. What is it I'm worried about exactly? she asked herself as she drove toward Meadowview, the trip back magically uncomplicated this time.

It was as if the unanswered questions were popping up

everywhere. Not that any one of them seemed to have anything to do with anything, she reassured herself, as she arrived home, pulled her jacket off and began boiling a pot of water for spaghetti.

But her anxiety seemed to grow. What was with Carol Anne this afternoon, and why on earth would Farrell have sent her kids off to stay with her on a school night, when they'd never gone there before? It was both odd and miraculously convenient that the children were out of the house on that terrible night. Had they been sleeping at home, the whole family would have died. She felt an icy stab of horror at the thought and pushed it away.

Lainey opened a box of linguine, pouring the entire pound in, just as Farrell had always done. Why did I do that? she thought sadly, remembering that only she and the two kids would eat tonight. In the old days, John Cole would have polished off half a box all by himself. She saw John in her mind's eye, reaching for his second, then third helping early Sunday evening, the children's homework lying about the table in untidy piles, Farrell dressed in jeans and a T-shirt, fresh from whatever Sunday afternoon game Tim or Riley had participated in. But the image of John brought up the other unanswered question, the fight Mrs. Miles had mentioned right before the accident.

Lainey sponged off the table and set down the plates and silverware, adding three paper napkins from a side drawer.

"Dinner in ten minutes," she called upstairs, hearing a light tap at the back door.

"Anybody home?"

Sugar Taplinger's unmistakable contralto rang out.

Lainey let her in, reaching out for the plate of chocolate chip cookies being offered as a prize.

Lainey sniffed in pleasure. "Just baked?" she asked, inhaling their warmth.

"Ten minutes ago," Sugar answered, walking over to the table and pulling out a chair. "What's for dinner?"

"Spaghetti," Lainey answered. "You interested?"

Sugar smiled cheerily. "Don't worry. I'm gone in one minute. Helmut's taking me out tonight. Open rib night at Smokey's."

"You really would be welcome."

Lainey sounded like some artificial version of herself, a fact that did not escape Sugar. She peered at Lainey.

"What's with you? Everything okay?"

Lainey started to demur, but stopped herself. In fact, she needed to talk about this, to make some kind of sense of things. She thought of asking about Carol Anne, then realized how catty it would sound.

"Sugar . . ." Lainey hesitated as she thought how to phrase it. "Do you mind if I ask you something?"

"Anything but my age or my weight," was Sugar's reply.

Lainey felt awkward suddenly. How could she trespass on John and Farrell this way? Yet she found herself going forward. "Was there anything . . . unusual going on with Farrell and John before the accident?"

"Unusual?" Sugar looked at her in surprise. "Why're you asking?"

Lainey shrugged. "I don't know," she said haltingly. "Actually, I had an odd conversation with Mrs. Miles. She said something about the two of them fighting, something to the effect of John not being quite himself."

Sugar looked at her thoughtfully. There seemed to be a long silence before she answered. "Well," she finally said, pushing herself out of the chair and coming over to Lainey, "as long as you're asking." She lowered her voice to a whisper. "I was plenty worried about Farrell right before they died. Not that there was anything wrong with her, mind you. But John—he was another story."

Lainey looked at her quizzically. "What do you mean?"

"Frankly, he was a madman, at her all the time, angry about nothing." Sugar crossed her arms in front of her massive chest. "You know," she said quietly, "the night they died, they'd been fighting like cats and dogs. I could hear them all the way across to my house. I hate to think that it was possible, but . . ."

Lainey felt herself go pale. "What are you suggesting?" she asked, afraid of what the answer would be.

Sugar looked her straight in the eye. "I've never said this out loud before, knowing what it could do to those kids." She inclined her head toward the ceiling as if to indicate the children upstairs. "The notion that John arranged for them to die that night, the very idea that their father could have murdered their mother. . . . Why, it would destroy Tim and Riley."

Lainey looked at her in horror.

"We'll never know," Sugar said sadly, turning away from Lainey. "No one will ever know."

Lainey barely noticed Sugar's walking out the back door; nor did she see the spaghetti starting to boil over the sides of the pot. It was only the sounds of Tim and Riley bounding down the stairway that reminded her to breathe.

Chapter 20

There was a rapid flurry of knocks on the door. Sugar crossed the room quickly to answer it, her mouth set in a frown at the knowledge of who it would be. Carol Anne had always been a colossal pain in the ass, which was pretty much what Sugar had expected when she initially recruited her. Still, in terms of the business, that was okay; Sugar knew how to handle Carol Anne's sort of jittery personality, and otherwise she was fine, just as Sugar had predicted she would be. But ever since the Coles' deaths, she had been driving Sugar crazy.

It's not like I had a choice, she thought. If there had been any other alternative, she never would have selected Carol Anne to be the one to call Farrell and invite her children to stay over that night. But there was no one else who could fit the bill in providing a place for those kids at the last minute, certainly no one else Farrell knew and trusted. Carol Anne had done what Sugar instructed her to do, but when the Coles were found dead the following day, she had gone completely to pieces.

Hell, she should be glad I didn't tell her what was going to happen, Sugar thought in annoyance. I spared her from having to worry about being an accomplice. Fortunately, Carol Anne's extensive debts—which she kept secret from her husband—ensured that she wasn't in a position to either quit the business or go to the police.

The whole thing had been so easy to pull off, really. She'd had a good plan, and she followed it. Appearing at the Coles' house on the pretense of dropping off the coffee cake, it had been a simple matter to tell Farrell she would let herself out, instead heading down to the basement to inspect the heating system and unlock the window so she could get back in later that night. When she returned after dark, she found it child's play to alter the damper. Years of being the sole caretaker of her mother's house had taught her a lot. That, plus a few hours at the Meadowview Public Library, had enabled her to make the furnace malfunction appear accidental. She had left the Coles' basement knowing that virtually no one would recognize it as having been tampered with.

But Carol Anne's spineless personality might lead her to give the whole thing away. So far she'd been all right. She'd even done a fairly convincing job when she told the police it was Farrell who had called *her* that night to ask if the kids could sleep over at the Gisondis', instead of the other way around. At first, she'd balked when Sugar informed her that that was the way it would have to go, but Sugar quickly illustrated how Carol Anne herself would become a suspect if everyone knew she had so deliberately removed the kids from harm's way that night.

It hadn't taken long for Carol Anne to understand that she had no choice but to go along. Sugar smiled as she recalled the flash of anger in Carol Anne's eyes when she finally realized exactly how trapped she was. First sign of spunk she ever showed, Sugar thought in amusement.

She opened the door to see Carol Anne standing there, dressed for her appointment with Lester Altman, her

Thursday afternoon regular. She had requested that Sugar meet her at the suite fifteen minutes early to discuss something. All the girls knew that Sugar rarely came to the suite herself when anyone else was around. She employed a maid to change the sheets and clean up frequently, a mousy-looking, quiet girl from Mexico, in the country illegally, and only too happy to take the large cash payments in return for her silence.

Sugar herself preferred to conduct business from the private telephone line she'd had installed in her office upstairs at home. It was a place into which Helmut rarely ventured. During the day, she set up appointments, went over the finances, and handled whatever else needed her attention. No one from her professional world was permitted to call her at night or on weekends, so appointments were generally scheduled in advance. She had assumed the arrangement would cost her business, and that was simply the price she'd have to pay. But it turned out that making it more difficult to schedule a session with one of her girls actually added to the cachet of her operation.

"Hi, hon," Sugar said warmly to Carol Anne, forcing a welcoming smile and extending an arm to usher her inside. "What's up?"

"Oh, Sugar." Carol Anne was obviously upset, but there was also relief on her face at the sight of the other woman, as if her problem would now be solved. "We have to talk."

Sugar helped Carol Anne take off her blue blazer. She wore an inexpensive beige silk shirtwaist dress. Sugar knew that beneath the dress was the red lace push-up bra and garter belt Lester Altman preferred, and Carol Anne would be wearing only those when she answered the door for him. Occasionally, Sugar wondered what the hell these men saw in the annoyingly nervous and boring Carol Anne. But she simply had to remind herself that some women's behavior in bed could be a big surprise, and, for whatever reason, Carol Anne fit into that category. She had three regular customers and very few complaints from any of the other men she entertained.

Carol Anne chewed unhappily on a fingernail as she dropped down onto the couch. "I ran into Lainey Wolfe here at the hotel yesterday. I couldn't help it—she was just there, smack dab right in front of me."

"And?" Sugar prodded, careful to cover her shock.

Carol Anne turned a worried face to Sugar. "She was asking me questions about what I was doing here, and what *Farrell* had been doing here."

Sugar took a few steps closer. "Farrell?" she responded sharply.

Carol Anne nodded. "She said we obviously were having a good time here, that we were up to something. She was smiling and going on about it. Sugar, *she knows*."

Sugar pursed her lips. "I don't believe it."

"But she *does*. She was being, like, subtle, but she was trying to let me know, I could tell. She even knew that Farrell had a key." Carol Anne got up and started pacing around the room, picking things up and putting them down again. "I knew something terrible would happen. People don't get away with"—her voice dropped down to a whisper—"things like this, like Farrell and John."

Anguished, she stopped and looked at Sugar. "Why did you do it? Those two children . . ."

Sugar could see from her eyes that Carol Anne was suddenly thinking of her own two children, wondering if they might wind up in the same situation as Farrell's. "Listen, I keep my mouth shut, although I know I'm going to hell for this. Straight to hell." She started to cry. "I'm just afraid I'm going to go to jail, too."

Sugar came over to put an arm around her. "Hon, you just let me take care of things. You're not going to hell, because you didn't do anything. All you did was help those children that night, keep them safe. Whatever else was going on isn't anything you want to know about. But believe me, what happened was absolutely necessary. If Farrell and John *hadn't* been stopped, you can be sure you *would* have wound up in jail. And where would that have left your kids?"

Carol Anne's face crumpled, the battle between her guilt and the desire to preserve herself plainly visible.

"Now, sweetheart," Sugar said soothingly, "you're getting all upset for no reason. Nothing's going to come of this. Forget about it. We can't undo the past." She patted Carol Anne's cheek. "You did the right thing by telling me."

Carol Anne gave her a wild look. "You're not going to do anything to Farrell's friend?"

Sugar laughed. "Don't be ridiculous."

"Oh, God, I can't stand it." Carol Anne sat down in a chair and stared at the floor in misery.

"Pull yourself together." Sugar picked up her purse and retrieved her raincoat from the closet. "Lester will be here soon, and you don't want him to see you like this. Think of the money you'll be making today. On top of that, he *is* a nice guy, isn't he?"

Carol Anne raised her head and looked over at Sugar dully.

"Talk to you later." Sugar gave her a gay wave before leaving.

It was only when she was alone in the elevator that Sugar dropped her cheerful expression and allowed herself to feel the force of her anger. Goddammit, it had been intolerably stupid of her to give Farrell that key. I *had* to go in for the overkill, she thought in fury. It had been fun that day, knowing Farrell would be even more spooked by the notion of having a key in order to come frequently to the suite; it was just the added bit of toying with Farrell's mind that Sugar hadn't been able to resist. She'd intended to get the key back. But how was she supposed to know all hell would break loose, and the chain of connections would go right back to John Cole and his bitch of a wife.

Now there was Lainey Wolfe to contend with. Sugar fumed, furious that she would have to worry about yet another meddling idiot. She had been careful to stay close to Farrell's friend, making herself useful, knowing it could be important to maintain access to the Cole household. Up until now, she believed everything was under control. It had been an unpleasant surprise when Lainey threw that question at her about Farrell and John fighting, but Sugar had been convinced she'd handled it perfectly. Suggesting that John had engineered the "accident" would have horrified Farrell's buddy just enough to make her drop the whole issue, of that Sugar was certain. She wasn't about to do in those two kids by broadcasting to the world that their father might be a killer.

But now Carol Anne was talking about Lainey's having the key to the suite. There was no way to know if she realized what it was for, or what Farrell had been doing there. Carol Anne was convinced that Lainey knew what was going on, but Carol Anne's judgment was hardly reliable.

Of course, that didn't mean Sugar could take any chances. By the time she got to her car, she knew what her next step had to be. Before she did anything else, she needed to get that key back. This was the perfect time, too. Lainey would be at work in New York, and the kids were still at school. The only potential problem was the housekeeper; Sugar didn't know which days she came. Well, she could easily come up with an excuse if she ran into the woman.

Going close to eighty on the highway, she pulled off at the exit for Meadowview, reviewing her options, her fury rising with every passing minute at the flood of trouble these people had brought to her door. She arrived at her house as quickly as the winding roads allowed, and parked her car in the garage. Pausing to take a few deep breaths, she slowed her pace in case anyone was watching, then casually crossed her backyard to come around to the Cole house. Trying the back door, she was pleased to find it unlocked, and let herself in.

"Hello? Anybody home?" she cheerfully called out.

Silence. Sugar closed the door behind her and went swiftly upstairs to Farrell's room. Looking around, she assessed the situation. Then she went over and yanked open the dresser's top drawer. Empty. Startled, Sugar stared into it for a moment. Then she pulled open the other drawers. All empty. But, of course, it made sense. By now, somebody would have gotten rid of their things. In fact, that was probably the way Lainey had come across the key, rummaging through Farrell's drawers.

But what had she done with it? Thrown it away? Without realizing it, Sugar shook her head as if answering her own question. No, not if Lainey thought it had some significance.

She stood there, considering. Then she turned and went to the guest room where she knew Lainey was sleeping. She surveyed the surfaces of the dresser and tables, then opened each of the four dresser drawers and inspected the clothes within, careful to leave it all undisturbed. Lainey's small jewelry box was in the lower drawer. Slowly, Sugar sifted through the chains and earrings, trying not to alter their casual arrangement. The key wasn't there either.

Frustrated, she turned to the closet. Most of the clothes were on hangers, but there were several hooks along one side of the wall where Lainey had hung a bathrobe, a nightshirt, and a pair of jeans. Sugar reached into the jeans' front pocket. Her fingers closed around a slender piece of metal. Definitely a key. Pulling it out, she turned it over to see the *ST-T* written in script.

She smiled.

Chapter 21

"NBC's lucky to have you." Doris Beckley took a last sip of her old-fashioned and tapped the empty glass on the table for emphasis.

"You're lucky to be young enough so they still want you."

Hugh Beckley's muttered response was just loud enough for Penn to catch. Good for you, woe is me. The familiar anthem Penn recalled from his youth hadn't changed by so much as a note.

Nor had the Wild Boar Inn, the restaurant the Beckley family had eaten in every Sunday night since Penn could remember. His mother would order the filet of sole, his father would pat his stomach and say, "Ah, I might as well go for it," then point to the standing rib roast on the menu and ask for it to be "done to a turn," whatever the hell that meant. And never once would either of his parents address a single remark to the other.

Penn wondered how they got there every Sunday since he and Farrell had moved out of the house. Did they just walk toward the garage at six twenty-five, or did one or the other actually utter a phrase like "shall we?" in the always silent house.

"Your father and I have something important to discuss with you."

Penn looked at his mother in surprise. Whatever it was she had in mind must be a whopper if they'd managed to talk to each other about it.

"You know how much we admire Lainey, how brave she is to turn her entire life around for our grandchildren . . ." Doris looked out the window as if the dark silhouette of trees could offer up the perfect phrase with which she could continue.

Penn waited her out patiently. He never filled in her sentences. In fact, he never listened to the words; it was the code that lay beneath the words that really mattered. Already, he could read the fact that she did not like Lainey Wolfe. The part about the grandchildren could go in any one of a hundred directions.

"Here's what your mother is trying to say."

Hugh Beckley didn't look at his wife as he took over her conversation. On the other hand, Penn acknowledged thankfully, at least his father wasn't a code kind of guy. Whatever it was he wanted to complain about, he was going to do it clearly enough so he wouldn't be misunderstood.

"Those kids belong with us."

Decoding complete, sir, Penn thought without much amusement.

"And why is that?" He tried to sound impartial, which was difficult given how appalled he was starting to feel.

"They're our grandchildren, damn it." Hugh's sudden burst of anger was quickly replaced by a polite smile as the waitress lay an enormous slab of gray beef in front of him.

All conversation ceased as she continued around the table, delivering a rare club steak to Penn and the pallid-looking sole to his mother. The moment the waitress walked back toward the kitchen, his father returned to his theme.

"It was hard enough to be screwed by *my* parents. I'll be damned if I'll sit by while my daughter screws me, too." As he spoke, Hugh seemed to get even angrier, his face reddening until it was the exact color of Penn's steak.

Penn was disgusted. He'd been hearing his father complain about his own parents all his life. And what had they done? They'd provided him with a highly paid vice presidency in a paper company that made several million dollars a year, and had flourished all the way through the Depression. What they hadn't provided him with was the chairmanship. Hugh Beckley's father had lived well into his nineties. By the time the job was open, Hugh was deemed too old to fill it.

So now, poor Hugh was forced to live on something like half a million dollars per year in interest from the millions he'd inherited at his father's death. That he loathed his wife and found little to occupy his time was, undoubtedly, also his father's doing.

This barely fazed Penn. It was, after all, a very old refrain. But the part about Farrell left him furious.

"What would you have had my sister do?" He rarely engaged in direct confrontation with his parents. But then, he used to drink, which made it so much easier to tune them out. His father would just grow more belligerent, while his mother would simply ignore whatever she didn't want to hear.

"Farrell and John should have wanted the best for their children, same as your mother and I tried to do for the two of you." This time, Hugh included his wife in his glance as he spoke. "Tim and Riley belong with us. End of story."

Penn couldn't keep the edge of anger out of his voice this time. "End of whose story?" he asked.

His father eyed him sharply. "Grandchildren belong with their grandparents," he said with finality.

"So they can sit in a big empty house, watching you two not speak to each other?"

Doris and Hugh both stared at him, his mother in surprise, his father enraged.

"Surely, you can't want your niece and nephew raised by a total stranger?" His father's eyes were burning now. "An unmarried woman in her thirties."

Penn couldn't believe his father's description of Lainey Wolfe. "You mean the stranger who spent half her childhood in your house, the one who was your daughter's best friend?" He placed his hand flat on the table, as if in preparation to stand up.

His mother lay a restraining hand on his. "Your father isn't saying anything against Lainey. We just want what's best for the children. She's not even the same religion."

Enough of this, Penn decided, throwing his napkin onto the table. "I'm glad you two have finally seen fit to speak to each other, but I'll be damned if this sudden unity is going to catapult my niece and nephew back into the mausoleum." He stood up and pushed his chair in to the table. Then he bent over so only his parents would hear what he was about to say. "Short of bringing their parents back to life, Lainey Wolfe is the best thing that could have happened to Tim and Riley. If you two are planning any interference with her guardianship, you'll have to get by me first."

He walked out of the restaurant without looking back. Neither of his parents called after him or made a move to stop him.

As the chill night air hit him, he thought about what he'd said. Well, it was true. Much to his surprise, Lainey had turned out to be terrific. He'd observed her day after day, week after week. However flaky she'd been as a teenager, the adult version had turned out just fine.

More than fine, he admitted to himself as he opened his car door and slid into the front seat.

He visualized her as he started up the engine and pulled out onto North Avenue. So different from Sarita. Different from any woman he'd ever dated. He'd always secretly admired her warmth, even when he'd been an older brother whose sole interest was torturing his sister's best friend. But over the past couple of months, as he'd watch her helping Riley with her spelling or trying to ease Tim out of his hostile gloom, he saw Lainey as simply beautiful.

Not that he ever let Lainey know what he was thinking. Sometimes he offered himself up as a sitter, but most nights, he got home from work and went straight to the carriage house, reading in the privacy of his room. For the past two days, he'd stayed in Manhattan, sleeping at the Stanhope, where the network maintained a room, at work from early in the morning until well into the night on a project involving the revolt at Attica years before. He hadn't even seen Lainey, let alone spoken to her, in days.

But tonight, he realized grimly, he'd better go home to Meadowview. He'd better share at least some of what his parents had said at dinner. If they felt strongly enough to engage in voluntary conversation with each other—as they clearly had since Farrell and John had died—they surely must be planning some kind of action.

It would be his job to protect his niece and nephew

from whatever that turned out to be. And that meant warning Lainey.

It was only nine-thirty when he pulled into the driveway. He could see Lainey through the living room window, seated on the couch, reading. He felt oddly touched by the sight of her, by the notion that Tim and Riley were fast asleep upstairs, that this was his home.

Dressed casually in blue jeans and a black wool pullover, Lainey looked beautiful in the hushed wash of light and shadow blended from various lamps around the room. It was a setting in which she should have looked relaxed, but instead, he noticed an unusual tension in her posture.

He wondered just how much to tell her, half wishing he could go right to bed and say nothing at all. But that wasn't an option. He knocked on the wall before entering the room.

"Knocking? Aren't we formal?" Lainey said sarcastically, looking up as she lay aside a letter on which there seemed to be formal printing.

He eased himself into a chair across from her. "Listen," he said, his voice serious, "I had an interesting conversation with the parents tonight."

Lainey looked at him curiously, although her mind seemed miles away. "And what would that be?"

"Not to scare you, but mater and pater seem to feel that the children belong with them."

"No!" she answered ironically, her eyes widening in mock amazement, as if he were telling her something she already knew. But, in contrast to her sardonic tone, there were tears in her eyes.

"I gather this isn't news." Penn spoke in a manner as guarded as her own, but, as her tears began trailing a path down her cheeks, he ached to comfort her.

Self-consciously wiping the tears away, Lainey held up the letter and passed it over to him. As he read its contents, he realized that his dinner conversation had only been a preview of the main event. This letter was not from them; instead it was from their lawyer, a letter of legal intention to remove custody from Lainey Wolfe and transfer it to Hugh and Doris Beckley. It suggested that if Lainey did not agree within thirty days, court proceedings would begin with all due haste.

When he finished the letter, he noticed Lainey lower her head, bringing her arms around her chest as if to stem her crying.

Penn couldn't stop himself. Within seconds, he had joined her on the couch, throwing his arms around her, comforting her as if she were a child.

"Lainey, honey," he crooned, his hands rising to smooth the hair back from her face, his mouth unexpectedly making contact with her neck as he whispered words of solace. He didn't understand quite why, maybe the honeyed fragrance of her perfume or the silky firmness of her skin, but suddenly he was kissing her, his lips traveling up her throat, his tongue gently tasting the delicacy of her lips before crushing her mouth with his own.

He felt her tongue meet his own in a fevered longing, as her arms wound around his neck. The passion came quickly, as if it were a continuation of their first time together. The swell of her breasts, the mysterious hollows beneath her neck. It was all so familiar, so incredibly right, as if they'd been together for all of time. For long moments, they clung together, tasting, exploring, savoring each other with every whispered caress. As they finally pulled apart, Penn looked deeply into her eyes, his gaze a reflection of all he knew he'd been feeling for so very long.

"Lainey, it's going to be all right. They can't get the kids away from you. They can't force you to do anything you don't want. I promise, we're going to make everything all right. You and Tim and Riley . . ." He paused with the struggle to find the right words. "You're the legal guardian, and there's nothing my parents can do about it, not if I have anything to say about it."

Lainey looked back at him as if in a daze. Her hands fell from around his neck, and she sat back, at a distance from him now.

"You don't understand," she said almost frantically.

His eyes were stubborn, as his hand once again trailed down her cheek. "Oh, yes, I do."

"Penn . . ." She took a last glance at him and stood up, moving away from the couch to stand behind a chair. "I'm not crying because I'm afraid of losing Tim and Riley. It's just that I think, maybe, your parents are right."

"What?" Unconsciously, Penn's fingers curled into a fist.

"I think I should probably take that job in California." Her eyes searched his face as if wishing she could remove the condemnation she was beginning to see there. "I mean, maybe I could take them with me while I worked on Marissa." Her words came in a rush now. "They would love Los Angeles . . . it's sunny and warm all the time, and maybe it would be good for them to get away from all the memories here."

He recognized the look on her face, that wounded deer effect she'd always had as a kid when Farrell was bullying her into some activity she wasn't quite ready to perform. But instead of sympathy, he felt a rising fury. Had he lost his mind? This woman cared nothing for him, and less for his niece and nephew.

"The terms of guardianship were absolutely clear," he said coldly as he, too, stood up. "You agreed to move into this house, to raise the children in circumstances that were warm and familiar. To love them as a parent." He glared at her. "I guess that concept is somewhere out of your reach."

Lainey's voice broke as she answered. "I *do* love them. I'm just not sure if that's enough." Her eyes beseeched him. "I'm not completely certain your parents are wrong."

"Fucking unbelievable." Penn shook his head. "You never change, do you?" His eyes blazed. "Well, I guess this time the joke's on me, because for once you had me fooled."

"Stop it," Lainey cried, covering her eyes with her hands.

Penn regarded her with disgust. "I actually thought you'd become an adult, but no." His voice rose to a shrill falsetto, a cruel imitation of her. "I can't marry you, Julian, I can't live up to your expectations, oh, Farrell, my best friend . . ."

That he was wounding Lainey horribly was obvious, but Penn couldn't stop. He didn't know who he was angrier at—Lainey for showing her habitual stripes or himself for falling for it. For falling for her, he acknowledged bitterly.

Well, that was over with, as of right now. "How did Farrell put up with you for all those years?" He strode to the far side of the room.

Lainey shuddered at the sound of her friend's name. Even in his anger, he could see the pain that comment had caused her. But that wasn't what she expressed when she answered him.

She stood, her feet firmly rooted on the carpet, still

holding the chair for support, but composed now. "And just who are you to judge?" The words came out icily. "I think those privileges are revoked when your blood alcohol level reaches a thousand." She folded the newspaper and stood up. Then she walked toward the doorway. Penn's voice reached her just before she was out of the room.

"If you ever paid attention to anyone other than yourself, you might have noticed that I've been sober since I returned from England."

Lainey looked back as if she were about to argue, then thought better of it.

"I'm sorry I was stupid enough to tell my parents that the kids were better off with you," he yelled. "I must have been out of my mind."

Without saying another word, he strode right past her and out of the room.

Penn heard the police siren screaming before he noticed the flashing red lights in his rearview mirror. He glanced at the speedometer before braking and pulling to the side of the parkway: eighty-eight miles per hour. That should be worth about two hundred bucks, if not a night in jail, he mused, not even particularly minding the thought. It would be an appropriate end to a spectacularly rotten evening.

"What's your hurry?" The young officer scanned the inside of the car as Penn rolled down the window.

Penn looked at him, McDonough, his nameplate read. He couldn't have been much over twenty-two. "The truth is, I'm not going anywhere at all." He grinned ruefully as he reached into his pocket and extracted his wallet, pulling out his license and registration and handing them through the window.

"Have you had anything to drink?" the policeman asked, leaning down and sniffing the air around Penn as if to answer his own question.

"Not in months," Penn answered.

Apparently satisfied, McDonough wrote up the speeding ticket and handed it to Penn, along with his papers. "The state limit's fifty-five. I advise you to stick to it in the future." He nodded sternly one more time before returning to his car and pulling away.

Penn stayed on the shoulder of the road. He didn't feel like driving anymore. He didn't feel much like anything except having a long drink.

What's the best antidote for a ticket? he wondered, draping his hands over the wheel and closing his eyes. Scotch, maybe. No, perhaps a vodka and tonic, he decided, imagining the pleasure of sitting at a bar and savoring each swallow, the tension easing from his body, the worry from his mind.

He could almost taste the cold liquid running down his throat, warming his chest, then his belly. Unbidden, the image of the tall glass was replaced by a vision of Lainey Wolfe. He could feel his mouth once again on her neck as he inhaled her sweetness, indulging in the pure pleasure of her.

Whoa, buddy, he thought, forcing his eyes open, opening the car door for air. When he saw the lights of an approaching car, he slammed the door shut and sat straight up at the wheel.

No more of this, he decided. One drink will hurt a lot less than fantasizing about goddamn Lainey Wolfe. He turned the key in the ignition and pulled onto the highway. O'Henry's would still be open, he thought, picturing the dark wooden bar with satisfaction. It took only five minutes to get to the exit, and another two to pull into the parking lot.

He could practically feel the alcohol going through him as he hurried out of the car in a haze of expectation. The raucous sounds of a live band assaulted him before he'd even reached the entrance, matched by the familiar odors of beer and perspiration as he pulled the door open.

"Hey, watch it!" A young man in a plaid shirt and jeans yelled, as Penn nearly collided with him.

The sound of the man's voice startled Penn. For a moment, he stood there, taking in the irate look on the man's face.

What am I doing? he thought suddenly, staring in at the dark, crowded bar as if wondering how he got there. He looked carefully around him, noticing now the loneliness and desperation clear on so many of the faces of the men lined up around the bar. He turned around and walked away, relieved not to have gotten any further.

He approached his car, not getting inside, but leaning against the hood. Breathing slowly, he tried to clear his head. He couldn't let himself do this. There were more important things than speeding tickets or rotten parents or even beautiful women. There was no way he could let his anger at Lainey allow him to slide back into drinking. No way at all.

With difficulty, he erased her image from his mind, replacing it with a picture of Tim and Riley. When she left, they would be his responsibility, one he had to live up to.

And he had to do it sober. He thought about what that meant. Most of the time, it wasn't so hard. But if a night like tonight could lead him to the doorstep of O'Henry's, maybe it was time to get some help. He glanced around the parking lot, his eyes alighting on the phone booth he remembered across the way. Fishing around his pocket for a quarter, he walked over to it and picked up the receiver.

Dialing the number for information, he felt only relief as he heard himself ask for the number of Alcoholics Anonymous.

Chapter 22

Lainey could hear Penn's voice coming from the family room as she hurried down the stairs, still in the process of buckling her belt.

"... the story is about accounting firms defrauding their corporate customers. It should air in another month or two."

Riley's high voice interrupted. "What's 'defrauding'?"

"Cheating, honey," Penn answered. "Anyway, that's where I met her, while I was producing this piece."

Charlie Cole spoke next in an amused tone. "Is she one of the cheating accountants?"

Penn laughed. "No, she's a friend of Tamara Bourne, one of our reporters. Tamara and I were working on the story when Nancy came to the office. They were supposed to have lunch together."

"And you wound up going along . . ." Charlie supplied knowingly.

"Right." Penn smiled.

"Is she a reporter, too, Uncle Penn?" Riley wanted to know.

"No, baby, she's actually a singer. She even has a record out."

Riley's voice rose in awe. "Really? A record?"

"She even has a record out." Lainey mimicked Penn's

words under her breath in a nasty singsong. Tugging on her shirt cuffs beneath her navy blue blazer, she stopped at John's study and stuck her head in the room. Tim was inside, sitting at John's desk, playing DOOM on his father's computer.

"I'm going now, sweetheart," she said to him.

"Okay." His attention riveted by the screen, he gave a brief wave without looking at her.

"Have fun with your uncle, but try to get to sleep before dawn."

He nodded, not listening. She shut the door. Unfortunately, there wasn't much chance the children would have even half that much fun with their Uncle Charlie. He had obviously been operating from his better instincts when he agreed to baby-sit, but, as with everything that had to do with Tim and Riley, he would have been delighted to find some way out of it. *I guess I should be grateful he actually showed up,* Lainey reflected.

She walked around the corner to the family room. Riley was sitting on the couch, her legs crossed underneath her, while the two men were standing near the television set, deep in conversation. Penn was freshly shaved, dressed casually but neatly in a light blue shirt and tweed jacket. He looked to Lainey just the way someone should look before going out on what promised to be a good date—*expectant* was the only word she could think of for it.

He gave her a quick once-over and smiled. Since their blowup the week before, they'd maintained an uneasy truce. "Well, Riley, look how lovely Lainey is this evening."

Lainey ignored him, turning to Charlie. "Thanks for helping out tonight. Just make sure Riley brushes her teeth before bed. They're very self-sufficient otherwise. I

left the number of the restaurant I'll be at on the kitchen
table if you need me for some reason."

"I'll leave my office number, too, if you want," Penn
offered. "I could check in a couple of times there."

Lainey shot him an annoyed glance. "That's not necessary. It doesn't make much sense to leave a message on
your voice mail, when I'll be just twenty minutes away."

Charlie was unconcerned. "Fine, whatever."

Lainey came over and knelt to give Riley a hug and
kiss. "Good night, honey pie. I love you and I'll come in
to kiss you when I get back."

Riley gave her a tight squeeze. "Night."

They all turned at the sound of a car honking outside.

"There's Megan." With a last smile for Riley, Lainey
started out of the room.

"Have a good time," Penn called out behind her.

Her response was biting. "I will. And I have no doubt
you will, too."

Opening the front door, she stepped outside and
paused. Why on earth am I being so much meaner to him
than usual? But, of course, she knew the answer. She'd
been unreasonably irritable ever since he had informed
her that he was going out on a date and couldn't baby-sit.

It was foolish of her to assume he would be available
to baby-sit on a Saturday night with just a week's notice.
But after continually telling Megan how much she would
like Carla Mirsky, Megan had finally suggested a night
out, and this was the one night all three of them could
make it. Penn had said he was sorry, but he and his date
were going to a dinner party, and he didn't feel he could
back out on such short notice. Megan had already hired
her own sitter, and Carla had shifted another dinner date
in order to drive up; Lainey really didn't want to cancel
on them. Luckily, Charlie called to ask about the kids—

an infrequent occurrence, although Lainey tried to give him credit for not disappearing altogether from their lives. She seized the opportunity to suggest he spend an evening with them.

But she'd been annoyed with Penn ever since. And it wasn't that she resented his being unavailable to baby-sit.

She approached Megan's car, parked at the end of the walk, and gave a smile and a wave. Christ, she thought, I can't believe it. I'm jealous. Penn has a date, and I don't want him to go. I want him to be in that house with me. I want him all to myself.

She reached for the car handle. Oh, boy, was she in trouble.

"*Yeah.* Die, you moron."

Tim kept up a steady stream of comments and sound effects as he jerked the mouse back and forth, watching the results of his motions on the computer screen. He'd been playing DOOM for over an hour now, and he was getting hungry, even though he'd had dinner before Lainey went out. Maybe he'd take a break and get something to eat, then come back for a while before he went to bed.

Riley, the one who would normally be at the computer on a Saturday night, was in the other room with Uncle Charlie. She was thrilled to spend time with him. Tim shook his head disgustedly. She didn't know enough to realize that Uncle Charlie didn't give a damn about the two of them. Tim had never realized it before, either, but it was pretty obvious now. Just because he was Dad's brother doesn't mean he has to love us, he told Riley silently.

He exited the game, playing distractedly with the

computer, calling up directories. Heck, he thought, what difference did it make? If Riley wanted to pretend Uncle Charlie cared, let her go ahead. It didn't—

Tim stopped and stared. The computer screen showed a directory of file names that were actually dates. He scanned them. 93JUNE. 94SEPT. The earliest seemed to be 92JAN. With his finger, he tracked them. There was 92FEB. 92MAR. They were all there, up to the present.

He had found his dad's computer diary.

He knew his father had kept a diary on the computer; he and Riley often heard him mention it. But they would never have dreamt of trying to read his files. When his father had first given them permission to use his computer, it was accompanied by a long lecture about responsibility. He could remember his dad's deep voice, telling them they were old enough to be held accountable if they erased anything. Of course, he had backups for everything important, but that wasn't the point, he reminded them. They were not to fool around on the machine, they were not to pry, they were to respect the fact that it was his computer. If they couldn't abide by those rules, that would be the end of their privileges on it. They had known he wasn't kidding, and they had been careful. Besides, they weren't interested in anything he might have on the computer; they had their own stuff they wanted to do.

Tim had always figured the diary was about business or law cases or something. He moved the cursor up and down, randomly selecting a file. 94JULY. *Retrieve.*

7/1 The Farmer case is dragging on, as I guessed it would, and Evan Palmer isn't working out the way I'd hoped.

Business, just like he thought. Boring. Tim exited the file. 94NOV. *Retrieve.*

11/1 To come home at the end of the day and see my kids is like a small miracle. Their battles to triumph in their world—it's beautiful and sad at the same time. When Tim showed me his new skates, he was so excited, I just wanted to hug him. But I knew he wouldn't like it if I did.

Tim leaned back in the chair, fighting the urge to cry. *Dad.* Swallowing hard, he got out of the file. Maybe he would look at that one another time.

February. He located it, but he hesitated for a moment. This was the last month of entries, the month they died. Maybe there was something in this file. . . . His heart began to beat faster. It could be a big mistake to look. Maybe it was better not to know. It was *definitely* better not to know. But he couldn't help himself.

Retrieve. He skipped down to the last page, then moved the cursor back up until he saw where that day's entry began. It was a short one.

2/16 It's too raw, now. I can't even get myself to write it down. It's as if Farrell purposely set out to destroy us. She's betrayed me and the kids, and I have no idea why. It makes me sick to think about it, so I'm desperately trying not to. I want to believe I can get past it, that somehow we can endure it and work things out. But the truth is, I'm so pissed off, I could kill her with my bare hands.

Tim stared at the screen, reading it a second time, his stomach knotting up with fear. *I could kill her.* So it was true. Whatever it was they had been fighting about that morning, his dad had been so furious, he had gone and done it. He had actually killed her. And killed himself right along with her.

Tim had known it all along.

"No, Dad, no," he whispered urgently, as if his words

could change what he saw in front of him. "Please. She didn't mean it, whatever it was, I know it."

Nothing happened. There was only the hum of the computer screen in the otherwise quiet room.

Tim felt numb. Another horrible thought occurred to him. If anybody else found out what his father had done . . . He shut his eyes, overwhelmed by the idea. No, he couldn't let that happen.

He tore open the desk drawer where he knew his father had kept the floppy discs. Selecting one, he quickly inserted it into the computer, and pressed a series of commands. It didn't take long. He copied February's file onto the floppy disc, and erased it completely from the computer's hard drive. If anyone called up this directory, they would find the files intact all the way up through last January. Only this one month's file was gone, and since it was the last thing to be entered, there was no gap in sequence. No one would know it had ever been there.

Sticking the floppy inside his shirt, he turned off the computer, then ran up to his room and hid the disc in the back of his closet, in the bottom of the box containing his old Power Ranger collection. There. The secret was still safe.

He heard Riley talking in the hall, being accompanied by Uncle Charlie as she went to brush her teeth. Tim stood there, thinking. Maybe Uncle Charlie could be of some use after all.

Waiting until Riley was in bed, Tim went downstairs to the family room, and waited on the couch for his uncle. The television was on, and when Charlie returned, he sat down, intending to watch.

"Hey, Tim," he said absently, as he settled himself into an armchair.

"Uncle Charlie, could I talk to you a minute?" Tim asked.

"Sure." His eyes still on the screen, Charlie reached for the open can of beer on the table nearby.

Tim hesitated, not even sure what it was he wanted to ask. "Did my parents fight?"

Charlie glanced over at him. "I don't know much about that area. They sure looked happy all the time, didn't they? But, Jeez, I never heard of a married couple who didn't fight, so I suppose, yeah, they must have."

Tim considered that. It wasn't much help. He guessed he was going to have to get into this a little further. He would have to ask about that particular fight, about what he knew was the key to the whole mess. Taking a deep breath, he came out with it.

"Did my dad like sweets?"

"Sweets?" Charlie gave him a puzzled look, then turned back to the television. "Sure." He must have been thinking about it, because, after a minute, he continued, his eyes still on the screen. "When we were kids, I liked chocolate more than he did. Ice cream was more his thing. He usually gave in if there was an extra Devil Dog or something. I'd want to wrestle him for it, but he didn't really seem to care." He gave a short laugh. "I always thought that was wimpy of him."

"But was there some kind of sweet he liked a whole lot, something that would be really important?" Tim urged.

"Huh?" Charlie finally fixed his full attention on Tim. "Like what?"

"Well, it's just that . . ." Tim realized he had no choice but to spell it out. "The day before they died, my parents were having a fight about a sweet. My dad was angry,

angrier than I ever heard him. I'm trying to figure out
why a sweet could get him so mad."

Charlie was staring at him. "The day before they
died?" He seemed to be turning things over in his mind,
but he didn't offer any conclusion. "I don't know," he
finally said quietly, as if talking more to himself than to
Tim. "They were fighting over food? That makes no
sense."

"It wasn't just food," Tim said. "It was something particular. I heard my dad say 'a sweet.' He didn't say what
it was, though."

"I don't know what it could have been about." Charlie
gave Tim a penetrating look. "Are you saying it had
something to do with them dying?"

"No, no," Tim said hastily. "That was an accident. I
was just wondering." Words tumbled out in his effort to
change his uncle's train of thought. "It was just too bad,
you know, them fighting on their last day together."

Charlie rested his head against the back of the chair
and sighed. Then he turned back to Tim with a shrug. "It
could have been anything. People fight all the time about
all sorts of things. I guess they were no different. Who
knows?"

Nobody, Tim thought miserably. Nobody but Mom
and Dad. All I know is that it made Dad mad enough to
do what he did.

He got up. "I'm going to bed."

Charlie took a sip of his beer. "Good night, sport."

Tim left. Please, God, he prayed silently as he trudged
upstairs, I'll do anything if you just make sure nobody
ever finds out what really happened. Dad wasn't a bad
guy, he wasn't. Something made him do it. *Something.*
Mom wasn't bad, either. She loved us. If she did something wrong, there was a reason for that, too.

Going into his room, he picked up the baseball mitt and ball that rested on his desk. He slipped on the glove as he sat down on a chair next to the window. Looking out at the night, he tossed the ball into his mitt over and over again.

Chapter 23

"But, Tim, it's your favorite!"

Doris Beckley's disappointment was almost palpable, as her grandson took the Power Ranger she'd given him and tucked it back inside its colorful container. All the birthday presents he'd received were lying neatly, untouched, in a large circle on the lawn.

The trees were in bloom all around the perimeter of the yard, and red and purple balloons and crepe paper made a festive addition to the spring flowers, the azalea and irises sprouting gracefully. But all the gifts in the world, all the colors in the rainbow weren't about to bring a smile to Tim Cole. He'd barely noticed the rollerblades Lainey had given him, and even the fishing trip to northern Maine proferred by Penn had elicited only the briefest of smiles.

Lainey watched the interaction between Tim and his grandmother carefully. She felt sorry for Doris Beckley. She should have been able to figure out that Power Rangers were something he'd outgrown years before, but the woman was obviously trying to please him, a task that had proved impossible for anyone over the past two days. Lainey had thought she'd seen some small signs of emotional recovery, but suddenly Tim seemed more unhappy than ever, as if his depression were bottomless.

And no one had been exempt from Tim's aggressive emptiness—not Lainey, not Riley, not even Uncle Penn the Great. Nonetheless, Lainey felt compelled to soften the blow for Doris Beckley. Perhaps a toy fit for a five-year-old, two pairs of flannel pajamas, and a cardigan sweater weren't going to make a ten-year-old's heart beat faster, but no grandmother deserved complete indifference as a thank you.

Lainey wandered over to Doris Beckley's side. "Those football pajamas are going to make him happy every time he puts them on," Lainey said, smiling self-consciously.

Doris looked at her coldly. "I know what my grandson likes," she said, turning away and leaving Lainey to her own devices.

Why did I bother? Lainey asked herself, walking across the lawn to help Riley cut her second piece of birthday cake.

"This is great, but when it's time for my birthday, can you make it strawberry frosting instead of chocolate?" Riley held out her plate, not even waiting for Lainey to lay it down before grabbing it out of her hands and biting into the cake. "Thanks," she said, her mouth stuffed, as she walked over to where Tim's friends were starting up a touch football game.

Penn strode up beside Lainey and took the knife out of her hands. "When it's time for her birthday, are you going to be within a fifty-mile radius?" He cut a vicious swipe from the devil's food center, still looking at her as if he wished it were she under the knife instead of the cake.

Lainey had no intention of getting into a fight. She'd been preparing this party for days, had invited everyone she could think of, including all the kids in Tim's class, his grandparents, even her own parents so he might feel special. She'd fixed two huge pots of chili, plus a pan of lasagna, carried cases of soda from the supermarket, and had been awake since five-thirty this morning fixing up the backyard so it looked celebratory.

To reward her for her efforts, she received two nasty phone calls from Al Smile, reminding her of the work she hadn't had time to finish on Friday before leaving early to prepare for this gala, she had the satisfaction of Tim's vacant glare from the time he woke up this morning through the entire party, and now she had the benefit of Penn Beckley's best wishes. Made a girl happy to be alive.

Lainey looked around the yard as the kids separated into teams and one pint-size quarterback bent over the football and yelled "hike!" She watched as the children advanced from one end of the "field," as marked by a green lawn chair, toward the carriage house, which would be official touchdown territory. Everywhere she looked she saw used soda cans and plastic glasses, paper plates covered with chocolate remnants, discarded wrapping paper, scores of balled-up napkins.

Megan Burke came over to survey the scene along with Lainey. "Come on," she said, "let's start to get the crap into the gaahbage. It'll make your evening much more pleasant if we cleaahh up the back forty right now."

Lainey smiled at her gratefully. How nice to have at least one guest who didn't have eating Lainey for breakfast on her personal agenda. Together, the two women began picking up the assortment of trash, and depositing it in a large shopping bag. With their hands full of additional bottles and plates, they walked to the back door.

"You do this every single year?" Lainey asked as she opened the door and held it for Megan.

"Two children, two parties," Megan said cheerfully. "It's the suburban equivalent of 'one man, one vote.' "

"Is the party planner allowed a coffee break with a friend during the event?" Lainey asked, putting down the load she was carrying before settling into a chair.

Megan lifted an eyebrow. "Actually, vodka is the break of choice at these events. You'd be amazed how much more energy and enjoyment the end of a party can hold when you've provided yourself with the proper lubrication."

Lainey looked across the kitchen toward the cabinet where a number of liquor bottles were stored. "You know, I don't think I can make it from here to there. Maybe I'll just stay put." She lay her head on the tabletop, offering Megan a sideways smile. "In forty or fifty years, they'll find me here, dead as a doornail. 'She gave it her all, but it just wasn't enough.' That's what they'll write on my gravestone."

Megan laughed appreciatively. "Before I got married, I used to think all of this child stuff was a breeze." She shook her head. "Hah!"

"I never thought any of it was a breeze," Lainey answered. "In fact, of all the things I watched Farrell do, the birthday parties always seemed the hardest. All those details. All those little faces depending on you to provide them with a good time." She raised her head and yawned ostentatiously. "Honestly, next to this party stuff, the rest of it seems like a picnic."

Megan squinted as if considering the issue seriously. "I don't know," she said finally. "I'd take the parties over the projectile vomiting." She tipped her head to one side.

"And I'd take the vomiting and the parties way before the pleasures of carpooling."

Lainey found herself giggling uncontrollably. She stopped abruptly, however, when Doris and Hugh Beckley marched into the room.

Farrell's father nodded to Megan before eyeing Lainey with severity. "My grandson is walking through his tenth birthday like a robot. I'm glad his pain hasn't interfered with your good time."

Megan looked up at him in surprise, then turned her head to Lainey, the offer of help clear in her eyes. Lainey shook her head almost imperceptibly, and Megan nodded in return.

"Excuse me," she said blandly, leaving and walking quickly back out to the yard.

Lainey stood up and started clearing away the extra items she and Megan had brought in from outside. She had no idea how to respond to Farrell's parents. She decided to say nothing.

As she swept the dirty plastic and paper into a large garbage bag, Doris Beckley reached out for her hand. "Lainey, let me apologize for my husband. I know—we both know—you're doing the best job you possibly can."

Lainey looked up, interested to read the face behind such apparent generosity of spirit. Doris's eyes were as cold as ice, but she attempted a reassuring smile.

"Thank you," Lainey said simply.

Hugh Beckley wasn't bothering with civility. "Your best job isn't good enough, and we all know it." Hugh's dark brown eyes bored into hers. "I suspect even you know it."

Lainey felt the prickle of anger awakening in her chest. "I don't know any such thing," she said as politely as she could.

Hugh's face had reddened. "Let's stop playing games," he snarled, one hand slicing through the air in front of him like a machete. He was too angry to notice Lainey's parents and Penn, who had entered the room behind him. "Why the hell should you be playing Mommy in my daughter's house when Doris and I are perfectly happy to step in. Tim and Riley belong with us. We're their grandparents, for Christ's sake."

Stung, Lainey tried to keep her tone even. "Your daughter and your son-in-law wanted the children right here in this house, and they wanted me with them."

Hugh was yelling now. "My daughter never knew what she wanted, and, evidently, her husband wasn't much better. Frankly, I think they were both nuts when they made these arrangements, and my lawyer thinks so, too." He looked at Lainey with contempt. "You, of all people, raising my grandchildren . . ." He made it sound like a curse.

Saul Wolfe stepped forward protectively, sheltering Lainey from Farrell's father. "Who are you to scream at my daughter?"

Helen Wolfe joined her husband, broadening the wedge between their daughter and the Beckleys. Meanwhile, Penn Beckley hoisted himself up onto a countertop, watching all the players as if he were at the theater.

"I'm not blaming Lainey for anything," Hugh said, trying for, but not quite achieving, a calm tone of voice. "I just want her to know what Doris and I have planned." He looked at his wife, who nodded her head in accord. "We know our grandchildren should be taken care of by their own, and we're in the process of making sure that happens."

He strode away from the Wolfes toward the back door.

Taking a brief, angry glance at Penn, he led his wife out of the room.

"What a putz," Lainey's father expostulated the minute the door closed behind them. He took a step toward Lainey, and enveloped her in a tight hug.

Lainey experienced a moment of relief before hearing the words that followed.

"Of course, he's absolutely right."

Lainey extricated herself from his arms. "Oh, not you, too."

"Oh, my darling"—it was her mother chiming in now—"you're doing an amazing job. But it shouldn't be *your* job."

Her father nodded vigorously in agreement. "If you had children of your own, and, God forbid, something happened to you, of course, your mother and I would expect to take over. After all, you're our baby."

Lainey looked at them openmouthed. "I'm your thirty-six-year-old *adult* daughter, for God's sake."

Her mother took on a more apologetic note. "You are absolutely an adult, a single woman who should be getting on with her own life, with her own husband and her own children."

Lainey felt as if she were about to explode. "Mom, Dad, I don't have time for this discussion. There are about thirty people outside, and they're my guests, so if you would be good enough to let me finish up in here, I'd really appreciate it."

"She always knows best," her mother said sharply before taking her husband's arm and escorting him outside.

I don't know best, Lainey thought helplessly, sinking back down in a chair as she watched them leave. I don't know anything at all. She wished she could blot it all out,

Hugh Beckley's rage, her own parents' smugness. But she couldn't lie to herself, and she couldn't stop thinking about what they'd said.

How wonderful it would be to escape from everything that was bothering her, the pressure of mothering two grief-stricken children, the difficulties of doing a job she'd always been good at in half as many hours with half as much success. How wonderful it would be, she thought, with an involuntary shiver, not having to worry about whether her best friend's husband had been a cold-blooded murderer.

"So, I guess when you pull out, you're going to make the older generation very happy."

Lainey had forgotten Penn was even in the room until she heard his voice.

"Don't you have anything more important to attend to?" she asked bitterly. "Some political figure who's about to be assassinated, or perhaps a supermodel with an unprecedented insight into foreign affairs?"

"I'm glad you haven't lost touch with your fantasy life. That was always your strong suit, wasn't it, the what-ifs, the if-onlys." He looked at her scornfully. "It's reality you have the problem with, like how those kids you claim to love so much are going to do under the reign of King Hugh and Queen Doris."

"Listen, Penn." Lainey was outraged. "You don't know the first thing about me, nor have I decided anything definite about Tim and Riley."

Penn eased himself off the countertop and walked over to her. His eyes were dangerously bright. Placing his hands on the back of Lainey's chair, he tipped it back, leaving her suspended and helpless. Silent, menacing, he was so close, she could almost feel his breathing.

For a split second, she had the crazy notion that he was

about to kiss her, the thought making her almost dizzy. But when he moved, it was to lower her chair abruptly back to the floor and stride out of the room.

"You can't get to me," she cried out as he disappeared, wondering if that were really true.

Chapter 24

Lainey consulted the attendance sheet on her clipboard as fifteen boys wearing powder blue MEADOWVIEW TIGERS T-shirts and baseball caps jostled and talked around her.

"Okay, listen up." Squinting into the bright sun, she raised her voice for all of them to hear. "Jordan's not here, so Dan's going to hit after Matthew. Got it? Everybody know where you're playing?" She waited, but no one voiced any questions. "Brian, you have the bases set out?"

Brian, a red-haired boy with dimples, nodded. Satisfied, she sent them off to warm up, and headed back to the bench. She sat down, watching Martin Crawley, the head coach and father of the team's pitcher, giving last-minute instructions to a few of the boys, while the others tossed balls back and forth to one another. Tim was playing his regular position at first base, effortlessly catching whatever was thrown his way. She watched him, pleased and proud. Thank God, his grief hadn't kept him from playing sports, and, more importantly, being able to get some pleasure from them.

She readjusted her own baseball cap, smoothing back her hair beneath it. If anyone had told me last spring I'd be an assistant coach to a team of ten-year-olds. . . . It hadn't been easy, making time to come to the weekly night practice, and now the Saturday morning games, but the whole thing had turned out to be a pleasant surprise. It was only when the father who was originally supposed to be assistant coach had to back out at the last minute that Lainey agreed to step in. Tim had told her that the team was having trouble recruiting another dad, and Lainey, bristling, asked why a mom couldn't do the job.

"Sure, I guess," Tim said, "but I've never seen a mom coach."

That was enough for Lainey. The surprise was how much she wound up enjoying the job. She had been an above-average ball player as a child, and she got a big kick out of reawakening her skills, tossing the ball around with the boys at practice. At games, she amazed herself with the way she jumped up and down to cheer like the most zealous parent.

Today's game was an important one. The Tigers were facing the Eagles, a team that had beaten them the last two times they'd played one another. Lainey paced nervously as she kept score on her clipboard.

"Mark, Richie, get your fingers out of the fence before they get hit," she called to two boys hanging on to the backstop, watching intently as one of their teammates swung and missed. The batter struck out on the next pitch. "Damn," she said fiercely.

Tim stepped up to the plate and positioned himself to hit.

"Let's do it," she yelled encouragingly.

Tim hit a double, eliciting wild cheers from both players and the crowd of parents watching.

"Way to go, guy." Happily, Lainey made a notation on the clipboard.

The Tigers had a great game, while the Eagles pitched poorly and made one error after another. The final score of 7–1 had the home team screaming with joy at their victory. Lainey high-fived all the celebrating kids around her.

"Okay, now," Martin Crawley yelled as he gathered the boys in a circle for the obligatory cheer for the other team, "let's hear it."

All fifteen boys stuck out their hands to meet in the center of the circle, and gave a halfhearted "Yay, Eagles." The answering "Yay, Tigers" from the losing team was even less spirited. Then the opposing teams formed two lines from the pitcher's mound to home plate, and the boys hurriedly slapped hands as they passed each other in the obligatory show of good sportsmanship. Watching them quickly dispersing with their parents and friends, Lainey wondered how many of them heard the head coach yelling that Thursday night's practice would be at six instead of six-thirty. She began gathering the team's equipment into a large black bag, which she would keep at home and bring back next time.

"Hey, Lainey, good game, huh?" Tim, who had been talking with some of the boys, came running over to help her carry the equipment to the car. He was glowing from his team's victory.

Lainey put an arm around him as they walked. "You were sensational."

He pulled away, not wanting the other boys to see her display of affection. "I was, wasn't I?" He grinned.

They both laughed as they approached the car. Settling the black bag in the trunk, they got in and headed for home. Tim continued to exult as they drove, and Lainey responded, delighting in his pleasure. There was definitely something to be said for life out here, she reflected.

I must be losing my edge, she thought with a smile. Well, maybe that wasn't the worst thing in the world.

Tim had quieted down and was looking out the window, lost in his own thoughts. Suddenly, Lainey recalled the task that was waiting for her back at the house. Her good mood began to dissipate.

This was the afternoon she had put aside to clean out Farrell's desk in the bedroom. Oh, God, she groaned inwardly. The job would be long, tedious, and, by the end, guaranteed to leave her crying yet again over the loss of her friend.

But it had to get done. Little by little, she was forcing herself to go through all of John and Farrell's things. This wasn't the first time she had noted the irony of her being the one to pore over the sea of files they had left. When she had lived alone, she would go to nearly any lengths to avoid doing her own paperwork. It wasn't that she enjoyed the consequences of overdue bills and lapsed insurance policies; it was just that she somehow never seemed to take care of those things in time, and could never remember what was due when.

But with every check she wrote for the household expenses, she felt the weight of her responsibilities as guardian and coexecutor of the estate. If she were going to be running these children's lives, she had to stay on top of it all.

As she turned the car onto Fielding Drive, she saw a blond-haired boy bicycling aimlessly back and forth in front of the Cole house.

"There's Shane," Tim said, rolling down his window and leaning out to call to his friend. "Hey!"

"Who's Shane?" Lainey asked as they turned into the driveway.

"From around the corner. Let me out here."

Lainey stopped the car and Tim jumped out, consulting with his friend before coming back to talk to her through the car window.

"I'm going over to his house to shoot some hoops, okay?"

Lainey nodded. "No lunch?"

Tim was already running toward the garage, where his own bicycle was leaning against the wall. "I'll eat there," he shouted over his shoulder.

Pleased, Lainey watched him pedal off, then pulled the car into the garage and went into the house. Other than going to school and playing sports, Tim had spent too much time alone in his room. Any enthusiasm he showed for getting together with other kids was a small miracle.

On the other hand, she thought with a smile, there goes any excuse I might have had for putting off what I have to do. Riley was over at her friend Emma's house, to be picked up at three. It's just me and a thousand papers, Lainey said to herself, pulling off her baseball cap and piling it on the kitchen table along with her jacket and purse. But, first, a shower. She grabbed a can of soda from the refrigerator and was heading out of the room, when the telephone rang.

Opening the can, she turned back and took a quick gulp of the cold soda as she reached for the receiver. "Hello."

"You have no idea how good it is to hear your voice."

Lainey's stomach flipped over. She set the can down on the counter. "Julian."

"Hi, darling. How are you?"

"Where are you calling from?"

Old habits die hard, she thought, realizing that her first reaction had been to wonder if his wife might find out he was calling her. But she had no reason to worry about it anymore. It was over.

"I was just out for a walk, and I wanted to hear your voice," Julian said. There was a pause. "Well, that's not true. I went out so I could call you."

"Oh." Lainey wished she knew how to handle this. It was surprising how little she had thought about him since she had ended the affair, and their interactions at the office were generally free of sexual undertones. But hearing his voice now, so intimate, so reminiscent of other secretive conversations they'd had in the past, stirred her somehow.

His voice dropped. "I miss you, baby."

"Julian, don't." She closed her eyes. Keep your head on straight, she admonished herself. She didn't want to marry him, and the only other option was to go back to the way it used to be.

"Why not, sweetheart?" he asked seductively.

For a split second, she ached for him, wanting nothing more than to run into his arms, to kiss him, to feel him kissing her back and wanting her. But she knew it was more about the fact that she was lonely, aching to be touched. No other man wanted to make love to her. Hell, no one else even wanted to pay any attention to her.

Here's the truth of it, she reminded herself. I mooned over this guy forever, then ran like the devil when he actually became available. I can go back to the safe, comfortable way it was, but I won't be able to pretend that it's healthy or normal anymore. Neurotic, sick, masochistic—pick one. That's what we're contemplating here. Not to mention how manipulative it would be toward him.

"Can't we get together, you know, just talk a little?" Julian interrupted her thoughts. "I'm free now. We could meet somewhere for a few hours."

Lainey could imagine the scene perfectly. A romantic

reunion complete with a trip to a nearby hotel. It sounded wonderful. A *very* bad move.

"I really don't think so," she said. "It's not—"

There was a loud knock, and the kitchen door was pushed open by Sugar Taplinger. Seeing that Lainey was on the telephone, she went over to sit down at the table, mouthing the words, "Take your time."

Instinctively, Lainey lowered her voice, even though she knew Sugar could still hear her. "This isn't a good time to talk." Struggling with herself, she finally got out the next words. "But we really shouldn't be talking at all, not about this. It would be a mistake."

"No, Lainey, it wouldn't," Julian replied forcefully.

"I'm sorry, we just can't do this now." Lainey was growing even more unsettled, fighting to resist Julian and feeling Sugar's eyes on her. "I've got to go now, Julian. Let's discuss this another time."

She heard his reluctant "All right" before hanging up. Sitting down at the table, she exhaled loudly, exasperated with herself and how shaken she felt.

"What's doing, hon?" Sugar asked in concern.

Lainey shook her head. "Oh, this man . . ."

"This Julian person?" Sugar asked. "Who is he?"

Lainey hesitated. "An old boyfriend."

Sugar smiled. "They can do you in, those old flames. Especially popping up out of nowhere. How long has it been since you last saw him?"

Lainey laughed. "A couple of days." She didn't feel like talking about Julian, but couldn't think of a graceful way not to. "Seeing him is sort of unavoidable," she said, a note of finality in her voice.

"Ahhh . . ." Sugar nodded. "A man you work with." She didn't wait for confirmation of her assumption, nor was she ready to leave the subject. "That makes it harder to break away. He wants to stay together?"

Lainey smiled ruefully. "Sure. But staying together doesn't mean what you think. He's married." She took another sip of her soda. "Let's talk about more pleasant things, shall we?" she said brightly.

It was Sugar's turn to laugh. "Whatever you want."

Lainey answered apologetically. "I'm sorry. It's embarrassing to think about my time with Julian. It evoked parts of my character I'm not exactly proud of."

Sugar nodded understandingly. "Well," she said, getting up, "we all have to do what we have to do. There's something to be said for a little companionship."

Lainey looked over in surprise. "You think I should continue to see him?"

"I'm not saying that, but I understand it's not such an easy decision." She smiled sympathetically as she headed for the door. "Being single is a lot harder than it looks sometimes."

"Thanks for saying that. And for not being shocked," Lainey said.

"Takes a lot more than that to shock me." Sugar gave a dismissive wave of her hand. "I came over here to see if you wanted anything from the Price Club. Helmut needed me to pick up some stuff for the cars, so since I'm making the drive over . . ."

"No, thanks very much." Lainey came over to open the door for her.

She waved as Sugar crossed the backyard to her own house.

Standing at the top of the basement stairs, Lainey raised one knee to help support the basket of laundry she held, and reached out with her free hand to feel around for the light switch. She switched it on, illuminating the large area below.

Farrell and John had talked about having the basement finished one day, turning it into a playroom for the kids. But everyone had been satisfied with the amount of space they had upstairs, so they had never bothered. Still, Farrell had maintained that they would want to do it when the children were teenagers. Standing there, Lainey recalled her words when they had discussed it one day.

"We'll want to keep those kids in the basement twirling hula hoops, playing Ping-Pong, and drinking soda," Farrell had laughed. "You know, kind of re-create the fifties, and trap them there. My goal is to make them think sex and drugs haven't been invented."

"I'm sure that will be *very* effective," Lainey had agreed facetiously.

She smiled at the memory until it suddenly occurred to her that, if she stayed, *she* would now have to be the one to deal with Tim and Riley discovering sex and drugs.

"Not a pretty picture," she muttered as she went down the steps. Mrs. Miles usually did the laundry in the middle of the week, but Lainey and the children had engaged in a marathon cake and cookie-baking session the night before, and Lainey decided to deal with the dried-on chocolate icing now, instead of leaving it to set into their clothes. Along with the stuff from last night, she'd grabbed whatever other clothing was in the hampers to make a full load.

She set the laundry basket down on top of the dryer, then opened up the washer, and began loading the clothes into it. Off to one side was a small workroom, and through its open door, Lainey could see the pegboard holding all of John's tools, each hung neatly, and next to that, a large wooden worktable. Gazing in, Lainey could almost see John standing there, bending over some household project, brandishing a screwdriver or a drill. Sadly, she turned back to what she was doing.

She went through the garments, turning them right side out, unfolding cuffs, taken up with her task, not thinking about anything at all. It was quiet and peaceful.

Reaching for the box of detergent, she nearly dropped it as the quiet was shattered by a sudden loud noise.

"Jesus." Whirling around, Lainey saw Riley in John's workroom, dropping down several inches from the window onto the table that was just beneath it. She had climbed in through the window, which opened directly into the yard.

Lainey put a hand over her heart. "Riley, you scared the wits out of me."

"Sorry." Riley sat down on the table, then slid off to stand on the floor.

"What are you doing coming in through the window? You don't like the door anymore?" Lainey turned back to get the detergent.

"I don't know." Riley shrugged, walking toward her. "It's just more interesting sometimes to come in that way. You know, we could never have done it before."

Lainey poured detergent into a measuring cup. "What do you mean?"

"It was always locked." Riley peered into the washing machine. "It's only been unlocked since . . . since . . . you know." It seemed to occur to her that she might be getting herself into trouble. "I didn't unlock it, Lainey, I swear. I found it that way. I just didn't lock it again."

As she tipped the powder into the machine, Lainey thought about what Riley was saying. John Cole had been a maniac about household security. Farrell often teased him about the way he went around the house every night, checking to make sure all the doors and windows were locked.

Lainey set the cup down and faced Riley. "It's all right, sweetheart. You didn't do anything wrong. When exactly did you find it that way?"

"Well . . ." Riley hung her head. "I know it was wrong but I just couldn't stand all the people anymore. It made Grandma mad, I remember."

"What did, honey?" Lainey asked patiently.

Riley looked at her unhappily. "It was the day they died. When Tim and I came home from our sleepover. You weren't here yet, but everybody else in the whole world was. I couldn't stand it, so I came down here to hide."

Lainey knelt down to give her a hug. "I'd have wanted to hide, too."

Riley put her arms around Lainey in return. "That's when. I was just kind of sitting on the table, looking out the window, and I saw the lock was open. Daddy would never have let that lock be open."

They were both silent for a moment.

"You know something?" Riley asked.

"What?"

"It was like—I don't know. Daddy had all these rules. But he was gone, and there was the window, just unlocked. . . . It was like all his rules were gone, too. Like they went away with him."

Lainey gave her a sad smile and kissed her cheek. "I understand."

"Anyway," Riley said, her tone lighter, as if she had put the topic behind her, "it's been open ever since, and sometimes I like to use it to get in and out. It's kind of fun."

She pulled away from Lainey and headed for the stairs. "Can I have some of the chocolate cake?"

"Not until dessert time, please," Lainey answered, but her mind wasn't on what she was saying.

As she trudged up the stairs, Riley's protest was weak enough to show she hadn't expected any other response. "Oh, phooey."

Lainey turned on the washing machine, then stood in front of it, immobile, thinking. The day after the Coles died, Riley had found an unlocked window in a house in which every ground-level window was always kept locked at night. She tried to picture what might have gone on the day they discovered John and Farrell upstairs. The house was filled with carbon monoxide, so she guessed the police or the fire department opened windows to air it out. They could have unlocked John's carefully closed windows. That was probably it.

But something kept her standing there, her mind still playing out the scenario, imagining what might have happened. Finally, she was able to put her finger on what was troubling her. Would anyone actually have bothered to go into the tiny workroom over there to open that window when there were four much larger ones right here in the main area of the basement? Under those circumstances, she doubted she herself would; it wouldn't be worth it.

She walked over to the doorway of the workroom and regarded the window more closely. It was clearly big enough for an adult to climb through, and it led directly from the yard into the basement. Right to the gas furnace that had malfunctioned, spewing the poisonous fumes that killed John and Farrell.

Lainey spun around to look at the furnace. Fear started

to rise in her throat. Maybe she'd been on the right track, and the whole thing hadn't been an accident.

And maybe it wasn't John who had made it happen. Someone else could have climbed in that window and deliberately tampered with the furnace.

But who?

Chapter 25

Lainey felt as if she were the most conspicuous person in the world as she pulled open the door to the Meadow-view Police Department. I'm probably being ridiculous by coming here, she thought. I'm going to make a complete fool of myself. Standing in the brightly lit entry area, she fought the impulse to turn around and leave.

She couldn't leave. That would mean being left alone with her imagination, having to deal with the same questions she had gone over in her mind again and again since finding out about the unlocked window in the basement. It would all probably add up to nothing, but she *had* to know, had to resolve the doubts that had been plaguing her. Coming here was the only way she could think of to do that.

"May I help you?" The officer behind the long counter to her left looked up from what he was writing to address her.

She walked over to him and smiled. "Hi. I was hoping to talk to someone about the Coles. You know, on Fielding Drive."

He looked at her questioningly.

"They died in a carbon monoxide accident."

Instantly, he knew who she meant. "Of course. Why don't you have a seat over here."

"Thanks." Lainey followed the direction his fingers were pointing, going over to sit down next to one of the large desks. All the other desks were occupied, most people either on the telephone or bent over paperwork. Nearby, she saw a well-dressed, middle-aged woman talking with a man who was probably a detective. The woman looked distraught, Lainey noted.

A tall, thin, dark-haired man in his early forties approached Lainey.

"I'm Detective Yates," he said, sticking out a hand for her to shake, and sitting down in the swivel chair facing her. "I handled the report on the Coles. How can I help you?"

Lainey felt herself practically squirming in her chair, hating to bring up what she was about to say, knowing she had no choice. Stop acting like a two-year-old, she told herself.

"I'm Lainey Wolfe. I was a friend of John and Farrell Cole, and I'm the guardian of their children. This may seem wildly far-fetched to you, but I just wanted to make sure—" She paused, uncertain how to go on. "I wanted to confirm that you were satisfied their deaths were an accident."

Detective Yates raised his eyebrows in surprise. "Excuse me?"

She continued unhappily. "There have been some things that have made me wonder if there might have been more to it. I'm sure I'm just being crazy."

"Like what?" he asked, leaning forward.

"I know this has nothing to do with anything, but I understand the Coles were having some difficulties just before their deaths. Some arguing, that sort of thing. And my friend, Farrell, had been acting a little bit strange. That may sound like nothing to you, but I've known her

since we were children, so it was pretty noticeable to
me." She paused, wondering whether any of this made
sense to the man. "Now, I've learned that there was a
window open in the basement. John Cole always kept
those windows locked, always. So I started thinking . . ."

The detective picked up a pen and started tapping it on
the desk. "I was in the basement myself, Miss Wolfe,
and, of course, the windows were opened. They were
opened all over the house to help get rid of the gas."

"Yes," Lainey said, "but this particular window was
away from the others in the basement. It's in a little room
that John Cole used, off to the side. There are other big
windows, so it didn't necessarily make sense that you
would have gone into that room."

Detective Yates leaned his chair way back and looked
up at the ceiling, recollecting. Then his eyes met hers
again. "Okay, I remember what you're talking about. We
were mostly concerned with the main part of the basement, but, yeah, there was some kind of side room. With
tools, right?" He shut his eyes for a moment, remembering again. "Nope, I'm reasonably sure none of my
people went in there."

Lainey tried not to let her face reveal how startled she
was to have her theory confirmed.

The detective observed her discomfort, then spoke
again. "If you have some reason to believe this was
something other than an accident, I hope you'll tell me
why. You say they were fighting before it happened,
which makes me think you're considering that one of
them was somehow responsible."

Lainey shook her head. "No, I might have thought that
at one time, but I don't anymore. You didn't know John
Cole. It's unthinkable."

He let out a humorless laugh. "Miss, I'll tell you, nine

times out of ten, we've got to look to the husband in cases like these. You'd be amazed at what husbands and wives can do to each other."

Lainey grimaced. Coming here had been a mistake. "I guess I'm letting my imagination get the better of me. You guys were convinced it was an accident."

He nodded. "You know, these kinds of accidents *do* happen. It's tragic, but it's not as if we've never seen such a thing before. The furnace's backdraft damper should have opened, and it failed, which kept the fumes from leaving the house the way they should have. But there were no marks or indications that anyone tampered with the wires. Our guess is that it wasn't installed properly, because a couple of the screws were loose. And very few people have those things inspected regularly. Unfortunately, one of the wires came loose as a result, and that broke the connection."

He pointed his index finger at her. "But if you know of someone who might have wanted to hurt these people, or you've got evidence of somebody fooling around in their house, I want to be the first to hear it."

Lainey stood up. "You will be. Thank you very much for your time."

Detective Yates opened a desk drawer to pull out a business card, and handed it to her. "My pleasure. Call me if you think of anything else."

Lainey dropped the card into her purse, and escaped from the building as quickly as she could. It had been unsettling to find out that the police hadn't touched that window. That meant that under normal conditions, it definitely would have been locked. On the other hand, they hadn't found any evidence of someone trying to kill John and Farrell. It was enough for them. It should be enough for her, too.

So why wasn't it?

* * *

Lainey burst into the house, running to the staircase and dropping her briefcase and purse on the bottom step.

"Mrs. Miles," she called, "I'm home."

The housekeeper appeared at the top of the stairs, hastening down toward Lainey.

"I'm so sorry I'm late," Lainey continued in a rush of words, "I know you have to get to your daughter's. The train was del—" She stopped short as she got a better look at the expression on Mrs. Miles's face. She was clearly upset. "What is it? Is something wrong?"

"Oh, that poor child," the older woman began, reaching the bottom steps. "Thank the Lord you're back."

Lainey grabbed the banister, ready to bolt upstairs. "Who is it? What happened?"

"Riley's in her room. But she's practically hysterical."

"Hysterical about what?" Lainey wanted to shake the woman to get the answer from her more quickly.

Mrs. Miles looked at her, surprised that Lainey didn't already know. "The newspaper, of course. All the children at school were talking about it today, teasing her. You can imagine how cruel . . ."

Lainey tried to keep her voice even. "Please tell me what you're talking about. Which newspaper and what was it?"

"The Meadowview paper. It was with the mail yesterday." She began walking toward the kitchen, Lainey right behind her. "I didn't see it myself."

There was a stack of mail from the day before next to the microwave. Lainey hadn't had a chance to go through it yet. She grabbed the local paper from the bottom of the stack and unfolded it, scanning the front page.

"What am I—" she started, then stopped as she reached the lower half of page one.

LOCAL DOUBLE DEATH MAY BE HOMICIDE/SUICIDE

She quickly scanned the article, which suggested that the classification of John and Farrell's deaths as accidental warranted a closer look. It went on to say that there was no hard evidence of foul play, but unconfirmed reports of serious trouble in the Coles' marriage indicated that further investigation might be in order to rule out any possibility of John Cole's direct involvement.

"Jesus Christ." Lainey tossed the paper down and headed back toward the stairs, calling out behind her as she went. "The kids saw this?"

Mrs. Miles nodded.

Lainey took the steps two at a time, going straight to Riley's room and throwing open the door. The seven-year-old was sprawled across her bed, facedown, crying. Lainey sat next to her, wordlessly gathering her up in her arms. She stroked her hair and rocked her, Riley's gut-wrenching sobs piercing Lainey's heart.

"It's all right, baby, it's all right," she murmured urgently. "It's not true."

Riley screamed out a sob in reply, and Lainey caught a glimpse of her distorted face, red, soaking wet with tears. Her body was in continual spasms from the force of her crying. Her own eyes welling up, Lainey fought not to break down herself. She hugged Riley more fiercely.

Riley struggled to get the words out. "They s-s-said Daddy . . ." She couldn't go on, letting out a chilling wail.

"Your mom and dad loved each other," Lainey said. "You know this isn't true."

She stopped, pressing her lips to Riley's hot forehead. Please, God, she prayed, don't let me be telling her a lie. Let it not be true. I know it's not, I'm sure it's not. But, please, let me be right.

She continued to talk over the noise of Riley's cries.

"Honey, newspapers say things, but that doesn't mean they're always true or right. And they only said there was talk, stupid talk, which means nothing. It's all ridiculous, it's not real."

Riley broke away from Lainey and buried her face in her pillow. "Leave me alone," she screamed.

Lainey heard the door to Tim's room being slammed. He was home early. If Riley had been subjected to everyone's gossip and teasing at school, then, of course, he would have been, too. But how the hell did it get into the paper to begin with?

"I'll be back soon, honey. If you want me, I'm here," she said soothingly to Riley before hastening out and downstairs.

She located her purse and dug around inside it until she found the detective's business card. She dialed the number.

"Detective Yates, please." She tapped her foot impatiently until she heard his voice on the line.

"Yates here."

"This is Lainey Wolfe," she said tersely. "Can you please tell me how our conversation got into the newspaper? Do you have any idea what this is going to do to the Cole children?"

He didn't seem to know what she was talking about. "I'm sorry, I'm not—"

She interrupted. "Have you seen the latest Meadowview paper?"

"No. I've been out all day. Hold on." She heard him yelling out to someone else. "Hey, you got the new *Ledger*?"

There was a pause. Then she heard him curse.

"Miss Wolfe?"

"I'm here."

"This is the first I've seen of it."

"How did it happen?" she demanded. "You're the only person I discussed this with, and after months of silence, suddenly this article right after we talk."

"Can you hang on?"

He covered the receiver with his hand, but she could hear muffled shouting on the other side. Finally, he was back.

"This is very unfortunate, but it seems that there was a woman here the same time you were. She was reporting a stolen car radio. Apparently, she overheard some of what we said."

"What woman?"

"Turns out she's married to a guy who writes for the paper."

Lainey's stomach dropped. The woman at the other desk who had looked so upset. "I don't believe this."

His tone was sympathetic. "I'm sorry it happened."

Lainey's temper flared. "So because of some eaves-dropping opportunist, we'll have the whole town making the worst kind of assumptions."

"You can't stop things from being printed. I wish I could. But it clearly states that there aren't any facts proving anything."

"A lot of good that does," she retorted furiously.

She hung up. I *knew* I should have kept my mouth shut, she thought, as angry with herself as with the whole situation. Hastily, she ran upstairs. Sticking her head into Riley's room, she saw that she was asleep, her face still streaked with tears, her breathing labored. All that crying has exhausted her, Lainey thought. Good, let her rest. Let her get away from this nightmare.

She went over to Tim's room, knocking on the door as she opened it, not waiting for his reply.

Tim was sitting in a chair, staring at the wall. He turned to her. He wasn't crying, but she saw the unbearable pain in his eyes. She was startled to see that the right side of his face and upper lip were swollen and bruised.

"Tim, honey." She came over and knelt down next to him.

"They think it's really *funny,* you know?" he said in a detached voice. "Like it's some TV show. Some of the kids were asking me stuff, like how he did it and how long it took them to die. Most of the others wouldn't even look at me."

"Oh, sweetheart, no," Lainey breathed, overwhelmed by the horror of what he must have endured.

She reached out to push his hair back off his forehead, but he pulled away, wincing, as if fearful she would touch the swollen part of his face.

"Tim, what happened to you?" she asked, putting her hand on his shoulder instead.

"I fell."

She was taken aback by how little effort he put into the lie. "No, you didn't," she said softly.

His eyes met hers. She felt her heart was being torn out by the hurt reflected in them. "I got beat up," he amended simply.

Lainey was stunned. "Today? Because of this?"

He shook his head, and gave her a bitter smile. "Just a coincidence. Remember the kids who were taking my allowance?"

Oh, Jesus. Lainey had forgotten about all that. Tim hadn't mentioned it for a while, and she'd somehow assumed the situation had resolved itself. Guiltily, she realized that his silence on the subject had enabled her to put it out of her mind and move on to the million other things that had demanded her attention.

"It's been going on all this time?"

"Yeah." He looked away, embarrassed. "They took my money this morning. Of course, they knew about the newspaper, so they used the opportunity to give me their opinion. That was how I found out, actually. Garth Hober wanted to know why Dad didn't just shoot her or cut her throat open."

Lainey groaned before she could stop herself.

"I was with Paul Russell." Tim turned back to her again. "They took his money, too. That was the only good thing, I guess. I found out I'm not the only one in my class."

"They've been taking money from a lot of kids?"

"Well, him at least." Tim dropped his gaze to his lap, and spoke quietly. "I got mad when they said that about Dad. I kind of tried to fight them."

Lainey saw his eyes glistening with tears, as he pointed to his cheek. "This is what happened." His voice descended to a whisper. "I guess I'm not much of a fighter."

"Tim, darling." Anguished, she encircled his slender shoulders with her arms, and he collapsed against her.

For the first time since his parents had died, he cried to her. His sobs came in great, heaving waves. Lainey cried along with him, burying her face in his hair, torn apart by the suffering of both children, so precious to her, so vulnerable to the world. *Why can't I protect them?* she asked silently, helplessly.

When she was finally able to compose herself, she whispered soothingly to him, letting him cry himself out. At last, he was quiet again. She put her hands on either side of his face and looked into his eyes.

"I'm so sorry about all of it. I'm sorry you have to put

up with people's stupid gossip. Which is all it is. None of it's true."

He stared at her, wiping his nose on his sleeve.

"And I'm sorry I didn't help you with those idiot boys. I feel terrible about that. You shouldn't have to deal with that sort of thing by yourself."

He drew back and gave a slight shrug. "There's nothing anyone can do."

She sat back on her haunches. "Well, wait a minute. I didn't say that. We haven't actually thought this through."

Rising, she got the chair from his desk and brought it over to sit directly across from him. She leaned forward, putting her hands on his knees. "There *are* answers to these kinds of problems, Tim. You don't have to put up with people victimizing you." She sat back. "And you know what? You're not going to."

He sighed. "I can't beat them up, and it's not like I'm going to talk them out of it."

"But you said you're not the only one. There may be more besides you and Paul, too."

"So? You want us to gang up on them?"

Lainey was thinking. "No, that's not the answer. But by yourself, it's your word against theirs. If there are more of you, you've got witnesses."

Tim made a face. "You're not gonna get a bunch of the guys to tattle like babies."

"No-o-o . . ." She furrowed her brow, considering. Then she smiled. "But what about this?"

His eyes never left her face as she laid out the details of her plan.

Tim and Paul Russell both struggled to appear nonchalant, resisting their mutual urge to walk more quickly.

Paul adjusted his backpack nervously. "So, what'd you think of that science homework?" The words came out stilted, his voice artificially loud.

Tim didn't answer. They were approaching the spot where Garth and Jay usually confronted him. He peered into the distance, trying to see to the end of the block. No sign of them. Then, suddenly, they were there, rounding the corner. Tim tensed.

"Up ahead," he muttered to Paul.

Startled, Paul stopped, trying to see to the street's end.

"Keep going," Tim hissed.

Paul fell in step beside him silently. Garth and Jay were sauntering, both peering at a comic book that Garth held open in his hand. Approaching Tim and Paul, they both looked up and smiled as if this were a spontaneous encounter.

"What a surprise," Jay said with a grin.

"Yeah, fancy meeting you here," added Garth.

Tim attempted to walk past them.

"Now hold on, Timmy," Garth said in a hurt voice. "You're not gonna talk with us?"

"I have to get to school," Tim said. "C'mon, Paul."

Paul looked from Tim to the bigger boys. He didn't move.

Jay put an arm around Paul. "Our friend here wants to spend some time with us. He's not gonna hurt our feelings, right, Paulie boy?"

Paul stared down at the ground.

"You stay, too, pal." Garth reached out to grab Tim's sleeve, but Tim immediately yanked his arm away.

Angered, Garth took a firmer hold of Tim with one hand. With the other, he swatted the side of his head. "Hey, jerk. Maybe we don't want to make conversation with you now that I think about it. Maybe you just want to hand over your allowance and get out of our sight."

Tim tried to keep from rubbing his stinging forehead. He drew himself up, speaking loudly. "I'm tired of giving you my allowance. I've given you money for too long, and I'm done."

Garth and Jay stared at each other in amused surprise.

"You hear that?" Jay said.

"I heard it, but I didn't believe it," Garth replied, with an exaggerated shake of his head.

Paul, emboldened by hearing Tim, took a step forward. "And I'm done, too. You've been stealing my allowance and hitting me. I don't want you to do it anymore."

Garth's eyes narrowed. "Listen, moron, you're gonna continue giving us your allowance until we say you can stop. And if we want to hit you, we'll hit you. Got it?"

"Got it. Thank you very much."

The voice came from behind the fence of a nearby house. Garth and Jay whirled around at the sound to see Henry Wyatt, one of the other fourth-graders, emerging, video camcorder in hand.

"I got it, too." Robbie Levy, another classmate of Tim's, appeared from behind the shrubbery of the house across the street, a camcorder in his hand as well. "I'm the backup," he explained politely to the two older boys. "You know, just in case."

Stunned displeasure evident on their faces, Garth and Jay watched as two other boys in Tim's class stepped out from their hiding places nearby.

Tim stepped up to the older boys and spoke in a loud, firm voice. "We have the whole thing on videotape now. If you touch any one of us again or try to take our money, or if we find out you touched anybody else, we'll take the tape to the police. Understand?"

Disbelief replacing his bravado, Garth tried to recover. "Hey, come on. The police?" His tone turned wheedling. "You wouldn't really do that."

Tim turned an icy gaze to him. "In a second."

"Jeez," Jay muttered in annoyance. "What a bunch of assholes."

"Yeah," Tim said, beginning to enjoy himself, "but assholes with a tape."

"Ahh, let's get outta here," Garth said in disgust to his friend, turning to go. Tim could see the fear in his eyes, despite the casual words.

The six younger boys watched their retreating backs without saying a word. When they had disappeared around the corner, the boys all let out whoops of joy, jumping up and down. They high-fived one another, cheering and slapping one another on the back.

Still talking excitedly, they began to move as a group down the street, heading for school. Tim was grinning from ear to ear. It worked, he thought. It actually *worked.* He felt like he was flying. He felt happier than he could remember feeling since . . . He pushed the other thought away. He had done this, he and his friends. He and Lainey.

He couldn't wait to tell her.

Chapter 26

"It's your stop, miss."

Lainey had been so preoccupied with the work she needed to finish, she hadn't noticed reaching her destination until the train's conductor touched her on the shoulder. Smiling up in thanks at the burly gray-haired man who had become a familiar face in the time she'd lived in Meadowview, Lainey gathered her belongings hastily. Once on the platform, she had to throw everything down on a bench, only then having the time to put on her jacket and neatly pile all her papers into her briefcase.

As she walked toward the parking lot where she had left her car, she realized it was a beautiful day, cool for late spring, abundant sun sparkling off every surface. Amazing, she thought. Here it was, already three o'clock in the afternoon, and only now did she notice the weather. Not that it was going to do much for her, she reflected, as she got into the car.

Even with Carpathia doing its employees the favor of letting them go early the Thursday before Memorial Day, Lainey felt so overbooked, she couldn't imagine how she would get everything done by the following Tuesday when work started up once more. For months she'd been juggling her responsibilities at the office with everything she had to do at home. Not that she had ever felt like a success at either end, but now things were completely out of hand.

At least the kids would be gone for the next day or so. Doris Beckley had called a full week earlier with an imperious demand for her grandchildren this weekend. The usual reserve in her voice had evolved into the entitled tones of a Czarina in the weeks since she'd stated her intention of pursuing legal custody of Tim and Riley. Ordinarily, Lainey might have resisted the ultimatum out of some childish spirit of rebellion, but she had decided on the one course of action that made her feel comfortable in relation to Farrell's parents. She would attempt to deal with them now exactly as she would have had they never threatened her at all.

Even if, every now and then, she felt impulses that were less than charitable, the fact was that Tim and Riley deserved a good relationship with the one set of grandparents they had left. Besides, maybe if Lainey acted like a reasonable human being, it would evoke the same behavior from Doris and Hugh.

Or, then again, maybe Penn was right, and she was the biggest bitch in the world. Maybe she was being generous with the Beckleys because she ultimately *wanted* them to take the children.

She couldn't bear to contemplate that question right now, feeling the dull headache that always accompanied this line of thought. There was too much to accomplish before the kids got back to the house. She thought about the sketches she owed Al Smile. Those would take at least three or four hours.

But far more interesting to her was the material Patrick Fouchard had sent down from the Chicago focus groups. All the hours of tape had been transcribed into over one hundred typed pages, and he'd asked her to go through them and write up an analysis of where Carpathia should be headed on Marissa.

Not that anyone is going to care what I think after June tenth, the date Fouchard had set as the deadline for her final decision on moving to California. It hung over her head like a sword, one that would slice her in two no matter what she decided. If she said yes to him, she could say hello to permanent guilt for the rest of her life. Already she was having nightmares in which Farrell appeared, furious in some, heartbroken in others. Lainey would wake up, shaking and sweaty, overwhelmed by shame.

Then again, if she turned Fouchard down, she was certain she'd regret it for the rest of her life. *Everything comes in cycles,* her mother used to say. But Lainey knew that wasn't true, at least not this time. Fouchard had given her, literally, a once-in-a-lifetime offer. When—if—she said no to Marissa, she would be forever entrenched in the world of the mundane.

The only imaginative use of her brain lately had been the cartoons that appeared in the local paper. She smiled as she thought of the last few she'd sent in to the *Ledger*. Although they still had their first appearances in the kids' lunch boxes, her latest cartoons dealt almost exclusively with life at the office. Unable to stop herself, she'd done a series featuring a character who looked suspiciously like Al Smile, with the words "Hey, you" leading off each one.

In the first, a harried, middle-aged man was trampling a group of female employees as he rushed through the entrance of a midtown building. Underneath the art was a single sentence: "It's considerate to be on time." In the next, the same man was in a large meeting. While everyone else in the room looked the other way, he was decapitating the man next to him with a machete. The caption read "How to get ahead."

Thank goodness for the *Ledger*, she thought as she pulled up to the red light at the Post Road. She glanced down at the sketches she'd begun for Al Smile, a few of which were sticking out of her briefcase. There was Patsy Pony in all her glory, on her way to the zoo. God, the final art they'd chosen was boring. In fact, she thought sadly, just about everything comprising her daily job at Carpathia was boring. The endless copying of other people's ideas in those horrible pastel colors, applied in the same dreary tints, for the same mugs and the same greeting cards. It was only developing a character like Marissa, extending that character into interesting situations that became a creative and artistic challenge.

She was so lost in gloom, it took the honking from the car behind hers to alert her to the light's having turned green. Crossing through the busy intersection, she considered how tedious the next few hours would be as she completed the Patsy sketches. She wished she could do just about anything else, but it would be ridiculous to put it off; then she'd not only have to do it later on, but she'd have the anxiety of missing the deadline as well.

It occurred to her that there was one legitimate activity she could engage in before facing up to her task. Quickly, she peered into the rearview mirror, then pulled the car around full circle, driving back to the Post Road. Nothing, she reasoned, was a more righteous use of her time than food shopping. She would use her propinquity to the Grand Union to put off her work for another half hour.

She swung into the parking lot of the supermarket,

easily finding an empty spot close to the entrance. As she got out of the car, she saw Carol Anne Gisondi pulling her station wagon into a space a few cars down. Lainey waved and caught up with Carol Anne right near the entrance.

"How's it going?" Lainey asked offhandedly, as they walked through the door.

Carol Anne smiled at her briefly, quickly heading toward the back of the supermarket. She's really warming up, Lainey thought sarcastically as she stood near the front, trying to remember what she needed to buy. As she was assessing what aisle to attack first, her eye fell on the newsstand, located just beyond the checkout lanes. The DOUBLE DEATH MAY BE HOMICIDE headline leapt out at her. Suddenly, all thoughts of shopping, all thoughts of work fled.

The banner headline seemed a personal accusation. I can't just stand by and do nothing, she said to herself, feeling the frustration and powerlessness that had become so familiar. She could almost hear Farrell and John calling out to her. *If you were a real friend, you wouldn't be letting this happen.* Suddenly, she thought of something she *could* do, and right this minute, too.

Hurrying toward the meat section, she searched for Carol Anne and found her in conversation with the store's butcher. Lainey waited impatiently as Carol Anne discussed the merits of ground beef versus ground chuck as they applied to lasagna, but as soon as the conversation was finished, she walked up beside her. Wasting no time, Lainey launched into the subject that had been worrying her all week.

"How come the kids were at your house the night of the accident?"

Carol Anne stood still, her hands on her cart, and stared back at her blankly.

Lainey forced herself to slow down. "Sorry for the inquisition, but there've been some confusing things lately." She smiled reassuringly at Carol Anne. "You know, the night Farrell and John died, the children were at your house. Was there some special reason why they were there that night?"

Carol Anne hesitated. "I don't honestly remember," she said finally, turning the cart around and pushing it toward the canned food aisle.

Lainey caught up with her easily. "I'd assumed they slept at your house all the time, but Riley tells me that's not true."

Carol Anne stopped again, and looked at her. "What exactly is it you're saying?"

Lainey laughed it off. "Oh, nothing, really. It's just with all these awful rumors going around, I want to understand everything I possibly can." She rolled her cart slowly next to Carol Anne's. "This has been so tough on Riley and Tim."

"Oh, it must be terrible for them," was Carol Anne's genuinely sympathetic response.

Lainey shook her head sadly. "You can't imagine. Well, of course, with two kids of your own, I guess you can."

"Well, yes," Carol Anne said earnestly.

Both women continued down the aisle, stopping for only a second or two as Lainey reached out for two cans of tomato sauce. "How did Farrell sound when she called you that night?" she asked, as she placed the cans in her cart.

Once more, Carol Anne gave her a blank look.

"You know, was she sad, was she angry? Was there

anything unusual in what she said?" Lainey searched
Carol Anne's face as she put the question to her.

The other woman looked as if she were trying hard to
recall, but, again, she finally shrugged. "It was so long
ago. All I really remember is her calling and asking if
they could sleep over."

"So there was nothing special about Farrell that night?
How about when she dropped the kids off at your house?
Or did you pick them up?"

Carol Anne answered sharply. "Lainey, you ask the
strangest questions." Nervously, her fingertips began to
tap the cart's metal handle. "Let me think back and see if
I come up with anything." She looked at her watch. "Oh,
my," she said brightly, "I'm so very late."

She turned away from Lainey and pushed her near-
empty cart toward the checkout lanes. "I promise I'll get
back to you with anything I remember." Without another
glance, she strode to the front, hurriedly paying for
her items and making her way out to the parking lot.

Curiouser and curiouser, Lainey thought, watching her
through the large glass windows until she was out of
sight. Haphazardly, she made her own way through the
store, quickly selecting what she needed, pausing in front
of the meat counter. She eyed the lamb chops, conjuring
up how pleased Riley would be if she served them for
dinner, pink and juicy, covered with mint jelly. Then she
remembered that the kids would be gone tonight. And the
Beckleys meant to keep them the next night as well.
Unexpectedly, the thought made Lainey lonely.

By the time she got home from the Grand Union, Mrs.
Miles had gone home, and the large house was empty
and silent. Lainey unpacked the grocery bags, then went
upstairs to change into jeans. She looked at the phone
machine, but there wasn't a single message. Fine, she

thought after a tiny pang, I'll just get down to work. She picked up her briefcase and carried it into the dining room, clearing a space for herself on the large, gleaming table.

Vowing to start with the part that was least interesting, she pulled out the Patsy sketches, her hands moving mechanically across the page. The actual work was so automatic, it left her mind free, all too free, she decided, as she kept thinking about the June tenth deadline Fouchard had insisted on. How can I stay, how can I leave? It was a relentless thread she couldn't let go of. Haunted by the question, she failed to notice the bead of black ink drip onto her sketch.

"Damn," she said out loud as she finally saw the blot spreading. She crumpled the paper in her hand and pushed it aside.

She tried to continue her efforts on the next piece of blank paper, but her hand refused to move. She felt oppressed by the almost total silence surrounding her. Outside of the occasional creaky old-house noises and the slight buzz of an electric clock on the breakfront, Lainey heard absolutely nothing. Maybe music would help, she decided, getting up and going into the living room.

She walked over and turned on the receiver, switching stations until she came to public radio. She recognized the strains of Shubert's Unfinished Symphony immediately, closing her eyes and listening with intent pleasure for only a minute or so, before the symphony trailed off. The sounds of an announcer beginning to talk unnerved her, and she began switching stations, trying to find something that would please her. But nothing did the trick, the country stations too whiny, the rock stations too brazen.

Fine, she decided, giving up and turning it off, I should be working anyway. But, back in the dining room, seated once again, she was as unwilling to pick up her pen as she had been before. Okay, she thought, tossing down her pen and giving in to her lethargy, I'll read a book instead. She returned to the living room, and gazed at the titles on the bookshelves, finding any number of volumes that should have held her interest, but not one of them did.

The loneliness she'd felt earlier returned with a vengeance, accompanied by the deadly inertia that used to dog her on long summer weekends. I *like* being alone, she insisted to herself, forcing herself to think about the irritation that accompanied an argument with Tim or some unpleasantness with Penn. The lady doth protest too much, she acknowledged silently.

The ring of the telephone came as a welcome interruption. Lainey rushed over to pick it up.

"Hello," she said cheerfully, her depression carefully hidden.

Riley's voice was instantly recognizable, although it was unusually quiet. "Hi."

"Well, hi yourself. What's going on?"

"Nothing."

Lainey was stung by the sadness she heard. "Hey, baby, what are Grandma and Grandpa doing with you two tonight?"

"Not much," was the muffled response. "Can you come here, too?"

The heartbreaking pain Lainey experienced shocked her. "Oh, honey," she said, longing to embrace the girl through the phone line, "this is your special time with your grandparents. It's gonna fly right by."

"Yeah." Riley sounded unconvinced.

"I promise," Lainey said emphatically. "In fact, I can think of something you might love to do with Grandma. Why don't you ask her to go through some of the albums they have from when Mommy and I were kids. There are all these pictures you'd love to look at."

She could hear the little girl's sharp intake of breath.

"Oh, that would be great. I'm gonna go ask Grandma."

Lainey almost hung up the phone when Tim's voice rang out in the background.

"Let me talk," she heard him say.

"Lainey . . ."

He had his grown-up voice on, the one he generally used when he was hiding something.

"Yes, Tim," she answered, smiling to herself.

"Umm . . . do you know where my basketball is?"

"Well, yes, I do. It's in the basement, on top of the Ping-Pong table." She chuckled softly. It was *always* on top of the Ping-Pong table. He must have needed to hear her voice, just as Riley had.

Tim cleared his throat. "Okay, well, see you tomorrow."

"See you tomorrow, honey." Lainey hung up, surprised to find she was crying.

What is this? she asked herself, grabbing a tissue out of her pocket. She didn't feel sad. In fact, she felt better than she had all day. She walked back to the dining room and sat down, pulling the Marissa pages out and flipping quickly through the thick transcription booklet. It seemed utterly pedestrian, as meaningless as the pallid sketches she'd been trying to get through earlier.

Suddenly, it was crystal clear. She wasn't going to California. She wasn't going anywhere. She wouldn't leave these kids if the President offered her a Cabinet post.

With no ambivalence at all, she went upstairs to her

bedroom and thumbed through her phone book. Now that she had made the decision, she was startled by how completely right it felt. Unhesitatingly, she dialed Patrick Fouchard's office number. There's no reason to wait until June tenth, she thought with immense satisfaction as she waited for someone to pick up. Idly, she wondered if he, too, would have left early, but he answered on the third ring.

"Patrick Fouchard." His voice rang out authoritatively.

"Lainey Wolfe," she said, "with an answer."

Fouchard responded cheerfully. "Well, given how ebullient you sound, I assume it's yes."

"Actually, I'm afraid it's no," Lainey said politely. "And this time it's final."

There was an ominous silence on the other end of the line. When Fouchard finally spoke, there was a new coldness in his tone. "I'm sorry to hear that. Frankly, given your unwillingness to grab the ball, I'm afraid you may not be what we were looking for after all."

"I'm sure you'll find someone much better qualified," Lainey said tactfully.

Again, a long silence preceded his response. "Well, Ms. Wolfe," he finally said, "I'm afraid you don't quite catch my drift. I think, under the circumstances, it's time for you to separate from Carpathia completely."

Lainey couldn't believe what she was hearing. "You mean I'm fired?" she asked, incredulous.

"Your decision to turn down this opportunity comes as a grave disappointment to me. At this point, I have to believe your talents would best be served elsewhere." Fouchard hung the phone up firmly.

Stunned, Lainey replaced the receiver. At first, she felt nothing at all, which surprised her. She might have expected to feel angry or sad or any number of things.

But an emotion that was almost completely foreign to her was beginning to bubble up. She was startled to realize it was pure elation.

She contemplated all the things she would have time for, the places she could take Tim and Riley, all the thought she could give to her own cartoons.

What am I really going to miss? she wondered, conjuring up instant images of Carla and Gail. Well, there was no reason to lose her friendship with those two. Not much else came to mind. Not even Julian. The idea of not having to run into him every day filled her with nothing but relief.

Suddenly, she felt completely energized, a picture of the children flying through the door filling her with pleasure. I think I'll make something special, she thought, envisioning a huge dish of spaghetti and meatballs or a thick pot roast, two meals they both loved.

But first, she might do some work on the *Ledger* cartoons. New ideas were flooding through her brain. Happily, she went downstairs and into the kitchen to grab a pad and a Magic Marker. Within minutes, she was deeply immersed in a cartoon, the words "Hey, you" already scrawled across the top of the page.

Chapter 27

Charlie Cole felt a blast of heat as he opened his front door and stepped through the thick pile of letters and newspapers that had been thrown through his mail slot since he'd left ten days before. He placed his suitcases down quickly and walked over to the air conditioner, turning it to its highest setting. Only then did he take his jacket off and flip on the overhead light.

He looked around the living room, thinking how dark and small it seemed suddenly. Every apartment he'd seen during his time in Miami had been bright and airy. He pictured the huge condo on Brickell and the beautiful young woman who owned it. Nothing like waking up to warm sunlit breezes blowing right in from the ocean, he thought, smiling at the other memorable aspects waking up in that apartment had held.

The apartment he'd rented for himself down there was much smaller, of course. It would take a while for him to establish himself, to build up enough of a financial nest egg so he could live as he really wished. But the deal his old college roommate had offered was a good one, and soon enough he would be perfectly comfortable.

Not that he'd ever considered the food business before, but The Sombrero South, when he finally got down there to see it, proved both more solid and more interesting than Charlie would have expected. Okay, he would never have the brains and focus his brother had had, but charm and energy were two things Charlie had in spades. And those qualities, unhindered by the self-destructiveness he'd made up his mind to leave behind, would serve him just fine. Ted would oversee the hotel, while Charlie would run the restaurant.

When Ted's father had run the place all through the seventies and eighties, it had catered to old people. Charlie remembered using it as a base during inter-session, junior year of college, he and Ted cruising for babes all night, then coming home at eight or nine in the morning and finding groups of white-haired senior citizens already set in their lawn chairs facing the ocean.

But that was the old South Beach. Now it had become one of the trendiest, hippest spots in the country, a major growth area for younger people, people like himself who had energy and creativity. No longer slow, no longer elderly, the population was charged with ambitious out-of-towners and Cuban emigrés, all seeking life at its most enterprising.

He frowned as he walked over to the refrigerator and drew out a cold bottle of Heineken. *Legal* life at its most enterprising, he thought, as he opened it and took a long gulp. He walked over to the brown velvet sofa and stretched out luxuriously. Tonight was for resting; tomorrow he would begin the moving arrangements, tomorrow he would implement the decisions he'd come to.

He'd been living life a little too close to the edge; it was time to stick to those rules he'd never given much thought to before. Breaking them had proven to be too dangerous. No more money laundering, no more dealing. From now on he was John Q Citizen.

It had been bad enough when Marina Paulsen was killed. At first, he'd only been frightened of being implicated in her financial dealings, especially after his brother's visit. But when John and Farrell turned up dead, that was another matter. Sure, it was unlikely that anyone would finger him for the money laundering if they hadn't caught up with him thus far, but three deaths—every one of which was connected with him— that was too close for comfort.

When he was a kid, his mother used to chide him about taking small sums from her purse or shoplifting a T-shirt or a pair of moccasins at the mall. Then, with his drug arrest, his father had started in on him. But actually he'd never taken either one of his parents' words very seriously. To him, it had been youthful hijinks. Even the stuff he'd done with Marina had started as more or less of a lark, as much to see if he could get away with it as for the extra income it afforded him.

But with the murders, everything had changed. And that was just what it was, he thought angrily, *murder*. He knew it, even if no one else had figured it out. John was Marina's attorney, and someone had gotten him out of the way, just as they'd done with her. Nothing else made sense. And nothing else had ever made him feel so rotten.

He never would have guessed how much he'd miss his brother. That they'd fought the very last time they'd spoken just about killed him. And that he couldn't figure out who had done it was even worse. Who the hell was it, he thought for the thousandth time, sitting up straight and resting his beer on the coffee table. Who even knew Marina, Farrell, and John? He'd pondered it every day since it happened, but time had delivered no further clarity.

Except, that is, the clarity of knowing when to move on

and change his life. Maybe he wasn't the genius who would solve his brother's murder, but at least he could live his life without a clear path to prison, or worse yet, to his own murder for God-knows-what.

Uncomfortable with his thoughts, he stood up and reached for the pile of mail, setting it on the kitchen counter. Then he went back, and started gathering all the newspapers. There would be no way to catch up on almost two weeks of news with all the packing he had in front of him; he might as well put them straight in the trash. After all, Ted wanted him down there for good within the next week or so.

It was only when he started stacking the newspapers in his arms that he found the headline: DOUBLE DEATH MAY BE HOMICIDE. He sat back down immediately, scanning the contents of the article.

"Oh, Jesus," he said out loud, as he came to the paragraph accusing his brother of murder and suicide. Horrified, he threw the paper onto the floor. Naming John Cole as a killer—it was ludicrous. Not in a million years.

There had to be plenty of other people who wanted Marina's lawyer out of the way, who would have been terrified at the information her papers might have contained. But there was no way he could suggest that to the police without divulging his own part in all of it. He stole another look at the headline, and was surprised to feel tears coming into his eyes.

His brother was a great guy, no matter how hard a time Charlie had given him at that last meeting. How could he let him stand convicted in the press? He thought about Tim and Riley. How could he let his niece and nephew think their father was capable of such an act?

He stood up and began pacing around his living room. No matter what he'd ever done, how many dances he'd performed with danger, Charlie had never been dishonest with himself. He knew his own worst instincts, his weakest links. But right now, he felt lower than he ever had in his life. He couldn't let things stand as they were. There had to be some way to fight this. Some way that did not include ending up in jail, he acknowledged with a stab of guilt. There had to be somebody who would push an investigation until it uncovered whatever the hell the truth was.

His pacing lasted over an hour, all thoughts of Florida temporarily out of his head. He finally decided on the one thing he could do, as meager as it might be.

His resolution brought him some relief as he walked over to the phone, carefully laying a handkerchief over the mouthpiece as he dialed a familiar number. He heard Lainey Wolfe's "hello" on the third ring.

Chances were, she wouldn't recognize his voice, but just to make sure, he lowered his range to an almost unintelligible growl.

"Your friends, the Coles," he whispered hoarsely. "Murdered, both of them. And the husband had nothing to do with it." Without another word, he hung the phone up, his hands shaking as he wiped the beads of sweat from his face.

A wave of humiliation flooded through him. He knew how half-assed, how cowardly the call had been. At least it's something, he rationalized. A step, okay, a small step, he acknowledged, but at least he hadn't done plug nothing.

Feeling a sliver of relief, he walked into the kitchen and reached into the refrigerator for another beer. If I work through the night, he thought as he took a long draw at the bottle, maybe I can get on a plane to Miami by tomorrow night.

Chapter 28

The person on the other end of the telephone had hung up. Lainey slammed down the receiver and stepped back in fright.

Who the hell was that? Someone was out there who knew that John and Farrell had been murdered. He might know who did it. He might know why. Maybe the man on the phone had done it himself.

She sank down on her bed, trying to sort out her thoughts. Thank God, she had been passing by her room when the phone rang, and was able to get it herself before one of the children picked it up. Would whoever it was have said all that to Tim or Riley? She shuddered slightly. And why was he calling here to begin with, instead of calling the police.

Because he wanted to talk to *her,* to tell her that the whole thing wasn't an accident. *The husband had nothing to do with it*. He wanted her to know that John wasn't involved. He must have seen the newspaper article.

She stood up, oddly queasy, and growing only more frightened. Someone was out there somewhere who knew what had happened. With that terrible voice, he had shattered her secret hope that she was only suffering from an overactive imagination. And he was telling her that she had better find a way to get at the answers, instead of just wondering. She needed to find out the truth before—

Before what?

Lainey went downstairs, a thousand thoughts colliding in her brain. She knew one thing; she could no longer afford to be so casual about the way she pursued this. It was time to get serious. Should she call the police? she asked herself. It certainly was tempting—not to be so alone in this. But why bother, she realized. She knew nothing more than she did the last time she went to them. And a fat lot of good that had done.

Below, Riley crossed in front of the staircase, on her way to the family room with a small bag of popcorn in her hand. She smiled up at Lainey, who smiled back absently. She was reminded that it was Riley who had inadvertently led her to the unlocked basement window. Maybe the children had other information that was important, things they might not know had any significance. Lainey hated to drag them into this, but she was going to have to find out.

"Honey, can I talk to you for a minute?" she asked, hurrying down to where Riley was, and putting an arm around her.

"Sure." Riley stuck her hand in the open bag and shoved a handful of popcorn in her mouth.

"It's about Mom and Dad."

Riley stopped chewing, and looked up at Lainey. Her voice lost its cheerfulness. "What?"

As she talked, Lainey walked her into the family room, and they sat down on the couch. "It would be really helpful if you could tell me about how your parents were doing. I mean, if they seemed happy or sad to you."

"Huh?" Riley looked at her in bewilderment.

I'm really botching this up, Lainey thought. I don't even know what the hell I'm trying to get at. She searched for the words that might trigger any sort of relevant recollections. "Before the accident, were things around here pretty normal, or did they seem different in any way? Like, were there any people visiting that maybe you and Tim didn't know?"

Riley was obviously still confused. "They had visitors all the time. We didn't know everybody who came here."

Lainey sighed. This wasn't leading anywhere. "I'm sorry. These questions don't make a lot of sense. It's just that I wondered what was going on in your parents' lives just before the accident happened."

"Oh." Riley ate some more popcorn, chewing reflectively. "They always seemed happy to me."

"You're right, honey." Lainey gave her a quick hug. "They *were* happy."

Lainey got up and began to walk out of the room, when Riley's voice stopped her.

"You could look in Dad's diary, I guess. Maybe he wrote stuff about being happy or sad around then."

Lainey turned around and stared. "Your dad kept a diary?"

Riley nodded. "On his computer." She dropped her gaze, embarrassed. "I read some of it once, a long time ago. We were never allowed to look at it, but I did." She brought her eyes up again to meet Lainey's. "A lot of it I didn't understand, because it was about his work and stuff. Some of it was about Mom, and Tim and me."

At the mention of her brother's name, she suddenly looked panicked. "Please don't tell Tim I read it. We weren't supposed to, and I know he didn't. I always told him I didn't either."

"Honey," Lainey said slowly, "could you show me this diary?"

"Sure," Riley replied, relieved that Lainey was uninterested in her confession. "Now?"

She got up and led Lainey into her father's study, dropping the popcorn bag on John's desk as she sat down in his chair.

"Let me just find it."

Lainey watched her, amazed at the speed and confidence with which the seven-year-old entered commands at the keyboard. Words and lists flashed on the screen as her fingers moved over the keys.

"Okay." She pushed the chair back so Lainey could come closer to see the directory on the screen.

Lainey stepped forward. Computer files divided by year and month. Of course, she thought, clear and logical like John himself. She scanned the list, looking for the month of their deaths.

"Do you see a file for last February?" she asked. "Maybe it's under a different name, although I don't know why that one month would be different."

Riley scrolled up and down the list, the two of them searching. "I guess not."

"Let's look at January then."

Riley opened the file for her, and Lainey scanned the daily entries. John had written about office politics, a case he was working on, the possibility of the family going to the south of France in June. He also made notes about what they were all doing as the weeks passed, dinners, sporting activities, a night at the theater. There was nothing out of the ordinary. But given that there was some sort of entry for every single day, Lainey decided it was unlikely he had just stopped writing altogether after

January. He would still have been writing in it during the month they died.

So where was the file?

"Thanks, Riley." Lainey kissed the top of her head quickly. "Good job, cyber whiz."

"You're done?"

Lainey nodded, and Riley hit a few more buttons before shutting the computer off.

"I hope it helped." Riley picked up her popcorn. "You want me for anything else?"

"No, sweetie."

Riley left as Lainey took her place in John's chair. She stared at the blank computer screen. The man kept a diary for years, as regular as clockwork. But the whole month leading up to the night he died—the night he was *murdered*—was nowhere to be seen.

Was it actually possible that someone had come in here, and erased that particular file?

Lainey swallowed, hating how frightened she felt. Someone coming into the house. Someone calling anonymously. It was scary and terrible, and, what was worse, it was no longer just her imagination roaming wild. It was real.

"Lainey, where are you?"

She heard Tim's voice, probably coming from the kitchen.

"In here, hon," she yelled out, quickly composing herself. "Dad's study."

He appeared in the doorway, taking in the sight of Lainey seated at the computer. "You doing something with that? Need some help?"

"No, thanks. I was just sitting here, thinking."

He came toward her. "Yeah?"

Well, she thought, Riley had led her to the diary. Who

knew what Tim might lead her to. Painful or not, she had
to ask him.

"Tim," she began, "I was curious about how things
were between your parents before the accident."

"Accident?" he echoed bitterly. "Nobody thinks it was
an accident, Lainey. Everyone knows Dad killed them
both."

"Oh, Tim." He had endured so much gossip after that
newspaper article, but it was still a shock to hear him say
the words himself. "You don't believe that, do you?"

"Sure, I do," he said. "Dad did it. Simple as that."

"Sweetheart, you can't believe what's in the papers."

He shrugged. "In this case, the papers are right."

Despite his tough words, Lainey noted that his eyes
were filling with tears.

"Honey." Lainey came over to put her arms around
him. "Why would you say such a thing? Your dad loved
your mom, and he loved you and Riley. He wouldn't, not
in a million years."

Tim turned his face to the side so she couldn't see it.
"You're wrong."

Her tone grew more stern. "I'm *not* wrong. No one
loved his family more than your father."

She was startled by the sound of a large sob escaping
from him. Kneeling, she brought his face to hers. "What
is it?"

"He *didn't* love us." Tim's voice was getting louder.
"At least, he didn't love *her*. He hated her." The next
words were blurted out. "He was so mad at her,
he wanted to kill her. *And he did.*"

Lainey pulled back, stunned. "That's not so," she said
urgently.

Tim continued to cry. "It's true. I heard them, the day
he did it. I came back home in the morning, but they

didn't see me. They were fighting. He was so mad—I'd never seen him so mad."

Lainey waited, seeing he was trying to calm himself down. Finally, she spoke again.

"Did you hear what they were fighting about?"

He took a deep, shaky breath. "I didn't understand. All I remember is that it was about a sweet."

"Sweets? Like candy?" Lainey racked her brain for any possible connection.

"I don't know," Tim answered miserably. "I keep trying to figure it out. He was yelling about a sweet. 'At least it's a sweet,' he said."

"A sweet," she echoed. "Wait a minute. Do you mean a suite, like a hotel suite?"

Startled, Tim stopped and stared at her. "I never thought of that." He shook his head. "What's the difference what he meant? I only know he was so mad that he made that gas leak happen himself. He *meant* for it to happen."

As the significance of what he was saying sank in, Lainey's voice dropped to a horrified whisper. "All along, you've thought your father did it? From the beginning?"

"Of course." He turned away as if embarrassed.

Lainey's mind flashed on the day of the funeral, Tim sitting stone-faced during the car ride home. Dear God, she thought, he believed his father murdered his mother, even before anyone else suggested such a thing. And he kept it a secret. She couldn't bear to think about what he must have been going through.

She knelt down beside him and took him in her arms. He didn't resist.

"Sweetheart," she said forcefully, "I swear to you that I will prove your father didn't do it. I know he didn't, just

as I know we're here together right now, and I love you."
She paused. "Do you believe me?"

He looked at her sadly. "I want to."

Lainey kissed his cheek. "I don't have the answer for
you now. But I will. I *swear* to you."

She hugged him to her, wondering how on earth she
was going to keep her promise.

It was the middle of the night when Lainey's eyes flew
open, and she was instantly wide awake, an image in her
mind of herself standing in front of the Hotel St.-Tropez,
talking to Carol Anne Gisondi. *A suite.* Farrell had a key
to a room in that hotel. And her friend Carol Anne was
also in that hotel, or at least had been on that one day.

Throwing back the covers, she turned on a light and
went over to her dresser, yanking open the top drawer to
peer in. What had she done with that key? Mentally
retracing her steps on the day she had found it, she realized she had never removed it from the pocket of that
particular pair of jeans. But they had been washed many
times since then, and Mrs. Miles had never returned a
key, the way she had several other items that Lainey
neglected to take out of her pockets.

She went over to her closet, locating the pants on a
hanger. Hurriedly, she stuck her hand in each of the front
and back pockets. Empty. The key had probably fallen out
en route to the washing machine, or maybe in the machine
itself. Unless, a small voice in her head added, someone
came up here and took it. Lord, no. She shivered.

"I'm not going to think stuff like that," she whispered
fiercely.

It had been a big silver key, she recalled. It had
St.-T written on one side, but on the other was a number.

The room number. She closed her eyes and concentrated: 1012. That was it.

She switched off the light and got back into bed. She couldn't imagine why Farrell would have a key to a local hotel. Who the hell kept keys to hotel rooms, anyway? And on the day of her death, her usually even-tempered husband had been yelling at her—had been absolutely *furious* with her, according to Tim—about a suite.

"Farrell," she whispered into the darkness, "what did you do?"

The elevator doors opened, and Lainey stepped out onto the tenth floor. She turned to the right, peering at the numbers on the doors as she walked. Finally, she stopped. Room 1012. *La Plage.* It was the last door in the row, and there seemed to be enough space between the door and the end of the hall to suggest that, behind the wall, 1012 might be a suite. But there was no way to know for certain.

She glanced around, trying to decide where to position herself. Although she had no idea what she was waiting for, she didn't want to stand right outside the room or even sit in as conspicuous a place as the armchair next to the window at the corridor's end. Going back just past the elevator, she saw the small open area containing the ice and soda machines. Perfect. She stepped inside.

The corridor was completely silent. Maybe there wasn't much activity in a hotel in the late afternoon. Well, she would have to wait there for however long it took. Whatever *it* was, she thought with a sigh. Opening her large shoulder bag, she fished out the *Time* magazine she had brought and began reading.

The sound of a door opening several minutes later startled her. Shoving the magazine back in her purse, she hesitated, then looked out. There was a woman leaving a room down at the opposite end of the hall. Lainey pretended to busy herself with the soda machine until the woman passed by. Breathing a sigh of relief, she went back to her magazine.

When she finished the final article, she closed the cover and glanced at her watch. Nearly half an hour had passed since she'd arrived. Maybe this was going to be a complete waste of time. But she couldn't think of any other way to find out what was going on here.

At that moment, a door opened. Lainey peeked out. Oh, God, she thought, her heart pounding, it was the last door, 1012. A man in a dark suit emerged. Lainey shrank back. She heard him laughing, then saying something she couldn't make out. A woman's voice responded to his words. Then the door was shut, and the man strode to the elevator. Lainey stood, frozen, trying not to breathe. Silently, the man waited for the elevator to arrive. It wasn't until he got inside and she heard the doors close that Lainey relaxed and took a deep breath.

A man and a woman were in that room. So what, she thought. That tells me nothing at all. She remained where she was, though, and five minutes later, she heard a door opening again. She peered out. 1012. An attractive blond-haired woman came out this time, pulling the door shut behind her, hurrying toward the elevator, her face down as she fussed with the contents of her purse.

I still know nothing, Lainey thought as she listened to the elevator doors close behind the woman. Now what? Disgustedly, she went into her wallet and extracted change to get herself a Coke from the machine. Popping open the can, she took a long swig. Remind me never to volunteer for any stakeouts with the cops, she told herself sardonically. A person could die of boredom, and without having learned a thing, no less.

The elevator was back. Carefully, Lainey looked out. A tall, dark-haired woman was walking down the hall, her back to Lainey. She watched as the woman stopped at Room 1012, pulled a key out of her jacket pocket, and unlocked the door, disappearing inside.

Lainey leaned against the wall. A man and a woman leave the room, and ten or fifteen minutes later, another woman comes to let herself in with a key. She narrowly—conveniently—misses the other couple. By accident or by design?

She waited. Finally, she heard the elevator open yet again. This time it was a short, heavyset man who went down the hall. Lainey's heart sank as she watched. She couldn't be seeing what she thought she was seeing. It wasn't possible. *Go to some other room,* she urged him silently. *Please, not there.*

He stopped at 1012, giving three short raps on the door. Lainey made out a woman's cheerful "Who is it?" coming from inside the room and heard him respond with a gruff, "It's me." The door opened, and she saw a woman's bare arm reach out to touch him, gently drawing him inside.

Lainey's stomach churned. Please, God, she prayed, let me think of some other explanation. Tell me this isn't a bunch of call girls and their customers. Tell me Farrell wasn't mixed up in this.

She rubbed her forehead. It wasn't possible. Farrell loved John and the kids. There was no reason in the world she would get involved in something like this. It wasn't as if she needed the money. Was it supposed to be fun?

Lainey's mind was suddenly full of memories from

Farrell's Christmas party. Farrell's preoccupation the entire evening, her asides to John about keeping her on the straight and narrow. More fragments of their conversation were coming back now, the two of them in the bedroom fixing Lainey's hair, Farrell talking about how she might have been in too much of a hurry to get married. *Sometimes I look at some guy and I think about all the stuff I'm not allowed to think about.*

Lainey shut her eyes. She had always assumed that, despite the occasional jokes, Farrell was happy with the life she chose, that she had voluntarily given up her wilder ways and had no regrets about it. Had she needed one last fling—or maybe more?

Lainey hurried over to the elevator and jabbed impatiently at the button over and over, wanting to get the hell away from this hotel. At the lobby, she bolted out, hurrying toward the exit. Then, she came to a dead halt. Walking toward her was Sugar Taplinger.

For a split second, Lainey saw displeasure in Sugar's eyes. But almost immediately, it was replaced by a broad smile.

"Hey, hon," she said effusively, putting a hand on Lainey's arm, "what a surprise. You here for the meeting?"

Lainey stared at her. "What meeting?" she finally got out.

"Well, the Senior Volunteer League Meeting, of course," Sugar answered cheerfully.

"No, no, I'm not." Lainey shook her head, frantically trying to come up with some plausible excuse for being at the hotel.

But Sugar didn't ask for any further explanation. "This is the league's big meeting for the year, you know," she said. "And I'm gonna be late if I don't get my behind in there." She moved past Lainey, smiling. "See you later."

Lainey stood there, staring after Sugar as she disappeared around a corner. Farrell, Carol Anne Gisondi, and Sugar Taplinger all coincidentally frequented a hotel several towns away from Meadowview. Lainey turned and strode over to the front entrance, quickly locating what she was looking for. Like many hotels, the St.-Tropez had a board on which they posted the day's events. There it was, the third item from the top: Senior Volunteer League, the Blue Room. So there really was a meeting.

Or Sugar just happened to know there was such a meeting. If Lainey were still upstairs, would she now be watching Sugar unlock the door to Room 1012?

Sugar pretended to observe herself in the gilded mirror next to the elevator, smoothing back her hair as if it were her most important concern. In fact, she was struggling to keep her fury from showing on her face.

There was no reason in the world for Lainey Wolfe to be in this damned hotel except for one. That idiot Carol Anne had been right. Lainey knew the truth. And Lainey was undoubtedly going to do something about it.

Chapter 29

Penn deposited his suitcases in the carriage house before going into the main house, pulling off his khaki suit jacket as he went and slinging it over his shoulder. Frowning, he hoped he would be able to see Tim and Riley without encountering Lainey. In the days after Tim's birthday, his interactions with her had been brief and icy, and then he'd left on assignment for Santa Fe. Since that time, he certainly had no reason to change his attitude toward her. She was the one about to take off into the blue horizon. In fact, *her* bags were probably already packed and waiting by the front door.

He rubbed his eyes, tired from the flight. It was a foregone conclusion they would have some kind of battle, but he didn't particularly feel like getting into it right now. He walked through the kitchen, disappointedly hearing the silence in the big house, sensing that the children weren't around anywhere.

He came upon Lainey in the living room, seated on an armchair, wearing faded blue jeans and a white V-neck T-shirt. She was frowning, holding a pen poised over the yellow legal pad resting on her lap. It annoyed him that she could look so innocent and so goddamn beautiful when she was about to get away with something so rotten.

She looked up as he entered, a guarded expression crossing her face as soon as she saw who it was.

"Where are the kids?" he asked curtly.

Anger flashed on her face. "And hello to you, too," she snapped. "They're out at a movie with Megan Burke and her kids. Thank you for inquiring. We've all been fine while you were away."

"You wish to exchange pleasantries?" His sarcasm was couched in a formal tone. "I beg your pardon. Lovely weather we're having, isn't it? Though not as nice as the weather in L.A., I suppose."

"I suppose not," she said, wondering what he was getting at. Her tone grew sharp once more. "Are you hinting that you're on your way out there next? A terrible loss, but we'll muddle through."

"On the contrary," he said, dropping his jacket over the arm of the couch. "I've arranged to stay put for the next couple of months. No more locations for right now. I'm sure it hadn't occurred to you, but it would be better for the kids if someone they felt comfortable with stayed around, rather than just their grandparents."

She gave a weary sigh. "Penn, I'm sorry, but I'm not in the mood for your oblique insults right now. I've got other things on my mind."

"Oh, I'm sure of that." He saw her draw back slightly at the anger in his voice. Damn. He hadn't wanted to get into this right now, but somehow he found it impossible to stop. "No doubt, you've got lists to make, which I presume you're working on right now. Important lists, like which clothes to pack and what new restaurants to try when you get there."

"When I get where?"

He shoved his hands in his pants pockets, walking, too restless to stand still. "Stop being coy, Lainey. We all know you're about to start your new career as a Hollywood mover and shaker. It's what, five or six days until the tenth? The great creative genius, starting up a new character, moving mountains, changing history. We wouldn't want two little kids to get in the way of *that,* now would we?"

She stared at him. "I don't remember mentioning the date."

He stopped and shrugged. "You've got some very chatty coworkers."

Her eyes narrowed. "Meaning what? You're not going to tell me you called my office to check up on what I've been doing? God help you if that's true."

He waved a hand at her dismissively. "Relax, nobody's checking up on you. I took a message for you one night, remember, from a woman you work with. Fran Morgan or Meyers or something, said she shared an office with you. She was only too glad to chat with me, tell me all about how excited she was for you, what a 'fabulous' summer you were going to have."

Lainey sounded disgusted. "Poor Fran was no match for your considerable charm over the telephone, I imagine."

He smiled. "Why, thank you," he said facetiously. "Anyway, she told me everyone was, quote, holding their breath, unquote, to find out what your decision would be on June tenth." He lowered his voice into a conspiratorial stage whisper. "She wondered if I might have the inside track on what you were thinking. But I said no, we were all holding our breath here, too."

He stopped directly in front of Lainey, his eyes boring into hers. "Of course, I didn't tell her that we didn't have to wonder about the answer. We all know you're only too glad to have this excuse to hightail it out of here. Not your fault, of course, nobody could pass up this kind of break. Nobody would even *expect* you to say no. And the grandparents are here, ready to force your hand anyway. So it all works out nice and neat. Doesn't it?"

He was startled to see her burst into laughter.

"So that's why you're so delightful tonight," she said, smiling. "But, as usual, you don't have the slightest clue what's really going on."

He bristled. "What the hell does that mean? Isn't the tenth the right day?"

She rose, transferring the pad and pen to one hand, and moved forward, about to walk past him. "Yes, it is," she said breezily.

Irritated beyond endurance, he grabbed her wrist as she crossed in front of him, stopping her, forcing her to look into his face. He was stunned to feel a charge of sexual desire so potent, it was all he could do not to push her back down onto the couch. God, how he wanted her.

He dropped her hand as quickly as if it were on fire.

Something flashed in her eyes in response to him, but she quickly averted her face. Her voice was quiet as she turned her gaze to him again.

"I turned down the Marissa project. I'm not going to Los Angeles. I'm not even working at Carpathia anymore. So I'm here and I intend to stay. Forever. I'm never leaving these kids. Not for a job, and not for your parents either, no matter how many high-priced attorneys they throw at me."

He took a step back, not trusting himself to stand so close to her, still taking in what she had just told him.

"You're staying?"

She nodded. "You're finally getting the picture."

Their eyes met. "Well," he said softly, "I'll be god-damned. I truly will be." Without thinking, he reached out and laid a gentle hand on her shoulder. "You surprise me. Yet again."

Her face flushed, and she pulled away hastily. "There's no reason to be so surprised," she said defensively.

This time it was his turn to laugh. "No, of course not. There was never a time when you considered giving up and leaving, or letting my parents have it their way. Never."

She winced. "Okay, I suppose you had to get that in sooner or later. Now you've had your fun, so knock it off. And now you won't have me to blame for keeping you from your precious assignments all over the globe, impressing the locals, sleeping with exotic women. You don't have to stick around waiting for me to disappear anymore, if that's what you've been doing."

He couldn't help himself. Moving closer, he put a hand out to touch her hair. "Maybe I want to be around."

They remained there, looking at each other, not moving. Then, the pen slid through Lainey's fingers onto the carpet. Quickly, she bent over to retrieve it. As she replaced it on the pad, she paused, gazing at what she had written on the top yellow page.

When she looked up again, her expression had turned grim.

"I guess it's time to tell you something. I made a promise to myself, but now the children are involved, and I can't wait around until the answer just comes to me. I need some help here."

He was puzzled. "Yes?"

"Sit down, Penn." Her tone softening, Lainey ushered him over to the couch. As they sat, she turned to face him, one leg tucked underneath her.

"What is this about the kids?" He laid one arm across the back of the couch.

She searched for the right words. "You saw that newspaper story, right? The one suggesting John was responsible for their deaths?"

"Lainey," he began in annoyance, "you can't possibly believe that. Somebody writes something in a paper—all of a sudden, it's real? No way. You know it, and I know it. Not John Cole."

She nodded. "I know that. But the children are suffering from the fallout of that article."

His eyes turned pained. "Oh, of course. The other kids—*damn it*."

"The point is, I have to prove that John didn't have anything to do with it for the children's sake."

"There's nothing you have to prove. The police believed it was an accident, and there's no reason to think John had—"

"Penn, listen," she interrupted fiercely. "It's not John I'm worried about. I think they both may have been murdered."

The silence was long and heavy as Penn stared at her. Finally, he shook his head. "I'm not getting this."

Lainey rubbed her eyes, as if prolonging the moments before her next words. She spoke so quietly, he had to strain to hear her. "I don't understand it all. But Farrell . . . She was involved in something not right, and I'm afraid there's a connection."

"Not right," he said sharply. "What do you mean, not right?"

"Oh, Penn," she said miserably. "I found a key to a hotel room in Farrell's things. I went there and watched. There were men and women coming and going. It was obvious."

"What was obvious?" he asked slowly, as if he really didn't want to know.

Lainey went on. "And something had been wrong between Farrell and John. Tim told me he heard them fighting the day before they died, and it was something to do with a suite. I'm guessing that's the same hotel suite."

His eyes locked on hers. "What the hell are you saying?"

She gazed down into her lap. "It was some kind of call girl operation. And Farrell was involved somehow."

Penn clenched his fists. "Have you lost your mind? What possible reason could she have had for getting into something like that?" His voice was growing more urgent. "My sister was a happily married woman."

Lainey bit her lip. "It's not the happily married Farrell who would have done it." Her voice dropped. "It's the old Farrell, our old Farrell. The one who loved to be wild."

Penn swallowed. He understood exactly what she meant. He felt a stab of fear at the idea that she might be right. "And?" he managed to get out.

"I don't see how it all fits together, but I can't help believing that it does. I don't think it was an accident, Penn. I believe somebody came into the house and tampered with that furnace because they wanted to kill Farrell. Or John. Or maybe both of them."

Penn shut his eyes, his horror mounting as he went over the days surrounding his sister's death, now recast in the light of a murder.

"That's what I've been doing," she went on, holding out the yellow pad slightly so he could see the scrawled notes on it. "Writing it all down. I'm trying to make sense of everything I know. Like, why is John's computer diary missing the whole month of February? And you weren't here when I got that call—someone calling to tell me it *was* murder, that John had nothing to do with it."

"What?" Penn exploded. "Are you serious?"

She nodded unhappily. "I've really come to believe someone killed them."

"Do you have any ideas who might have done it?" he said hoarsely.

"Not really, no."

"What about the police? Do they know about this?"

"I went to them. But it was before I found out about Farrell and the hotel. I just went to ask if they had any reason to think it might not have been an accident." She looked pained. "The only thing that came of it was that article in the local paper accusing John."

He nodded, attempting to compose himself. Finally, he took a deep breath and exhaled slowly. "Well, if it's true, then we're going to find the person who did it. Together."

Lainey had barely enough time to fill Penn in on the details of what she had discovered so far before Tim and Riley returned home from the movies, Megan sticking her head in to shout a quick hello, then driving off. It wasn't until the children were settled into bed for the night that Lainey and Penn finally convened again in the living room to discuss what their next step might be.

"You don't think I'm crazy, do you?" Lainey asked him as she dropped down onto the couch. "I really wish you would tell me I am. Maybe all those things—running into Sugar and Carol Anne at that hotel, all the other stuff I told you—maybe none of it means anything."

He shook his head. "If it turns out to be a wild series of coincidences, that would be great. But, hell, what I do for a living is investigate things, so we're going to get working until we figure out what was going on here, once and for all."

She sighed. "It may be worse to know."

He ignored her remark. "I've got several ideas of where to start. First of all, we have to decide who might have been the intended target. Farrell or John?"

"Or both," Lainey offered.

"Right."

Penn sat down next to her and placed his hand on her arm. She felt a jolt at his touch. *Cut it out,* she told herself adamantly. This wasn't the time to be entertaining notions of kissing him, holding him. He didn't even seem to notice he was touching her. Make him stop, she begged silently. Make him go on forever.

"We should be going through all their things first," he said almost to himself. He turned away, removing his hand, apparently oblivious to the fact that he had touched her at all.

Concentrate, she admonished herself again. He's playing games with you, just like that first time. Penn Beckley loved nothing better than turning his charm on some poor female. She flooded red with embarrassment as she thought about that night months before, here on the same couch. Caresses, soft words. It had meant absolutely nothing.

Nothing to him, she acknowledged, knowing, deep inside, where it had lain hidden since that night, that, in fact, it had meant quite a lot to her. She was startled to realize that that one night was burned more deeply into her memory than any ten nights with Julian Kroll. Or with anyone else, for that matter.

Which leaves me where, she thought, watching Penn get up to pace. Exactly where I was before. Alone. As always. Forever.

Not true, she realized, thinking of the two children she'd committed herself to. That's right, she thought with sudden pride, *committed* myself to.

She shook her head clear of her thoughts. Right now, it was time to set the record straight for Farrell and John. She got up and came around to stand in front of Penn.

"I've gone through most of their things," she said. "John kept some business papers here, but I didn't notice anything out of the ordinary about them. Of course, I just glanced at that stuff. If you want to go through those more carefully, they're pretty easy to pull together."

"Let's do it."

They went into John's study, pulling boxes out of the cabinets, and files from the drawers. Spreading out on the floor, they began poring over the documents, searching for anything at all that might stand out.

They worked silently, one or the other occasionally making an observation, looking hard for any possible links. Penn had a thick stack of file folders from the lower right-hand drawer of John's desk, and he had been patiently going through them for nearly two hours when he stopped, letting out a long, low whistle. He held up a white piece of paper with typing on it.

"What is it?" Lainey asked.

"A list of people." Penn handed it over for Lainey to examine. "It's from a file marked Marina Paulsen, some policewoman John represented. I don't know what it means, but take a look."

Lainey ran her eyes down the page. She didn't recognize any of them, a seemingly random assortment of names in no particular order that she could discern. It was—

She stopped and stared at the name, fourth from the bottom.

Sugar Taplinger.

Lainey felt sick to her stomach. She looked over at Penn. "It wasn't a coincidence that I saw her in the hotel," she said. "Somehow, this all fits together."

Penn retrieved the piece of paper from her. "It looks that way. But what's the connection?"

Lainey was trying to make sense of it all. "I figured she had something to do with the . . . that business at the hotel. But what is her name doing in John's files?"

Penn gave her a questioning glance. "And in a file relating to a cop, no less." He looked at the name on the file again. "Marina Paulsen. Maybe this was all a lot less innocent than it appeared."

Lainey turned a confused face to Penn. "Could she be on a list of intended victims? Maybe all the women involved in that call girl ring are in trouble."

Penn stood, stretching his cramped legs. "Here's what we'll do. I'm going to take tomorrow off, and we're going to split up to pursue whatever we've got."

"Well, I'm certainly going to see what else I can find out about Sugar Taplinger," Lainey said. She got up and took a deep breath. "This woman was Farrell's *next door neighbor*. Some nice lady in the suburbs who makes incredible cakes and sandwiches." She suddenly looked wild-eyed as she turned to Penn. "Who's over here all the time, offering me help. She's saved my ass more than once when I needed someone to take the kids. . . .

"God, Penn." Her voice was anguished. "Who *is* this woman? Either she's mixed up in some incredibly dirty mess. Or worse—what if she actually had some part in killing Farrell and John?"

She covered her face with her hands. Penn came to stand beside her. He put his arms around her comfortingly. She felt his lips brush her forehead. "It'll be all right, Lainey," he murmured. "It's better to find out the truth."

She wanted to stay there, wrapped in his arms, for the rest of her life. She felt completely safe for the first time in—it struck her like a blow that she had never before felt as safe in the arms of any man.

But when she looked up, she saw that there was hurt in his eyes. Farrell was his little sister. As upsetting as it may have been for Lainey, she had had time to adjust to each new piece of the puzzle as it presented itself. Penn had just had it all thrust at him at once, the shock of what Farrell was doing, the suggestion that she had been deliberately killed. It had to be tearing him apart.

Lainey forced a small smile.

"You're right. It's better to know the truth."

They picked up the files and put them away, doing their best to leave the room looking undisturbed so the children wouldn't notice anything amiss in the morning. Lainey saw the combination of pain and determination on his face as he said good night. She watched him leave, her heart aching for him, aching for herself.

Chapter 30

Lainey thought she would burst with impatience, waiting for Penn to get home the next afternoon. She had spent most of the day in the Meadowview Library, and her shock over what she had found left her jumpy and distracted.

She was relieved to learn from Mrs. Miles that Riley had gone over to a friend's house for some kind of meeting with a few of the kids in her computer club, and Tim had called to say he was staying at school for an impromptu softball game. Thank goodness, Lainey thought, saying good-bye to the housekeeper until the next day. It meant she and Penn were free to do whatever came next. But where the hell was he?

Grabbing the checkbook and a bunch of bills from a basket in one of the kitchen cabinets, she sat down at the table to make some use of her time while she waited. She picked up a pen, and started going over the electric bill. But Farrell's face was there before her, more vivid than ever. Lainey felt a surge of anger within her.

"Why, why, why?" she asked the image, her frustration mounting. Would she ever find out what had really happened? Had Farrell gone to that hotel to meet men once or a hundred times? Did she do it because she enjoyed it?

"Why couldn't you tell me?" Lainey whispered,

acknowledging for the first time how hurt she was that Farrell hadn't wanted to confide in her, or hadn't felt that she could. Lainey chewed on her thumbnail, wondering what she would have said if she *had* known.

Frustrated, she pushed her chair away from the table. A car was pulling up outside. At last, Penn was back. She hurried to meet him at the front door.

"You won't believe what I saw at the library," she said urgently, coming up to him and reaching out with both hands to grab onto his forearms. "I'm so glad you're finally here."

She saw him glance down at her hands, saw the smile that flickered across his face. Embarrassed, she broke away.

"Did you find out anything?" she asked brusquely.

He nodded, putting his hand lightly on the small of her back and steering her into the family room. "But you go first."

They sat down, facing each other on the couch. Lainey's words came tumbling out. "I did what you suggested and went through all the Meadowview newspapers for the six months before February. There was nothing, nothing, nothing. And then, just a few weeks before Farrell and John died, I found it. Her picture and everything."

"What?" Penn urged.

"Marina Paulsen, the policewoman whose file we were going through last night. Penn, she *died* just before they did. The paper said her car went off the road and crashed. But it was the woman with the list that had Sugar's name on it. I mean, I know it was an accident and all, but don't you think that's an odd coincidence?"

"Jesus Christ." Penn digested this. "Of course, Farrell and John were also supposed to be an accident."

Lainey nodded. "And, besides that, I did research into Sugar. Her maiden name was Lawton, and her real first name is Beatrice."

"Beatrice?" Penn asked sharply.

"Yes." Lainey waited, but he didn't say anything else. "Anyway, I remembered two useful things she'd said. First of all, she had made a joke at last year's Christmas party here about some football player she dated at Penn State. So I get on the telephone to Penn State, and it turns out there's no record of Beatrice Lawton or Sugar Taplinger or anybody remotely like that in any years it might have been possible for her to be in college."

"Goes along with the whole picture," Penn interjected.

"And then," Lainey continued, "she also mentioned once that she had been a paralegal at a law firm in New York before she married Helmut, you know, explaining that she used to work before they moved up here. The only reason I remembered this was because the name struck me. She'd said the firm was Gardner, Burnett and something or other."

"You remembered that?" Penn asked skeptically. "Why would you?"

Lainey smiled. "Frances Hodgson Burnett was the author of *The Secret Garden,* which was my favorite book when I was a kid. Gardner, Garden. Burnett. I might not remember my own phone number, but you could ask me that when I'm eighty, and I'd still know it. I thought it was a pretty funny coincidence, though I didn't say anything about it to Sugar."

"Yeah, I remember Farrell reading that over and over when we were kids," Penn recalled with a quiet chuckle.

"Anyway," Lainey said, "I checked, and there's no such firm in New York."

Penn gazed at her admiringly. "Nice work for a morning."

Lainey was mortified to feel herself blushing under his praise. She cleared her throat to disguise her discomfort.

"And what did you come up with?"

"Well, once you pointed it out to me last night, I was really struck by how the kids were out of the house when it happened. I was always so grateful for that, I never thought that you could also look at it as being way too convenient." Penn frowned. "So I started by talking to a guy I know at the phone company, somebody I interviewed a long time ago for research on a story. Guess what?"

Lainey waited, not moving.

"Farrell didn't make that call to the Gisondi woman to ask her to take the kids overnight. The call came from the Gisondi phone *into* this house. *She* called Farrell."

"I knew it," Lainey breathed. "Damn it, I *knew* Carol Anne was lying. The whole thing with those kids being friends was wrong from the start."

She sat there, thinking, then spoke again. "So that means Carol Anne was somehow in this, and she was at the hotel because she's one of the women . . ."

"That's right," Penn assented.

"I don't believe it. That little nervous, mousy woman." Lainey's shoulders sagged. "I feel like I'll never really know anything about anybody for the rest of my life."

"That's not all. I went to the St.-Tropez. At first, I couldn't get anywhere, and I had to go up a few layers to one of the more senior managers. But I found out about that suite, albeit with the help of a five-hundred-dollar bribe and the threat of going to the police to expose their respectable little hotel."

Lainey snapped to attention. "Tell me."

"The room is registered to a Jeanette Beatrice. That's why I was surprised when you told me Sugar's real name was Beatrice. I don't know who the hell Jeanette's supposed to be."

"The room is registered to Sugar?"

Penn nodded. "The guy finally coughed up her real name. She'd never told anyone at the hotel, just went by the alias, but he made it his business to find out who she really was. The hotel has permitted this racket to go on— for years, he tells me—and they take the cash and make like they don't know a thing. He told me Sugar's always been the one to pay the bills."

Lainey ran her hand through her hair. "In other words, Sugar runs the whole thing. She's not just one of the women there. She's the head of it."

Penn nodded, then held up one hand, ticking off the points on his fingers as he spoke. "And she's on a list of names drawn up by a cop who dies just before Farrell and John. The list is in John's possession. Farrell is part of the circle of call girls." He winced at the words he had just said, then went on, dropping his hand back into his lap. "The connections are all there, although I could come up with several different scenarios explaining them."

The two of them sat quietly for a while. Finally, Lainey broke the silence. "What do we do now? There are all these links, but I don't see what you'd call real proof that Sugar's the one."

"Right," Penn said with a nod. "We need to find out for certain. And I've been tossing over an idea in my mind while I was driving home."

"Yes?"

"I'm going to talk to Helmut Taplinger."

Lainey looked at him questioningly. "Do you think he'd inform on his own wife?"

"I don't know." Penn shook his head. "Who knows if he has any information to give. Does he even know about his wife's extracurricular activities?" He looked at Lainey as if she might supply the answer.

Lainey just shrugged.

Penn smiled. "But the one thing I do know about Helmut is that he's a guy who likes the sound of his own voice. Even if he knows nothing, he may let out some interesting information. And there's certainly no use going back to Carol Anne."

Lainey nodded in agreement, then stood up and walked across the room. As she turned to face him, Penn could sense her anxiety.

"What's the matter?" he asked, leaning back against the couch and trying to read her expression.

"Nothing," she answered a little too quickly.

He stood up and came over to her. "What?" he demanded more insistently.

"I'm thinking about what Sugar might do if Helmut tells her about your suspicions." Lainey's fear was apparent. "Who knows what Carol Anne has already said to her?" Her voice had taken on a fevered quality.

Penn draped one arm lightly around her shoulders. "Don't worry, Lainey," he said almost jovially, "I'll protect you."

"And exactly who's going to protect *you*?" she asked, extracting herself from his hold and walking several feet away.

"Sugar isn't going to do anything to either one of us, I swear it," he answered more seriously.

He'd meant to reassure her, but Lainey seemed to be growing more upset with each passing second.

"God, Penn, please. This woman may be dangerous. This could be the person who killed Farrell and John. I don't want you interrogating Helmut, practically *asking* her to kill you, too. You can't!"

He stood before her, an expression on his face she couldn't read. "Why can't I? Think how wonderful it would be if she succeeded, all the peace and quiet you'd have around here."

"Don't joke about it!" Lainey felt an unbearable clutch of alarm at the idea of what might happen. She couldn't bear to lose him, too.

But who was she kidding? she thought suddenly. No matter what happened, she would lose him in the end. He would go back to London or some such place. Coming and going was what his life had always been about.

In fact, he had been living at the house nearly as long as she had, but there was an unspoken agreement that his stay here was temporary. She pictured what it was going to be like when he left, of how empty the house would be, how empty her own life would be. The realization stung like a blow.

"Who cares what you do," she exclaimed angrily. "You're halfway out of here anyway." Without realizing what she was doing, her hands formed into fists, and she started to raise them. In her deep hurt, she felt an atavistic urge to punish him.

But his arms came around her, and he drew her to him, hard, his mouth coming down on hers. The hunger of their kiss was so powerful, Lainey felt as if she were being pulled under by some force that blacked out everything around them and left her with only the feel of him, the taste of him, the need to be with him.

They sank down onto the soft carpet, their kisses still ferocious but their bodies gently molding together, as if the moment were fragile. Then, she felt his hand moving to stroke her cheek, running along her shoulder and arm, down to her thigh. She uttered a gasp, feeling him claim her, rocked by how much she wanted him. She pressed herself against him, the gentleness of the moment before completely gone now as their need for each other overtook them.

They were struggling out of their clothes, exquisitely tortured by the delay of buttons and zippers, their mouths never parting.

"Lainey," he sighed slowly, reverently, as she finally shrugged off the last garment and was naked against him. He ran his hands along the curve of her back and up her sides to the fullness of her breasts. She shuddered with the pleasure of it.

I love you, she thought, suddenly knowing it was useless to pretend it wasn't so, holding onto him as if for dear life.

He moved over her, and she urged him with her body to continue. But he stopped to take her face in both his hands and gaze into her eyes, his desire plainly visible, yet held at bay.

"I can't help it," he said softly. "I love you."

Lainey thought her heart had stopped. She didn't breathe.

"I guess I always have." He spoke almost wonderingly, then brought his mouth to meet hers once more, this time in a kiss so tender, it left no room for doubt.

They moved together, Lainey drowning in the flood of her feelings and thoughts. Exhilarated by his words, she was also terrified of what had to be coming next, the fear that was as well-known to her as an old friend. It was the same fear that had made her run from Julian's proposal, that had tormented her in the first weeks of living with

Chapter 31

"So, this young upstart sits there in my office, insisting that he deserves a job at the magazine"—Helmut poked his index finger out so firmly, it threatened to insert itself into Penn's chest—"*and then he mispronounces my name.*" Helmut shook his head in disgust. " 'Taplinger,' I told him. 'Like *linger,* not like *binger.*' " This time, Helmut punched his finger into the air three times in a row for emphasis. "Well," he continued, his face reddening and his thatch of white hair sticking straight up from his head, "if this kid can't even remember that much, how am I supposed to trust him to edit a scholarly magazine."

In his frenzy, Helmut had begun to look to Penn like something midway between a beet and a scallion. He had all he could do to keep from laughing. Finally, he managed to summon a "Well . . ." in response.

Helmut nodded as if Penn's reply had been a vote of absolute support.

Penn looked around the Taplingers' kitchen, wondering how to turn the conversation where he needed it to go. It had been twenty minutes at least since he'd accidentally on purpose run into Helmut in the yard, quizzing him on issues related to *Armchair General,* and getting himself invited in for a cup of coffee. Penn had observed

Sugar leaving before he came over, and he wanted to finish up before her return.

"My brother-in-law was a great fan of your magazine," Penn said earnestly.

Helmut looked up, a proud smile lighting his face. "Well, I can't say I knew that, but it shouldn't surprise me. You know, we've turned a profit every year since I arrived."

"He was one of the smartest guys I ever knew," Penn said sadly. "Not that my sister was any slouch." He reached for the white porcelain mug on the table in front of him.

Helmut looked appropriately sympathetic. "They were fine people," he agreed.

"But, every now and then," Penn said, after taking a long sip of coffee, "I wonder how happy they were with each other."

Helmut looked up in surprise. "They seemed quite happy to me."

Penn nodded. "It's just, well, they were married a long time, and they were both so young . . . and, to tell you the truth, we found some surprising stuff when we were clearing out their bedroom. A key from the St.-Tropez Hotel, for example . . ."

Helmut's shocked intake of breath did not escape Penn's notice. He decided to press on.

"You know, Lainey ran into your wife there one day not so long ago. What is it with that place?" Penn's voice was pleasant enough, but his sharp gaze never left Helmut's face.

"I don't know what you're talking about," Helmut answered briskly, taking a look at his watch and jumping out of his chair. "You'll have to pardon me, but I have several articles to finish and only a few hours left." He walked toward his back door purposefully, pulling it open and standing beside it.

Penn stood and joined his host at the door. The two men shook hands, and Helmut closed the door firmly behind him.

Well, Penn thought as he walked across the yard, one thing had definitely been established. Helmut Taplinger knew about his wife's activities at the St.-Tropez. Was he involved in the murders as well? That, Penn was less sure of. One thing he did acknowledge—he had enjoyed his host's discomfort. Not that he was exactly sure of what he'd accomplished by rattling Helmut's cage, but something was bound to come out of this.

"I tell you he knows everything."

Helmut had been hysterical since Sugar walked in the door, pacing around the kitchen as she put away groceries, his spindly voice rising in pitch as he worked himself up even further. His obvious frustration grew even stronger as Sugar hid her concern.

"Darling," she said, smiling, her expression composed and calm, "I don't know what you think he knows, but it couldn't matter less."

"Believe me, he knows about the St.-Tropez, that much was clear." Helmut looked at Sugar beseechingly. "What else could he know about? What haven't you told me?"

Sugar picked up a container of cottage cheese and walked over to the refrigerator. "What in the world would be so terrible that I wouldn't tell you?" Her face was turned away from him, but she listened intently for his answer.

"I don't know." Helmut sounded almost afraid.

Could he even imagine the truth? Sugar wondered as she noted his hesitancy. When she turned around, she gave him a glance so nakedly appraising, it started him blathering apologies.

Her voice was fierce as she walked over to him and spoke quietly into his ear. "Whatever it is you're thinking, it's only going to cause you pain. I have done nothing, absolutely nothing, that I'm ashamed of." She glanced at him disparagingly. "I have never hidden my activities from you, nor have I ever embarrassed you with them." She walked away from him, grabbing a large Cadbury bar from one of the shopping bags and tearing it open. Voraciously, she took a large bite, chewing it thoroughly as she looked squarely at her husband.

Helmut stood where he was, his expression both frightened and crestfallen. "I know, Sugar. I'm sorry. I didn't mean to accuse you. I'm just . . ."

"You're just behind in your work and anxious to get back to it," she finished the sentence for him.

Helmut looked as if he wanted to say more, but finally he shuffled out of the kitchen. Sugar heard his footsteps as he climbed the stairway, undoubtedly to hide away in his office.

When she heard the door close, she sank onto a kitchen chair. If only she felt as confident as she sounded. Of course, Penn knew about the business. Lainey had obviously figured it out and spread the news.

She took another bite of the chocolate. Which probably meant that they suspected the murders as well. Screw Lainey Wolfe. Moves to town just to make trouble for Sugar Taplinger. Chewing slowly, she thought of the people who'd made trouble for her in the past. It was a long parade of faces. She imagined an enormous tidal wave sweeping them all away, their futile cries for help filling the air as they were swept out to sea. Grinning, she crumpled up the candy bar wrapper and deposited it in the trash basket.

Chapter 32

As the sunlight streamed in through the bedroom window, Helmut turned over and looked at the clock. Eight forty-five, he thought with alarm. Getting out of bed quickly, he noticed with surprise that Sugar's side of the bed seemed undisturbed.

Where was she all night? he thought irritably. How could she have let me oversleep like this? He walked to the door and called out her name twice, without getting any response.

"Damn," he said out loud, walking into the bathroom.

Ten minutes later, scrubbed clean, his white hair plastered wetly to his head, he walked into the kitchen, annoyed to see that the kitchen table had not been set.

"Sugar," he called out once more, only then noticing the pale blue envelope with his name on it in her handwriting, left on top of the stove.

Abruptly recalling his fears from the day before, he opened it hesitantly.

> Helmut,
>   I'm sorry about what I have to tell you. You were so right yesterday, right about everything you were too decent to say. What I did to Farrell and John Cole is too awful to live with. Yes, I murdered them,

*and now I owe them—and, my beloved, you—my life
as well. Please forgive me for what I have to do. And
know that this note is for you only, just as our love
was between you and I. I go to my death safe and
happy in that knowledge.*

> *Yours forever,*
> *S*

Helmut felt the heavy sobs as they rose through his
body. "Between you and *me*," he heard himself repeating
over and over as the grief began to pour out of his eyes.

"I'm sorry, Mr. Taplinger," the shorter officer in the
blue seersucker suit said, not for the first time.

"What time did the car go into the water?" Helmut
asked helplessly, as he slumped into a chair in the living
room. "How long did it take you to get it out?"

The two policemen had arrived just before ten in the
morning in response to Helmut's telephone call. They'd
returned around three to pick him up and take him to
Sugar's car, which she'd driven off the boardwalk in
neighboring Lyonsport sometime during the night.
Helmut had had to identify the Jeep as one that had
belonged to him and his wife. At first, not having to identify Sugar's body had been a relief.

It was only now, after the officers had accompanied
him home, with sunset leaving its dark imprint on everything that had happened, that Helmut found himself
unable to face being left alone.

He asked question after question in an effort to keep
the two men there with him. Why hadn't the body sur-
faced yet? Where would it show up if it took another
twelve hours? Another day? Another week?

The taller officer, a black man in his early forties,

shook his head and walked over to the wet bar in the corner, pouring out a glass of Scotch. "Here, try this," he said kindly, holding the glass out to Helmut.

Gratefully, he accepted it, drinking it down in one gulp. He found himself slightly dizzy, a reverberating buzz of pain boring into his head.

"I'm sorry for your loss," the white policeman said one more time, "but Seth and I have to get back to the station to write up the report."

The two officers looked at each other and made their way to the front door. Helmut realized he had no way of stopping them and slumped farther into his seat.

He thought about all the things he should be doing, people he should be calling, legal details that had to be seen to, but he couldn't get himself to move. Only after half an hour did he rouse himself from the chair, going up the stairs to stand in the doorway of Sugar's office.

The piles of paper were neatly stacked as usual, notepads and folders aligned in order of size. He walked over to her brown leather swivel chair, the indentation of her body permanently worn into it.

Her body, he thought, aching inside. Where was her body? Would it wash up soon, or would he be racked by uncertainty forever? He couldn't bear to think about it, her essence, floating in the vastness of the chilly water, lost to him, lost to heaven.

A bullet of anguish exploded in his belly. How could she have done this? He would have forgiven her anything; she must have known that. He had always been there for her. She couldn't have doubted it.

The pain he felt was unbearable. There had to be something he could do, he thought miserably, something he could accomplish that would lessen the agony. Idly, he noticed that the door to the room's small closet was open. Out of habit, he walked over to close it.

Your wife is dead, and you're worried about a door being left open! he thought, shutting the door so ferociously that it swung open once again. He reached out, intending to close it firmly this time, when his eye fell on the back of the closet. It was so clean, so empty.

Had it always been that way? he wondered, scanning the bare flooring. Frowning, he shut the door and walked over to her desk, this time sitting in her chair. For several moments, he stared vacantly at the wall above her desk. Had she had anything in there before? he wondered, wishing with all his heart that he'd shown more interest in her affairs while she'd been alive.

But a knot of fear was starting to form. As little time as he'd spent in her office, he could swear that closet floor had contained any number of things. Why would she clean out that closet before committing suicide? It just didn't make any sense.

Helmut stood up and shook his head. He was being ridiculous. Who cared if she cleaned out a closet sometime in the past couple of months? Sugar was dead. That was the only thing that mattered.

But he found himself obsessed with thoughts of that cleared space when he fell into bed a few minutes later. Could she have been wearing something from that closet when she drove the car into the water?

He might never know. Her body might never be found. The officers had said as much earlier that evening.

No body.

His breath suddenly caught in his throat. What if there were no body?

What if only the car was in the water? What if Sugar

had simply been sick of *him*? What if she were out there somewhere making a whole new life for herself?

She would never do that to me, he reasoned, turning on the light and sitting up. He punched up the pillows and tried to make himself more comfortable. He reached for the copy of David Donald's Lincoln biography, which he'd left on the night table, trying desperately to immerse himself in the chapter detailing young Abe's relationship with his stepmother. But it was no use. The lines seemed to blur together to form an indistinguishable mush. Finally, he laid the book facedown on his stomach and stared into the darkness.

"She loved me," he assured himself in the silence of the empty house.

Lainey looked back toward the Taplinger house, wondering if Helmut had fallen asleep yet. All day long, she'd debated calling him, but she couldn't make herself dial the number.

The news of Sugar's suicide had come with a phone call from the Meadowview police, informing Lainey of the contents of the note she had left. But the arrival of the *Ledger* in the middle of the afternoon still came as a shock.

MEADOWVIEW MATRON A SUICIDE! the headline screamed in big black letters, a sizable picture of Sugar right next to it.

Lainey and Penn had spent the bulk of the afternoon trying to figure out how much to tell the children. If they had their way, Tim and Riley would never know of Farrell's participation in the activities at the St.-Tropez, but the news that Sugar had killed their parents wasn't something to hide. By the time the children had gotten home from school, she and Penn had decided exactly what words to use. They'd relayed their abbreviated version of the story as gently as possible. Tim and Riley had reacted by becoming very quiet, and they'd stayed that way for the rest of the afternoon, both of them eating little at dinner and apparently glad to go to bed early that evening.

Penn had gone back to Manhattan. He'd spent far too much time investigating Sugar; he had work to do. There were a million things for Lainey to do in the house, and this was the perfect opportunity to get them done. She could even luxuriate in a warm bubble bath or get into the stack of magazines at the foot of the bed.

But it was impossible. Her mind refused to let go of the thought that had been haunting her. She would never have frightened the children by saying it out loud. But she couldn't lie to herself. She just didn't believe what the police were saying. Sugar Taplinger was not a woman ashamed of her actions. She was a cold-blooded murderer, incapable of that kind of personal sacrifice.

Lainey could believe that Sugar had disappeared. But nothing could convince her that Sugar would take her own life.

Chapter 33

Sugar sat at the wheel of the white Oldsmobile she'd rented, her shoulders thick with tension, the pains shooting down the back of her neck making her long for the aspirin she hadn't thought to take with her. She surveyed the scene around her, the park few people bothered to visit and nobody seemed to take care of. There were empty soda cans littering the dense underbrush and plastic bags with the rotting remains of half-consumed family lunches.

She had driven here the morning before, intending to camp out in the woods until she decided exactly how to proceed. If only I could have brought everything I needed, she thought, annoyed at the discomfort she'd had to endure. Without a blanket or a change of clothes, she'd had to sleep in the back of the car, not an easy task for a woman her size.

It was foresight, not luck, she thought with satisfaction, that made her stockpile identification under the name Beatrice Samuels. Not that she knew for sure that something would happen; but if and when it did, she would be ready. And, she thought with pride, she had been ready, even if she hadn't been able to take much besides the bags of cash she'd kept stored away all these years.

Well, that's all I need anyway, she thought, opening the car door and getting out to stretch.

She lifted her arms over her head, then brought them back to her sides. Not much of an outfit for exercise, she thought, amused as she looked down at her bright red silk caftan. She began to walk in a small circle, moving her shoulders up and down, in and out, in an effort to get the kinks out, but it did little to ease her discomfort.

She slid back into the front seat, tapping her fingernails impatiently on the steering wheel. She knew she ought to drive as far from Meadowview as possible, but she couldn't bring herself to do it. Not that she regretted writing the note to Helmut and pushing the car into the water. She just couldn't face leaving that damned Lainey Wolfe and those bratty little kids to live America's most perfect life. Sleep had come hard in the confines of the Olds, but that was okay with her, just as long as the plan she'd spent most of the night developing allowed her to leave Meadowview in a manner she could look back on with satisfaction.

Why, in her entire life, she reflected, no one had left her in peace. If only Lainey had been smart enough to keep out of it. Now she would have to punish her. And not just Lainey, either. She would have to deal with the kids, too. It wasn't as if she had anything against Tim and Riley. For God's sake, she moved them out of harm's way once before. No time for pity, she decided, pushing the thought out of her mind.

Lainey, she didn't feel sorry for at all. Sugar chuckled as she thought of the weapon Lainey had put in her hand all that time before. Julian Kroll. It had been so easy

Chapter 34

Lainey came into the kitchen, grabbing a paper towel to wipe the perspiration from her forehead after her three-mile run. She went through a mental list of all the things she had to do today.

All day yesterday had been devoted to the horror of Sugar Taplinger's suicide. Not that in her heart of hearts Lainey believed she had really done it, but finally, in the light of day, after a lengthy discussion with Penn, she had come to the conclusion that, even if she were alive, Sugar would be hightailing it out of the country. She was effectively out of their lives forever.

The ringing of the telephone interrupted her thoughts.

"I'll get it," she called out, knowing Mrs. Miles was somewhere else in the house.

"Hello."

There was a deep male voice on the other end. "Hello, may I speak to Lainey Wolfe?"

"Speaking. Who is this?"

"Ms. Wolfe, this is Oscar Shaw. We've never met, but we're sort of neighbors. I live over on Pine Lane."

"Oh," she said.

"I apologize if I'm disturbing you, but I just tracked down your number, and I didn't want to put it off. The reason I'm calling is that I've been following your cartoons in the *Ledger*. I think they're brilliant."

"Well, thank you. That's very kind of you." Lainey was flattered and a bit surprised that some guy in Meadowview had gone to the trouble of contacting her personally with his compliment.

"I'd like to see more of them if I could. As soon as possible, in fact."

She shifted her weight, and her tone grew more guarded. "Well, they'll certainly continue to be in the paper."

"No, no, we'd like to do this faster," he replied. There was a pause. "I'm sorry. I'm not being clear. I'm an executive vice president in the creative department at Dorset Enterprises. We've got a group of people who want to get together with you. You see, I brought a bunch of the cartoons into a meeting and they got a terrific response."

Dorset. Startled, Lainey was momentarily at a loss for words. Carpathia's biggest competitor had been following her little "Hey, you!" cartoons in the Meadowview paper. *I'll be goddamned.*

Apparently realizing she wasn't going to say anything, he went on. "Dorset is heavily involved in syndication, and we feel your strip is an excellent candidate. We'd want to work it all out with an eye toward merchandising the character. She's got some great potential."

"Really?" Lainey hoped she sounded nonchalant, but she doubted it.

"So, you think we might set up a meeting to talk about all this?"

Lainey broke into a broad grin. "Absolutely."

"Good. I'll have my secretary call you on Monday to arrange a time."

"That will be fine, Mr. Shaw."

"I look forward to meeting you."

Lainey hung up the telephone and stared at it. Slowly, a huge grin spread across her face.

"Someone named Maria Kroll called," Mrs. Miles said, entering the kitchen.

Her joy suddenly dissipated, and all the air seemed to leave Lainey's lungs.

"You're supposed to meet her at three-thirty at that old diner near the parkway." Mrs. Miles shook her head. "I told her you'd be picking up the kids from that awards assembly, but she wouldn't take no for an answer. Claimed you'd 'handle it,' whatever that means."

"And you'll handle it perfectly, whatever it is you're supposed to be doing," Penn said jovially, coming into the kitchen from the other end of the room, and planting a quick kiss on Lainey's nose. "Who are you supposed to be meeting there?"

Lainey didn't answer him at first. Instead, she looked at her watch and addressed her attention once again to the housekeeper. "What old diner is that?" she asked, wishing Penn were not in the room.

"It's the one near the arboretum, you know, up past Belmont Hill."

Penn looked at Lainey curiously. "What're you doing at the arboretum?"

Lainey looked pointedly at Mrs. Miles. She wished she could not answer, but realized that no answer at all would only make it sound worse than it was. "Maria Kroll called," she said as matter-of-factly as she could. "She wants me to meet her in an hour or so." Breathlessly, she hurried on, longing to change the subject. "And you won't believe what happened today. This guy from Dorset called about my cartoons . . ."

It had taken Penn a minute to figure out who Maria Kroll was, but when he did, his response was adamant. "Julian's wife? There's no reason for you to meet Maria Kroll."

Mrs. Miles looked up in surprise. Raising one eyebrow, she gazed from Penn to Lainey. "I'll be upstairs if you need me," she said tactfully, going out toward the stairway.

Lainey turned to Penn. "I don't see that I have any choice. It's not as if I want to go."

"Excuse me," Penn said harshly. "We humans always have a choice."

Lainey looked at him in dismay. "You don't understand—"

"Oh, yes, I do," Penn interjected. He walked over to Lainey and placed his arms around her. "Honey," he said, his voice conciliatory, "Julian was your past. This is your future. There's no reason to look back."

Lainey extricated herself from his arms. "It's not a question of looking back. It's just, well, I owe this woman something."

Penn shrugged. "You owe her not seeing her husband anymore. As far as I know, you've been acting on that fact for the past couple of months." He frowned. "But, maybe I don't know everything there is to know."

"Oh, Penn, don't be ridiculous," Lainey said irritably. "You know damn well I haven't spoken to Julian."

His mouth thinned disdainfully. "What's ridiculous is going on some wild-goose chase with your ex-lover's wife. If you no longer cared for Julian Kroll, you wouldn't feel this compelling need to chase down the missus."

"I acted badly, and there are amends to make." Lainey approached him, taking his hand and holding it within both of hers. "Listen," she said sadly, "I don't know why Julian's wife is suddenly calling me, but I can't just leave her waiting at some diner in the middle of nowhere. I've done enough to her already."

Penn pulled back his hand. "Fine. I'll pick up Tim and Riley." He looked at her impatiently. "You go looking for trouble, as you always do."

This time it was Lainey's turn to walk out of the room.

Chapter 35

Just put one foot in front of the other, Lainey thought to herself as she saw the ramshackle old wood-paneled diner up ahead. She tried to take comfort from the beauty of the surroundings. The large sign reading SEMINOLE ARBORETUM was a few yards behind the diner, but the mile-long approach to it had been spectacular. As she got out of the car, she noticed a sign to two different hiking trails, one called FOREST DRIVE, the other OVERLOOK HEIGHTS.

If only I were coming here to hike, she thought, coming up to the door and resting one hand on the knob. She looked around her one last time. The early summer shrubbery was a hundred different shades of green, the verdant wooded hills and barely audible buzz of insects suggesting complete serenity.

Stay calm, she instructed herself, turning the knob and entering the diner.

Lainey walked into the diner, taking in the forest theme of the room. Murals of trees and flowers had been painted on all the walls, probably thirty or forty years before, Lainey thought, noticing the chips and cracks. There was a long counter, with high-backed stools lined up in front, plus eight or ten wooden booths with red plastic seating.

Lainey looked around, halfheartedly hoping that Maria Kroll had changed her mind and gone back to Westchester. There were very few customers. One elderly couple sat in a booth at the back, and one young man, attired in shorts and a dull green T-shirt, his well-used backpack lying at his feet, sat at the counter eating a huge stack of French toast.

There was a shuffling noise off to her left, and with a sinking sensation in her stomach she saw the pretty dark-haired woman sitting in the booth just off to her right.

"Maria," Lainey said softly, hoping not to attract the attention of the other people in the diner.

The woman looked at her blankly.

Lainey called her name once more, a little louder this time.

"You Lainey somebody?" A waitress, portly and tall, her stiff beehive held in place with a pencil, called out loudly to Lainey, the door marked women closing behind her.

Lainey nodded.

"Your friend went up to the Overlook Trail. Says you should go find her."

Lainey looked apologetically at the woman who obviously wasn't Maria Kroll and walked out of the diner. She started toward the sign that led to where Maria said she'd be, then stopped.

Driving here, Lainey had been so caught up in her guilt and fear in confronting Maria, and her frustration with Penn, she hadn't really considered things very clearly. Why would Maria Kroll come here now? she wondered, leaning her shoulder against a tall oak tree and peering up at the trail. It just didn't make sense. Once Lainey had ended it, she and Julian hadn't had anything to do with each other. In fact, she thought, remembering numerous

conversations on the subject, Julian had insisted that his
wife knew nothing about his extracurricular activities.
And Lainey had believed him. If Maria had found out
after it was all over, it seemed slightly ridiculous for her
to come looking for Lainey.

So why here, why now?

A horrible thought came into her mind. What if it
weren't Maria Kroll who was out there looking for her?

Sugar Taplinger crouched patiently as she waited for
Lainey. In her hand was the rifle she'd taken from the
trunk of Helmut's Jeep. Two boxes of shells, one already
opened, sat at her feet.

It had all been so easy, so very easy. She'd gotten to
the Meadowview elementary school well before three.
Thanks to the information Mrs. Miles had so nicely supplied, getting the children out had been no problem. A
well-brought-up ten-year-old girl had gone inside and
delivered the note Sugar had prepared. She was certain
the principal hadn't hesitated for a moment before
announcing that Tim and Riley Cole were wanted outside
by their grandmother.

And weren't they pleased as punch, Sugar chuckled to
herself sarcastically, when they found her waiting for
them. She had thrown the two of them, their faces turning
white with fear and confusion, into her car almost before
they knew what was happening. No, the children had presented no problem and nor would Lainey.

Sugar listened intently. She thought she heard a noise
from the direction of the diner. She stood stock-still for
several minutes, but there was nothing except the rustling
of trees. Then, suddenly, there it was, the sound of
someone stepping on a branch. But it hadn't come from
the direction of the diner. Whoever was creeping around

was somewhere up high, in the thick of trees that hung well above where she was hidden.

Why, you sneaky bitch, Sugar thought, holding her hand above her eyes and peering at the horizon. Sneaky, but not smart, she reflected. Smiling grimly, she turned around and looked down at the small clearing thirty feet or so down the hill. Tim and Riley Cole, their hands and feet tied, their mouths bound with scarves, sat, immobile, on the ground. Lainey had stupidly put Sugar right smack between herself and what she cared about most.

Lainey cursed silently as her foot broke the slender branch in half. She stayed where she was, holding her breath, afraid to move. Slowly, she surveyed the area below her, her eyes scanning the forest.

Suddenly, she saw a glimmer of red. Yes, she thought as the image moved. There she was, Sugar Taplinger, like a flash of fire in her crimson silk.

Lainey debated her next move. Should she creep back to the diner and alert the police, or would Sugar stop her before she got near the place?

"It's over, Lainey!" Sugar's loud voice came as a shock in the muted silence of the woods.

Lainey froze but didn't answer, her heart pounding painfully in her chest.

"Look down, all the way down," Sugar cackled absurdly from her leafy shelter below Lainey.

Lainey peered down toward the trail. She squinted in the sunlight, trying to find whatever it was Sugar wanted her to see.

Suddenly she saw them, Tim and Riley, scarily still, all the way down the hill. She gasped, her heart clutching painfully with fear. Even from this distance, she could feel their terror.

"I'll shoot them," Sugar yelled triumphantly, standing now and holding a rifle out so Lainey could see it.

Blindly, frantically, Lainey searched around for a weapon of some kind. Without much thought, she grabbed a rock from near her feet and started racing down the hill. She couldn't think about the target she was making of herself as she ran toward Sugar, wouldn't allow herself to consider the retaliation she might be bringing upon herself. All she knew was she had to get to the children.

When she was forty or fifty feet from Sugar, the woman turned away from her, raising the rifle to her shoulder and aiming it below.

"No!" Lainey screamed in anguish, as she heard the gun go off.

Rushing forward, she hurled the rock at Sugar's back, barely noticing the woman stumble in surprise as the rock connected with her shoulder. Lainey jumped on her, pummeling her with her fists, then twisting her arm around Sugar's neck. The two of them fell to the ground. The sound of Tim screaming assailed Lainey's ears, but she wouldn't give up her hold. She slammed Sugar's arm against the ground over and over, trying to break the stronghold she had on the rifle.

Lainey had never seen the kind of fury that was now on Sugar's face, giving her the strength to fight back with such venom. But Lainey was fighting with the force of her own fury, an anger so powerful, she knew she could kill this woman with her bare hands. Sugar had shot her Tim. With a ferocious grunt, Lainey rammed Sugar's elbow hard to the ground. Sugar cried out in pain, and the rifle flew out of her grip at last.

Lainey leaped up, grabbing the rifle and aiming it straight at Sugar's head.

For a long moment, they looked at each other. Then Sugar lumbered to her feet, her caftan torn and streaked with dirt, her fleshy body heaving up and down as she fought for breath. Appearing shocked, she blinked three times in a row, as if in wonderment that this could have happened to her.

Gasping for breath herself, Lainey struggled for control, fighting the terrible impulse to shoot this woman, wanting to throw down the gun and run to Tim, knowing she had to think clearly now. She forced herself to calm down. She would take Sugar back to the diner and get help for the boy there.

"Let's go—"

Lainey's instructions were interrupted by an explosion of sound coming from below.

Without understanding what had happened, Lainey saw Sugar drop to the ground. Too startled to move, she stood there helplessly, watching the wet trail of blood spread grotesquely across the silk fabric of Sugar's caftan.

Lainey heard footsteps trudging up the hill. Staring, waiting, she was too shocked to even wonder who it could be.

Helmut Taplinger emerged from behind the trees, a large revolver in his right hand, tears streaming down his face.

He walked over to where Sugar lay, carefully setting his gun down as he dropped to his knees beside her. Lainey watched as he reached down to envelop her in his arms, cradling her head.

"Why did you do this to me?" he asked over and over again as the life drained from Sugar's body.

Epilogue

"Check."

Lainey stood in the doorway to Tim's room, laughing, as Riley removed Tim's queen from the chessboard victoriously. The little girl was seated at the end of the bed, allowing Tim to lie there as they played, his shoulder swathed in thick white bandages, three pillows tucked behind his head for comfort.

Penn's arms embraced her, and she turned around, burying herself in his warmth. He hadn't left her side for more than a few minutes since he'd rushed to the hospital two days before. The sound of the doorbell interrupted their silent communion.

"Arm yourself," Penn said lightly. "That'll be the 'rents." He kissed the top of Lainey's head and pulled away.

Lainey grinned at him. "After the events of the past few days, I don't see Doris and Hugh as that much of a threat."

Together, they descended the stairs. Lainey stayed on the bottom step, while Penn went to open the door.

"Mother," he said gravely, as Doris Beckley rushed past him toward the stairway, stopping when she saw Lainey.

Doris tilted her head a fraction of an inch in greeting,

and went on upstairs. Hugh followed close behind, calling words of encouragement out to his grandson well before he reached his room.

Within moments, the two were back downstairs.

"They hardly talked to us," Doris said testily.

Lainey smiled at her. "They're in the middle of a game. Chess is very serious to those two."

"Besides, we've got some other important matters to discuss," Penn said solemnly, ushering his parents into the living room. He gestured them toward the couch, then walked back to Lainey, putting his arm around her waist.

Doris looked at them curiously.

"Am I supposed to gather something from this display?" she asked unpleasantly.

Penn ignored the question.

"How far has your lawyer gotten in filing for custody?" he asked.

Hugh looked at his son in disdain. "I see that we're supposed to answer your questions, but you're exempt from that responsibility."

Penn tried to hide his growing impatience. "In answer to Mother's question, yes, there's something to be gathered here, something I'll be more than happy to explain when we finish this discussion."

Hugh smacked his hand on the arm of the couch in disgust. "I see that you both believe you're being very grown-up and sophisticated, but people on opposite sides of a lawsuit don't generally socialize."

Penn took Lainey's hand and led her near to where his parents sat. He looked intently at his father. "I don't think there's going to be a lawsuit."

The flash of anger in his mother's pale blue eyes indicated just how strongly she felt. "There not only will be a lawsuit—there *is* one. Expect to be served with the papers within the next week. We saw Harold Itkin yesterday, and he's fully prepared to move ahead."

"I'm glad your grandson's hospitalization didn't interfere with your daily activities," Penn said dryly.

With some satisfaction, he noted his mother avert her eyes in embarrassment.

His father was another matter. "If Tim is badly hurt, that's all the more reason to get this settled," he said irritably.

Penn kept his voice steady. "And did Mr. Itkin give you any notion of how long this lawsuit would take?" He hesitated for a moment before going on. "That is, with the layers of appeal Lainey and I are prepared to come back with, if—and that's a mighty big if—you actually win."

Hugh stayed silent. Penn could see his father weighing the situation, considering the expensive and unpleasant process ahead. But the undiluted belligerence in his eyes indicated that he wasn't about to give up.

"And did he mention what the odds were of your winning if Lainey were married to their uncle?" Penn went on relentlessly. "The uncle who also happens to be coexecutor of their parents' will?"

Hugh looked at his wife in dismay.

"Don't ask me," she exclaimed, turning to regard Lainey and Penn, shock on her face.

"Grandma, Grandpa, we're finished. Come on up." Tim's voice rang out.

Doris stood up, obviously glad to follow the boy's wishes and put an end to the conversation.

Hugh stood up as well. "We'll talk about this later," he said, aiming his words somewhere over Penn's head.

"No," Penn replied, moving to block their way. "We'll finish this now."

He laced his fingers with Lainey's. "I'd like you to be happy about this, but happy or not, you're going to hear it. Lainey is my wife."

Doris gasped, while Hugh's face darkened with annoyance.

"Nice thing to do," he muttered. "Wreck your damn life to prevent a lawsuit."

Lainey finally spoke. "You don't understand," she said, her voice cracking with emotion. "We didn't get married to prevent a custody suit. We got married because we love each other."

Penn nodded. "And we're going to raise Tim and Riley because we want to. Not because we have to, not because we're supposed to. Because they're ours and we love them."

Lainey spoke now. "We want you in their lives, too. They need grandparents, grandparents who love them as much as we do."

Doris looked down at her lap, folding and unfolding her hands, her mouth set. "You always had to shock us, Penn. You could never do anything we expected."

Hugh rose. "Well, we're going to need some time to think about this." He turned to his wife. "Come on. Let's go back upstairs."

Lainey and Penn moved to one side, enabling his parents to walk past them.

"There are a whole lot of Christmases and Easters, not to mention graduations and weddings coming in the next few years," Penn called out as he watched his parents climb the stairs.

Hugh stopped and looked back at his son. Then, slowly, he nodded before continuing up the stairs.

Penn turned to Lainey. "I think it's over," he said, putting his arms around her tightly. "Or, at least, it's the beginning of the end. I think they'll come around if we give them some time."

Riley's voice floated down from upstairs. "Lainey, bring up the Gameboy."

Her demand made Lainey smile. God, how she loved these children. Thank you, Farrell, she thought, thank you for giving them to me, for trusting me. I won't let you down.

A wide grin spread across her face as she looked at Penn. "Can you hang on while I run to fulfill her highness's demands?"

He paused, taking in the radiance on her face. For a brief moment, he just stood, watching her. But when he spoke, his tone was teasing.

"I've hung on for you this long. I can hang on forever."

She laughed. "And I intend to see that you do."

She spied the electronic toy across the room and went over to retrieve it. "Okaaay," she said, walking back to Penn and pulling him toward the stairway. "Let's get this show on the road."

If you enjoyed
What Matters Most,
be sure to look for
Cynthia Victor's dazzling
new novel in which a woman
betrayed discovers that her own
success is truely the best revenge!

Turn the page
for a special preview of

The Secret

A Dutton hardcover
on sale in July of 1997.

Gazing at her reflection in the bathroom mirror, Miranda Shaeffer reviewed everything she had done in the past hour. Dinner was in the oven, hors d'oeuvres were assembled on heavy silver trays, the brie soft and creamy, the vegetable platter lined with ice chips to keep everything crisp. Every available lamp in the West End Avenue apartment was turned on, their beams throwing cheerful light across the plates of cheeses and patés scattered on various tables in the large living room. She had gotten all three children to sleep—the two boys in the larger bedroom, Sophie in the room that for another family might have functioned as a maid's room. Now, she thought, evaluating her pale skin and shoulder-length brown hair, all I have to worry about is my face.

As she stroked rose blush along her cheekbone, Miranda heard her in-laws enter the apartment, their voices tired after a day of touring both the Metropolitan Museum and the Whitney. Hurriedly, she applied some mascara, then added some gray shadow above her green eyes. She was dotting her lips with a sheer gloss when she heard her husband mention her name. His footsteps echoed in the long hallway as he came toward the bathroom.

"Honey, the adoring throngs are waiting for the

empress to alight," he said only slightly impatiently, bending down to kiss the top of her head.

"I'm practically there." She brushed her hair one last time.

Stephen straightened the stiff white collar of her navy blue dress. "You know, if you organized things a bit more stringently, you might get to your own parties on time."

Miranda stuck her tongue out at him in the mirror. "Why is it you only use words like 'stringently' when your parents are here?"

He put his right hand up in the air, as if in surrender. "Caught. Guilty. If you shoot me right now, I don't have to die a year older." He draped his arm affectionately over her shoulder and turned her toward him. "After all, my birthday's not until tomorrow."

"Such a shame to lose a gifted author at such an early age," she said, placing her arms around his neck.

Stephen pulled her closer, his voice dropping to a whisper. "That is our secret, and only our secret." He held her at a distance suddenly. "You haven't gone and told anyone, have you?"

Miranda looked reproachful at the accusation. "Honey, when I make a promise, I keep it." She rubbed his cheek tenderly, trying to ease a smile out of him.

Stephen looked relieved as they walked out of the bathroom to join the party. Miranda watched him contentedly as he mingled among the party guests. The Belkers and the Lights, their friends from Jack's school, stood in one corner of the room, hovering over the food, drinking wine and smiling relaxedly. Miranda understood what pleasure uninterrupted adult company and leisurely eating were for parents of small children.

Stephen's parents sat on the couch, eagerly discussing

the paintings they'd seen that afternoon with the art
director of Colby and Cummings, the advertising agency
where Stephen worked. Miranda would have marveled
more at the depth of erudition displayed by both his parents if she hadn't had to sit through countless such lec-
tures since the Shaeffers had moved to New York to take
teaching posts at Columbia University four years before.
Miranda was still fond enough of her in-laws, but their
pomposity had grown with their professional reputations,
and more and more often she found them difficult to take.

No, she realized, it was more than that. Disembow-
eling was more like it. Not that their piercing remarks
hurt her; it was their effect on Stephen that was the real
problem.

Stephen's book was a perfect example. When she had
teased him about keeping it a secret from them, back
when he first started writing it, she'd only been half kidding. She knew how disapproving they would be of
Stranger from the East, a light adventure story without
much deeper meaning. She could only imagine their
reaction, their son producing such a novel. And she knew
their disapproval was the thing Stephen most dreaded in
the world.

But her husband had cleverly skirted the problem with
an ingenious idea.

Stephen had decided to submit the manuscript entirely
in secret, to keep his identity a mystery to the whole
world. He sent the four-hundred-page manuscript through
the mail to a selected group of literary agents, using the
pen name Forrestor. There was no return address except
a post office box in lower Manhattan, miles from their
apartment. The mystery piqued the interest of several
agents, and the one who wound up taking it on generated

enough talk about it to get Highland Press to agree to publish it.

No one—not the agent, not the editor at Highland—no one except Miranda knew who Forrestor actually was. When Stephen's editor at Highland, Paul Harlow, wished to communicate with his author, he sent notes to the post office box. Eventually, the two men began to communicate by E-mail. But from the first draft through galley corrections, page proofs, and the final finished book right off the press, only "Forrestor" responded to everyone involved.

The people at Highland Press had been clever enough to capitalize on this as a publicity angle when the book came out, and several newspapers had included stories about the mysterious new writer on the popular fiction scene. Even *People* had picked up on it, printing a tiny paragraph about Forrestor in the issue that came out the week of the book's publication.

Stephen had been so tickled by seeing the book in stores, he'd bought half a dozen copies, which he and Miranda had admired lovingly in the privacy of their bedroom. The book had been out for almost a month, but both of them still felt a thrill when they'd see it in their neighborhood bookstore. There it was, with a shiny red jacket, a picture of a man's face half-hidden in shadow, and the title in raised gold-foil lettering.

The extra money was fun, too—not that it amounted to very much. The day Stephen brought home his check, an advance against future sales, he also picked up a bottle of Dom Perignon. He and Miranda had joked that between the agent taking his fifteen percent, and the cost of the champagne, there was barely anything left. But they had stayed up late that night, drinking the champagne and planning how to spend the remainder of his five-thousand-dollar advance.

What had amazed them both was that, even before his first book came out, the publisher had offered him forty thousand dollars to write another one. It seemed like a small fortune to both of them. Just that afternoon when they had returned from Fairway, the kids retreating exhaustedly to the television set in the living room, Stephen had urged Miranda to consider giving up her job. She'd have more time for the kids, he'd reasoned. Time to play bridge even. She'd smiled when he said that. After all, it was her passion for the game that had brought them together in college.

But giving up her job was such a big step. It wasn't that writing for Unity bank was so fascinating. How many ways were there to brag about interest rates and location convenience? Still, she liked being part of the working world, mingling with people whose shoelaces she wasn't expected to tie, whose hair she didn't have to comb.

On the other hand, her life had become so hopelessly complicated. She often felt stretched to the breaking point, and, worse, as though she was cheating everyone—her children, her co-workers, even her employers. And there wasn't a single minute that she couldn't have laid her head down on any available surface and gone straight to sleep. Rest was one indulgence she never got to experience.

She gazed around the living room, making sure her guests were all involved in conversation. What would it be like to have all day to herself? she wondered. Not exactly to herself, she amended, spying one of Sophie's stickers adorning the side of the cd player. But it was an interesting thought. Enough time for each of her three children, enough time for a quiet cup of coffee once in a while. Imagine, she chuckled, how wonderful a man Forrestor must be to afford his wife such luxuries.

The copy of *Stranger from the East* that Stephen had bought that afternoon lay on the coffee table, tossed with seeming casualness between a four-volume Mark Twain set and a pile of *Scientific Americans*. Miranda saw her husband's eyes dart repeatedly toward the bright red jacket as he discussed art and politics with his parents. Every now and then, she caught herself looking at it as well, and their eyes would meet. They laughed silently together, feeling deliciously alone in the crowded room. They were smiling at each other when Stephen's father noticed the volume, picked it up, and then tossed it back on the table with disgust.

"This is exactly the kind of trash that is celebrated in America today," he said vociferously, his head bobbing up and down, his narrow-eyed disapproval making his face look almost feral. "Why do you even have it in your house, Stephen?"

Miranda turned to her father-in-law, hiding a smile as she managed to say mildly, "I don't know, Pop. I read it and it's pretty entertaining."

He gave her a look of disdain.

Miranda smiled broadly. "Intelligent, really. You'd be surprised at just how well written it is."

She stifled the urge to wink at Stephen, though she hoped he was finding the exchange as enjoyable as she was.

Stephen, however, stayed silent. In fact, as she turned back to him, she saw that he looked stricken. Moving quickly to his side, she linked her arm through his, although her next remarks were aimed at her father-in-law.

"Pop, I bet if you picked it up, you wouldn't be able to put it down." She smile sardonically, trying to enlist Stephen in her private pleasure, but he pulled away from her.

"Hello, all." Lydia Greenfield entered the room with her customary grace, despite the bulky Sunday *Times* she carried under one arm. She walked across to Miranda, wincing as she passed the platters of creamy dips and chocolate truffles. Placing most of the news sections down on a wooden chair, she extracted the *Book Review,* holding the front page up for everyone to see.

"May I point to page one," she announced theatrically. "The very bulimic and talentless prima ballerina who vomited in every backstage bathroom across the forty-eight states has written her story for all the world to enjoy. Or, I should say, has spilled her guts to a ghost writer for all the world to bow down to." Disgustedly, she dropped the section on top of the rest of the news-paper. "Not only can she not actually *write,* but she could not actually *dance* when we started together at the Miami Ballet. Of all people to get this kind of attention."

Miranda watched Stephen, still disgruntled from his father's words, pick up the book section, absently turning the pages. Suddenly, she saw his expression change to one of near wonder. Without a word to their visitors, he pulled her from the room, walking to the kitchen, and slamming the door behind them.

"My God, look," he said, his eyes alive with excitement.

Miranda took the proffered page and turned it toward her. It was the hardcover bestseller list. And there, nestled in at number five in its first appearance, was *Stranger from the East* by Forrestor.